PRAISE FROM THE CRITICS
FOR *A RAISIN IN THE SUN*:

John Chapman, *New York Daily News*—
"A beautiful, lovable play. It is affectionately human, funny and touching. . . . A work of theatrical magic in which the usual barrier between audience and stage disappears."

Walter Kerr, *New York Herald Tribune*—
"An honest, intelligible, and moving experience."

Robert Coleman, *New York Mirror*—
"Miss Hansberry has etched her characters with understanding, and told her story with dramatic impact. She has a keen sense of humor, an ear for accurate speech and compassion for people."

John McClain, *New York Journal American*—
"A wonderfully emotional evening."

LORRAINE HANSBERRY

touched the taproots of American life as never before in *A Raisin in the Sun* which won the New York Drama Critics Circle Award for the 1958-1959 season. A writer who penetrated beyond the racial to create universal characters, a writer deeply committed to "the *how* of living"—she enriched the American theater for all time with the greatness of her understanding and talent.

The film version of the play was also an outstanding success. The later musical version, titled RAISIN, won the theater's coveted Tony Award as Best Musical. It ran for over 2 years in New York and on national tour.

A
Raisin In
The Sun

LORRAINE HANSBERRY

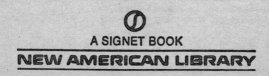

A SIGNET BOOK

NEW AMERICAN LIBRARY

To Mama:

in gratitude for the dream

What happens to a dream deferred?
Does it dry up
Like a raisin in the sun?
Or fester like a sore—
And then run?
Does it stink like rotten meat?
Or crust and sugar over—
Like a syrupy sweet?

Maybe it just sags
Like a heavy load.

Or does it explode?

—Langston Hughes

A RAISIN IN THE SUN *was first presented by Philip Rose and David J. Cogan at the Ethel Barrymore Theatre, New York City, March 11, 1959, with the following cast:* (*In order of appearance*)

RUTH YOUNGER	Ruby Dee
TRAVIS YOUNGER	Glynn Turman
WALTER LEE YOUNGER (BROTHER)	Sidney Poitier
BENEATHA YOUNGER	Diana Sands
LENA YOUNGER (MAMA)	Claudia McNeil
JOSEPH ASAGAI	Ivan Dixon
GEORGE MURCHISON	Louis Gossett
KARL LINDNER	John Fiedler
BOBO	Lonne Elder III
MOVING MEN	Ed Hall, Douglas Turner

Directed by Lloyd Richards

Designed and lighted by Ralph Alswang

Costumes by Virginia Volland

The action of the play is set in Chicago's Southside, sometime between World War II and the present.

ACT ONE

SCENE 1. Friday morning.
SCENE 2. The following morning.

ACT TWO

SCENE 1. Later, the same day.
SCENE 2. Friday night, a few weeks later.
SCENE 3. Moving day, one week later.

ACT THREE

An hour later.

ACT I

Scene One

The YOUNGER *living room would be a comfortable and well-ordered room if it were not for a number of indestructible contradictions to this state of being. Its furnishings are typical and undistinguished and their primary feature now is that they have clearly had to accommodate the living of too many people for too many years—and they are tired. Still, we can see that at some time, a time probably no longer remembered by the family (except perhaps for* MAMA) *the furnishings of this room were actually selected with care and love and even hope—and brought to this apartment and arranged with taste and pride.*

That was a long time ago. Now the once loved pattern of the couch upholstery has to fight to show itself from under acres of crocheted doilies and couch covers which have themselves finally come to be more important than the upholstery. And here a table or a chair has been moved to disguise the worn places in the carpet; but the carpet has fought back by showing its weariness, with depressing uniformity, elsewhere on its surface.

Weariness has, in fact, won in this room. Everything has been polished, washed, sat on, used, scrubbed too

11

often. All pretenses but living itself have long since vanished from the very atmosphere of this room.

Moreover, a section of this room, for it is not really a room unto itself, though the landlord's lease would make it seem so, slopes backward to provide a small kitchen area, where the family prepares the meals that are eaten in the living room proper, which must also serve as dining room. The single window that has been provided for these "two" rooms is located in this kitchen area. The sole natural light the family may enjoy in the course of a day is only that which fights its way through this little window.

At left, a door leads to a bedroom which is shared by MAMA *and her daughter,* BENEATHA. *At right, opposite, is a second room (which in the beginning of the life of this apartment was probably a breakfast room) which serves as a bedroom for* WALTER *and his wife,* RUTH.

Time: Sometime between World War II and the present.

Place: Chicago's Southside.

At Rise: It is morning dark in the living room. TRAVIS *is asleep on the make-down bed at center. An alarm clock sounds from within the bedroom at right, and presently* RUTH *enters from that room and closes the door behind her. She crosses sleepily toward the window. As she passes her sleeping son she reaches down and shakes him a little. At the window she raises the shade and a dusky Southside morning light comes in feebly. She fills a pot with water and puts it on to boil. She calls to the boy, between yawns, in a slightly muffled voice.*

RUTH *is about thirty. We can see that she was a pretty girl, even exceptionally so, but now it is apparent that life has been little that she expected, and disappointment has already begun to hang in her face. In a few years, before thirty-five even, she will be known among her people as a "settled woman."*

She crosses to her son and gives him a good, final, rousing shake.

RUTH Come on now, boy, it's seven thirty! (*Her son sits up at last, in a stupor of sleepiness*) I say hurry up, Travis! You ain't the only person in the world got to use a bathroom! (*The child, a sturdy, handsome little boy of ten or eleven, drags himself out of the bed and almost blindly takes his towels and "today's clothes" from drawers and a closet and goes out to the bathroom, which is in an outside hall and which is shared by another family or families on the same floor.* RUTH *crosses to the bedroom door at right and opens it and calls in to her husband*) Walter Lee! . . . It's after seven thirty! Lemme see you do some waking up in there now! (*She waits*) You better get up from there, man! It's after seven thirty I tell you. (*She waits again*) All right, you just go ahead and lay there and next thing you know Travis be finished and Mr. Johnson'll be in there and you'll be fussing and cussing round here like a mad man! And be late too! (*She waits, at the end of patience*) Walter Lee—it's time for you to get up!

> (*She waits another second and then starts to go into the bedroom, but is apparently satisfied that her husband has begun to get up. She stops, pulls the door to, and returns to the kitchen area. She wipes her face with a moist cloth and runs her fingers through her sleep-disheveled hair in a vain effort and ties an apron around her housecoat. The bedroom door at right opens and her husband stands in the doorway in his pajamas, which are rumpled and mismated. He is a lean, intense young man in his middle thirties, inclined to quick nervous movements and erratic speech habits— and always in his voice there is a quality of indictment*)

WALTER Is he out yet?

RUTH What you mean *out?* He ain't hardly got in there good yet.

WALTER   (*Wandering in, still more oriented to sleep than to a new day*) Well, what was you doing all that yelling for if I can't even get in there yet? (*Stopping and thinking*) Check coming today?

RUTH   They *said* Saturday and this is just Friday and I hopes to God you ain't going to get up here first thing this morning and start talking to me 'bout no money— 'cause I 'bout don't want to hear it.

WALTER   Something the matter with you this morning?

RUTH   No—I'm just sleepy as the devil. What kind of eggs you want?

WALTER   Not scrambled. (RUTH *starts to scramble eggs*) Paper come? (RUTH *points impatiently to the rolled up* Tribune *on the table, and he gets it and spreads it out and vaguely reads the front page*) Set off another bomb yesterday.

RUTH (*Maximum indifference*) Did they?

WALTER (*Looking up*)   What's the matter with you?

RUTH   Ain't nothing the matter with me. And don't keep asking me that this morning.

WALTER   Ain't nobody bothering you. (*Reading the news of the day absently again*) Say Colonel McCormick is sick.

RUTH (*Affecting tea-party interest*)   Is he now? Poor thing.

WALTER (*Sighing and looking at his watch*) Oh, me. (*He waits*) Now what is that boy doing in that bathroom all this time? He just going to have to start getting up earlier. I can't be being late to work on account of him fooling around in there.

RUTH (*Turning on him*)   Oh, no he ain't going to be get-

ting up no earlier no such thing! It ain't his fault that
he can't get to bed no earlier nights 'cause he got a
bunch of crazy good-for-nothing clowns sitting up running their mouths in what is supposed to be his bedroom after ten o'clock at night ...

WALTER That's what you mad about, ain't it? The things
I want to talk about with my friends just couldn't be
important in your mind, could they?
    (*He rises and finds a cigarette in her handbag on
    the table and crosses to the little window and looks
    out, smoking and deeply enjoying this first one*)

RUTH (*Almost matter of factly, a complaint too automatic
to deserve emphasis*) Why you always got to smoke
before you eat in the morning?

WALTER (*At the window*) Just look at 'em down there
... Running and racing to work ... (*He turns and
faces his wife and watches her a moment at the stove,
and then, suddenly*) You look young this morning, baby.

RUTH (*Indifferently*) Yeah?

WALTER Just for a second—stirring them eggs. It's gone
now—just for a second it was—you looked real young
again. (*Then, drily*) It's gone now—you look like yourself again.

RUTH Man, if you don't shut up and leave me alone.

WALTER (*Looking out to the street again*) First thing
a man ought to learn in life is not to make love to no
colored woman first thing in the morning. You all some
evil people at eight o'clock in the morning.
    (TRAVIS *appears in the hall doorway, almost fully
    dressed and quite wide awake now, his towels and
    pajamas across his shoulders. He opens the door
    and signals for his father to make the bathroom
    in a hurry*)

TRAVIS (*Watching the bathroom*) Daddy, come on!
(WALTER *gets his bathroom utensils and flies out to the bathroom*)

RUTH Sit down and have your breakfast, Travis.

TRAVIS Mama, this is Friday. (*Gleefully*) Check coming tomorrow, huh?

RUTH You get your mind off money and eat your breakfast.

TRAVIS (*Eating*) This is the morning we supposed to bring the fifty cents to school.

RUTH Well, I ain't got no fifty cents this morning.

TRAVIS Teacher say we have to.

RUTH I don't care what teacher say. I ain't got it. Eat your breakfast, Travis.

TRAVIS I *am* eating.

RUTH Hush up now and just eat!
(*The boy gives her an exasperated look for her lack of understanding, and eats grudgingly*)

TRAVIS You think Grandmama would have it?

RUTH No! And I want you to stop asking your grandmother for money, you hear me?

TRAVIS (*Outraged*) Gaaaleee! I don't ask her, she just gimme it sometimes!

RUTH Travis Willard Younger—I got too much on me this morning to be—

TRAVIS Maybe Daddy—

RUTH *Travis!*
(*The boy hushes abruptly. They are both quiet and tense for several seconds*)

TRAVIS (*Presently*) Could I maybe go carry some groceries in front of the supermarket for a little while
after school then?

RUTH Just hush, I said. (*Travis jabs his spoon into his
cereal bowl viciously, and rests his head in anger upon
his fists*) If you through eating, you can get over there
and make up your bed.
> (*The boy obeys stiffly and crosses the room, al-
> most mechanically, to the bed and more or less
> carefully folds the covering. He carries the bedding
> into his mother's room and returns with his books
> and cap*)

TRAVIS (*Sulking and standing apart from her unnaturally*)
I'm gone.

RUTH (*Looking up from the stove to inspect him automatically*) Come here. (*He crosses to her and she
studies his head*) If you don't take this comb and fix
this here head, you better! (*TRAVIS puts down his books
with a great sigh of oppression, and crosses to the
mirror. His mother mutters under her breath about his
"slubbornness"*) 'Bout to march out of here with that
head looking just like chickens slept in it! I just don't
know where you get your slubborn ways . . . And get
your jacket, too. Looks chilly out this morning.

TRAVIS (*With conspicuously brushed hair and jacket*) I'm
gone.

RUTH Get carfare and milk money—(*Waving one finger*)
—and not a single penny for no caps, you hear me?

TRAVIS (*With sullen politeness*) Yes'm.
> (*He turns in outrage to leave. His mother watches
> after him as in his frustration he approaches the
> door almost comically. When she speaks to him,
> her voice has become a very gentle tease*)

RUTH (*Mocking; as she thinks he would say it*) Oh, Mama makes me so mad sometimes, I don't know what to do! (*She waits and continues to his back as he stands stock-still in front of the door*) I wouldn't kiss that woman good-bye for nothing in this world this morning! (*The boy finally turns around and rolls his eyes at her, knowing the mood has changed and he is vindicated; he does not, however, move toward her yet*) Not for nothing in this world! (*She finally laughs aloud at him and holds out her arms to him and we see that it is a way between them, very old and practiced. He crosses to her and allows her to embrace him warmly but keeps his face fixed with masculine rigidity. She holds him back from her presently and looks at him and runs her fingers over the features of his face. With utter gentleness—*) Now—whose little old angry man are you?

TRAVIS (*The masculinity and gruffness start to fade at last*) Aw gaalee—Mama . . .

RUTH (*Mimicking*) Aw—gaaaaalleeeee, Mama! (*She pushes him, with rough playfulness and finality, toward the door*) Get on out of here or you going to be late.

TRAVIS (*In the face of love, new aggresiveness*) Mama, could I *please* go carry groceries?

RUTH Honey, it's starting to get so cold evenings.

WALTER (*Coming in from the bathroom and drawing a make-believe gun from a make-believe holster and shooting at his son*) What is it he wants to do?

RUTH Go carry groceries after school at the supermarket.

WALTER Well, let him go . . .

TRAVIS (*Quickly, to the ally*) I *have* to—she won't gimme the fifty cents . . .

WALTER (*To his wife only*) Why not?

RUTH (*Simply, and with flavor*) 'Cause we don't have it.

WALTER (*To* RUTH *only*) What you tell the boy things
like that for? (*Reaching down into his pants with a
rather important gesture*) Here, son—
    (*He hands the boy the coin, but his eyes are di-
rected to his wife's.* TRAVIS *takes the money happily*)

TRAVIS Thanks, Daddy.
    (*He starts out.* RUTH *watches both of them with
murder in her eyes.* WALTER *stands and stares
back at her with defiance, and suddenly reaches
into his pocket again on an afterthought*)

WALTER (*Without even looking at his son, still staring
hard at his wife*) In fact, here's another fifty cents . . .
Buy yourself some fruit today—or take a taxicab to
school or something!

TRAVIS Whoopee—
    (*He leaps up and clasps his father around the
middle with his legs, and they face each other in
mutual appreciation; slowly* WALTER LEE *peeks
around the boy to catch the violent rays from his
wife's eyes and draws his head back as if shot*)

WALTER You better get down now—and get to school,
man.

TRAVIS (*At the door*) O.K. Good-bye.
    (*He exits*)

WALTER (*After him, pointing with pride*) That's *my* boy.
(*She looks at him in disgust and turns back to her
work*) You know what I was thinking 'bout in the bathroom this morning?

RUTH No.

WALTER   How come you always try to be so pleasant!

RUTH   What is there to be pleasant 'bout!

WALTER   You want to know what I was thinking 'bout in the bathroom or not!

RUTH   I know what you thinking 'bout.

WALTER (*Ignoring her*)   'Bout what me and Willy Harris was talking about last night.

RUTH (*Immediately—a refrain*)   Willy Harris is a good-for-nothing loud mouth.

WALTER   Anybody who talks to me has got to be a good-for-nothing loud mouth, ain't he? And what you know about who is just a good-for-nothing loud mouth? Charlie Atkins was just a "good-for-nothing loud mouth" too, wasn't he! When he wanted me to go in the dry-cleaning business with him. And now—he's grossing a hundred thousand a year. A hundred thousand dollars a year! You still call *him* a loud mouth!

RUTH (*Bitterly*)   Oh, Walter Lee . . .
         (*She folds her head on her arms over the table*)

WALTER (*Rising and coming to her and standing over her*)   You tired, ain't you? Tired of everything. Me, the boy, the way we live—this beat-up hole—everything. Ain't you? (*She doesn't look up, doesn't answer*) So tired—moaning and groaning all the time, but you wouldn't do nothing to help, would you? You couldn't be on my side that long for nothing, could you?

RUTH   Walter, please leave me alone.

WALTER   A man needs for a woman to back him up . . .

RUTH   Walter—

WALTER   Mama would listen to you. You know she listen to you more than she do me and Bennie. She think more of you. All you have to do is just sit down with her when you drinking your coffee one morning and talking 'bout things like you do and—(*He sits down beside her and demonstrates graphically what he thinks her methods and tone should be*)—you just sip your coffee, see, and say easy like that you been thinking 'bout that deal Walter Lee is so interested in, 'bout the store and all, and sip some more coffee, like what you saying ain't really that important to you— And the next thing you know, she be listening good and asking you questions and when I come home—I can tell her the details. This ain't no fly-by-night proposition, baby. I mean we figured it out, me and Willy and Bobo.

RUTH (*With a frown*) Bobo?

WALTER Yeah. You see, this little liquor store we got in mind cost seventy-five thousand and we figured the initial investment on the place be 'bout thirty thousand, see. That be ten thousand each. Course, there's a couple of hundred you got to pay so's you don't spend your life just waiting for them clowns to let your license get approved—

RUTH You mean graft?

WALTER (*Frowning impatiently*) Don't call it that. See there, that just goes to show you what women understand about the world. Baby, don't *nothing* happen for you in this world 'less you pay *somebody* off!

RUTH Walter, leave me alone! (*She raises her head and stares at him vigorously—then says, more quietly*) *Eat* your eggs, they gonna be cold.

WALTER (*Straightening up from her and looking off*) That's it. There you are. Man say to his woman: I got me a dream. His woman say: Eat your eggs. (*Sadly, but gaining in power*) Man say: I got to take hold of this here world, baby! And a woman will say: Eat your eggs and go to work. (*Passionately now*) Man say: I got to change my life, I'm choking to death, baby! And his woman say——(*In utter anguish as he brings his fists down on his thighs*)——Your eggs is getting cold!

RUTH (*Softly*) Walter, that ain't none of our money.

WALTER (*Not listening at all or even looking at her*) This morning, I was lookin' in the mirror and thinking about it . . . I'm thirty-five years old; I been married eleven years and I got a boy who sleeps in the living room—— (*Very, very quietly*)——and all I got to give him is stories about how rich white people live . . .

RUTH Eat your eggs, Walter.

WALTER *Damn my eggs . . . damn all the eggs that ever was!*

RUTH Then go to work.

WALTER (*Looking up at her*) See——I'm trying to talk to you 'bout myself——(*Shaking his head with the repetition*) ——and all you can say is eat them eggs and go to work.

RUTH (*Wearily*) Honey, you never say nothing new. I listen to you every day, every night and every morning, and you never say nothing new. (*Shrugging*) So you would rather *be* Mr. Arnold than be his chauffeur. So— I would *rather* be living in Buckingham Palace.

WALTER That is just what is wrong with the colored woman in this world . . . Don't understand about building their men up and making 'em feel like they somebody. Like they can do something.

RUTH (*Drily, but to hurt*) There *are* colored men who do things.

WALTER No thanks to the colored woman.

RUTH Well, being a colored woman, I guess I can't help myself none.

(*She rises and gets the ironing board and sets it up and attacks a huge pile of rough-dried clothes, sprinkling them in preparation for the ironing and then rolling them into tight fat balls*)

WALTER (*Mumbling*)   We one group of men tied to a race of women with small minds.

(*His sister* BENEATHA *enters. She is about twenty, as slim and intense as her brother. She is not as pretty as her sister-in-law, but her lean, almost intellectual face has a handsomeness of its own. She wears a bright-red flannel nightie, and her thick hair stands wildly about her head. Her speech is a mixture of many things; it is different from the rest of the family's insofar as education has permeated her sense of English—and perhaps the Midwest rather than the South has finally—at last —won out in her inflection; but not altogether, because over all of it is a soft slurring and transformed use of vowels which is the decided influence of the Southside. She passes through the room without looking at either* RUTH *or* WALTER *and goes to the outside door and looks, a little blindly, out to the bathroom. She sees that it has been lost to the Johnsons. She closes the door with a sleepy vengeance and crosses to the table and sits down a little defeated*)

BENEATHA   I am going to start timing those people.

WALTER   You should get up earlier.

BENEATHA (*Her face in her hands. She is still fighting the urge to go back to bed*)   Really— would you suggest dawn? Where's the paper?

WALTER (*Pushing the paper across the table to her as he studies her almost clinically, as though he has never seen her before*)   You a horrible-looking chick at this hour.

BENEATHA (*Drily*)   Good morning, everybody.

WALTER (*Senselessly*)   How is school coming?

BENEATHA (*In the same spirit*)   Lovely. Lovely. And you know, biology is the greatest. (*Looking up at him*) I dissected something that looked just like you yesterday.

WALTER   I just wondered if you've made up your mind and everything.

BENEATHA (*Gaining in sharpness and impatience*)   And what did I answer yesterday morning—and the day before that?

RUTH (*From the ironing board, like someone disinterested and old*)   Don't be so nasty, Bennie.

BENEATHA (*Still to her brother*)   And the day before that and the day before that!

WALTER (*Defensively*)   I'm interested in you. Something wrong with that? Ain't many girls who decide—

WALTER *and* BENEATHA (*In unison*)   —"to be a doctor." (*Silence*)

WALTER   Have we figured out yet just exactly how much medical school is going to cost?

RUTH   Walter Lee, why don't you leave that girl alone and get out of here to work?

BENEATHA (*Exits to the bathroom and bangs on the door*) Come on out of there, please!
      (*She comes back into the room*)

WALTER (*Looking at his sister intently*)   You know the check is coming tomorrow.

BENEATHA (*Turning on him with a sharpness all her own*) That money belongs to Mama, Walter, and it's for her to decide how she wants to use it. I don't care if she wants to buy a house or a rocket ship or just nail it up somewhere and look at it. It's hers. Not ours—*hers*.

WALTER (*Bitterly*) Now ain't that fine! You just got your mother's interest at heart, ain't you, girl? You such a nice girl—but if Mama got that money she can always take a few thousand and help you through school too —can't she?

BENEATHA I have never asked anyone around here to do anything for me!

WALTER No! And the line between asking and just accepting when the time comes is big and wide—ain't it!

BENEATHA (*With fury*) What do you want from me, Brother—that I quit school or just drop dead, which!

WALTER I don't want nothing but for you to stop acting holy 'round here. Me and Ruth done made some sacrifices for you—why can't you do something for the family?

RUTH Walter, don't be dragging me in it.

WALTER You are in it— Don't you get up and go work in somebody's kitchen for the last three years to help put clothes on her back?

RUTH Oh, Walter—that's not fair . . .

WALTER It ain't that nobody expects you to get on your knees and say thank you, Brother; thank you, Ruth; thank you, Mama—and thank you, Travis, for wearing the same pair of shoes for two semesters—

BENEATHA (*Dropping to her knees*) Well—I *do*—all right?—thank everybody . . . and forgive me for ever wanting to be anything at all . . . forgive me, forgive me!

RUTH   Please stop it! Your mama'll hear you.

WALTER   Who the hell told you you had to be a doctor?
If you so crazy 'bout messing 'round with sick people
—then go be a nurse like other women—or just get
married and be quiet . . .

BENEATHA   Well—you finally got it said . . . It took you
three years but you finally got it said. Walter, give up;
leave me alone—it's Mama's money.

WALTER   *He was my father, too!*

BENEATHA   So what? He was mine, too—and Travis'
grandfather—but the insurance money belongs to
Mama. Picking on me is not going to make her give it
to you to invest in any liquor stores—(*Underbreath,
dropping into a chair*)—and I for one say, God bless
Mama for that!

WALTER (*To* RUTH)   See—did you hear? Did you hear!

RUTH   Honey, please go to work.

WALTER   Nobody in this house is ever going to understand me.

BENEATHA   Because you're a nut.

WALTER   Who's a nut?

BENEATHA   You—you are a nut. Thee is mad, boy.

WALTER (*Looking at his wife and his sister from the door,
very sadly*)   The world's most backward race of people, and that's a fact.

BENEATHA (*Turning slowly in her chair*)   And then there
are all those prophets who would lead us out of the
wilderness—(WALTER *slams out of the house*)—into
the swamps!

RUTH   Bennie, why you always gotta be pickin' on your

brother? Can't you be a little sweeter sometimes? (*Door opens.* WALTER *walks in*)

WALTER (*To Ruth*)   I need some money for carfare.

RUTH (*Looks at him, then warms; teasing, but tenderly*) Fifty cents? (*She goes to her bag and gets money*) Here, take a taxi.

> (WALTER *exits.* MAMA *enters. She is a woman in her early sixties, full-bodied and strong. She is one of those women of a certain grace and beauty who wear it so unobtrusively that it takes a while to notice. Her dark-brown face is surrounded by the total whiteness of her hair, and, being a woman who has adjusted to many things in life and over-come many more, her face is full of strength. She has, we can see, wit and faith of a kind that keep her eyes lit and full of interest and expectancy. She is, in a word, a beautiful woman. Her bearing is perhaps most like the noble bearing of the women of the Hereros of Southwest Africa— rather as if she imagines that as she walks she still bears a basket or a vessel upon her head. Her speech, on the other hand, is as careless as her carriage is precise—she is inclined to slur everything —but her voice is perhaps not so much quiet as simply soft*)

MAMA   Who that 'round here slamming doors at this hour?

> (*She crosses through the room, goes to the window, opens it, and brings in a feeble little plant growing doggedly in a small pot on the window sill. She feels the dirt and puts it back out*)

RUTH   That was Walter Lee. He and Bennie was at it again.

MAMA   My children and they tempers. Lord, if this little

old plant don't get more sun than it's been getting it ain't never going to see spring again. (*She turns from the window*) What's the matter with you this morning, Ruth? You looks right peaked. You aiming to iron all them things? Leave some for me. I'll get to 'em this afternoon. Bennie honey, it's too drafty for you to be sitting 'round half dressed. Where's your robe?

BENEATHA   In the cleaners.

MAMA   Well, go get mine and put it on.

BENEATHA   I'm not cold, Mama, honest.

MAMA   I know—but you so thin . . .

BENEATHA (*Irritably*)   Mama, I'm not cold.

MAMA (*Seeing the make-down bed as* TRAVIS *has left it*) Lord have mercy, look at that poor bed. Bless his heart—he tries, don't he?
(*She moves to the bed* TRAVIS *has sloppily made up*)

RUTH   No—he don't half try at all 'cause he knows you going to come along behind him and fix everything. That's just how come he don't know how to do nothing right now—you done spoiled that boy so.

MAMA   Well—he's a little boy. Ain't supposed to know 'bout housekeeping. My baby, that's what he is. What you fix for his breakfast this morning?

RUTH (*Angrily*)   I feed my son, Lena!

MAMA   I ain't meddling—(*Underbreath; busy-bodyish*) I just noticed all last week he had cold cereal, and when it starts getting this chilly in the fall a child ought to have some hot grits or something when he goes out in the cold—

RUTH (*Furious*)   I gave him hot oats—is that all right!

MAMA I ain't meddling. (*Pause*) Put a lot of nice butter on it? (RUTH *shoots her an angry look and does not reply*) He likes lots of butter.

RUTH (*Exasperated*) Lena—

MAMA (*To* BENEATHA. MAMA *is inclined to wander conversationally sometimes*) What was you and your brother fussing 'bout this morning?

BENEATHA It's not important, Mama.
        (*She gets up and goes to look out at the bathroom, which is apparently free, and she picks up her towels and rushes out*)

MAMA What was they fighting about?

RUTH Now you know as well as I do.

MAMA (*Shaking her head*) Brother still worrying hisself sick about that money?

RUTH You know he is.

MAMA You had breakfast?

RUTH Some coffee.

MAMA Girl, you better start eating and looking after yourself better. You almost thin as Travis.

RUTH Lena—

MAMA Un-hunh?

RUTH What are you going to do with it?

MAMA Now don't you start, child. It's too early in the morning to be talking about money. It ain't Christian.

RUTH It's just that he got his heart set on that store—

MAMA You mean that liquor store that Willy Harris want him to invest in?

RUTH   Yes—

MAMA   We ain't no business people, Ruth. We just plain working folks.

RUTH   Ain't nobody business people till they go into business. Walter Lee say colored people ain't never going to start getting ahead till they start gambling on some different kinds of things in the world—investments and things.

MAMA   What done got into you, girl? Walter Lee done finally sold you on investing.

RUTH   No. Mama, something is happening between Walter and me. I don't know what it is—but he needs something—something I can't give him any more. He needs this chance, Lena.

MAMA   (*Frowning deeply*)   But liquor, honey—

RUTH   Well—like Walter say—I spec people going to always be drinking themselves some liquor.

MAMA   Well—whether they drinks it or not ain't none of my business. But whether I go into business selling it to 'em *is*, and I don't want that on my ledger this late in life. (*Stopping suddenly and studying her daughter-in-law*) Ruth Younger, what's the matter with you today? You look like you could fall over right there.

RUTH   I'm tired.

MAMA   Then you better stay home from work today.

RUTH   I can't stay home. She'd be calling up the agency and screaming at them, "My girl didn't come in today—send me somebody! My girl didn't come in!" Oh, she just have a fit . . .

MAMA   Well, let her have it. I'll just call her up and say you got the flu—

RUTH (*Laughing*) Why the flu?

MAMA 'Cause it sounds respectable to 'em. Something white people get, too. They know 'bout the flu. Otherwise they think you been cut up or something when you tell 'em you sick.

RUTH I got to go in. We need the money.

MAMA Somebody would of thought my children done all but starved to death the way they talk about money here late. Child, we got a great big old check coming tomorrow.

RUTH (*Sincerely, but also self-righteously*) Now that's your money. It ain't got nothing to do with me. We all feel like that—Walter and Bennie and me—even Travis.

MAMA (*Thoughtfully, and suddenly very far away*) Ten thousand dollars—

RUTH Sure is wonderful.

MAMA Ten thousand dollars.

RUTH You know what you should do, Miss Lena? You should take yourself a trip somewhere. To Europe or South America or someplace—

MAMA (*Throwing up her hands at the thought*) Oh, child!

RUTH I'm serious. Just pack up and leave! Go on away and enjoy yourself some. Forget about the family and have yourself a ball for once in your life—

MAMA (*Drily*) You sound like I'm just about ready to die. Who'd go with me? What I look like wandering 'round Europe by myself?

RUTH Shoot—these here rich white women do it all the time. They don't think nothing of packing up they suit-

cases and piling on one of them big steamships and—
swoosh!—they gone, child.

MAMA   Something always told me I wasn't no rich
white woman.

RUTH   Well—what are you going to do with it then?

MAMA   I ain't rightly decided. (*Thinking. She speaks now
with emphasis*) Some of it got to be put away for
Beneatha and her schoolin'—and ain't nothing going to
touch that part of it. Nothing. (*She waits several seconds, trying to make up her mind about something,
and looks at* RUTH *a little tentatively before going on*)
Been thinking that we maybe could meet the notes on a
little old two-story somewhere, with a yard where Travis
could play in the summertime, if we use part of the
insurance for a down payment and everybody kind of
pitch in. I could maybe take on a little day work again,
few days a week—

RUTH   (*Studying her mother-in-law furtively and concentrating on her ironing, anxious to encourage without
seeming to*) Well, Lord knows, we've put enough
rent into this here rat trap to pay for four houses by
now . . .

MAMA   (*Looking up at the words "rat trap" and then
looking around and leaning back and sighing—in a
suddenly reflective mood—*) "Rat trap"—yes, that's
all it is. (*Smiling*) I remember just as well the day me
and Big Walter moved in here. Hadn't been married
but two weeks and wasn't planning on living here no
more than a year. (*She shakes her head at the dissolved
dream*) We was going to set away, little by little, don't
you know, and buy a little place out in Morgan Park.
We had even picked out the house. (*Chuckling a little*)
Looks right dumpy today. But Lord, child, you should
know all the dreams I had 'bout buying that house and

fixing it up and making me a little garden in the back—
(*She waits and stops smiling*) And didn't none of it
happen.

(*Dropping her hands in a futile gesture*)

RUTH (*Keeps her head down, ironing*)   Yes, life can be
a barrel of disappointments, sometimes.

MAMA   Honey, Big Walter would come in here some
nights back then and slump down on that couch there
and just look at the rug, and look at me and look at
the rug and then back at me—and I'd know he was
down then . . . really down. (*After a second very long
and thoughtful pause; she is seeing back to times that
only she can see*) And then, Lord, when I lost that
baby—little Claude—I almost thought I was going to
lose Big Walter too. Oh, that man grieved hisself! He
was one man to love his children.

RUTH   Ain't nothin' can tear at you like losin' your baby.

MAMA   I guess that's how come that man finally worked
hisself to death like he done. Like he was fighting
his own war with this here world that took his baby
from him.

RUTH   He sure was a fine man, all right. I always liked
Mr. Younger.

MAMA   Crazy 'bout his children! God knows there was
plenty wrong with Walter Younger—hard-headed,
mean, kind of wild with women—plenty wrong with
him. But he sure loved his children. Always wanted
them to have something—be something. That's where
Brother gets all these notions, I reckon. Big Walter
used to say, he'd get right wet in the eyes sometimes,
lean his head back with the water standing in his eyes
and say, "Seem like God didn't see fit to give the
black man nothing but dreams—but He did give us
children to make them dreams seem worth while."

(*She smiles*) He could talk like that, don't you know.

RUTH Yes, he sure could. He was a good man, Mr. Younger.

MAMA Yes, a fine man—just couldn't never catch up with his dreams, that's all.
(BENEATHA *comes in, brushing her hair and looking up to the ceiling, where the sound of a vacuum cleaner has started up*)

BENEATHA What could be so dirty on that woman's rugs that she has to vacuum them every single day?

RUTH I wish certain young women 'round here who I could name would take inspiration about certain rugs in a certain apartment I could also mention.

BENEATHA (*Shrugging*) How much cleaning can a house need, for Christ's sakes.

MAMA (*Not liking the Lord's name used thus*) Bennie!

RUTH Just listen to her—just listen!

BENEATHA Oh, God!

MAMA If you use the Lord's name just one more time—

BENEATHA (*A bit of a whine*) Oh, Mama—

RUTH Fresh—just fresh as salt, this girl!

BENEATHA (*Drily*) Well—if the salt loses its savor—

MAMA Now that will do. I just ain't going to have you 'round here reciting the scriptures in vain—you hear me?

BENEATHA How did I manage to get on everybody's wrong side by just walking into a room?

RUTH If you weren't so fresh—

BENEATHA Ruth, I'm twenty years old.

MAMA   What time you be home from school today?

BENEATHA   Kind of late. (*With enthusiasm*) Madeline is going to start my guitar lessons today.

(MAMA *and* RUTH *look up with the same expression*)

MAMA   Your *what* kind of lessons?

BENEATHA   Guitar.

RUTH   Oh, Father!

MAMA   How come you done taken it in your mind to learn to play the guitar?

BENEATHA   I just want to, that's all.

MAMA (*Smiling*)   Lord, child, don't you know what to do with yourself? How long it going to be before you get tired of this now—like you got tired of that little play-acting group you joined last year? (*Looking at Ruth*) And what was it the year before that?

RUTH   The horseback-riding club for which she bought that fifty-five-dollar riding habit that's been hanging in the closet ever since!

MAMA (*To* BENEATHA)   Why you got to flit so from one thing to another, baby?

BENEATHA (*Sharply*)   I just want to learn to play the guitar. Is there anything wrong with that?

MAMA   Ain't nobody trying to stop you. I just wonders sometimes why you has to flit so from one thing to another all the time. You ain't never done nothing with all that camera equipment you brought home—

BENEATHA   I don't flit! I—I experiment with different forms of expression—

RUTH   Like riding a horse?

BENEATHA —People have to express themselves one way or another.

MAMA What is it you want to express?

BENEATHA (*Angrily*) Me! (MAMA *and* RUTH *look at each other and burst into raucous laughter*) Don't worry— I don't expect you to understand.

MAMA (*To change the subject*) Who you going out with tomorrow night?

BENEATHA (*With displeasure*) George Murchison again.

MAMA (*Pleased*) Oh—you getting a little sweet on him?

RUTH You ask me, this child ain't sweet on nobody but herself—(*Underbreath*) Express herself!
    (*They laugh*)

BENEATHA Oh—I like George all right, Mama. I mean I like him enough to go out with him and stuff, but—

RUTH (*For devilment*) What does *and stuff* mean?

BENEATHA Mind your own business.

MAMA Stop picking at her now, Ruth. (*A thoughtful pause, and then a suspicious sudden look at her daughter as she turns in her chair for emphasis*) What *does* it mean?

BENEATHA (*Wearily*) Oh, I just mean I couldn't ever really be serious about George. He's—he's so shallow.

RUTH Shallow—what do you mean he's shallow? He's *Rich!*

MAMA Hush, Ruth.

BENEATHA I know he's rich. He knows he's rich, too.

RUTH Well—what other qualities a man got to have to satisfy you, little girl?

BENEATHA You wouldn't even begin to understand. Anybody who married Walter could not possibly understand.

MAMA (*Outraged*) What kind of way is that to talk about your brother?

BENEATHA Brother is a flip—let's face it.

MAMA (*To* RUTH, *helplessly*) What's a flip?

RUTH (*Glad to add kindling*) She's saying he's crazy.

BENEATHA Not crazy. Brother isn't really crazy yet—he—he's an elaborate neurotic.

MAMA Hush your mouth!

BENEATHA As for George. Well. George looks good—he's got a beautiful car and he takes me to nice places and, as my sister-in-law says, he is probably the richest boy I will ever get to know and I even like him sometimes—but if the Youngers are sitting around waiting to see if their little Bennie is going to tie up the family with the Murchisons, they are wasting their time.

RUTH You mean you wouldn't marry George Murchison if he asked you someday? That pretty, rich thing? Honey, I knew you was odd—

BENEATHA No I would not marry him if all I felt for him was what I feel now. Besides, George's family wouldn't really like it.

MAMA Why not?

BENEATHA Oh, Mama—The Murchisons are honest-to-God-real-*live*-rich colored people, and the only people in the world who are more snobbish than rich white people are rich colored people. I thought everybody knew that. I've met Mrs. Murchison. She's a scene!

MAMA   You must not dislike people 'cause they well off, honey.

BENEATHA   Why not? It makes just as much sense as disliking people 'cause they are poor, and lots of people do that.

RUTH (*A wisdom-of-the-ages manner. To* MAMA)   Well, she'll get over some of this—

BENEATHA   Get over it? What are you talking about, Ruth? Listen, I'm going to be a doctor. I'm not worried about who I'm going to marry yet—if I ever get married.

MAMA *and* RUTH   *If!*

MAMA   Now, Bennie—

BENEATHA   Oh, I probably will . . . but first I'm going to be a doctor, and George, for one, still thinks that's pretty funny. I couldn't be bothered with that. I am going to be a doctor and everybody around here better understand that!

MAMA (*Kindly*)   'Course you going to be a doctor, honey, God willing.

BENEATHA (*Drily*)   God hasn't got a thing to do with it.

MAMA   Beneatha—that just wasn't necessary.

BENEATHA   Well—neither is God. I get sick of hearing about God.

MAMA   Beneatha!

BENEATHA   I mean it! I'm just tired of hearing about God all the time. What has He got to do with anything? Does he pay tuition?

MAMA   You 'bout to get your fresh little jaw slapped!

RUTH   That's just what she needs, all right!

BENEATHA   Why? Why can't I say what I want to around here, like everybody else?

MAMA   It don't sound nice for a young girl to say things like that—you wasn't brought up that way. Me and your father went to trouble to get you and Brother to church every Sunday.

BENEATHA   Mama, you don't understand. It's all a matter of ideas, and God is just one idea I don't accept. It's not important. I am not going out and be immoral or commit crimes because I don't believe in God. I don't even think about it. It's just that I get tired of Him getting credit for all the things the human race achieves through its own stubborn effort. There simply is no blasted God—there is only man and it is he who makes miracles!

> (MAMA *absorbs this speech, studies her daughter and rises slowly and crosses to* BENEATHA *and slaps her powerfully across the face. After, there is only silence and the daughter drops her eyes from her mother's face, and* MAMA *is very tall before her*)

MAMA   Now—you say after me, in my mother's house there is still God. (*There is a long pause and* BENEATHA *stares at the floor wordlessly.* MAMA *repeats the phrase with precision and cool emotion*) In my mother's house there is still God.

BENEATHA   In my mother's house there is still God.
> (*A long pause*)

MAMA (*Walking away from* BENEATHA, *too disturbed for triumphant posture. Stopping and turning back to her daughter*)   There are some ideas we ain't going to have in this house. Not long as I am at the head of this family.

BENEATHA   Yes, ma'am.
> (MAMA *walks out of the room*)

RUTH (*Almost gently, with profound understanding*)
You think you a woman, Bennie—but you still a little
girl. What you did was childish—so you got treated
like a child.

BENEATHA   I see. (*Quietly*) I also see that everybody
thinks it's all right for Mama to be a tyrant. But all the
tyranny in the world will never put a God in the
heavens!
    (*She picks up her books and goes out*)

RUTH (*Goes to* MAMA's *door*)   She said she was sorry.

MAMA (*Coming out, going to her plant*)   They frightens
me, Ruth. My children.

RUTH   You got good children, Lena. They just a little
off sometimes—but they're good.

MAMA   No—there's something come down between me
and them that don't let us understand each other and
I don't know what it is. One done almost lost his mind
thinking 'bout money all the time and the other done
commence to talk about things I can't seem to understand in no form or fashion. What is it that's changing,
Ruth?

RUTH (*Soothingly, older than her years*)   Now . . . you
taking it all too seriously. You just got strong-willed
children and it takes a strong woman like you to keep
'em in hand.

MAMA (*Looking at her plant and sprinkling a little water
on it*)   They spirited all right, my children. Got to admit they got spirit—Bennie and Walter. Like this little
old plant that ain't never had enough sunshine or nothing—and look at it . . .
    (*She has her back to* RUTH, *who has had to stop
    ironing and lean against something and put the
    back of her hand to her forehead*)

RUTH *(Trying to keep* MAMA *from noticing)* You . . . sure . . . loves that little old thing, don't you? . . .

MAMA Well, I always wanted me a garden like I used to see sometimes at the back of the houses down home. This plant is close as I ever got to having one. *(She looks out of the window as she replaces the plant)* Lord, ain't nothing as dreary as the view from this window on a dreary day, is there? Why ain't you singing this morning, Ruth? Sing that "No Ways Tired." That song always lifts me up so—*(She turns at last to see that* RUTH *has slipped quietly into a chair, in a state of semiconsciousness)* Ruth! Ruth honey—what's the matter with you . . . Ruth!

Curtain

Scene Two

It is the following morning; a Saturday morning, and house cleaning is in progress at the YOUNGERS. *Furniture has been shoved hither and yon and* MAMA *is giving the kitchen-area walls a washing down.* BENEATHA, *in dungarees, with a handkerchief tied around her face, is spraying insecticide into the cracks in the walls. As they work, the radio is on and a Southside disk-jockey program is inappropriately filling the house with a rather exotic saxophone blues.* TRAVIS, *the sole idle one, is leaning on his arms, looking out of the window.*

TRAVIS Grandmama, that stuff Bennie is using smells awful. Can I go downstairs, please?

MAMA Did you get all them chores done already? I ain't seen you doing much.

TRAVIS Yes'm—finished early. Where did Mama go this morning?

MAMA (*Looking at* BENEATHA) She had to go on a little errand.

TRAVIS Where?

MAMA To tend to her business.

TRAVIS Can I go outside then?

MAMA Oh, I guess so. You better stay right in front of the house, though . . . and keep a good lookout for the postman.

TRAVIS   Yes'm. (*He starts out and decides to give his* AUNT BENEATHA *a good swat on the legs as he passes her*) Leave them poor little old cockroaches alone, they ain't bothering you none.

>   (*He runs as she swings the spray gun at him both viciously and playfully.* WALTER *enters from the bedroom and goes to the phone*)

MAMA   Look out there, girl, before you be spilling some of that stuff on that child!

TRAVIS (*Teasing*)   That's right—look out now!
>   (*He exits*)

BENEATHA (*Drily*)   I can't imagine that it would hurt him —it has never hurt the roaches.

MAMA   Well, little boys' hides ain't as tough as Southside roaches.

WALTER (*Into phone*)   Hello—Let me talk to Willy Harris.

MAMA   You better get over there behind the bureau. I seen one marching out of there like Napoleon yesterday.

WALTER   Hello, Willy? It ain't come yet. It'll be here in a few minutes. Did the lawyer give you the papers?

BENEATHA   There's really only one way to get rid of them, Mama—

MAMA   How?

BENEATHA   Set fire to this building.

WALTER   Good. Good. I'll be right over.

BENEATHA   Where did Ruth go, Walter?

WALTER   I don't know.
>   (*He exits abruptly*)

BENEATHA   Mama, where did Ruth go?

MAMA (*Looking at her with meaning*)   To the doctor, I think.

BENEATHA   The doctor? What's the matter? (*They exchange glances*) You don't think—

MAMA (*With her sense of drama*)   Now I ain't saying what I think. But I ain't never been wrong 'bout a woman neither.

(*The phone rings*)

BENEATHA (*At the phone*)   Hay-lo . . . (*Pause, and a moment of recognition*) Well—when did you get back! . . . And how was it? . . . Of course I've missed you— in my way . . . This morning? No . . . house cleaning and all that and Mama hates it if I let people come over when the house is like this . . . You *have*? Well, that's different . . . What is it— Oh, what the hell, come on over . . . Right, see you then.

(*She hangs up*)

MAMA (*Who has listened vigorously, as is her habit*)   Who is that you inviting over here with this house looking like this? You ain't got the pride you was born with!

BENEATHA   Asagai doesn't care how houses look, Mama —he's an intellectual.

MAMA   *Who?*

BENEATHA   Asagai—Joseph Asagai. He's an African boy I met on campus. He's been studying in Canada all summer.

MAMA   What's his name?

BENEATHA   Asagai, Joseph. Ah-sah-guy . . . He's from Nigeria.

MAMA   Oh, that's the little country that was founded by slaves way back . . .

BENEATHA   No, Mama—that's Liberia.

MAMA   I don't think I never met no African before.

BENEATHA   Well, do me a favor and don't ask him a whole lot of ignorant questions about Africans. I mean, do they wear clothes and all that—

MAMA   Well, now, I guess if you think we so ignorant 'round here maybe you shouldn't bring your friends here—

BENEATHA   It's just that people ask such crazy things. All anyone seems to know about when it comes to Africa is Tarzan—

MAMA   (*Indignantly*)   Why should I know anything about Africa?

BENEATHA   Why do you give money at church for the missionary work?

MAMA   Well, that's to help save people.

BENEATHA   You mean save them from *heathenism*—

MAMA (*Innocently*)   Yes.

BENEATHA   I'm afraid they need more salvation from the British and the French.

> (RUTH *comes in forlornly and pulls off her coat with dejection. They both turn to look at her*)

RUTH (*Dispiritedly*)   Well, I guess from all the happy faces—everybody knows.

BENEATHA   You pregnant?

MAMA   Lord have mercy, I sure hope it's a little old girl. Travis ought to have a sister.

> (BENEATHA *and* RUTH *give her a hopeless look for this grandmotherly enthusiasm*)

BENEATHA   How far along are you?

RUTH   Two months.

BENEATHA   Did you mean to? I mean did you plan it or was it an accident?

MAMA   What do you know about planning or not planning?

BENEATHA   Oh, Mama.

RUTH (*Wearily*)   She's twenty years old, Lena.

BENEATHA   Did you plan it, Ruth?

RUTH   Mind your own business.

BENEATHA   It is my business—where is he going to live, on the *roof*? (*There is silence following the remark as the three women react to the sense of it*) Gee—I didn't mean that, Ruth, honest. Gee, I don't feel like that at all. I—I think it is wonderful.

RUTH (*Dully*)   Wonderful.

BENEATHA   Yes—really.

MAMA (*Looking at* RUTH, *worried*)   Doctor say everything going to be all right?

RUTH (*Far away*)   Yes—she says everything is going to be fine . . .

MAMA (*Immediately suspicious*)   "She"— What doctor you went to?
      (RUTH *folds over, near hysteria*)

MAMA (*Worriedly hovering over* RUTH)   Ruth honey— what's the matter with you—you sick?
      (RUTH *has her fists clenched on her thighs and is fighting hard to suppress a scream that seems to be rising in her*)

BENEATHA   What's the matter with her, Mama?

MAMA (*Working her fingers in* RUTH'S *shoulder to relax her*) She be all right. Women gets right depressed sometimes when they get her way. (*Speaking softly, expertly, rapidly*) Now you just relax. That's right . . . just lean back, don't think 'bout nothing at all . . . nothing at all—

RUTH I'm all right . . .
(*The glassy-eyed look melts and then she collapses into a fit of heavy sobbing. The bell rings*)

BENEATHA Oh, my God—that must be Asagai.

MAMA (*To* RUTH) Come on now, honey. You need to lie down and rest awhile . . . then have some nice hot food.
(*They exit,* RUTH'S *weight on her mother-in-law.* BENEATHA, *herself profoundly disturbed, opens the door to admit a rather dramatic-looking young man with a large package*)

ASAGAI Hello, Alaiyo—

BENEATHA (*Holding the door open and regarding him with pleasure*) Hello . . . (*Long pause*) Well—come in. And please excuse everything. My mother was very upset about my letting anyone come here with the place like this.

ASAGAI (*Coming into the room*) You look disturbed too . . . Is something wrong?

BENEATHA (*Still at the door, absently*) Yes . . . we've all got acute ghetto-itus. (*She smiles and comes toward him, finding a cigarette and sitting*) So—sit down! How was Canada?

ASAGAI (*A sophisticate*) Canadian.

BENEATHA (*Looking at him*) I'm very glad you are back.

ASAGAI (*Looking back at her in turn*)   Are you really?

BENEATHA   Yes—very.

ASAGAI   Why—you were quite glad when I went away. What happened?

BENEATHA   You went away.

ASAGAI   Ahhhhhhhh.

BENEATHA   Before—you wanted to be so serious before there was time.

ASAGAI   How much time must there be before one knows what one feels?

BENEATHA (*Stalling this particular conversation. Her hands pressed together, in a deliberately childish gesture*)   What did you bring me?

ASAGAI (*Handing her the package*)   Open it and see.

BENEATHA (*Eagerly opening the package and drawing out some records and the colorful robes of a Nigerian woman*)   Oh, Asagai! . . . You got them for me! . . . How beautiful . . . and the records too! (*She lifts out the robes and runs to the mirror with them and holds the drapery up in front of herself*)

ASAGAI (*Coming to her at the mirror*)   I shall have to teach you how to drape it properly. (*He flings the material about her for the moment and stands back to look at her*)   Ah—Oh-pay-gay-day, oh-gbah-mu-shay. (*A Yoruba exclamation for admiration*)   You wear it well . . . very well . . . mutilated hair and all.

BENEATHA (*Turning suddenly*)   My hair—what's wrong with my hair?

ASAGAI (*Shrugging*)   Were you born with it like that?

BENEATHA (*Reaching up to touch it*)   No . . . of course not.

(*She looks back to the mirror, disturbed*)

ASAGAI (*Smiling*) How then?

BENEATHA You know perfectly well how . . . as crinkly as yours . . . that's how.

ASAGAI And it is ugly to you that way?

BENEATHA (*Quickly*) Oh, no—not ugly . . . (*More slowly, apologetically*) But it's so hard to manage when it's, well—raw.

ASAGAI And so to accommodate that—you mutilate it every week?

BENEATHA It's not mutilation!

ASAGAI (*Laughing aloud at her seriousness*) Oh . . . please! I am only teasing you because you are so very serious about these things. (*He stands back from her and folds his arms across his chest as he watches her pulling at her hair and frowning in the mirror*) Do you remember the first time you met me at school? . . . (*He laughs*) You came up to me and you said—and I thought you were the most serious little thing I had ever seen—you said: (*He imitates her*) "Mr. Asagai—I want very much to talk with you. About Africa. You see, Mr. Asagai, I am looking for my *identity!*"
    (*He laughs*)

BENEATHA (*Turning to him, not laughing*) Yes—
    (*Her face is quizzical, profoundly disturbed*)

ASAGAI (*Still teasing and reaching out and taking her face in his hands and turning her profile to him*) Well . . . it is true that this is not so much a profile of a Hollywood queen as perhaps a queen of the Nile—(*A mock dismissal of the importance of the question*) But what does it matter? Assimilationism is so popular in your country.

BENEATHA (*Wheeling, passionately, sharply*)   I am not an assimilationist!

ASAGAI (*The protest hangs in the room for a moment and* ASAGAI *studies her, his laughter fading*)   Such a serious one. (*There is a pause*) So—you like the robes? You must take excellent care of them—they are from my sister's personal wardrobe.

BENEATHA (*With incredulity*)   You—you sent all the way home—for me?

ASAGAI (*With charm*)   For you—I would do much more . . . Well, that is what I came for. I must go.

BENEATHA   Will you call me Monday?

ASAGAI   Yes . . . We have a great deal to talk about. I mean about identity and time and all that.

BENEATHA   Time?

ASAGAI   Yes. About how much time one needs to know what one feels.

BENEATHA   You never understood that there is more than one kind of feeling which can exist between a man and a woman—or, at least, there should be.

ASAGAI (*Shaking his head negatively but gently*)   No. Between a man and a woman there need be only one kind of feeling. I have that for you . . . Now even . . . right this moment . . .

BENEATHA   I know—and by itself—it won't do. I can find that anywhere.

ASAGAI   For a woman it should be enough.

BENEATHA   I know—because that's what it says in all the novels that men write. But it isn't. Go ahead and laugh—but I'm not interested in being someone's little episode in America or—(*With feminine vengeance*)—

one of them! (ASAGAI *has burst into laughter again*)
That's funny as hell, huh!

ASAGAI   It's just that every American girl I have known
has said that to me. White—black—in this you are all
the same. And the same speech, too!

BENEATHA (*Angrily*)   Yuk, yuk, yuk!

ASAGAI   It's how you can be sure that the world's most
liberated women are not liberated at all. You all talk
about it too much!

> (MAMA *enters and is immediately all social charm
> because of the presence of a guest*)

BENEATHA   Oh—Mama—this is Mr. Asagai.

MAMA   How do you do?

ASAGAI (*Total politeness to an elder*)   How do you do,
Mrs. Younger. Please forgive me for coming at such
an outrageous hour on a Saturday.

MAMA   Well, you are quite welcome. I just hope you
understand that our house don't always look like this.
(*Chatterish*) You must come again. I would love to
hear all about—(*Not sure of the name*)—your country. I think it's so sad the way our American Negroes
don't know nothing about Africa 'cept Tarzan and all
that. And all that money they pour into these churches
when they ought to be helping you people over there
drive out them French and Englishmen done taken
away your land.

> (*The mother flashes a slightly superior look at
> her daughter upon completion of the recitation*)

ASAGAI (*Taken aback by this sudden and acutely unrelated expression of sympathy*)   Yes . . . yes . . .

MAMA (*Smiling at him suddenly and relaxing and looking him over*)   How many miles is it from here to
where you come from?

ASAGAI   Many thousands.

MAMA (*Looking at him as she would* WALTER)   I bet you don't half look after yourself, being away from your mama either. I spec you better come 'round here from time to time and get yourself some decent home-cooked meals . . .

ASAGAI (*Moved*)   Thank you. Thank you very much. (*They are all quiet, then*—) Well . . . I must go. I will call you Monday, Alaiyo.

MAMA   What's that he call you?

ASAGAI   Oh—"Alaiyo." I hope you don't mind. It is what you would call a nickname, I think. It is a Yoruba word. I am a Yoruba.

MAMA (*Looking at* BENEATHA)   I—I thought he was from—

ASAGAI (*Understanding*)   Nigeria is my country. Yoruba is my tribal origin—

BENEATHA   You didn't tell us what Alaiyo means . . . for all I know, you might be calling me Little Idiot or something . . .

ASAGAI   Well . . . let me see . . . I do not know how just to explain it . . . The sense of a thing can be so different when it changes languages.

BENEATHA   You're evading.

ASAGAI   No—really it is difficult . . . (*Thinking*) It means . . . it means One for Whom Bread—Food—Is Not Enough. (*He looks at her*) Is that all right?

BENEATHA (*Understanding, softly*)   Thank you.

MAMA (*Looking from one to the other and not under-standing any of it*)   Well . . . that's nice . . . You must come see us again—Mr.—

ASAGAI   Ah-sah-guy ...

MAMA   Yes ... Do come again.

ASAGAI   Good-bye.
      (*He exits*)

MAMA (*After him*)   Lord, that's a pretty thing just went
   out here! (*Insinuatingly, to her daughter*) Yes, I guess
   I see why we done commence to get so interested in
   Africa 'round here. Missionaries my aunt Jenny!
      (*She exits*)

BENEATHA   Oh, Mama! ...
      (*She picks up the Nigerian dress and holds it up
      to her in front of the mirror again. She sets the
      headdress on haphazardly and then notices her
      hair again and clutches at it and then replaces the
      headdress and frowns at herself. Then she starts
      to wriggle in front of the mirror as she thinks a
      Nigerian woman might. TRAVIS enters and re-
      gards her*)

TRAVIS   You cracking up?

BENEATHA   Shut up.
      (*She pulls the headdress off and looks at herself
      in the mirror and clutches at her hair again and
      squinches her eyes as if trying to imagine some-
      thing. Then, suddenly, she gets her raincoat and
      kerchief and hurriedly prepares for going out*)

MAMA (*Coming back into the room*)   She's resting now.
   Travis, baby, run next door and ask Miss Johnson to
   please let me have a little kitchen cleanser. This here
   can is empty as Jacob's kettle.

TRAVIS   I just came in.

MAMA   Do as you told. (*He exits and she looks at her
   daughter*) Where you going?

BENEATHA (*Halting at the door*)   To become a queen of the Nile!

> (*She exits in a breathless blaze of glory.* RUTH *appears in the bedroom doorway*)

MAMA   Who told you to get up?

RUTH   Ain't nothing wrong with me to be lying in no bed for. Where did Bennie go?

MAMA (*Drumming her fingers*)   Far as I could make out—to Egypt. (RUTH *just looks at her*) What time is it getting to?

RUTH   Ten twenty. And the mailman going to ring that bell this morning just like he done every morning for the last umpteen years.

> (TRAVIS *comes in with the cleanser can*)

TRAVIS   She say to tell you that she don't have much.

MAMA (*Angrily*)   Lord, some people I could name sure is tight-fisted! (*Directing her grandson*) Mark two cans of cleanser down on the list there. If she that hard up for kitchen cleanser, I sure don't want to forget to get her none!

RUTH   Lena—maybe the woman is just short on cleanser—

MAMA (*Not listening*)   —Much baking powder as she done borrowed from me all these years, she could of done gone into the baking business!

> (*The bell sounds suddenly and sharply and all three are stunned—serious and silent—mid-speech. In spite of all the other conversations and distractions of the morning, this is what they have been waiting for, even* TRAVIS, *who looks helplessly from his mother to his grandmother.* RUTH *is the first to come to life again*)

RUTH (*To* TRAVIS) *Get down them steps, boy!*
   (TRAVIS *snaps to life and flies out to get the mail*)

MAMA (*Her eyes wide, her hand to her breast*) You mean it done really come?

RUTH (*Excited*) Oh, Miss Lena!

MAMA (*Collecting herself*) Well . . . I don't know what we all so excited about 'round here for. We known it was coming for months.

RUTH That's a whole lot different from having it come and being able to hold it in your hands . . . a piece of paper worth ten thousand dollars . . . (TRAVIS *bursts back into the room. He holds the envelope high above his head, like a little dancer, his face is radiant and he is breathless. He moves to his grandmother with sudden slow ceremony and puts the envelope into her hands. She accepts it, and then merely holds it and looks at it*) Come on! Open it . . . Lord have mercy, I wish Walter Lee was here!

TRAVIS Open it, Grandmama!

MAMA (*Staring at it*) Now you all be quiet. It's just a check.

RUTH Open it . . .

MAMA (*Still staring at it*) Now don't act silly . . . We ain't never been no people to act silly 'bout no money—

RUTH (*Swiftly*) We ain't never had none before—*open it!*
   (MAMA *finally makes a good strong tear and pulls out the thin blue slice of paper and inspects it closely. The boy and his mother study it raptly over* MAMA'S *shoulders*)

MAMA Travis! (*She is counting off with doubt*) Is that the right number of zeros.

TRAVIS Yes'm . . . ten thousand dollars. Gaalee, Grand-mama, you rich.

MAMA (*She holds the check away from her, still looking at it. Slowly her face sobers into a mask of unhappiness*) Ten thousand dollars. (*She hands it to* RUTH) Put it away somewhere, Ruth. (*She does not look at* RUTH; *her eyes seem to be seeing something somewhere very far off*) Ten thousand dollars they give you. Ten thousand dollars.

TRAVIS (*To his mother, sincerely*) What's the matter with Grandmama—don't she want to be rich?

RUTH (*Distractedly*) You go on out and play now, baby. (TRAVIS *exits.* MAMA *starts wiping dishes absently, humming intently to herself.* RUTH *turns to her, with kind exasperation*) You've gone and got yourself upset.

MAMA (*Not looking at her*) I spec if it wasn't for you all . . . I would just put that money away or give it to the church or something.

RUTH Now what kind of talk is that. Mr. Younger would just be plain mad if he could hear you talking foolish like that.

MAMA (*Stopping and staring off*) Yes . . . he sure would. (*Sighing*) We got enough to do with that money, all right. (*She halts then, and turns and looks at her daughter-in-law hard;* RUTH *avoids her eyes and* MAMA *wipes her hands with finality and starts to speak firmly to* RUTH) Where did you go today, girl?

RUTH To the doctor.

MAMA (*Impatiently*) Now, Ruth . . . you know better than that. Old Doctor Jones is strange enough in his way but there ain't nothing 'bout him make somebody slip and call him "she"—like you done this morning.

RUTH   Well, that's what happened—my tongue slipped.

MAMA   You went to see that woman, didn't you?

RUTH   (*Defensively, giving herself away*)   What woman you talking about?

MAMA   (*Angrily*)   That woman who—
        (WALTER *enters in great excitement*)

WALTER   Did it come?

MAMA   (*Quietly*)   Can't you give people a Christian greeting before you start asking about money?

WALTER   (*To* RUTH)   Did it come? (RUTH *unfolds the check and lays it quietly before him, watching him intently with thoughts of her own.* WALTER *sits down and grasps it close and counts off the zeros*) Ten thousand dollars—(*He turns suddenly, frantically to his mother and draws some papers out of his breast pocket*) Mama—look. Old Willy Harris put everything on paper—

MAMA   Son—I think you ought to talk to your wife . . . I'll go on out and leave you alone if you want—

WALTER   I can talk to her later— Mama, look—

MAMA   Son—

WALTER   WILL SOMEBODY PLEASE LISTEN TO ME TODAY!

MAMA   (*Quietly*)   I don't 'low no yellin' in this house, Walter Lee, and you know it—(WALTER *stares at them in frustration and starts to speak several times*) And there ain't going to be no investing in no liquor stores. I don't aim to have to speak on that again.
        (*A long pause*)

WALTER   Oh—so you don't aim to have to speak on that again? So *you* have decided . . . (*Crumpling his papers*) Well, *you* tell that to my boy tonight when you put him to sleep on the living-room couch . . . (*Turning to* MAMA *and speaking directly to her*) Yeah— and tell it to my wife, Mama, tomorrow when she has to go out of here to look after somebody else's kids. And tell it to *me*, Mama, every time we need a new pair of curtains and I have to watch *you* go out and work in somebody's kitchen. Yeah, you tell me then!

(WALTER *starts out*)

RUTH   Where you going?

WALTER   I'm going out!

RUTH   Where?

WALTER   Just out of this house somewhere—

RUTH (*Getting her coat*)   I'll come too.

WALTER   I don't want you to come!

RUTH   I got something to talk to you about, Walter.

WALTER   That's too bad.

MAMA (*Still quietly*)   Walter Lee—(*She waits and he finally turns and looks at her*) Sit down.

WALTER   I'm a grown man, Mama.

MAMA   Ain't nobody said you wasn't grown. But you still in my house and my presence. And as long as you are—you'll talk to your wife civil. Now sit down.

RUTH (*Suddenly*)   Oh, let him go on out and drink himself to death! He makes me sick to my stomach! (*She flings her coat against him*)

WALTER (*Violently*)   And you turn mine too, baby! (RUTH *goes into their bedroom and slams the door behind her*) That was my greatest mistake—

MAMA (*Still quietly*) Walter, what is the matter with you?

WALTER Matter with me? Ain't nothing the matter with *me!*

MAMA Yes there is. Something eating you up like a crazy man. Something more than me not giving you this money. The past few years I been watching it happen to you. You get all nervous acting and kind of wild in the eyes—(WALTER *jumps up impatiently at her words*) I said sit there now, I'm talking to you!

WALTER Mama—I don't need no nagging at me today.

MAMA Seem like you getting to a place where you always tied up in some kind of knot about something. But if anybody ask you 'bout it you just yell at 'em and bust out the house and go out and drink somewheres. Walter Lee, people can't live with that. Ruth's a good, patient girl in her way—but you getting to be too much. Boy, don't make the mistake of driving that girl away from you.

WALTER Why—what she do for me?

MAMA She loves you.

WALTER Mama—I'm going out. I want to go off somewhere and be by myself for a while.

MAMA I'm sorry 'bout your liquor store, son. It just wasn't the thing for us to do. That's what I want to tell you about—

WALTER I got to go out, Mama—
        (*He rises*)

MAMA It's dangerous, son.

WALTER What's dangerous?

MAMA   When a man goes outside his home to look for peace.

WALTER (*Beseechingly*) Then why can't there never be no peace in this house then?

MAMA   You done found it in some other house?

WALTER No—there ain't no woman! Why do women always think there's a woman somewhere when a man gets restless. (*Coming to her*) Mama—Mama—I want so many things . . .

MAMA   Yes, son—

WALTER I want so many things that they are driving me kind of crazy . . . Mama—look at me.

MAMA   I'm looking at you. You a good-looking boy. You got a job, a nice wife, a fine boy and—

WALTER A job. (*Looks at her*) Mama, a job? I open and close car doors all day long. I drive a man around in his limousine and I say, "Yes, sir; no, sir; very good, sir; shall I take the Drive, sir?" Mama, that ain't no kind of job . . . that ain't nothing at all. (*Very quietly*) Mama, I don't know if I can make you understand.

MAMA   Understand what, baby?

WALTER (*Quietly*) Sometimes it's like I can see the future stretched out in front of me—just plain as day. The future, Mama. Hanging over there at the edge of my days. Just waiting for me—a big, looming blank space—full of *nothing*. Just waiting for *me*. (*Pause*) Mama—sometimes when I'm downtown and I pass them cool, quiet-looking restaurants where them white boys are sitting back and talking 'bout things . . . sitting there turning deals worth millions of dollars . . . sometimes I see guys don't look much older than me—

MAMA Son—how come you talk so much 'bout money?

WALTER (*With immense passion*) Because it is life, Mama!

MAMA (*Quietly*) Oh—(*Very quietly*) So now it's life. Money is life. Once upon a time freedom used to be life—now it's money. I guess the world really do change . . .

WALTER No—it was always money, Mama. We just didn't know about it.

MAMA No . . . something has changed. (*She looks at him*) You something new, boy. In my time we was worried about not being lynched and getting to the North if we could and how to stay alive and still have a pinch of dignity too . . . Now here come you and Beneatha—talking 'bout things we ain't never even thought about hardly, me and your daddy. You ain't satisfied or proud of nothing we done. I mean that you had a home; that we kept you out of trouble till you was grown; that you don't have to ride to work on the back of nobody's streetcar— You my children—but how different we done become.

WALTER You just don't understand, Mama, you just don't understand.

MAMA Son—do you know your wife is expecting another baby? (WALTER *stands, stunned, and absorbs what his mother has said*) That's what she wanted to talk to you about. (WALTER *sinks down into a chair*) This ain't for me to be telling—but you ought to know. (*She waits*) I think Ruth is thinking 'bout getting rid of that child.

WALTER (*Slowly understanding*) No — no — Ruth wouldn't do that.

MAMA When the world gets ugly enough—a woman

will do anything for her family. *The part that's already living.*

WALTER   You don't know Ruth, Mama, if you think she would do that.

>   (RUTH *opens the bedroom door and stands there a little limp*)

RUTH (*Beaten*)   Yes I would too, Walter. (*Pause*) I gave her a five-dollar down payment.

>   (*There is total silence as the man stares at his wife and the mother stares at her son*)

MAMA (*Presently*)   Well — (*Tightly*) Well — son, I'm waiting to hear you say something . . . I'm waiting to hear how you be your father's son. Be the man he was . . . (*Pause*) Your wife say she going to destroy your child. And I'm waiting to hear you talk like him and say we a people who give children life, not who destroys them—(*She rises*) I'm waiting to see you stand up and look like your daddy and say we done give up one baby to poverty and that we ain't going to give up nary another one . . . I'm waiting.

WALTER   Ruth—

MAMA   If you a son of mine, tell her! (WALTER *turns, looks at her and can say nothing. She continues, bitterly*) You . . . you are a disgrace to your father's memory. Somebody get me my hat.

Curtain

A RAISIN IN THE SUN

will do anything for her family. The part that's about
living.

WALTER You don't know Ruth, Mama, if you think

ACT II

Scene I

Time: Later the same day.

At rise: RUTH *is ironing again. She has the radio going. Presently* BENEATHA'S *bedroom door opens and* RUTH'S *mouth falls and she puts down the iron in fascination.*

RUTH What have we got on tonight!

BENEATHA (*Emerging grandly from the doorway so that we can see her thoroughly robed in the costume Asagai brought*) You are looking at what a well-dressed Nigerian woman wears—(*She parades for* RUTH, *her hair completely hidden by the headdress; she is coquettishly fanning herself with an ornate oriental fan, mistakenly more like Butterfly than any Nigerian that ever was*) Isn't it beautiful? (*She promenades to the radio and, with an arrogant flourish, turns off the good loud blues that is playing*) Enough of this assimilationist junk! (*RUTH follows her with her eyes as she goes to the phonograph and puts on a record and turns and waits ceremoniously for the music to come up. Then, with a shout—*) OCOMOGOSIAY!

(RUTH *jumps. The music comes up, a lovely Ni-gerian melody.* BENEATHA *listens, enraptured, her eyes far away—"back to the past." She begins to dance.* RUTH *is dumfounded*)

RUTH   What kind of dance is that?

BENEATHA   A folk dance.

RUTH (*Pearl Bailey*)   What kind of folks do that, honey?

BENEATHA   It's from Nigeria. It's a dance of welcome.

RUTH   Who you welcoming?

BENEATHA   The men back to the village.

RUTH   Where they been?

BENEATHA   How should I know—out hunting or some-thing. Anyway, they are coming back now . . .

RUTH   Well, that's good.

BENEATHA (*With the record*)
   Alundi, alundi
   Alundi alunya
   Jop pu a jeepua
   Ang gu soooooooooo

   Ai yai yae . . .
   Ayehaye—alundi . . .
   (WALTER *comes in during this performance; he has obviously been drinking. He leans against the door heavily and watches his sister, at first with distaste. Then his eyes look off—"back to the past"—as he lifts both his fists to the roof, screaming*)

WALTER   YEAH . . . AND ETHIOPIA STRETCH FORTH HER HANDS AGAIN! . . .

RUTH (*Drily, looking at him*)   Yes—and Africa sure is

claiming her own tonight. (*She gives them both up and starts ironing again*)

WALTER (*All in a drunken, dramatic shout*) Shut up! . . . I'm digging them drums . . . them drums move me! . . . (*He makes his weaving way to his wife's face and leans in close to her*) In my *heart of hearts*—(*He thumps his chest*)—I am much warrior!

RUTH (*Without even looking up*) In your heart of hearts you are much drunkard.

WALTER (*Coming away from her and starting to wander around the room, shouting*) Me and Jomo . . . (*Intently, in his sister's face. She has stopped dancing to watch him in this unknown mood*) That's my man, Kenyatta. (*Shouting and thumping his chest*) FLAMING SPEAR! HOT DAMN! (*He is suddenly in possession of an imaginary spear and actively spearing enemies all over the room*) OCOMOGOSIAY . . . THE LION IS WAKING . . . OWIMOWEH! (*He pulls his shirt open and leaps up on a table and gestures with his spear. The bell rings. RUTH goes to answer*)

BENEATHA (*To encourage WALTER, thoroughly caught up with this side of him*) OCOMOGOSIAY, FLAMING SPEAR!

WALTER (*On the table, very far gone, his eyes pure glass sheets. He sees what we cannot, that he is a leader of his people, a great chief, a descendant of Chaka, and that the hour to march has come*) Listen, my black brothers—

BENEATHA OCOMOGOSIAY!

WALTER —Do you hear the waters rushing against the shores of the coastlands—

BENEATHA OCOMOGOSIAY!

WALTER   —Do you hear the screeching of the cocks in
   yonder hills beyond where the chiefs meet in council
   for the coming of the mighty war—

BENEATHA   OCOMOGOSIAY!

WALTER   —Do you hear the beating of the wings of the
   birds flying low over the mountains and the low places
   of our land—
      (RUTH *opens the door.* GEORGE MURCHISON *en-
      ters*)

BENEATHA   OCOMOGOSIAY!

WALTER   —Do you hear the singing of the women, singing the war songs of our fathers to the babies in the
   great houses . . . singing the sweet war songs? OH,
   DO YOU HEAR, MY BLACK BROTHERS!

BENEATHA (*Completely gone*)   We hear you, Flaming
   Spear—

WALTER   Telling us to prepare for the greatness of the
   time—(*To* GEORGE) Black Brother!
      (*He extends his hand for the fraternal clasp*)

GEORGE   Black Brother, hell!

RUTH (*Having had enough, and embarrassed for the
   family*)   Beneatha, you got company—what's the matter with you? Walter Lee Younger, get down off that
   table and stop acting like a fool . . .
      (WALTER *comes down off the table suddenly and
      makes a quick exit to the bathroom*)

RUTH   He's had a little to drink . . . I don't know what
   her excuse is.

GEORGE (*To* BENEATHA)   Look honey, we're going *to*
   the theatre—we're not going to be *in* it . . . so go
   change, huh?

Scenes on this and the following pages are from the motion picture. Columbia Pictures presents SIDNEY POITIER in A RAISIN IN THE SUN, co-starring Claudia MacNeil and Ruby Dee. Screenplay by Lorraine Hansberry. Directed by Daniel Petrie. A David Susskind-Philip Rose production.

Printed in the U.S.A.

BENEATHA: What do you want from me, Brother—that I quit school or just drop dead, which!

WALTER: I don't want nothing but for you to stop acting holy 'round here. Me and Ruth done made some sacrifices for you—why can't you do something for the family?

MAMA: She be all right. Women gets right depressed sometimes when they get her way.

WALTER: Ten thousand dollars—

RUTH: Honey . . . life don't have to be like this. I mean sometimes people can do things so that things are better . . . You remember how we used to talk when Travis was born . . .

BENEATHA: Talk about—olddddddddddd-fashionedddddddd —Negroes!

WALTER: Yeah, they said they can't hardly wait to see your face.

MAMA: What's the matter with you all?

WALTER: You trust me like that, Mama?

MAMA: I ain't never stop trusting you. Like
I ain't never stop loving you.

WALTER: Open it, Mama. It's for you.

WALTER: Ruth made up the note—read it . . .

MAMA: "To our own Mrs. Miniver—Love from Brother, Ruth and Beneatha." Ain't that lovely . . .

MAMA: Oh, God . . . Look down here—and show me the strength.

MAMA: Four o six Clybourne Street, Clybourne Park.

RUTH: Clybourne Park? Mama, there ain't no colored people living in Clybourne Park.

RUTH   You expect this boy to go out with you looking like that?

BENEATHA (*Looking at* GEORGE)   That's up to George. If he's ashamed of his heritage—

GEORGE   Oh, don't be so proud of yourself, Bennie—just because you look eccentric.

BENEATHA   How can something that's natural be eccentric?

GEORGE   That's what being eccentric means—being natural. Get dressed.

BENEATHA   I don't like that, George.

RUTH   Why must you and your brother make an argument out of everything people say?

BENEATHA   Because I hate assimilationist Negroes!

RUTH   Will somebody please tell me what assimila-who-ever means!

GEORGE   Oh, it's just a college girl's way of calling people Uncle Toms—but that isn't what it means at all.

RUTH   Well, what does it mean?

BENEATHA (*Cutting* GEORGE *off and staring at him as she replies to* RUTH)   It means someone who is willing to give up his own culture and submerge himself completely in the dominant, and in this case, *oppressive* culture!

GEORGE   Oh, dear, dear, dear! Here we go! A lecture on the African past! On our Great West African Heritage! In one second we will hear all about the great Ashanti empires; the great Songhay civilizations; and the great sculpture of Bénin—and then some poetry in the Bantu—and the whole monologue will end with the word *heritage!* (*Nastily*) Let's face it, baby, your heritage is nothing but a bunch of raggedy-assed spirituals and some grass huts!

BENEATHA   *Grass huts!* (RUTH *crosses to her and forcibly pushes her toward the bedroom*) See there . . . you are standing there in your splendid ignorance talking about people who were the first to smelt iron on the face of the earth! (RUTH *is pushing her through the door*) The Ashanti were performing surgical operations when the English—(RUTH *pulls the door to, with* BENEATHA *on the other side, and smiles graciously at* GEORGE. BENEATHA *opens the door and shouts the end of the sentence defiantly at* GEORGE)—were still tatooing themselves with blue dragons . . . (*She goes back inside*)

RUTH   Have a seat, George. (*They both sit.* RUTH *folds her hands rather primly on her lap, determined to demonstrate the civilization of the family*) Warm, ain't it? I mean for September. (*Pause*) Just like they always say about Chicago weather: If it's too hot or cold for you, just wait a minute and it'll change. (*She smiles happily at this cliché of clichés*) Everybody say it's got to do with them bombs and things they keep setting off. (*Pause*) Would you like a nice cold beer?

GEORGE   No, thank you. I don't care for beer. (*He looks at his watch*) I hope she hurries up.

RUTH   What time is the show?

GEORGE   It's an eight-thirty curtain. That's just Chicago, though. In New York standard curtain time is eight forty.
        (*He is rather proud of this knowledge*)

RUTH (*Properly appreciating it*)   You get to New York a lot?

GEORGE (*Offhand*)   Few times a year.

RUTH   Oh—that's nice. I've never been to New York.
(WALTER *enters. We feel he has relieved himself,
but the edge of unreality is still with him*)

WALTER   New York ain't got nothing Chicago ain't. Just
a bunch of hustling people all squeezed up together—
being "Eastern."
(*He turns his face into a screw of displeasure*)

GEORGE   Oh—you've been?

WALTER   *Plenty* of times.

RUTH (*Shocked at the lie*)   Walter Lee Younger!

WALTER (*Staring her down*)   Plenty! (*Pause*) What we
got to drink in this house? Why don't you offer this
man some refreshment. (*To* GEORGE) They don't know
how to entertain people in this house, man.

GEORGE   Thank you—I don't really care for anything.

WALTER (*Feeling his head; sobriety coming*)   Where's
Mama?

RUTH   She ain't come back yet.

WALTER (*Looking* MURCHISON *over from head to toe,
scrutinizing his carefully casual tweed sports jacket over
cashmere V-neck sweater over soft eyelet shirt and tie,
and soft slacks, finished off with white buckskin shoes*)
Why all you college boys wear them fairyish-looking
white shoes?

RUTH   Walter Lee!
(GEORGE MURCHISON *ignores the remark*)

WALTER (*To* RUTH)   Well, they look crazy as hell—
white shoes, cold as it is.

RUTH (*Crushed*)   You have to excuse him—

WALTER   No he don't! Excuse me for what? What you
always excusing me for! I'll excuse myself when I needs
to be excused! (*A pause*) They look as funny as them
black knee socks Beneatha wears out of here all the
time.

RUTH   It's the college *style*, Walter.

WALTER   Style, hell. She looks like she got burnt legs or
something!

RUTH   Oh, Walter—

WALTER (*An irritable mimic*)   Oh, Walter! Oh, Walter!
(*To* MURCHISON) How's your old man making out? I
understand you all going to buy that big hotel on the
Drive? (*He finds a beer in the refrigerator, wanders
over to* MURCHISON, *sipping and wiping his lips with
the back of his hand, and straddling a chair backwards to talk to the other man*) Shrewd move. Your
old man is all right, man. (*Tapping his head and half
winking for emphasis*) I mean he knows how to oper-
ate. I mean he thinks *big*, you know what I mean, I
mean for a *home*, you know? But I think he's kind of
running out of ideas now. I'd like to talk to him. Listen, man, I got some plans that could turn this city
upside down. I mean I think like he does. *Big*. Invest
big, gamble big, hell, lose *big* if you have to, you know
what I mean. It's hard to find a man on this whole
Southside who understands my kind of thinking—you
dig? (*He scrutinizes* MURCHISON *again, drinks his beer,
squints his eyes and leans in close, confidential, man
to man*) Me and you ought to sit down and talk sometimes, man. Man, I got me some ideas . . .

MURCHISON (*With boredom*)   Yeah — sometimes we'll
have to do that, Walter.

WALTER (*Understanding the indifference, and offended*)

Yeah—well, when you get the time, man. I know you a busy little boy.

RUTH Walter, please—

WALTER (*Bitterly, hurt*) I know ain't nothing in this world as busy as you colored college boys with your fraternity pins and white shoes . . .

RUTH (*Covering her face with humiliation*) Oh, Walter Lee—

WALTER I see you all all the time—with the books tucked under your arms—going to your (*British A—a mimic*) "clahsses." And for what! What the hell you learning over there? Filling up your heads—(*Counting off on his fingers*)—with the sociology and the psychology—but they teaching you how to be a man? How to take over and run the world? They teaching you how to run a rubber plantation or a steel mill? Naw—just to talk proper and read books and wear white shoes . . .

GEORGE (*Looking at him with distaste, a little above it all*) You're all wacked up with bitterness, man.

WALTER (*Intently, almost quietly, between the teeth, glaring at the boy*) And you—ain't you bitter, man? Ain't you just about had it yet? Don't you see no stars gleaming that you can't reach out and grab? You happy?—You contented son-of-a-bitch—you happy? You got it made? Bitter? Man, I'm a volcano. Bitter? Here I am a giant—surrounded by ants! Ants who can't even understand what it is the giant is talking about.

RUTH (*Passionately and suddenly*) Oh, Walter—ain't you with nobody!

WALTER (*Violently*) No! 'Cause ain't nobody with me! Not even my own mother!

RUTH Walter, that's a terrible thing to say!
(BENEATHA *enters, dressed for the evening in a cocktail dress and earrings*)

GEORGE Well—hey, you look great.

BENEATHA Let's go, George. See you all later.

RUTH Have a nice time.

GEORGE Thanks. Good night. (*To* WALTER, *sarcastically*) Good night, *Prometheus*.
(BENEATHA *and* GEORGE *exit*)

WALTER (*To* RUTH) Who is Prometheus?

RUTH I don't know. Don't worry about it.

WALTER (*In fury, pointing after* GEORGE) See there—they get to a point where they can't insult you man to man—they got to go talk about something ain't nobody never heard of!

RUTH How do you know it was an insult? (*To humor him*) Maybe Prometheus is a nice fellow.

WALTER Prometheus! I bet there ain't even no such thing! I bet that simple-minded clown—

RUTH Walter—
(*She stops what she is doing and looks at him*)

WALTER (*Yelling*) Don't start!

RUTH Start what?

WALTER Your nagging! Where was I? Who was I with? How much money did I spend?

RUTH (*Plaintively*) Walter Lee—why don't we just try to talk about it . . .

WALTER (*Not listening*) I been out talking with people who understand me. People who care about the things I got on my mind.

RUTH (*Wearily*) I guess that means people like Willy Harris.

WALTER Yes, people like Willy Harris.

RUTH (*With a sudden flash of impatience*) Why don't you all just hurry up and go into the banking business and stop talking about it!

WALTER Why? You want to know why? 'Cause we all tied up in a race of people that don't know how to do nothing but moan, pray and have babies!
(*The line is too bitter even for him and he looks at her and sits down*)

RUTH Oh, Walter . . . (*Softly*) Honey, why can't you stop fighting me?

WALTER (*Without thinking*) Who's fighting you? Who even cares about you?
(*This line begins the retardation of his mood*)

RUTH Well—(*She waits a long time, and then with resignation starts to put away her things*) I guess I might as well go on to bed . . . (*More or less to herself*) I don't know where we lost it . . . but we have . . . (*Then, to him*) I—I'm sorry about this new baby, Walter. I guess maybe I better go on and do what I started . . . I guess I just didn't realize how bad things was with us . . . I guess I just didn't really realize—(*She starts out to the bedroom and stops*) You want some hot milk?

WALTER Hot milk?

RUTH Yes—hot milk.

WALTER Why hot milk?

RUTH 'Cause after all that liquor you come home with you ought to have something hot in your stomach.

WALTER I don't want no milk.

RUTH You want some coffee then?

WALTER No, I don't want no coffee. I don't want nothing hot to drink. (*Almost plaintively*) Why you always trying to give me something to eat?

RUTH (*Standing and looking at him helplessly*) What else can I give you, Walter Lee Younger?
(*She stands and looks at him and presently turns to go out again. He lifts his head and watches her going away from him in a new mood which began to emerge when he asked her "Who cares about you?"*)

WALTER It's been rough, ain't it, baby? (*She hears and stops but does not turn around and he continues to her back*) I guess between two people there ain't never as much understood as folks generally thinks there is. I mean like between me and you—(*She turns to face him*) How we gets to the place where we scared to talk softness to each other. (*He waits, thinking hard himself*) Why you think it got to be like that? (*He is thoughtful, almost as a child would be*) Ruth, what is it gets into people ought to be close?

RUTH. I don't know, honey. I think about it a lot.

WALTER On account of you and me, you mean? The way things are with us. The way something done come down between us.

RUTH There ain't so much between us, Walter . . . Not when you come to me and try to talk to me. Try to be with me . . . a little even.

WALTER (*Total honesty*) Sometimes . . . sometimes . . . I don't even know how to try.

RUTH Walter—

WALTER Yes?

RUTH (*Coming to him, gently and with misgiving, but coming to him*) Honey . . . life don't have to be like this. I mean sometimes people can do things so that things are better . . . You remember how we used to talk when Travis was born . . . about the way we were going to live . . . the kind of house . . . (*She is stroking his head*) Well, it's all starting to slip away from us . . .
      (MAMA *enters, and* WALTER *jumps up and shouts at her*)

WALTER Mama, where have you been?

MAMA My—them steps is longer than they used to be. Whew! (*She sits down and ignores him*) How you feeling this evening, Ruth?
      (RUTH *shrugs, disturbed some at having been prematurely interrupted and watching her husband knowingly*)

WALTER Mama, where have you been all day?

MAMA (*Still ignoring him and leaning on the table and changing to more comfortable shoes*) Where's Travis?

RUTH I let him go out earlier and he ain't come back yet. Boy, is he going to get it!

WALTER Mama!

MAMA (*As if she has heard him for the first time*) Yes, son?

WALTER Where did you go this afternoon?

MAMA I went downtown to tend to some business that I had to tend to.

WALTER What kind of business?

MAMA   You know better than to question me like a child, Brother.

WALTER (*Rising and bending over the table*) Where were you, Mama? (*Bringing his fists down and shouting*) Mama, you didn't go do something with that insurance money, something crazy?

(*The front door opens slowly, interrupting him, and* TRAVIS *peeks his head in, less than hopefully*)

TRAVIS (*To his mother*)   Mama, I—

RUTH   "Mama I" nothing! You're going to get it, boy! Get on in that bedroom and get yourself ready!

TRAVIS   But I—

MAMA   Why don't you all never let the child explain hisself.

RUTH   Keep out of it now, Lena.

(MAMA *clamps her lips together, and* RUTH *advances toward her son menacingly*)

RUTH   A thousand times I have told you not to go off like that—

MAMA (*Holding out her arms to her grandson*) Well— at least let me tell him something. I want him to be the first one to hear . . . Come here, Travis. (*The boy obeys, gladly*) Travis—(*She takes him by the shoulder and looks into his face*)—you know that money we got in the mail this morning?

TRAVIS   Yes'm—

MAMA   Well—what you think your grandmama gone and done with that money?

TRAVIS   I don't know, Grandmama.

MAMA (*Putting her finger on his nose for emphasis*) She went out and she bought you a house! (*The explosion comes from* WALTER *at the end of the revelation and he jumps up and turns away from all of them in a fury.* MAMA *continues, to* TRAVIS) You glad about the house? It's going to be yours when you get to be a man.

TRAVIS Yeah—I always wanted to live in a house.

MAMA All right, gimme some sugar then—(TRAVIS *puts his arms around her neck as she watches her son over the boy's shoulder. Then, to* TRAVIS, *after the embrace*) Now when you say your prayers tonight, you thank God and your grandfather—'cause it was him who give you the house—in his way.

RUTH (*Taking the boy from* MAMA *and pushing him toward the bedroom*) Now you get out of here and get ready for your beating.

TRAVIS Aw, Mama—

RUTH Get on in there—(*Closing the door behind him and turning radiantly to her mother-in-law*) So you went and did it!

MAMA (*Quietly, looking at her son with pain*) Yes, I did.

RUTH (*Raising both arms classically*) Praise God! (*Looks at* WALTER *a moment, who says nothing. She crosses rapidly to her husband*) Please, honey—let me be glad . . . you be glad too. (*She has laid her hands on his shoulders, but he shakes himself free of her roughly, without turning to face her*) Oh, Walter . . . a home . . . *a home.* (*She comes back to* MAMA) Well —where is it? How big is it? How much it going to cost?

MAMA Well—

RUTH When we moving?

MAMA (*Smiling at her*) First of the month.

RUTH (*Throwing back her head with jubilance*)   Praise God!

MAMA (*Tentatively, still looking at her son's back turned against her and* RUTH)   It's—it's a nice house too . . . (*She cannot help speaking directly to him. An imploring quality in her voice, her manner, makes her almost like a girl now*) Three bedrooms—nice big one for you and Ruth. . . . Me and Beneatha still have to share our room, but Travis have one of his own—and (*With difficulty*) I figure if the—new baby—is a boy, we could get one of them double-decker outfits . . . And there's a yard with a little patch of dirt where I could maybe get to grow me a few flowers . . . And a nice big basement . . .

RUTH   Walter honey, be glad—

MAMA (*Still to his back, fingering things on the table*) 'Course I don't want to make it sound fancier than it is . . . It's just a plain little old house—but it's made good and solid—and it will`be *ours*. Walter Lee—it makes a difference in a man when he can walk on floors that belong to *him* . . .

RUTH   Where is it?

MAMA (*Frightened at this telling*)   Well—well—it's out there in Clybourne Park—
        (RUTH's *radiance fades abruptly, and* WALTER *finally turns slowly to face his mother with incredulity and hostility*)

RUTH   Where?

MAMA (*Matter-of-factly*)   Four o six Clybourne Street, Clybourne Park.

RUTH   Clybourne Park? Mama, there ain't no colored people living in Clybourne Park.

MAMA (*Almost idiotically*) Well, I guess there's going to be some now.

WALTER (*Bitterly*) So that's the peace and comfort you went out and bought for us today!

MAMA (*Raising her eyes to meet his finally*) Son—I just tried to find the nicest place for the least amount of money for my family.

RUTH (*Trying to recover from the shock*) Well—well—'course I ain't one never been 'fraid of no crackers, mind you—but—well, wasn't there no other houses nowhere?

MAMA Them houses they put up for colored in them areas way out all seem to cost twice as much as other houses. I did the best I could.

RUTH (*Struck senseless with the news, in its various degrees of goodness and trouble, she sits a moment, her fists propping her chin in thought, and then she starts to rise, bringing her fists down with vigor, the radiance spreading from cheek to cheek again*) Well —well!—All I can say is—if this is my time in life— my time—to say good-bye—(*And she builds with momentum as she starts to circle the room with an exuberant, almost tearfully happy release*)—to these Goddamned cracking walls!—(*She pounds the walls*) —and these marching roaches!—(*She wipes at an imaginary army of marching roaches*)—and this cramped little closet which ain't now or never was no kitchen! . . . then I say it loud and good, Hallelujah! and good-bye misery . . . I don't never want to see your ugly face again! (*She laughs joyously, having practically destroyed the apartment, and flings her arms up and lets them come down happily, slowly, reflectively, over her abdomen, aware for the first time perhaps that the life therein pulses with happiness and not despair*) Lena?

MAMA (*Moved, watching her happiness*)   Yes, honey?

RUTH (*Looking off*)   Is there—is there a whole lot of
sunlight?

MAMA (*Understanding*)   Yes, child, there's a whole lot
of sunlight.
    (*Long pause*)

RUTH (*Collecting herself and going to the door of the
room* TRAVIS *is in*)   Well—I guess I better see 'bout
Travis. (*To* MAMA) Lord, I sure don't feel like whip-
ping nobody today!
    (*She exits*)

MAMA (*The mother and son are left alone now and the
mother waits a long time, considering deeply, before
she speaks*)   Son—you—you understand what I done,
don't you? (WALTER *is silent and sullen*) I—I just
seen my family falling apart today . . . just falling to
pieces in front of my eyes . . . We couldn't of gone on
like we was today. We was going backwards 'stead of
forwards—talking 'bout killing babies and wishing each
other was dead . . . When it gets like that in life—you
just got to do something different, push on out and do
something bigger . . . (*She waits*) I wish you say something, son . . . I wish you'd say how deep inside you
you think I done the right thing—

WALTER (*Crossing slowly to his bedroom door and finally
turning there and speaking measuredly*)   What you
need me to say you done right for? *You* the head of this
family. You run our lives like you want to. It was
your money and you did what you wanted with it. So
what you need for me to say it was all right for? (*Bitterly, to hurt her as deeply as he knows is possible*)
So you butchered up a dream of mine—you—who always talking 'bout your children's dreams . . .

MAMA Walter Lee—
        (*He just closes the door behind him.* MAMA *sits alone, thinking heavily*)

Curtain

Scene II

Time: Friday night. A few weeks later.

At rise: Packing crates mark the intention of the family to move. BENEATHA *and* GEORGE *come in, presumably from an evening out again.*

GEORGE O.K. . . . O.K., whatever you say . . . (*They both sit on the couch. He tries to kiss her. She moves away*) Look, we've had a nice evening; let's not spoil it, huh? . . .

> (*He again turns her head and tries to nuzzle in and she turns away from him, not with distaste but with momentary lack of interest; in a mood to pursue what they were talking about*)

BENEATHA I'm *trying* to talk to you.

GEORGE We always talk.

BENEATHA Yes—and I love to talk.

GEORGE (*Exasperated; rising*) I know it and I don't mind it sometimes . . . I want you to cut it out, see— The moody stuff, I mean. I don't like it. You're a nice-looking girl . . . all over. That's all you need, honey, forget the atmosphere. Guys aren't going to go for the atmosphere—they're going to go for what they see. Be glad for that. Drop the Garbo routine. It doesn't go with you. As for myself, I want a nice—(*Groping*) —simple (*Thoughtfully*)—sophisticated girl . . . not a poet—O.K.?

> (*She rebuffs him again and he starts to leave*)

82

BENEATHA Why are you angry?

GEORGE Because this is stupid! I don't go out with you to discuss the nature of "quiet desperation" or to hear all about your thoughts—because the world will go on thinking what it thinks regardless—

BENEATHA Then why read books? Why go to school?

GEORGE (*With artificial patience, counting on his fingers*) It's simple. You read books—to learn facts—to get grades—to pass the course—to get a degree. That's all —it has nothing to do with thoughts.
        (*A long pause*)

BENEATHA I see. (*A longer pause as she looks at him*) Good night, George.
        (GEORGE *looks at her a little oddly, and starts to exit. He meets* MAMA *coming in*)

GEORGE Oh—hello, Mrs. Younger.

MAMA Hello, George, how you feeling?

GEORGE Fine—fine, how are you?

MAMA Oh, a little tired. You know them steps can get you after a day's work. You all have a nice time to-night?

GEORGE Yes—a fine time. Well, good night.

MAMA Good night. (*He exits.* MAMA *closes the door behind her*) Hello, honey. What you sitting like that for?

BENEATHA I'm just sitting.

MAMA Didn't you have a nice time?

BENEATHA No.

MAMA No? What's the matter?

BENEATHA Mama, George is a fool—honest. (*She rises*)

MAMA (*Hustling around unloading the packages she has entered with. She stops*) Is he, baby?

BENEATHA Yes.
(BENEATHA *makes up* TRAVIS' *bed as she talks*)

MAMA You sure?

BENEATHA Yes.

MAMA Well—I guess you better not waste your time with no fools.
(BENEATHA *looks up at her mother, watching her put groceries in the refrigerator. Finally she gathers up her things and starts into the bedroom. At the door she stops and looks back at her mother*)

BENEATHA Mama—

MAMA Yes, baby—

BENEATHA Thank you.

MAMA For what?

BENEATHA For understanding me this time.
(*She exits quickly and the mother stands, smiling a little, looking at the place where* BENEATHA *just stood.* RUTH *enters*)

RUTH Now don't you fool with any of this stuff, Lena—

MAMA Oh, I just thought I'd sort a few things out.
(*The phone rings.* RUTH *answers*)

RUTH (*At the phone*) Hello—Just a minute. (*Goes to door*) Walter, it's Mrs. Arnold. (*Waits. Goes back to the phone. Tense*) Hello. Yes, this is his wife speaking . . . He's lying down now. Yes . . . well, he'll be in tomorrow. He's been very sick. Yes—I know we should have called, but we were so sure he'd be able to come in today. Yes—yes, I'm very sorry. Yes . . . Thank you very much. (*She hangs up.* WALTER *is*

standing in the doorway of the bedroom behind her)
That was Mrs. Arnold.

WALTER (*Indifferently*)   Was it?

RUTH   She said if you don't come in tomorrow that they
are getting a new man . . .

WALTER   Ain't that sad—ain't that crying sad.

RUTH   She said Mr. Arnold has had to take a cab for
three days . . . Walter, you ain't been to work for three
days! (*This is a revelation to her*) Where you been,
Walter Lee Younger? (WALTER *looks at her and starts
to laugh*) You're going to lose your job.

WALTER   That's right . . .

RUTH   Oh, Walter, and with your mother working like
a dog every day—

WALTER   That's sad too— Everything is sad.

MAMA   What you been doing for these three days, son?

WALTER   Mama—you don't know all the things a man
what got leisure can find to do in this city . . . What's
this—Friday night? Well—Wednesday I borrowed Willy
Harris' car and I went for a drive . . . just me and myself and I drove and drove . . . Way out . . . way past
South Chicago, and I parked the car and I sat and
looked at the steel mills all day long. I just sat in the
car and looked at them big black chimneys for hours.
Then I drove back and I went to the Green Hat.
(*Pause*) And Thursday—Thursday I borrowed the car
again and I got in it and I pointed it the other way and
I drove the other way—for hours—way, way up to
Wisconsin, and I looked at the farms. I just drove and
looked at the farms. Then I drove back and I went to
the Green Hat. (*Pause*) And today—today I didn't
get the car. Today I just walked. All over the South-

side. And I looked at the Negroes and they looked at
me and finally I just sat down on the curb at Thirty-
ninth and South Parkway and I just sat there and
watched the Negroes go by. And then I went to the
Green Hat. You all sad? You all depressed? And you
know where I am going right now—

(RUTH *goes out quietly*)

MAMA   Oh, Big Walter, is this the harvest of our days?

WALTER   You know what I like about the Green Hat?
(*He turns the radio on and a steamy, deep blues pours
into the room*) I like this little cat they got there who
blows a sax . . . He blows. He talks to me. He ain't
but 'bout five feet tall and he's got a conked head and
his eyes is always closed and he's all music—

MAMA (*Rising and getting some papers out of her hand-
bag*) Walter—

WALTER   And there's this other guy who plays the piano
. . . and they got a sound. I mean they can work on
some music . . . They got the best little combo in the
world in the Green Hat . . . You can just sit there and
drink and listen to them three men play and you realize that don't nothing matter worth a damn, but just
being there—

MAMA   I've helped do it to you, haven't I, son? Walter,
I been wrong.

WALTER   Naw—you ain't never been wrong about nothing, Mama.

MAMA   Listen to me, now. I say I been wrong, son. That
I been doing to you what the rest of the world been
doing to you. (*She stops and he looks up slowly at her
and she meets his eyes pleadingly*) Walter—what you
ain't never understood is that I ain't got nothing, don't
own nothing, ain't never really wanted nothing that

wasn't for you. There ain't nothing as precious to me . . . There ain't nothing worth holding on to, money, dreams, nothing else—if it means—if it means it's going to destroy my boy. (*She puts her papers in front of him and he watches her without speaking or moving*) I paid the man thirty-five hundred dollars down on the house. That leaves sixty-five hundred dollars. Monday morning I want you to take this money and take three thousand dollars and put it in a savings account for Beneatha's medical schooling. The rest you put in a checking account—with your name on it. And from now on any penny that come out of it or that go in it is for you to look after. For you to decide. (*She drops her hands a little helplessly*) It ain't much, but it's all I got in the world and I'm putting it in your hands. I'm telling you to be the head of this family from now on like you supposed to be.

WALTER (*Stares at the money*) You trust me like that, Mama?

MAMA I ain't never stop trusting you. Like I ain't never stop loving you.

> (*She goes out, and* WALTER *sits looking at the money on the table as the music continues in its idiom, pulsing in the room. Finally, in a decisive gesture, he gets up, and, in mingled joy and desperation, picks up the money. At the same moment,* TRAVIS *enters for bed*)

TRAVIS What's the matter, Daddy? You drunk?

WALTER (*Sweetly, more sweetly than we have ever known him*) No, Daddy ain't drunk. Daddy ain't going to never be drunk again. . . .

TRAVIS Well, good night, Daddy.

> (*The* FATHER *has come from behind the couch and leans over, embracing his son*)

WALTER   Son, I feel like talking to you tonight.

TRAVIS   About what?

WALTER   Oh, about a lot of things. About you and what kind of man you going to be when you grow up. . . . Son—son, what do you want to be when you grow up?

TRAVIS   A bus driver.

WALTER   (*Laughing a little*) A what? Man, that ain't nothing to want to be!

TRAVIS   Why not?

WALTER   'Cause, man—it ain't big enough—you know what I mean.

TRAVIS   I don't know then. I can't make up my mind. Sometimes Mama asks me that too. And sometimes when I tell you I just want to be like you—she says she don't want me to be like that and sometimes she says she does. . . .

WALTER   (*Gathering him up in his arms*) You know what, Travis? In seven years you going to be seventeen years old. And things is going to be very different with us in seven years, Travis. . . . One day when you are seventeen I'll come home—home from my office downtown somewhere—

TRAVIS   You don't work in no office, Daddy.

WALTER   No—but after tonight. After what your daddy gonna do tonight, there's going to be offices—a whole lot of offices. . . .

TRAVIS   What you gonna do tonight, Daddy?

WALTER   You wouldn't understand yet, son, but your daddy's gonna make a transaction . . . a business transaction that's going to change our lives. . . . That's

how come one day when you 'bout seventeen years old
I'll come home and I'll be pretty tired, you know what
I mean, after a day of conferences and secretaries getting things wrong the way they do . . . 'cause an executive's life is hell, man—(*The more he talks the farther
away he gets*) And I'll pull the car up on the driveway
. . . just a plain black Chrysler, I think, with white
walls—no—black tires. More elegant. Rich people
don't have to be flashy . . . though I'll have to get
something a little sportier for Ruth—maybe a Cadillac
convertible to do her shopping in. . . . And I'll come
up the steps to the house and the gardener will be clip-
ping away at the hedges and he'll say, "Good evening,
Mr. Younger." And I'll say, "Hello, Jefferson, how are
you this evening?" And I'll go inside and Ruth will
come downstairs and meet me at the door and we'll kiss
each other and she'll take my arm and we'll go up to
your room to see you sitting on the floor with the cata-
logues of all the great schools in America around you.
. . . All the great schools in the world! And—and I'll
say, all right son—it's your seventeenth birthday, what
is it you've decided? . . . Just tell me where you want to
go to school and you'll *go*. Just tell me, what it is you
want to be—and you'll *be* it. . . . Whatever you want
to be—Yessir! (*He holds his arms open for* TRAVIS)
You just name it, son . . . (TRAVIS *leaps into them*) and
I hand you the world!

(WALTER's *voice has risen in pitch and hysterical
promise and on the last line he lifts* TRAVIS *high*)

(*Blackout*)

Scene III

Time: Saturday, moving day, one week later.

Before the curtain rises, RUTH'S *voice, a strident, dramatic church alto, cuts through the silence.*

It is, in the darkness, a triumphant surge, a penetrating statement of expectation: "Oh, Lord, I don't feel no ways tired! Children, oh, glory hallelujah!"

As the curtain rises we see that RUTH *is alone in the living room, finishing up the family's packing. It is moving day. She is nailing crates and tying cartons.* BENEATHA *enters, carrying a guitar case, and watches her exuberant sister-in-law.*

RUTH   Hey!

BENEATHA (*Putting away the case*)   Hi.

RUTH (*Pointing at a package*)   Honey—look in that package there and see what I found on sale this morning at the South Center. (RUTH *gets up and moves to the package and draws out some curtains*) Lookahere— hand-turned hems!

BENEATHA   How do you know the window size out there?

RUTH (*Who hadn't thought of that*)   Oh— Well, they bound to fit something in the whole house. Anyhow, they was too good a bargain to pass up. (RUTH *slaps her head, suddenly remembering something*) Oh, Bennie—I meant to put a special note on that carton over there. That's your mama's good china and she wants 'em to be very careful with it.

BENEATHA I'll do it.

> (BENEATHA *finds a piece of paper and starts to draw large letters on it*)

RUTH You know what I'm going to do soon as I get in that new house?

BENEATHA What?

RUTH Honey—I'm going to run me a tub of water up to here . . . (*With her fingers practically up to her nostrils*) And I'm going to get in it—and I am going to sit . . . and sit . . . and sit in that hot water and the first person who knocks to tell *me* to hurry up and come out—

BENEATHA Gets shot at sunrise.

RUTH (*Laughing happily*) You said it, sister! (*Noticing how large* BENEATHA *is absent-mindedly making the note*) Honey, they ain't going to read that from no airplane.

BENEATHA (*Laughing herself*) I guess I always think things have more emphasis if they are big, somehow.

RUTH (*Looking up at her and smiling*) You and your brother seem to have that as a philosophy of life. Lord, that man—done changed so 'round here. You know—you know what we did last night? Me and Walter Lee?

BENEATHA What?

RUTH (*Smiling to herself*) We went to the movies. (*Looking at* BENEATHA *to see if she understands*) We went to the movies. You know the last time me and Walter went to the movies together?

BENEATHA No.

RUTH Me neither. That's how long it been. (*Smiling again*) But we went last night. The picture wasn't much

good, but that didn't seem to matter. We went—and
we held hands.

BENEATHA　Oh, Lord!

RUTH　We held hands—and you know what?

BENEATHA　What?

RUTH　When we come out of the show it was late and
dark and all the stores and things was closed up . . .
and it was kind of chilly and there wasn't many people
on the streets . . . and we was still holding hands, me
and Walter.

BENEATHA　You're killing me.
(WALTER *enters with a large package. His happiness is deep in him; he cannot keep still with his
new-found exuberance. He is singing and wiggling
and snapping his fingers. He puts his package in
a corner and puts a phonograph record, which he
has brought in with him, on the record player. As
the music comes up he dances over to* RUTH *and
tries to get her to dance with him. She gives in at
last to his raunchiness and in a fit of giggling allows herself to be drawn into his mood and together they deliberately burlesque an old social
dance of their youth*)

BENEATHA (*Regarding them a long time as they dance,
then drawing in her breath for a deeply exaggerated
comment which she does not particularly mean*)　Talk
about—oldddddddddd-fashionedddddddd—Negroes!

WALTER (*Stopping momentarily*)　What kind of Negroes?
(*He says this in fun. He is not angry with her
today, nor with anyone. He starts to dance with
his wife again*)

BENEATHA　Old-fashioned.

WALTER (*As he dances with* RUTH) You know, when
these *New Negroes* have their convention—(*Pointing at
his sister*)—that is going to be the chairman of the
Committee on Unending Agitation. (*He goes on dancing, then stops*) Race, race, race! . . . Girl, I do believe you are the first person in the history of the entire human race to successfully brainwash yourself.
(BENEATHA *breaks up and he goes on dancing. He
stops again, enjoying his tease*) Damn, even the N
double A C P takes a holiday sometimes! (BENEATHA
and RUTH *laugh. He dances with* RUTH *some more and
starts to laugh and stops and pantomimes someone over
an operating table*) I can just see that chick someday
looking down at some poor cat on an operating table
before she starts to slice him, saying . . . (*Pulling his
sleeves back maliciously*) "By the way, what are your
views on civil rights down there? . . ."

(*He laughs at her again and starts to dance happily. The bell sounds*)

BENEATHA Sticks and stones may break my bones but
. . . words will never hurt me!
(BENEATHA *goes to the door and opens it as*
WALTER *and* RUTH *go on with the clowning.* BE-
NEATHA *is somewhat surprised to see a quiet-
looking middle-aged white man in a business suit
holding his hat and a briefcase in his hand and
consulting a small piece of paper*)

MAN Uh—how do you do, miss. I am looking for a
Mrs.—(*He looks at the slip of paper*) Mrs. Lena
Younger?

BENEATHA (*Smoothing her hair with slight embarrassment*) Oh—yes, that's my mother. Excuse me (*She
closes the door and turns to quiet the other two*) Ruth!
Brother! Somebody's here. (*Then she opens the door.*

The man casts a curious quick glance at all of them)
Uh—come in please.

MAN (*Coming in*) Thank you.

BENEATHA My mother isn't here just now. Is it business?

MAN Yes . . . well, of a sort.

WALTER (*Freely, the Man of the House*) Have a seat.
I'm Mrs. Younger's son. I look after most of her business matters.
         (RUTH *and* BENEATHA *exchange amused glances*)

MAN (*Regarding* WALTER, *and sitting*) Well— My name
is Karl Lindner . . .

WALTER (*Stretching out his hand*) Walter Younger. This
is my wife—(RUTH *nods politely*)—and my sister.

LINDNER How do you do.

WALTER (*Amiably, as he sits himself easily on a chair,
leaning with interest forward on his knees and looking
expectantly into the newcomer's face*) What can we
do for you, Mr. Lindner!

LINDNER (*Some minor shuffling of the hat and briefcase
on his knees*) Well—I am a representative of the Clybourne Park Improvement Association—

WALTER (*Pointing*) Why don't you sit your things on
the floor?

LINDER Oh—yes. Thank you. (*He slides the briefcase
and hat under the chair*) And as I was saying—I am
from the Clybourne Park Improvement Association and
we have had it brought to our attention at the last meeting that you people—or at least your mother—has
bought a piece of residential property at—(*He digs for
the slip of paper again*)—four o six Clybourne Street . . .

WALTER That's right. Care for something to drink? Ruth, get Mr. Lindner a beer.

LINDNER (*Upset for some reason*) Oh—no, really. I mean thank you very much, but no thank you.

RUTH (*Innocently*) Some coffee?

LINDNER Thank you, nothing at all.
(BENEATHA *is watching the man carefully*)

LINDNER Well, I don't know how much you folks know about our organization. (*He is a gentle man; thoughtful and somewhat labored in his manner*) It is one of these community organizations set up to look after—oh, you know, things like block upkeep and special projects and we also have what we call our New Neighbors Orientation Committee . . .

BENEATHA (*Drily*) Yes—and what do they do?

LINDNER (*Turning a little to her and then returning the main force to* WALTER) Well—it's what you might call a sort of welcoming committee, I guess. I mean they, we, I'm the chairman of the committee—go around and see the new people who move into the neighborhood and sort of give them the lowdown on the way we do things out in Clybourne Park.

BENEATHA (*With appreciation of the two meanings, which escape* RUTH *and* WALTER) Un-huh.

LINDNER And we also have the category of what the association calls—(*He looks elsewhere*)—uh—special community problems . . .

BENEATHA Yes—and what are some of those?

WALTER Girl, let the man talk.

LINDNER (*With understated relief*) Thank you. I would

sort of like to explain this thing in my own way. I mean I want to explain to you in a certain way.

WALTER   Go ahead.

LINDNER   Yes. Well. I'm going to try to get right to the point. I'm sure we'll all appreciate that in the long run.

BENEATHA   Yes.

WALTER   Be still now!

LINDNER   Well—

RUTH (*Still innocently*)   Would you like another chair— you don't look comfortable.

LINDNER (*More frustrated than annoyed*)   No, thank you very much. Please. Well—to get right to the point I—(*A great breath, and he is off at last*) I am sure you people must be aware of some of the incidents which have happened in various parts of the city when colored people have moved into certain areas—(BE-NEATHA *exhales heavily and starts tossing a piece of fruit up and down in the air*) Well—because we have what I think is going to be a unique type of organiza-tion in American community life—not only do we deplore that kind of thing—but we are trying to do something about it. (BENEATHA *stops tossing and turns with a new and quizzical interest to the man*) We feel —(*gaining confidence in his mission because of the in-terest in the faces of the people he is talking to*)—we feel that most of the trouble in this world, when you come right down to it—(*He hits his knee for emphasis*) —most of the trouble exists because people just don't sit down and talk to each other.

RUTH (*Nodding as she might in church, pleased with the remark*)   You can say that again, mister.

LINDNER (*More encouraged by such affirmation*)   That

we don't try hard enough in this world to understand
the other fellow's problem. The other guy's point of
view.

RUTH Now that's right.

(BENEATHA *and* WALTER *merely watch and listen
with genuine interest*)

LINDNER Yes—that's the way we feel out in Clybourne
Park. And that's why I was elected to come here this
afternoon and talk to you people. Friendly like, you
know, the way people should talk to each other and see
if we couldn't find some way to work this thing out. As
I say, the whole business is a matter of *caring* about
the other fellow. Anybody can see that you are a nice
family of folks, hard working and honest I'm sure.
(BENEATHA *frowns slightly, quizzically, her head tilted
regarding him*) Today everybody knows what it means
to be on the outside of *something*. And of course, there
is always somebody who is out to take the advantage
of people who don't always understand.

WALTER What do you mean?

LINDNER Well—you see our community is made up of
people who've worked hard as the dickens for years
to build up that little community. They're not rich and
fancy people; just hard-working, honest people who
don't really have much but those little homes and a
dream of the kind of community they want to raise
their children in. Now, I don't say we are perfect and
there is a lot wrong in some of the things they want.
But you've got to admit that a man, right or wrong, has
the right to want to have the neighborhood he lives in
a certain kind of way. And at the moment the overwhelming majority of our people out there feel that
people get along better, take more of a common interest
in the life of the community, when they share a common background. I want you to believe me when I

tell you that race prejudice simply doesn't enter into it. It is a matter of the people of Clybourne Park believing, rightly or wrongly, as I say, that for the happiness of all concerned that our Negro families are happier when they live in their *own* communities.

BENEATHA (*With a grand and bitter gesture*) This, friends, is the Welcoming Committee!

WALTER (*Dumfounded, looking at* LINDNER) Is this what you came marching all the way over here to tell us?

LINDNER Well, now we've been having a fine conversation. I hope you'll hear me all the way through.

WALTER (*Tightly*) Go ahead, man.

LINDNER You see—in the face of all things I have said, we are prepared to make your family a very generous offer . . .

BENEATHA Thirty pieces and not a coin less!

WALTER Yeah?

LINDNER (*Putting on his glasses and drawing a form out of the briefcase*) Our association is prepared, through the collective effort of our people, to buy the house from you at a financial gain to your family.

RUTH Lord have mercy, ain't this the living gall!

WALTER All right, you through?

LINDNER Well, I want to give you the exact terms of the financial arrangement—

WALTER We don't want to hear no exact terms of no arrangements. I want to know if you got any more to tell us 'bout getting together?

LINDNER (*Taking off his glasses*) Well—I don't suppose that you feel . . .

WALTER   Never mind how I feel—you got any more to say 'bout how people ought to sit down and talk to each other? . . . Get out of my house, man.
(*He turns his back and walks to the door*)

LINDNER (*Looking around at the hostile faces and reaching and assembling his hat and briefcase*)   Well—I don't understand why you people are reacting this way. What do you think you are going to gain by moving into a neighborhood where you just aren't wanted and where some elements—well—people can get awful worked up when they feel that their whole way of life and everything they've ever worked for is threatened.

WALTER   Get out.

LINDNER (*At the door, holding a small card*)   Well—I'm sorry it went like this.

WALTER   Get out.

LINDNER (*Almost sadly regarding* WALTER)   You just can't force people to change their hearts, son.
(*He turns and put his card on a table and exits. WALTER pushes the door to with stinging hatred, and stands looking at it. RUTH just sits and BENEATHA just stands. They say nothing. MAMA and TRAVIS enter*)

MAMA   Well—this all the packing got done since I left out of here this morning. I testify before God that my children got all the energy of the dead. What time the moving men due?

BENEATHA   Four o'clock. You had a caller, Mama.
(*She is smiling, teasingly*)

MAMA   Sure enough—who?

BENEATHA (*Her arms folded saucily*)   The Welcoming Committee.
(WALTER *and* RUTH *giggle*)

MAMA (*Innocently*) Who?

BENEATHA The Welcoming Committee. They said they're sure going to be glad to see you when you get there.

WALTER (*Devilishly*) Yeah, they said they can't hardly wait to see your face.
  (*Laughter*)

MAMA (*Sensing their facetiousness*) What's the matter with you all?

WALTER Ain't nothing the matter with us. We just telling you 'bout the gentleman who came to see you this afternoon. From the Clybourne Park Improvement Association.

MAMA What he want?

RUTH (*In the same mood as* BENEATHA *and* WALTER) To welcome you, honey.

WALTER He said they can't hardly wait. He said the one thing they don't have, that they just *dying* to have out there is a fine family of colored people! (*To* RUTH *and* BENEATHA) Ain't that right!

RUTH *and* BENEATHA (*Mockingly*) Yeah! He left his card in case—
  (*They indicate the card, and* MAMA *picks it up and throws it on the floor—understanding and looking off as she draws her chair up to the table on which she has put her plant and some sticks and some cord*)

MAMA Father, give us strength. (*Knowingly—and without fun*) Did he threaten us?

BENEATHA Oh—Mama—they don't do it like that any more. He talked Brotherhood. He said everybody ought to learn how to sit down and hate each other with good Christian fellowship.

(*She and* WALTER *shake hands to ridicule the remark*)

MAMA (*Sadly*)   Lord, protect us . . .

RUTH   You should hear the money those folks raised to buy the house from us. All we paid and then some.

BENEATHA   What they think we going to do—eat 'em?

RUTH   No, honey, marry 'em.

MAMA (*Shaking her head*)   Lord, Lord, Lord . . .

RUTH   Well—that's the way the crackers crumble. Joke.

BENEATHA (*Laughingly noticing what her mother is doing*)   Mama, what are you doing?

MAMA   Fixing my plant so it won't get hurt none on the way . . .

BENEATHA   Mama, you going to take *that* to the new house?

MAMA   Un-huh—

BENEATHA   That raggedy-looking old thing?

MAMA (*Stopping and looking at her*)   It expresses *me*.

RUTH (*With delight, to* BENEATHA)   So there, Miss Thing!

(WALTER *comes to* MAMA *suddenly and bends down behind her and squeezes her in his arms with all his strength. She is overwhelmed by the suddenness of it and, though delighted, her manner is like that of* RUTH *with* TRAVIS)

MAMA   Look out now, boy! You make me mess up my thing here!

WALTER (*His face lit, he slips down on his knees beside her, his arms still about her*)   Mama . . . you know what it means to climb up in the chariot?

MAMA (*Gruffly, very happy*)   Get on away from me now . . .

RUTH (*Near the gift-wrapped package, trying to catch* WALTER's *eye*)   Psst—

WALTER   What the old song say, Mama . . .

RUTH   Walter— Now?
(*She is pointing at the package*)

WALTER (*Speaking the lines, sweetly, playfully, in his mother's face*)
I got wings . . . you got wings . . .
All God's Children got wings . . .

MAMA   Boy—get out of my face and do some work . . .

WALTER
When I get to heaven gonna put on my wings,
Gonna fly all over God's heaven . . .

BENEATHA (*Teasingly, from across the room*)   Everybody talking 'bout heaven ain't going there!

WALTER (*To* RUTH, *who is carrying the box across to them*)   I don't know, you think we ought to give her that . . . Seems to me she ain't been very appreciative around here.

MAMA (*Eying the box, which is obviously a gift*)   What is that?

WALTER (*Taking it from* RUTH *and putting it on the table in front of* MAMA)   Well—what you all think? Should we give it to her?

RUTH   Oh—she was pretty good today.

MAMA   I'll good you—
(*She turns her eyes to the box again*)

BENEATHA   Open it, Mama.

(*She stands up, looks at it, turns and looks at all of them, and then presses her hands together and does not open the package*)

WALTER (*Sweetly*)   Open it, Mama. It's for you. (MAMA *looks in his eyes. It is the first present in her life without its being Christmas. Slowly she opens her package and lifts out, one by one, a brand-new sparkling set of gardening tools.* WALTER *continues, prodding*) Ruth made up the note—read it . . .

MAMA (*Picking up the card and adjusting her glasses*) "To our own Mrs. Miniver—Love from Brother, Ruth and Beneatha." Ain't that lovely . . .

TRAVIS (*Tugging at his father's sleeve*)   Daddy, can I give her mine now?

WALTER   All right, son. (TRAVIS *flies to get his gift*) Travis didn't want to go in with the rest of us, Mama. He got his own. (*Somewhat amused*) We don't know what it is . . .

TRAVIS (*Racing back in the room with a large hatbox and putting it in front of his grandmother*)   Here!

MAMA   Lord have mercy, baby. You done gone and bought your grandmother a hat?

TRAVIS (*Very proud*)   Open it!
        (*She does and lifts out an elaborate, but very elaborate, wide gardening hat, and all the adults break up at the sight of it*)

RUTH   Travis, honey, what is that?

TRAVIS (*Who thinks it is beautiful and appropriate*)   It's a gardening hat! Like the ladies always have on in the magazines when they work in their gardens.

BENEATHA (*Giggling fiercely*)   Travis—we were trying to make Mama Mrs. Miniver—not Scarlett O'Hara!

MAMA (*Indignantly*) What's the matter with you all!
This here is a beautiful hat! (*Absurdly*) I always
wanted me one just like it!
>(*She pops it on her head to prove it to her grand-
>son, and the hat is ludicrous and considerably
>oversized*)

RUTH Hot dog! Go, Mama!

WALTER (*Doubled over with laughter*) I'm sorry, Mama
—but you look like you ready to go out and chop you
some cotton sure enough!
>(*They all laugh except* MAMA, *out of deference to*
>TRAVIS' *feelings*)

MAMA (*Gathering the boy up to her*) Bless your heart
—this is the prettiest hat I ever owned— (WALTER,
RUTH *and* BENEATHA *chime in—noisily, festively and
insincerely congratulating* TRAVIS *on his gift*) What are
we all standing around here for? We ain't finished
packin' yet. Bennie, you ain't packed one book.
>(*The bell rings*)

BENEATHA That couldn't be the movers . . . it's not
hardly two good yet—
>(BENEATHA *goes into her room.* MAMA *starts for
>door*)

WALTER (*Turning, stiffening*) Wait—wait—I'll get it.
>(*He stands and looks at the door*)

MAMA You expecting company, son?

WALTER (*Just looking at the door*) Yeah—yeah . . .
>(MAMA *looks at* RUTH, *and they exchange inno-
>cent and unfrightened glances*)

MAMA (*Not understanding*) Well, let them in, son.

BENEATHA (*From her room*) We need some more string.

MAMA Travis—you run to the hardware and get me
some string cord.

(MAMA *goes out and* WALTER *turns and looks at* RUTH. TRAVIS *goes to a dish for money*)

RUTH   Why don't you answer the door, man?

WALTER   (*Suddenly bounding across the floor to her*) 'Cause sometimes it hard to let the future begin! (*Stooping down in her face*)
  I got wings! You got wings!
  All God's children got wings!
(*He crosses to the door and throws it open. Standing there is a very slight little man in a not too prosperous business suit and with haunted frightened eyes and a hat pulled down tightly, brim up, around his forehead.* TRAVIS *passes between the men and exits.* WALTER *leans deep in the man's face, still in his jubilance*)
  When I get to heaven gonna put on my wings,
  Gonna fly all over God's heaven . . .
(*The little man just stares at him*)
  Heaven—
(*Suddenly he stops and looks past the little man into the empty hallway*) Where's Willy, man?

BOBO   He ain't with me.

WALTER   (*Not disturbed*)   Oh—come on in. You know my wife.

BOBO   (*Dumbly, taking off his hat*)   Yes—h'you, Miss Ruth.

RUTH   (*Quietly, a mood apart from her husband already, seeing* BOBO)   Hello, Bobo.

WALTER   You right on time today . . . Right on time. That's the way! (*He slaps* BOBO *on his back*) Sit down . . . lemme hear.
      (RUTH *stands stiffly and quietly in back of them, as though somehow she senses death, her eyes fixed on her husband*)

BOBO   (*His frightened eyes on the floor, his hat in his*

hands)   Could I please get a drink of water, before I
tell you about it, Walter Lee?

(WALTER *does not take his eyes off the man*. RUTH
*goes blindly to the tap and gets a glass of water
and brings it to* BOBO)

WALTER   There ain't nothing wrong, is there?

BOBO   Lemme tell you—

WALTER   Man—didn't nothing go wrong?

BOBO   Lemme tell you—Walter Lee. (*Looking at* RUTH
and talking to her more than to WALTER) You know
how it was. I got to tell you how it was. I mean first
I got to tell you how it was all the way . . . I mean
about the money I put in, Walter Lee . . .

WALTER (*With taut agitation now*)   What about the
money you put in?

BOBO   Well—it wasn't much as we told you—me and
Willy—(*He stops*) I'm sorry, Walter. I got a bad feeling about it. I got a real bad feeling about it . . .

WALTER   Man, what you telling me about all this for?
. . . Tell me what happened in Springfield . . .

BOBO   Springfield.

RUTH (*Like a dead woman*)   What was supposed to
happen in Springfield?

BOBO (*To her*)   This deal that me and Walter went into
with Willy— Me and Willy was going to go down to
Springfield and spread some money 'round so's we
wouldn't have to wait so long for the liquor license
. . . That's what we were going to do. Everybody said
that was the way you had to do, you understand, Miss
Ruth?

WALTER   Man—what happened down there?

BOBO (*A pitiful man, near tears*) I'm trying to tell you, Walter.

WALTER (*Screaming at him suddenly*) THEN TELL ME, GODDAMMIT . . . WHAT'S THE MATTER WITH YOU?

BOBO Man . . . I didn't go to no Springfield, yesterday.

WALTER (*Halted, life hanging in the moment*) Why not?

BOBO (*The long way, the hard way to tell*) 'Cause I didn't have no reasons to . . .

WALTER Man, what are you talking about!

BOBO I'm talking about the fact that when I got to the train station yesterday morning—eight o'clock like we planned . . . Man—*Willy didn't never show up.*

WALTER Why . . . where was he . . . where is he?

BOBO That's what I'm trying to tell you . . . I don't know . . . I waited six hours . . . I called his house . . . and I waited . . . six hours . . . I waited in that train station six hours . . . (*Breaking into tears*) That was all the extra money I had in the world . . . (*Looking up at* WALTER *with the tears running down his face*) Man, *Willy is gone.*

WALTER Gone, what you mean Willy is gone? Gone where? You mean he went by <u>himself</u>. You mean he went off to Springfield by himself—to take care of getting the license—(*Turns and looks anxiously at* RUTH) You mean maybe he didn't want too many people in on the business down there? (*Looks to* RUTH *again, as before*) You know Willy got his own ways. (*Looks back to* BOBO) Maybe you was late yesterday and he just went on down there without you. Maybe—maybe —he's been callin' you at home tryin' to tell you what happened or something. Maybe—maybe—he just got sick. He's somewhere—he's got to be somewhere. We just got to find him—me and you got to find him. (*Grabs* BOBO *senselessly by the collar and starts to shake him*) We got to!

BOBO (*In sudden angry, frightened agony*) What's the matter with you, Walter! *When a cat take off with your money he don't leave you no maps!*

WALTER (*Turning madly, as though he is looking for* WILLY *in the very room*) Willy! . . . Willy . . . don't do it . . . Please don't do it . . . Man, not with that money . . . Man, please, not with that money . . . Oh, God . . . Don't let it be true . . . (*He is wandering around, crying out for* WILLY *and looking for him or perhaps for help from God*) Man . . . I trusted you . . . Man, I put my life in your hands . . . (*He starts to crumple down on the floor as* RUTH *just covers her face in horror.* MAMA *opens the door and comes into the room, with* BENEATHA *behind her*) Man . . . (*He starts to pound the floor with his fists, sobbing wildly*) That money is made out of my father's flesh . . .

BOBO (*Standing over him helplessly*) I'm sorry, Walter . . . (*Only* WALTER's *sobs reply.* BOBO *puts on his hat*) I had my life staked on this deal, too . . .
        (*He exits*)

MAMA (*To* WALTER) Son—(*She goes to him, bends down to him, talks to his bent head*) Son . . . Is it gone? Son, I gave you sixty-five hundred dollars. Is it gone? All of it? Beneatha's money too?

WALTER (*Lifting his head slowly*) Mama . . . I never . . . went to the bank at all . . .

MAMA (*Not wanting to believe him*) You mean . . . your sister's school money . . . you used that too . . . Walter? . . .

WALTER   Yessss! . . . All of it . . . It's all gone . . .
          (*There is total silence.* RUTH *stands with her face
          covered with her hands;* BENEATHA *leans forlornly
          against a wall, fingering a piece of red ribbon from
          the mother's gift.* MAMA *stops and looks at her son
          without recognition and then, quite without think-
          ing about it, starts to beat him senselessly in the
          face.* BENEATHA *goes to them and stops it*)

BENEATHA   Mama!
          (MAMA *stops and looks at both of her children
          and rises slowly and wanders vaguely, aimlessly
          away from them*)

MAMA   I seen . . . him . . . night after night . . . come
       in . . . and look at that rug . . . and then look at me
       . . . the red showing in his eyes . . . the veins moving in
       his head . . . I seen him grow thin and old before he
       was forty . . . working and working and working like
       somebody's old horse . . . killing himself . . . and you
       —you give it all away in a day . . .

BENEATHA   Mama—

MAMA   Oh, God . . . (*She looks up to Him*) Look down
       here—and show me the strength.

BENEATHA   Mama—

MAMA (*Folding over*)   Strength . . .

BENEATHA (*Plaintively*)   Mama . . .

MAMA   Strength!

Curtain

ACT III

An hour later.

At curtain, there is a sullen light of gloom in the living room, gray light not unlike that which began the first scene of Act One. At left we can see WALTER *within his room, alone with himself. He is stretched out on the bed, his shirt out and open, his arms under his head. He does not smoke, he does not cry out, he merely lies there, looking up at the ceiling, much as if he were alone in the world.*

In the living room BENEATHA *sits at the table, still surrounded by the now almost ominous packing crates. She sits looking off. We feel that this is a mood struck perhaps an hour before, and it lingers now, full of the empty sound of profound disappointment. We see on a line from her brother's bedroom the sameness of their attitudes. Presently the bell rings and* BENEATHA *rises without ambition or interest in answering. It is* ASAGAI, *smiling broadly, striding into the room with energy and happy expectation and conversation.*

ASAGAI   I came over . . . I had some free time. I thought I might help with the packing. Ah, I like the look of packing crates! A household in preparation for a journey! It depresses some people . . . but for me . . . it is another feeling. Something full of the flow of life, do you understand? Movement, progress . . . It makes me think of Africa.

BENEATHA Africa!

ASAGAI What kind of a mood is this? Have I told you how deeply you move me?

BENEATHA He gave away the money, Asagai . . .

ASAGAI Who gave away what money?

BENEATHA The insurance money. My brother gave it away.

ASAGAI Gave it away?

BENEATHA He made an investment! With a man even Travis wouldn't have trusted.

ASAGAI And it's gone?

BENEATHA Gone!

ASAGAI I'm very sorry . . . And you, now?

BENEATHA Me? . . . Me? . . . Me I'm nothing . . . Me. When I was very small . . . we used to take our sleds out in the wintertime and the only hills we had were the ice-covered stone steps of some houses down the street. And we used to fill them in with snow and make them smooth and slide down them all day . . . and it was very dangerous you know . . . far too steep . . . and sure enough one day a kid named Rufus came down too fast and hit the sidewalk . . . and we saw his face just split open right there in front of us . . . And I remember standing there looking at his bloody open face thinking that was the end of Rufus. But the ambulance came and they took him to the hospital and

they fixed the broken bones and they sewed it all up
. . . and the next time I saw Rufus he just had a little
line down the middle of his face . . . I never got over
that . . .

(WALTER *sits up, listening on the bed. Throughout
this scene it is important that we feel his reaction
at all times, that he visibly respond to the words
of his sister and* ASAGAI)

ASAGAI   What?

BENEATHA   That that was what one person could do for
another, fix him up—sew up the problem, make him
all right again. That was the most marvelous thing in
the world . . . I wanted to do that. I always thought
it was the one concrete thing in the world that a human
being could do. Fix up the sick, you know—and make
them whole again. This was truly being God . . .

ASAGAI   You wanted to be God?

BENEATHA   No—I wanted to cure. It used to be so important to me. I wanted to cure. It used to matter. I
used to care. I mean about people and how their bodies
hurt . . .

ASAGAI   And you've stopped caring?

BENEATHA   Yes—I think so.

ASAGAI   Why?

(WALTER *rises, goes to the door of his room and is
about to open it, then stops and stands listening,
leaning on the door jamb*)

BENEATHA   Because it doesn't seem deep enough, close
enough to what ails mankind—I mean this thing of
sewing up bodies or administering drugs. Don't you
understand? It was a child's reaction to the world. I
thought that doctors had the secret to all the hurts. . . .
That's the way a child sees things—or an idealist.

ASAGAI Children see things very well sometimes—and idealists even better.

BENEATHA I know that's what you think. Because you are still where I left off—you still care. This is what you see for the world, for Africa. You with the dreams of the future will patch up all Africa—you are going to cure the Great Sore of colonialism with Independence——

ASAGAI Yes!

BENEATHA Yes—and you think that one word is the penicillin of the human spirit: "Independence!" But then what?

ASAGAI That will be the problem for another time. First we must get there.

BENEATHA And where does it end?

ASAGAI End? Who even spoke of an end? To life? To living?

BENEATHA An end to misery!

ASAGAI (*Smiling*) You sound like a French intellectual.

BENEATHA No! I sound like a human being who just had her future taken right out of her hands! While I was sleeping in my bed in there, things were happening in this world that directly concerned me—and nobody asked me, consulted me—they just went out and did things—and changed my life. Don't you see there isn't any real progress, Asagai, there is only one large circle that we march in, around and around, each of us with our own little picture—in front of us—our own little mirage that we think is the future.

ASAGAI That is the mistake.

BENEATHA What?

ASAGAI What you just said—about the circle. It isn't a circle—it is simply a long line—as in geometry, you know, one that reaches into infinity. And because we cannot see the end—we also cannot see how it changes. And it is very odd but those who see the changes are called "idealists"—and those who cannot, or refuse to think, they are the "realists." It is very strange, and amusing too, I think.

BENEATHA You—you are almost religious.

ASAGAI Yes . . . I think I have the religion of doing what is necessary in the world—and of worshipping man—because he is so marvelous, you see.

BENEATHA Man is foul! And the human race deserves its misery!

ASAGAI You see: *you* have become the religious one in the old sense. Already, and after such a small defeat, you are worshipping despair.

BENEATHA From now on, I worship the truth—and the truth is that people are puny, small and selfish. . . .

ASAGAI Truth? Why is it that you despairing ones always think that only you have the truth? I never thought to see *you* like that. You! Your brother made a stupid, childish mistake—and you are grateful to him. So that now you can give up the ailing human race on account of it. You talk about what good is struggle; what good is anything? Where are we all going? And why are we bothering?

BENEATHA *And you cannot answer it!* All your talk and dreams about Africa and Independence. Independence and then what? What about all the crooks and petty thieves and just plain idiots who will come into power to steal and plunder the same as before—only now

they will be black and do it in the name of the new
Independence— You cannot answer that.

ASAGAI (*Shouting over her*)   *I live the answer!* (*Pause*)
In my village at home it is the exceptional man who
can even read a newspaper . . . or who ever *sees* a
book at all. I will go home and much of what I will
have to say will seem strange to the people of my village . . . But I will teach and work and things will
happen, slowly and swiftly. At times it will seem that
nothing changes at all . . . and then again . . . the
sudden dramatic events which make history leap into
the future. And then quiet again. Retrogression even.
Guns, murder, revolution. And I even will have moments when I wonder if the quiet was not better than
all that death and hatred. But I will look about my village at the illiteracy and disease and ignorance and I
will not wonder long. And perhaps . . . perhaps I will
be a great man . . . I mean perhaps I will hold on to
the substance of truth and find my way always with the
right course . . . and perhaps for it I will be butchered
in my bed some night by the servants of empire . . .

BENEATHA   *The martyr!*

ASAGAI   . . . or perhaps I shall live to be a very old man,
respected and esteemed in my new nation . . . And
perhaps I shall hold office and this is what I'm trying
to tell you, Alaiyo; perhaps the things I believe now for
my country will be wrong and outmoded, and I will not
understand and do terrible things to have things my
way or merely to keep my power. Don't you see that
there will be young men and women, not British sol-
diers then, but my own black countrymen . . . to step
out of the shadows some evening and slit my then
useless throat? Don't you see they have always been
there . . . that they always will be. And that such a

thing as my own death will be an advance? They who
might kill me even . . . actually replenish me!

BENEATHA   Oh, Asagai, I know all that.

ASAGAI   Good! Then stop moaning and groaning and tell
me what you plan to do.

BENEATHA   Do?

ASAGAI   I have a bit of a suggestion.

BENEATHA   What?

ASAGAI   (*Rather quietly for him*)   That when it is all over
—that you come home with me—

BENEATHA   (*Slapping herself on the forehead with exasperation born of misunderstanding*)   Oh—Asagai—at this
moment you decide to be romantic!

ASAGAI   (*Quickly understanding the misunderstanding*)
My dear, young creature of the New World—I do not
mean across the city—I mean across the ocean; home—
to Africa.

BENEATHA   (*Slowly understanding and turning to him with
murmured amazement*)   To—to Nigeria?

ASAGAI   Yes! . . . (*Smiling and lifting his arms playfully*)
Three hundred years later the African Prince rose up
out of the seas and swept the maiden back across the
middle passage over which her ancestors had come—

BENEATHA   (*Unable to play*)   Nigeria?

ASAGAI   Nigeria. Home. (*Coming to her with genuine romantic flippancy*)   I will show you our mountains and
our stars; and give you cool drinks from gourds and
teach you the old songs and the ways of our people—
and, in time, we will pretend that—(*Very softly*)—you
have only been away for a day—

(*She turns her back to him, thinking. He swings her around and takes her full in his arms in a long embrace which proceeds to passion*)

BENEATHA (*Pulling away*) You're getting me all mixed up—

ASAGAI Why?

BENEATHA Too many things—too many things have happened today. I must sit down and think. I don't know what I feel about anything right this minute.
(*She promptly sits down and props her chin on her fist*)

ASAGAI (*Charmed*) All right, I shall leave you. No—don't get up. (*Touching her, gently, sweetly*) Just sit awhile and think . . . Never be afraid to sit awhile and think. (*He goes to door and looks at her*) How often I have looked at you and said, "Ah—so this is what the New World hath finally wrought . . ."
(*He exits. BENEATHA sits on alone. Presently WALTER enters from his room and starts to rummage through things, feverishly looking for something. She looks up and turns in her seat*)

BENEATHA (*Hissingly*) Yes—just look at what the New World hath wrought! . . . Just look! (*She gestures with bitter disgust*) There he is! *Monsieur le petit bourgeois noir*—himself! There he is—Symbol of a Rising Class! Entrepreneur! Titan of the system! (*WALTER ignores her completely and continues frantically and destructively looking for something and hurling things to floor and tearing things out of their place in his search. BENEATHA ignores the eccentricity of his actions and goes on with the monologue of insult*) Did you dream of yachts on Lake Michigan, Brother? Did you see yourself on that Great Day sitting down at the Conference

Table, surrounded by all the mighty bald-headed men in America? All halted, waiting, breathless, waiting for your pronouncements on industry? Waiting for you—Chairman of the Board? (WALTER *finds what he is looking for—a small piece of white paper—and pushes it in his pocket and puts on his coat and rushes out without ever having looked at her. She shouts after him*) I look at you and I see the final triumph of stupidity in the world!

(*The door slams and she returns to just sitting again.* RUTH *comes quickly out of* MAMA'S *room*)

RUTH   Who was that?

BENEATHA   Your husband.

RUTH   Where did he go?

BENEATHA   Who knows—maybe he has an appointment at U.S. Steel.

RUTH (*Anxiously, with frightened eyes*)   You didn't say nothing bad to him, did you?

BENEATHA   Bad? Say anything bad to him? No—I told him he was a sweet boy and full of dreams and everything is strictly peachy keen, as the ofay kids say!

(MAMA *enters from her bedroom. She is lost, vague, trying to catch hold, to make some sense of her former command of the world, but it still eludes her. A sense of waste overwhelms her gait; a measure of apology rides on her shoulders. She goes to her plant, which has remained on the table, looks at it, picks it up and takes it to the window sill and sits it outside, and she stands and looks at it a long moment. Then she closes the window, straightens her body with effort and turns around to her children*)

MAMA Well—ain't it a mess in here, though? (*A false cheerfulness, a beginning of something*) I guess we all better stop moping around and get some work done. All this unpacking and everything we got to do. (RUTH *raises her head slowly in response to the sense of the line; and* BENEATHA *in similar manner turns very slowly to look at her mother*) One of you all better call the moving people and tell 'em not to come.

RUTH Tell 'em not to come?

MAMA Of course, baby. Ain't no need in 'em coming all the way here and having to go back. They charges for that too. (*She sits down, fingers to her brow, thinking*) Lord, ever since I was a little girl, I always remembers people saying, "Lena—Lena Eggleston, you aims too high all the time. You needs to slow down and see life a little more like it is. Just slow down some." That's what they always used to say down home—"Lord, that Lena Eggleston is a high-minded thing. She'll get her due one day!"

RUTH No, Lena . . .

MAMA Me and Big Walter just didn't never learn right.

RUTH Lena, no! We gotta go. Bennie—tell her . . . (*She rises and crosses to* BENEATHA *with her arms outstretched.* BENEATHA *doesn't respond*) Tell her we can still move . . . the notes ain't but a hundred and twenty-five a month. We got four grown people in this house—we can work . . .

MAMA (*To herself*) Just aimed too high all the time—

RUTH (*Turning and going to* MAMA *fast—the words pouring out with urgency and desperation*) Lena—I'll work . . . I'll work twenty hours a day in all the kitchens in Chicago . . . I'll strap my baby on my back if I have

to and scrub all the floors in America and wash all the
sheets in America if I have to—but we got to move
. . . We got to get out of here . . .

(MAMA *reaches out absently and pats* RUTH's
hand)

MAMA   No—I sees things differently now. Been thinking
'bout some of the things we could do to fix this place
up some. I seen a second-hand bureau over on Max-
well Street just the other day that could fit right there.
(*She points to where the new furniture might go.* RUTH
wanders away from her) Would need some new handles
on it and then a little varnish and then it look like
something brand-new. And—we can put up them new
curtains in the kitchen . . . Why this place be looking
fine. Cheer us all up so that we forget trouble ever
came . . . (*To* RUTH) And you could get some nice
screens to put up in your room round the baby's bassi-
net . . . (*She looks at both of them, pleadingly*) Sometimes you just got to know when to give up some
things . . . and hold on to what you got.

(WALTER *enters from the outside, looking spent
and leaning against the door, his coat hanging
from him*)

MAMA   Where you been, son?

WALTER   (*Breathing hard*)   Made a call.

MAMA   To who, son?

WALTER   To The Man.

MAMA   What man, baby?

WALTER   The Man, Mama. Don't you know who The
Man is?

RUTH   Walter Lee?

WALTER *The Man.* Like the guys in the streets say—
The Man. Captain Boss—Mistuh Charley . . . Old
Captain Please Mr. Bossman . . .

BENEATHA (*Suddenly*) Lindner!

WALTER That's right! That's good. I told him to come
right over.

BENEATHA (*Fiercely, understanding*) For what? What
do you want to see him for!

WALTER (*Looking at his sister*) We going to do business with him.

MAMA What you talking 'bout, son?

WALTER Talking 'bout life, Mama. You all always telling me to see life like it is. Well—I laid in there on
my back today . . . and I figured it out. Life just like it
is. Who gets and who don't get. (*He sits down with his
coat on and laughs*) Mama, you know it's all divided
up. Life is. Sure enough. Between the takers and the
"tooken." (*He laughs*) I've figured it out finally. (*He
looks around at them*) Yeah. Some of us always getting
"tooken." (*He laughs*) People like Willy Harris, they
don't never get "tooken." And you know why the rest
of us do? 'Cause we all mixed up. Mixed up bad. We
get to looking 'round for the right and the wrong; and
we worry about it and cry about it and stay up nights
trying to figure out 'bout the wrong and the right of
things all the time . . . And all the time, man, them
takers is out there operating, just taking and taking.
Willy Harris? Shoot—Willy Harris don't even count.
He don't even count in the big scheme of things. But
I'll say one thing for old Willy Harris . . . he's taught
me something. He's taught me to keep my eye on
what counts in this world. Yeah—(*Shouting out a little*)
Thanks, Willy!

RUTH   What did you call that man for, Walter Lee?

WALTER   Called him to tell him to come on over to the
show. Gonna put on a show for the man. Just what
he wants to see. You see, Mama, the man came here
today and he told us that them people out there where
you want us to move—well they so upset they willing
to pay us not to move out there. (*He laughs again*)
And—and oh, Mama—you would of been proud of
the way me and Ruth and Bennie acted. We told him
to get out . . . Lord have mercy! We told the man
to get out. Oh, we was some proud folks this afternoon, yeah. (*He lights a cigarette*) We were still full
of that old-time stuff . . .

RUTH (*Coming toward him slowly*)   You talking 'bout
taking them people's money to keep us from moving in
that house?

WALTER   I ain't just talking 'bout it, baby—I'm telling
you that's what's going to happen.

BENEATHA   Oh, God! Where is the bottom! Where is the
real honest-to-God bottom so he can't go any farther!

WALTER   See—that's the old stuff. You and that boy that
was here today. You all want everybody to carry a
flag and a spear and sing some marching songs, huh?
You wanna spend your life looking into things and trying to find the right and the wrong part, huh? Yeah.
You know what's going to happen to that boy someday
—he'll find himself sitting in a dungeon, locked in
forever—and the takers will have the key! Forget it,
baby! There ain't no causes—there ain't nothing but
taking in this world, and he who takes most is smartest
—and it don't make a damn bit of difference *how*.

MAMA   You making something inside me cry, son. Some
awful pain inside me.

WALTER   Don't cry, Mama. Understand. That white man is going to walk in that door able to write checks for more money than we ever had. It's important to him and I'm going to help him . . . I'm going to put on the show, Mama.

MAMA   Son—I come from five generations of people who was slaves and sharecroppers—but ain't nobody in my family never let nobody pay 'em no money that was a way of telling us we wasn't fit to walk the earth. We ain't never been that poor. (*Raising her eyes and looking at him*) We ain't never been that dead inside.

BENEATHA   Well—we are dead now. All the talk about dreams and sunlight that goes on in this house. All dead.

WALTER   What's the matter with you all! I didn't make this world! It was give to me this way! Hell, yes, I want me some yachts someday! Yes, I want to hang some real pearls 'round my wife's neck. Ain't she supposed to wear no pearls? Somebody tell me—tell me, who decides which women is suppose to wear pearls in this world. I tell you I am a *man*—and I think my wife should wear some pearls in this world!
       (*This last line hangs a good while and* WALTER *begins to move about the room. The word "Man" has penetrated his consciousness; he mumbles it to himself repeatedly between strange agitated pauses as he moves about*)

MAMA   Baby, how you going to feel on the inside?

WALTER   Fine! . . . Going to feel fine . . . a man . . .

MAMA   You won't have nothing left then, Walter Lee.

WALTER (*Coming to her*) I'm going to feel fine, Mama. I'm going to look that son-of-a-bitch in the eyes and say—(*He falters*)—and say, "All right, Mr. Lindner—

(*He falters even more*)—that's your neighborhood out there. You got the right to keep it like you want. You got the right to have it like you want. Just write the check and—the house is yours." And, and I am going to say—(*His voice almost breaks*) And you—you people just put the money in my hand and you won't have to live next to this bunch of stinking niggers! . . . (*He straightens up and moves away from his mother, walking around the room*) Maybe—maybe I'll just get down on my black knees . . . (*He does so;* RUTH *and* BENNIE *and* MAMA *watch him in frozen horror*) Captain, Mistuh, Bossman. (*He starts crying*) A-hee-hee-hee! (*Wringing his hands in profoundly anguished imitation*) Yasssssuh! Great White Father, just gi' ussen de money, fo' God's sake, and we's ain't gwine come out deh and dirty up yo' white folks neighborhood . . .

> (*He breaks down completely, then gets up and goes into the bedroom*)

BENEATHA That is not a man. That is nothing but a toothless rat.

MAMA Yes—death done come in this here house. (*She is nodding, slowly, reflectively*) Done come walking in my house. On the lips of my children. You what supposed to be my beginning again. You—what supposed to be my harvest. (*To* BENEATHA) You—you mourning your brother?

BENEATHA He's no brother of mine.

MAMA What you say?

BENEATHA I said that that individual in that room is no brother of mine.

MAMA That's what I thought you said. You feeling like you better than he is today? (BENEATHA *does not answer*) Yes? What you tell him a minute ago? That he wasn't a man? Yes? You give him up for me? You done wrote his epitaph too—like the rest of the world? Well, who give you the privilege?

BENEATHA   Be on my side for once! You saw what he just did, Mama! You saw him—down on his knees. Wasn't it you who taught me—to despise any man who would do that. Do what he's going to do.

MAMA   Yes—I taught you that. Me and your daddy. But I thought I taught you something else too . . . I thought I taught you to love him.

BENEATHA   Love him? There is nothing left to love.

MAMA   There is always something left to love. And if you ain't learned that, you ain't learned nothing. (*Looking at her*) Have you cried for that boy today? I don't mean for yourself and for the family 'cause we lost the money. I mean for him; what he been through and what it done to him. Child, when do you think is the time to love somebody the most; when they done good and made things easy for everybody? Well then, you ain't through learning—because that ain't the time at all. It's when he's at his lowest and can't believe in hisself 'cause the world done whipped him so. When you starts measuring somebody, measure him right, child, measure him right. Make sure you done taken into account what hills and valleys he come through before he got to wherever he is.

(TRAVIS *bursts into the room at the end of the speech, leaving the door open*)

TRAVIS   Grandmama—the moving men are downstairs! The truck just pulled up.

MAMA (*Turning and looking at him*)   Are they, baby? They downstairs?

(*She sighs and sits.* LINDNER *appears in the door-*

way. He peers in and knocks lightly, to gain at-
tention, and comes in. All turn to look at him)

LINDNER (*Hat and briefcase in hand*) Uh—hello . . .
(RUTH *crosses mechanically to the bedroom door*
and opens it and lets it swing open freely and
slowly as the lights come up on WALTER *within,*
still in his coat, sitting at the far corner of the
room. He looks up and out through the room to
LINDNER)

RUTH He's here.
(*A long minute passes and* WALTER *slowly gets*
up)

LINDNER (*Coming to the table with efficiency, putting his*
briefcase on the table and starting to unfold papers and
unscrew fountain pens) Well, I certainly was glad to
hear from you people. (WALTER *has begun the trek out*
of the room, slowly and awkwardly, rather like a small
boy, passing the back of his sleeve across his mouth
from time to time) Life can really be so much simpler
than people let it be most of the time. Well—with
whom do I negotiate? You, Mrs. Younger, or your
son here? (MAMA *sits with her hands folded on her*
lap and her eyes closed as WALTER *advances.* TRAVIS
goes close to LINDNER *and looks at the papers curi-*
ously) Just some official papers, sonny.

RUTH Travis, you go downstairs.

MAMA (*Opening her eyes and looking into* WALTER's)
No. Travis, you stay right here. And you make him
understand what you doing, Walter Lee. You teach
him good. Like Willy Harris taught you. You show
where our five generations done come to. Go ahead,
son—

WALTER (*Looks down into his boy's eyes.* TRAVIS *grins at*
him merrily and WALTER *draws him beside him with*

his arm lightly around his shoulders) Well, Mr. Lindner. (BENEATHA *turns away*) We called you—(*There
is a profound, simple groping quality in his speech*)—
because, well, me and my family (*He looks around and
shifts from one foot to the other*) Well—we are very
plain people . . .

LINDNER Yes—

WALTER I mean—I have worked as a chauffeur most of
my life—and my wife here, she does domestic work in
people's kitchens. So does my mother. I mean—we are
plain people . . .

LINDNER Yes, Mr. Younger—

WALTER (*Really like a small boy, looking down at his
shoes and then up at the man*) And—uh—well, my
father, well, he was a laborer most of his life.

LINDNER (*Absolutely confused*) Uh, yes—

WALTER (*Looking down at his toes once again*) My
father almost beat a man to death once because this
man called him a bad name or something, you know
what I mean?

LINDNER No, I'm afraid I don't.

WALTER (*Finally straightening up*) Well, what I mean
is that we come from people who had a lot of pride.
I mean—we are very proud people. And that's my sister over there and she's going to be a doctor—and we
are very proud—

LINDNER Well—I am sure that is very nice, but—

WALTER (*Starting to cry and facing the man eye to eye*)
What I am telling you is that we called you over here
to tell you that we are very proud and that this is—
this is my son, who makes the sixth generation of our
family in this country, and that we have all thought
about your offer and we have decided to move into

our house because my father—my father—he earned it. (MAMA *has her eyes closed and is rocking back and forth as though she were in church, with her head nodding the amen yes*) We don't want to make no trouble for nobody or fight no causes—but we will try to be good neighbors. That's all we got to say. (*He looks the man absolutely in the eyes*) We don't want your money.
    (*He turns and walks away from the man*)

LINDNER (*Looking around at all of them*) I take it then that you have decided to occupy.

BENEATHA That's what the man said.

LINDNER (*To* MAMA *in her reverie*) Then I would like to appeal to you, Mrs. Younger. You are older and wiser and understand things better I am sure . . .

MAMA (*Rising*) I am afraid you don't understand. My son said we was going to move and there ain't nothing left for me to say. (*Shaking her head with double meaning*) You know how these young folks is nowadays, mister. Can't do a thing with 'em. Good-bye.

LINDNER (*Folding up his materials*) Well—if you are that final about it . . . There is nothing left for me to say. (*He finishes. He is almost ignored by the family, who are concentrating on* WALTER LEE. *At the door* LINDNER *halts and looks around*) I sure hope you people know what you're doing.
    (*He shakes his head and exits*)

RUTH (*Looking around and coming to life*) Well, for God's sake—if the moving men are here—LET'S GET THE HELL OUT OF HERE!

MAMA (*Into action*) Ain't it the truth! Look at all this here mess. Ruth, put Travis' good jacket on him . . . Walter Lee, fix your tie and tuck your shirt in, you look just like somebody's hoodlum. Lord have mercy, where is my plant? (*She flies to get it amid the gen-*

*eral bustling of the family, who are deliberately trying
to ignore the nobility of the past moment*) You all
start on down . . . Travis child, don't go empty-handed
. . . Ruth, where did I put that box with my skillets
in it? I want to be in charge of it myself . . . I'm going
to make us the biggest dinner we ever ate tonight . . .
Beneatha, what's the matter with them stockings? Pull
them things up, girl . . .

> (*The family starts to file out as two moving men
> appear and begin to carry out the heavier pieces
> of furniture, bumping into the family as they move
> about*)

BENEATHA   Mama, Asagai—asked me to marry him today and go to Africa—

MAMA (*In the middle of her getting-ready activity*)   He
did? You ain't old enough to marry nobody—(*Seeing
the moving men lifting one of her chairs precariously*)
Darling, that ain't no bale of cotton, please handle it so
we can sit in it again. I had that chair twenty-five
years . . .

> (*The movers sigh with exasperation and go on
> with their work*)

BENEATHA (*Girlishly and unreasonably trying to pursue
the conversation*)   To go to Africa, Mama—be a
doctor in Africa . . .

MAMA (*Distracted*)   Yes, baby—

WALTER   Africa! What he want you to go to Africa for?

BENEATHA   To practice there . . .

WALTER   Girl, if you don't get all them silly ideas out
your head! You better marry yourself a man with some
loot . . .

BENEATHA (*Angrily, precisely as in the first scene of the
play*)   What have you got to do with who I marry!

WALTER   Plenty. Now I think George Murchison—
(*He and* BENEATHA *go out yelling at each other vigorously;* BENEATHA *is heard saying that she would not marry* GEORGE MURCHISON *if he were Adam and she were Eve, etc. The anger is loud and real till their voices diminish.* RUTH *stands at the door and turns to* MAMA *and smiles knowingly*)

MAMA (*Fixing her hat at last*)   Yeah—they something all right, my children . . .

RUTH   Yeah—they're something. Let's go, Lena.

MAMA (*Stalling, starting to look around at the house*)   Yes—I'm coming. Ruth—

RUTH   Yes?

MAMA (*Quietly, woman to woman*)   He finally come into his manhood today, didn't he? Kind of like a rainbow after the rain . . .

RUTH (*Biting her lip lest her own pride explode in front of* MAMA)   Yes, Lena.
(WALTER'S *voice calls for them raucously*)

MAMA (*Waving* RUTH *out vaguely*)   All right, honey—go on down. I be down directly.
(RUTH *hesitates, then exits.* MAMA *stands, at last alone in the living room, her plant on the table before her as the lights start to come down. She looks around at all the walls and ceilings and suddenly, despite herself, while the children call below, a great heaving thing rises in her and she puts her fist to her mouth, takes a final desperate look, pulls her coat about her, pats her hat and goes out. The lights dim down. The door opens and she comes back in, grabs her plant, and goes out for the last time*)

Curtain

STALKING THE JOB JUNGLE:
WOMEN IN THE MARKETPLACE

"Revolutionary . . . with enough clout to radically alter the contemporary job market."

—*BOOK VIEWS*

"Disturbing case studies and interviews . . ."
—Sunday *Sun Times,* Chicago

"Compelling . . ."
—*St. Louis Post-Dispatch*

"A *persuasive* . . . argument that women are frequently discriminated against at work by a male-provoked conflict between the importance of keeping their jobs . . . and their self-respect."

—*Parents*

"This is an angry book, but also a *well-documented and thoughtful* one, an offshoot of studies conducted by Cornell's Human Affairs Program, in which the author taught."

—*Publishers Weekly*

"This is an *excellent, incisive, thoroughly readable* study of a harrowing problem. . . . a clear and powerful argument for a new kind of labor movement which will demand respect and decent working conditions for working women."

—Andrea Dworkin, author of WOMAN HATING and OUR BLOOD: PROPHECIES AND DISCOURSES ON SEXUAL POLITICS

"Comprehensive . . . admirable in its completeness and its exposure of an inexcusable situation."
—*King Features Syndicate*

Sexual Shakedown

The Sexual Harassment of Women on the Job

by Lin Farley

WARNER BOOKS

A Warner Communications Company

WARNER BOOKS EDITION

ISBN 0-446-91251-4

This Warner Books Edition is published by
arrangement with McGraw-Hill Book Company,
1221 Avenue of the Americas, New York, N.Y. 10019

Cover design by Gene Light

Cover photo by Jerry West

Warner Books, Inc., 75 Rockefeller Plaza, New York, N.Y. 10019

Ⓦ A Warner Communications Company

Printed in the United States of America

First Printing: January, 1980

10 9 8 7 6 5 4 3 2 1

The author is grateful to the following for permission to quote from
copyrighted material:

ART News Associates for "Sexual Art-Politics" by Elizabeth C. Baker
from Art and Sexual Politics, edited by Elizabeth C. Baker and Thomas
B. Hess, copyright © 1973.
AP Newsfeatures and the Associated Press for "Sex Goes to Races,"
from the Los Angeles Times, copyright © June 4, 1976, and Linda Fill-
more for "Women's Work Around Track Never Done," from the Los
Angeles Times, copyright © May 19, 1976.
Chicago Tribune/New York News Syndicate, Inc. for an excerpt from
"Cartoon Quips," by Pete Hansen, in the Reader's Digest, copyright ©
August, 1970.
Chronicle Publishing Company for an excerpt from "Laughter the
Best Medicine," by Gene Bannon, in the Reader's Digest, copyright ©
October 1970.
Daily News for "HEW Officials Here Being Probed" by William
Federici, copyright © January 21, 1977.
Greenwood Press, Inc. for excerpts from Prisoners of Poverty by Helen
Campbell, copyright © 1970, 1975.
Grove Press, Inc. for The Story of O by Pauline Reage, copyright ©
1965 by Grove Press, Inc.
Harper & Row, Publishers, Inc. for excerpts from "The Politics of
Touch" by Nancy M. Henley in Radical Psychology, edited by Phil
Brown, copyright © 1973.

This book is dedicated to working people,
particularly my mother and my father,
and the working women of America
—in whose company I cannot fail
to raise my voice in indignation.

ACKNOWLEDGMENTS

For help with research I owe an invaluable debt to Sarah Elbert at SUNY, Binghamton; Frieda S. Rozen at the Pennsylvania State University; Robin Jacoby at the University of Michigan; Mae R. Carter at the University of Delaware; Martin Kasindorf of *Newsweek;* Barbara Wertheimer of Cornell University's Trade Union Women's Studies in New York City; and the understanding staff at the fine libraries of Cornell University.

For her early aid to the idea of a book, thanks to Mary Bralove of *The Wall Street Journal.*

Judy Burns, Cindy Carr, and Stevye Closterchiu are warmly thanked for their technical collaboration; and for their generous hospitality to me while traveling, a special thank-you to James Ford and Tammy Damon of San Francisco; Lexie Freeman in Washington, D.C.; Rue Wise in Los Angeles; Martha Steinhagen and Joan Nelson in Ann Arbor, Michigan.

Robert Fitch is remembered for a wonderful bedside manner toward work in progress, Dr. Harriet Connolly for her intellectual clarity, attorney Bonnie Brower for her commitment to justice and her excellence, and Maida Gierasch for sharing this work with her friends.

James Seligmann, my agent, is owed a deep debt of gratitude for his integrity.

My fondest and most heartfelt regards to Betsy Damon, my loving critic, who also frequently fed me, always listened, and never failed in her encouragement. Grateful thanks also to Edith Rosenthal, who took the manuscript to task, thoughtfully, and to Janet Derderian and Linda Montegrano among the many co-counselors who saw me through my personal doubts.

I want to thank Barbara Grant at McGraw-Hill for her valuable assistance. Blessings also to all the persons who consented to go on the record in connection with a controversial subject.

Finally, to all the working women who share something of their lives in this book I want to express my boundless appreciation for their courage, their honesty, and their faith in themselves.

Contents

Preface   11
Introduction   14

Part One

1 Two Instances of Sexual Harassment   21
2 Sexual Harassment: A Profile   30

How Does It Work?   33
How Widespread Is It?   37
How Do Women React?   41
3 The Historical Imperative   49

Modern Male Control of Female Labor   50
A History of Sexual Harassment   56
The Practice Against White Women   60
The Practice Against Black Women   63
The Cover-up   65
4 The Contemporary Economic Influence   69

5 Sexual Harassment in Nontraditional Jobs 78

    All-Male Fields 80
    Mostly Male Fields 90
    Training 93
    Academic Preparation 99
    College Teaching 108
    The Professions 110

6 Sexual Harassment in Traditional Jobs 124

    Hiring Policies 126
    Older Working Women 131
    Job-Hunting 138
    The Revolving-Door Attitude 140
    The Pattern of Male Retribution 142
    Waitress Work 143
    The Young Working Woman 148

Part Two

7 The Law: Civil Remedies 165
8 Employers 192
9 Unions 203
10 Men 218
11 Social Coercion I: The Casting Couch 233
12 Social Coercion II: The Washington Sex Scandals 252
13 The Future 261
14 Eleven Ways to Fight Sexual Harassment 266
    Notes 270
    Index 280

Preface

In the fall of 1974 I commenced teaching an extensive field-study course on Women and Work at Cornell University. Preparing for this moment had proved difficult because of a scarcity in analytical literature. As Elizabeth M. Almquist has explained: ". . . the research in the field is curiously devoid of theory, lacks policy implications. . . . Prestigious journals simply do not publish 'think pieces' that would direct the search for meaning and insight in the morass of facts and figures that are already available.[1]"* Faced with this reality I turned, as many women before me, to consciousness-raising, a remarkable tool for unlocking that vast storehouse of knowledge, women's own experiences.

Our first "C-R" session was devoted to work, and my students and I determined at the outset to discipline ourselves to focus on what had happened to us on our jobs because we were women. As we each took our turn speaking, I was a peer; the group was a nearly equal division of black and white, with economic backgrounds ranging from very affluent to poor. Still, when we had finished, there was an unmistakable pattern to our employment. Something absent in all the literature, something I had never seen although I had observed it many times, was newly exposed. Each one of us had already quit or been fired from a job at least once because we

*Notes will be found on page 266.

11

had been made too uncomfortable by the behavior of men.

Provided with this insight, I investigated the possibility of this kind of pattern to women's employment with scores of other working women. The male behavior eventually required a name, and *sexual harassment* seemed to come about as close to symbolizing the problem as the language would permit. Months went by and, everywhere I raised the issue—by recounting their experiences —women continued to confirm this to be the reality of their working lives. There seemed little doubt a pattern existed. The important questions now were how widespread it was and what exactly it meant.

Susan Meyer, Karen Sauvigne, and Carmita Wood joined with me in seeking the answers to these questions. At this juncture it took a certain measure of courage to declare publicly the name of something never before identified; Carmita Wood, a hard-working forty-four-year-old mother of four from the town of Ithaca, New York, suffered the destruction of her reputation in the process. We were doubted. However, more often we were aided by those who recognized the problem. Among these were Eleanor Holmes Norton, at that time Director of the New York City Human Rights Commission; Karen DeCrow, at that time NOW's National President; and Enid Nemy of *The New York Times,* who published the first nationally syndicated article about male sexual harassment.

It wasn't too long before all kinds of working women who had never before identified themselves with the fight for women's rights were involved in the effort to bring this issue to light. With their help, the Women's Section at Cornell's Human Affairs Program distributed the first questionnaire ever devoted solely to this topic and almost simultaneously mounted a legal appeal, prepared by Ellen Yackin, contesting the denial of unemployment compensation in a sexual harassment case. These women also helped to organize the first Speak-Out

12

on Sexual Harassment, and many of those who "testified" that day will be found in the pages of this book.

The Speak-Out marked the beginning of a grassroots organization of working women committed to fighting male sexual harassment. Jean McPheeters, Heather Thomas, Sandy Rubaii, Connie Korbel, Patricia Dougher, Diedre Silverman, Glo Webel, Lorraine Hodgson, Jody Berg, Susan Madar, and many more women than can be named here began to contribute to the process of better documenting the significance of this male behavior. We were soon joined, as a result of the *New York Times* article, by working women from across the nation. They sent us their experiences and their ideas; the mailbox bulged with news and information, including a letter that enclosed a twenty-dollar bill. The message was brief: "To help with the fight against sexual harassment. I can't sign my name."

The Human Affairs Program was terminated by Cornell University at the close of the 1976 school year. It was the end of the beginning of this book. I have shared this beginning for many reasons, not the least of which has been to acknowledge the working women who made it possible. However, I have also become alarmed over the years by an attitude that, because it probably would have happened anyway, the origin of this issue isn't worth remembering. This attitude ignores human initiative; breakthroughs in information with which to shape our future do not just accrue by osmosis even when we are inhaling the air of the right historical period. Moreover, the history of our process and our victories can never be inconsequential because it combats the tendency to resignation, which is how we all cope much too often. In essence, then, when we dismiss our history, we are abandoning the opportunity to reinforce a tradition without which we cannot bring our subjugation to an end.

New York City
1978

Introduction

For almost two decades our society has been undergoing a changing social awareness about what constitutes acceptable standards of behavior between the sexes. New information by women about the quality of their lives has often been the catalyst for this new consciousness. The sexual harassment of women on-the-job is the most recent illustration of this process. By testifying in their own behalf working women have begun to lay bare the male coercion, often masquerading as sexual initiative and frequently backed by the force of higher rank at work, which has been their daily fare on-the-job. Such male behavior is in sharp violation of ideas of equality, and the neutrality of work. Among the many concerns of this book are the psychological, sociological, ideological, ethical, legal and economic questions which are now being brought to bear in this new controversy, but underlying all of them there is still one central issue. Do women have to acquiesce to sex or sexual behavior from men-on-the-job in order to participate in wage-work in our society?

Public exposure of this abuse has been permeated by a notion that the sexual harassment of working women is of only minor concern in comparison with the whole battery of injustices that beset women at work, particularly the lack of equal pay with men. However, there is no aspect of women's deplorable situation at work today, be it economic or otherwise, that has not either been created

14

or maintained by this behavior and the way working women respond to it. This is because patriarchal relations, not capitalism, are at the root of working women's problems.

To begin at the beginning, although it cannot be said often enough, our society is first, last and foremost a patriarchy. Essentially, this means that it is a social system organized according to a principle of male rule and that it is this principle that shapes the matrix of systems such as democracy and capitalism which for the present characterize our particular kind of patriarchy. Throughout successive epochs the patriarchy has maintained itself by generating ideas that legitimize, i.e. make acceptable, the very conditions which make this rule possible. Enter male sexual harassment, which has until recently been a completely acceptable idea—although it is by this fiat that male aggression toward working women has been extensively practiced, a pratice that has kept working women both individually and collectively locked into a position of economic inferiority. Men accordingly have successfully insured their domination of modern work, hence society, because the patriarchy cannot lose control of its material base. The sexual harassment of working women is an issue of enormous significance. In light of this, underrating the extent and importance of the abuse is probably a result of an historically inadequate analysis of women and work which has continued right up to the present day.

As an example of this, much has been written over the last decade about a feminist success in women's employment; this is largely measured by the increased numbers of women who are working outside the home. However, this is less a result of feminism than it is a consequence of the expansion of the service sector in our increasingly service-oriented economy. In addition, women's overall employment conditions compared to those of men have deteriorated. The head of the department of Economics at American University, Nancy Smith Barrett, in a reference to women's increased labor force participation in the sixties wrote, ". . . the average job status of women relative to men actually declined during the period and the male-female earnings gap widened."[1] This is not surprising. The concentration of working women in a few over-crowded job categories which is the cause of these problems is virtually the same as it was in 1900. Edward Gross has explained this in an "index of segregation." By computing the percentage of women in the labor force who would have to change jobs in order for the occupational distribution of women workers to match that of men, Gross's index showed that female sex segregation was 66.9 in 1900, 68.4 in 1960 and the index had not substantially altered in 1974.[2]

The only major feminist success in recent women's employment, then, is what Barrett went on to describe as "a growing recognition that a problem existed."[3] This is true and this recognition of inequality resulted in three federal mandates to guarantee women equal pay and equal employment opportunity. The enforcement of these three mandates, the Equal Pay Act of 1963, Title VII of the 1964 Civil Rights Act and Executive Order Number Four began in some cases with sweeping court suits to repair damages to female employees and to correct sex discrimination in the future. Affirmative action plans have resulted and these plans in conjunction with what would have to be rather stringent enforcement are now considered the primary hope for women's employment opportunities.

Unfortunately, this strategy ignores the way men have patriarchalized capitalism and as a consequence the optimism is poorly grounded. Unequal pay, lack of promotion and poor opportunities are often only symptoms. Meanwhile, job segregation by sex is to a large degree sustained by male sexual harassment. This abuse is already rolling back the momentum of affirmative action and it will continue to coerce women by the means of severe economic and emotional abuse into over-crowded, sexually-segregated job categories. These occupations are tantamount to a female job ghetto and this is a primary cause of women's low wages. At the same time the abuse also impacts destructively within this ghetto, disrupting female job attachment, promoting female unemployment and inhibiting female solidarity. Until we understand sexual harassment, its historical function, the way it has been used to keep women 'in line' and the way this coercion interacts with women's employment conditions, women will remain an exploited underclass, the female workhorses in a male-managed economy.

PART ONE

It is a subject on which nothing final can be known,
so long as those who alone can really know it,
women themselves, have given but little testimony,
and that little, mostly suborned.

—John Stuart Mill
On the Subjection of Women

1
Two Instances of
Sexual Harassment

She was a twenty-seven-year-old receptionist for a Northern California dentist. In 1972 the victim called the Redwood City Police Department after her boss attempted to molest her sexually in the office. She had worked for the guy for about two months. She didn't run away because she needed the job to support herself and her child. He had chased her around the office, pushed her against a wall, and tried to make penetration. She refused, but he persisted and pulled her onto the floor, where he unzipped her dress. He tried repeatedly to make penetration. She was injured and bleeding vaginally. All the time he was telling her that this was why he hired her and that it was only a matter of time. She said she wanted nothing to do with it. When the phone rang he stopped and then he left for lunch. She went to lunch also and thought over whether or not to go back. She said, "I came back because I can't afford to leave my job." When she went back he tried it all over again and she left.

—Detective Richard Hamilton,
Redwood City Police Department

Dick Hamilton is thirty-nine years old. He's been a detective with the Redwood City Police Department for seventeen years. Explaining the disposition of this woman's case, he said,

Of course, the fact is the dentist was not arrested. It wound up a hearing for the D.A.'s office. There was no proof; it was his word against hers. She didn't report the case for ten days afterward and it was resolved through a citation hearing. It's like a slap on the wrist. He was advised of what could happen, of what the penalties are, and advised not to do it again.

Hamilton hasn't had that much experience with sexual harassment cases: "It's not the kind of thing that law enforcement gets normally." However, in his mind this case is analogous to rape and should be treated similarly.

There's just no question it's parallel to rape. In rape you have to prove force and fear. It's the same thing. This is economic force and fear. . . . You hear about these situations all the time, but nobody ever comes to us. I guess I can understand why. We had a prostitute who was raped and wanted to go to court. God, did she have a hard time. She said later she'd never report anything like that again. Now, here's a woman who knows the scene, who knows the score, and she can't take it. But if that's her attitude, you can just imagine what some receptionist or file clerk is feeling. They just won't come forward; it's too hard.

Prosecution of sexual harassment is also difficult.

"You are going to get into a gray area in both cases," Hamilton says. "It always boils down to a difference of opinion and any kind of evidence helps. In this harassment tapes are a big help. This thing may not be one big event like it is with rape. It's like he can harass you for days on end. 'Well, are you going to sleep with me tonight?' The time factor can be an advantage, though, if the woman uses that time to gather evidence. If she gets people for witnesses or if she can get tapes."

The restaurant is along the El Camino Real, the road of the missions in northern California; on Tuesday, July 1, 1975, the manager was booked in San Mateo County Jail for soliciting for prostitution. The following day the Redwood City *Tribune* reported that the twenty-six-year-old manager was arrested by Redwood City de-

22

tectives after he "allegedly told female job applicants that their sexual favors were a mandatory requirement for employment." Dick Hamilton was the arresting officer:

We had gotten a call from a woman who was upset because her seventeen-year-old daughter had applied for a job at this place and been propositioned. We were concerned because, one, a lot of young people were working there. If he tried it with one he might be trying it with others, might have even already tried it, and, two, the whole thing incensed me. That a guy would place restrictions like that on getting a job. There's a lot of young kids out there who'll do anything for a job. It's just not right.

Hamilton visited at her home with the girl who, after reluctantly agreeing to talk with him, corroborated her mother's complaint. "There just didn't seem any two ways about it," he said, "any lewd act for money or compensation is soliciting for prostitution; the guy was soliciting for an act of prostitution." Hamilton went "shopping" for a deputy district attorney who would prosecute the case if he made an arrest. "There wasn't any point in trying to do anything if we couldn't get someone to prosecute." It took some time, but he finally found a female deputy district attorney who said she would file the case. After deputizing a young girl and wiring her with a microphone, Hamilton accompanied the girl to the parking lot of the fast-food restaurant. A cover story, typical of the circumstances of many young female job-seekers had been worked out in advance and the new deputy entered the restaurant to apply for a job. What follows is excerpted from a transcript of this job interview. It ended with the manager's arrest (M is for manager, FA for female applicant):

    M: You're going to school right now?
    FA: I'm finished for the summer.
    M: You go again in the fall?
    FA: I'm not sure. I have to move out of the house.

M: You have to find a place?

FA: Um, um [yes].

M: Have you been really looking hard or. . . .

FA: Yeah.

M: I can give you an application and talk to you. . . . You want to come back and talk to me?

FA: Okay. Sure. Thank you.

M: So, in case you got a job, you're planning on moving out of the house, right?

FA: Yeah.

M: Can I ask you if it's too personal to talk about?

FA: No. It's just my parents and I don't get along any more and they think it's time I got out. . . .

M: Yeah, go out on your own. . . . You're twenty years old?

FA: Um, um.

M: How much business have you had in school?

FA: I've taken all business courses. I've taken EDP, all the office procedures, you know, shorthand.

M: Then you've never worked before at all?

FA: No.

M: No work, that's what's making it tough on you, huh?

FA: Yeah.

M: Well, did you ever, you know, babysit?

FA: Oh yes, I babysat.

M: And clean houses?

FA: Oh, my mother's house. I also worked up at Sequoia Hospital as a volunteer. That was when I was fifteen.

M: Right now you'd take anything you got, right?

FA: I enjoy working with people.

M: Is that why you're going to fast-food places?

FA: Well, you do get every type of person.

M: What is your big career goal?

FA: I really don't have one.

M: Are you the type a lady that wants to work all her life or are you looking for a husband and settle down?

FA: No, I just want to keep on working and enjoy life.

24

M: You're not a homebody type?

FA: No, not really.

M: Outgoing, kind of romantic?

FA: Yeah. Yeah.

M: When you do a job, do you do it thorough?

FA: Yeah, I follow through with it.

M: How long have you been looking—since school got out?

FA: Yeah, a couple of weeks.

M: And you're applying at fast foods.

FA: Yeah, you know, because I don't have the experience and all that.

M: Tell me more about yourself. What do you like to do?

FA: You mean hobbies?

M: Yeah.

FA: Oh, water-ski, horseback riding, archery.

M: I always ask about social life. If you had to work Friday and Saturday night, would that . . .

FA: No, it wouldn't bother me.

M: You have boyfriends or one steady . . .

FA: No, just whenever I feel like going out, I go out.

M: I'm thinking, I'm thinking.

FA: Yeah. Nervous.

M: Oh, don't be nervous with me! I'm just me, a dirty old hippy. I'll tell you something about the shop, okay? Me and my assistant do most of the cooking, but I expect employees to be all positions. Like this afternoon, I'm going to leave one of the girls here by herself and she's going to do everything by herself. Don't let the oil freak you out—I mean that it's hot.

FA: No, well anything you do in life, you know, you gotta take a chance.

M: Right, but, you know, I mean, knowing that you're going to burn yourself.

FA: You just have to be careful.

M: Well, you can't help it sometimes. There's also a lot of cleaning, and if you're not working you're cleaning. I'm not quite that bad; you'd be working

25

cash register. You don't have any qualms about cleaning messes, as far as cleaning toilets or stuff like that?

FA: That's just like cleaning my mother's house.

M: Okay, I try to give people the discouraging points. So you'd have to make, say, how much money? I mean I do have to take that into consideration. It'd have to be more full-time, right? You do have to make enough to support yourself.

FA: Well, that. I was going to move in with some girl-friends, you know.

M: I'm going through the whole store in my mind, that's what I'm doing. You know, we're a pretty loose organization. We've got loose people here. I don't expect people to work all the time when they're here, like sometimes there's a party. Are you a partier?

FA: Yes.

M: What do you think of marijuana?

FA: It's got its pros and cons. I really don't know.

M: Well, if somebody was sitting back here smoking, it wouldn't bother you?

FA: It wouldn't bother me. It's nothing to do with me. You see it every place you go.

M: Yeah, okay. Well, that's all. I'll put it [application] with the rest. And, you know, maybe I'll call you. I won't say that I'll call you and tell you I might not hire you, so you might try back or I might hire you or whatever.

FA: Okay.

M: Would it bother you if I was a dirty old man?

FA: Well, it all depends.

M: On what?

FA: On what you're suggesting.

M: What would you say if I'll give you the job if you go to bed with me? What would you say?

FA: That all depends. Is it going to be a permanent situation or what?

M: I don't know. Would it matter? Why would it matter? I wouldn't say every day or anything like that. I say once a week. What do you think?

26

FA: That's not bad.

 M: Want to shut the door and talk about it?

FA: Well, I don't care.

 M: Okay, come on in. You sure are pretty.

FA: Thank you.

 M: You sure have pretty legs.

FA: Thank you.

 M: So. I am going to be hiring somebody and I wouldn't mind a little something on the side. We'd work around your life and we'd work around my life. And you're interested in that and it doesn't upset you?

FA: Yeah. No.

 M: How about a kiss?

FA: I'm just nervous now, okay?

 M: Okay, so when can we get together?

FA: When do you want to?

 M: Soon. What about this afternoon at two o'clock. You can meet me at—well, wait, first let's talk about this. Okay. I'll start you out and we'll start out while I'm training you. . . .

After his arrest, the manager didn't stay in the station house long; the owner of the franchise rushed to bail him out almost immediately.

His boss didn't care [Hamilton said]. The really bewildering thing was nobody seemed to care. I thought it was newsworthy. I thought the press would really be interested in this, like they would say, "Hey, look at what this dirty old man is doing to these young girls." It wasn't like that at all. The press attitude was "Oh, well, big deal!" I couldn't get over it. I finally called some friends and they said the same thing. It was like everybody's attitude was: So the guy was propositioning her, so what else is new? I tried to explain that it seemed like a problem, but they didn't do much. They treated it as just routine.

The courts were an even bigger disappointment. Before the case came up for trial the female district attorney

27

had been transferred, and while Hamilton himself was busy with another case a different deputy district attorney agreed to a deal whereby the manager paid a $125 fine and returned to his job. Hamilton says, "The guy was arrested for pandering, which is a felony; he was charged with pandering, which is a felony; but they let him plea-bargain to a misdemeanor. He was convicted of disturbing the peace. The guy practically walked away scot-free. I just can't see it. Extortion is extortion and extortion is wrong."

If the attitude of the press and the courts bothered Hamilton, there was an additional eyeopener, from the California State Department of Labor:

I guess the thing that really amazed me is there's nothing in the labor code against it. We've done other cases with the state department of labor, but in this case we called them and they said there's nothing to stop it. I can't understand it. You'd think there would be something you could do if their hiring practices are so unfair and outrageous. There just isn't much recourse. You can turn down the job—that's about it. The whole point, though, is that it's just wrong. I guess that's why I think we should hear about a lot more of these cases. My attitude is that there's a lot of ways to hurt people. You can beat them with a club, but it's exactly the same thing if you force somebody to do something they don't want to do.

I wouldn't be a bit surprised if enough time hasn't passed that we could go back there and find the guy doing the same thing. We've even got the usual guys around here who say "Nothing wrong with that!" There's a part of society that goes along. There's some women who try to use sex to their advantage too. And they make it bad for all women. But I think they are a minority, a real small group. The thing is that they give all women a bad name. Of course, the real problem with an issue like this is it winds up as a women's rights issue and it's not—it's a matter of common sense and human dignity. It's just simple justice.

Because of his sensitive understanding of the coercion involved in sexual harassment, Hamilton is extraordinary. His attitudes are in sharp contrast to those of nearly every person or agency with whom he came in contact in the course of his involvement with these cases, and as these general social attitudes are explored throughout this book, the extent to which he should be commended rises immeasurably.

However, sexual harassment cannot be eliminated by relying on the enforcement of laws which do not completely fit the crime. In the history of men's misuse of women this abuse is a relatively recent arrival and is related to man's need to preserve his dominion over modern work. In this light, neither male rape nor female prostitution adequately define this new crime. The end result of male sexual harassment of women on the job is the extortion of female subservience at work. As a consequence, the broad range of male aggression brought to bear against working women—which includes, but is not limited to, forced sex either by rape or in exchange for work—cannot be seen as anything more (or less) than the means by which this extortion is effected.

Work is the key element in understanding sexual harassment, because this is the prize men are controlling through their extortion. This is clear from the preceding incidents; in both these cases women were forced out of jobs. And that penalty was barely touched upon by those I spoke with. The consequences of such extortion —being denied work or being forced out of work or being intimidated on the job as a result of male sexual aggression—are at the heart of the problem of sexual harassment.

2
Sexual Harassment:
A Profile

The sexual harassment of working women has been practiced by men since women first went to work for wages. It is a practice that until now has gone virtually unchallenged, largely as the result of a wide social acceptance of such behavior. For evidence of this we have only to refer to the countless jokes and cartoons about women and work that characterize much of our popular culture. A random survey of two 1970 issues of *Reader's Digest*, probably the most widely read compendium of American humor, turned up the following:

One shapely young secretary to another: "I like my longer midi dress, especially when it comes to taking dictation. The boss's letters are so much shorter."
—From "Cartoon Quips"[1]*

The discouraging rumor that United Air Lines would lower the hemlines on stewardesses' uniforms to a point well below the knee prompted this agonized question: "May we no longer eye the friendly thighs of United?"
—From "Laughter the Best Medicine"[2]

Both these jokes imply that men will express their time-honored right of sexual initiative toward working women, and it is the power to do this that provides the

*Notes begin on page 266.

axis on which the humor turns. In the first joke we laugh at the victim's puny effort to subvert this power; in the second we are expected to laugh at the cute male reproach that this power should be encroached upon. Also, in the latter joke the real feelings of the women involved are completely ignored, as if irrelevant.

We have here a re-enactment of social attitudes about sexual harassment; either women's feelings about it don't matter or, even if women don't like it, there is no escape from it. The humor is both a function of our identification with power in a male supremacist culture and a mask for hiding the widespread damage done to the majority of working women as a result of sexual harassment.

The use of humor à la ridicule and satire to keep oppressed people in their place is well known; the Step-'n-Fetch-It of yesteryear is only one familiar example. This image, whose purpose is to reinforce abuse and degradation by seeming to invite it, has a female equivalent in the dumb, big-busted secretary—a deliberate male caricature whose sole purpose is to reinforce the right of men to harass, control, and/or abuse working women sexually. It accomplishes this by undermining woman's role as worker, then reinforcing their use as sex objects by implying that they invite it. The message is conveyed that if women are going to make themselves sexual game, men have a license, even an obligation, to hunt. There is no glimpse here of the real working woman, a hard-working and important contributor to the work force; only a derisive facsimile drawn to the specifications of male desire. As with all stereotypes, this myth has been widely promulgated until it is believed as true. This deception has provided a cover for men to assert their sexual claims with impunity so long as the price in human suffering was smothered in hilarious laughter.

The turning point occurred when working women stopped laughing. On September 30, 1976, anyone who cared to dial New York Telephone's Dial-a-Joke could hear Milton Berle give the following discourse on secretaries:

One guy I know has a secretary with measurements of 45–23–45, and she's an expert touch typist. She's got to be. She can't see the keys. But this guy's really got trouble. His wife walked in on him one day and saw his secretary sitting on his lap. She said, "What does this mean?" And he said, "Dear, business has been so lousy I'm studying to be a ventriloquist."

Failing to laugh on cue, a group of working women from the Women Office Workers of New York City scheduled an unsmiling visit with the director of Dial-a-joke. It was the end of all such "jokes" to be aired by the New York Telephone Company.[3]

This particular company wasn't the first to find its sense of humor out of line. It was almost as if America went to bed one night laughing its collective head off only to wake up and find it had insulted two-fifths of the work force. Sheer numbers began to force a new sensibility about female workers; it was strengthened by the impact of ideas spilling over from the women's movement. Blasts at male mythology continued. Although the dumb, big-busted stereotypical female worker and her constellation of power/sex scenarios were never directly assaulted, the male joke that produced them went on the defensive. This retreat of male humor combined with the new sensibility about working women to permit the first widespread public rebuke of sexual harassment.

The full importance of this must not be underestimated; it is a radical change. The phrase *sexual harassment* is the first verbal description of women's feelings about this behavior and it unstintingly conveys a negative perception of male aggression in the workplace. With this new awareness, sociologists, psychologists, and management experts are now re-examining the matrix of male-female relations in the workplace. Working women are becoming more outspoken and the legality of male aggression at work is being challenged. And for the first time, studies documenting a wide pattern of sexual coercion are being publicized. The significance of these developments for working women is almost unfathomable. Our understanding of men, women, and work will never be the same again.

HOW DOES IT WORK?

Sexual harassment is best described as unsolicited nonreciprocal male behavior that asserts a woman's sex role over her function as worker. It can be any or all of the following: staring at, commenting upon, or touching a woman's body; requests for acquiescence in sexual behavior; repeated nonreciprocated propositions for dates; demands for sexual intercourse; and rape. These forms of male behavior frequently rely on superior male status in the culture, sheer numbers, or the threat of higher rank at work to exact compliance or levy penalties for refusal. The variety of penalties include verbal denigration of a woman sexually; noncooperation from male co-workers; negative job evaluations or poor personnel recommendations; refusal of overtime; demotions; injurious transfers and reassignments of shifts, hours, or locations of work, loss of job training; impossible performance standards and outright termination of employment. Sexual harassment also frequently influences many hiring situations, as when companies employ across-the-board policies of hiring only those women who are attractive sex objects regardless of skills, or where there will be an outright demand for some form of sexual behavior which will result in the reward of the job while refusal will result in a nonhire.

Disapproval of sexual harassment tends to focus on demands for sex as a condition of hiring as well as for keeping a job. These are considered serious manifestations of sexual coercion, while generalized staring, commenting, touching, and other forms of male familiarity are regarded as merely annoying and of little consequence. The outright demand for sex appears more serious because the economic penalties for noncompliance are easily discernible and the consequences to both the woman who refuses and the woman who submits against her will are easily imagined. Sexual harassment is nevertheless an act of aggression at any stage of its expression, and in all its forms it contributes to the ultimate goal of keeping women subordinate at work.

Adrienne Rich has written that men maintain the patriarchy in part through "etiquette."[4] Her choice of words in this context is interchangeable with what psychologist Nancy Henley has described as the "micropolitics" of human interactions.[5] A close look at male sexual harassment leaves no doubt the name of the game is dominance. As Erving Goffman has explained in *The Nature of Deference and Demeanor,* superordinates can often be identified by the exercising of familiarities which the subordinate is not allowed to reciprocate. He cites these familiarities as touching, teasing, informal demeanor, using familiar address, and asking for personal information.[6] Further clues to the communication of power between persons have been established by Michael Argyle. These include: bodily contact, physical proximity and position, gestures, posture, nodding or smiling, and silences or interruptions.[7] It is also generally agreed that those who communicate dominance will initiate standing closer, precipitate touching, and interrupt freely.

Eye contact is another dimension important to any micropolitical power analysis. In this realm, according to George Maclay and Humphry Knipe, staring can be characterized as a *threat display.*[8] Henley has also described touching as "one of the closer invasions of one's personal space. . . . It is even more a physical threat than space violation, pointing, or staring, perhaps a vestige of the days when dominance was determined by physical prowess."[9]

In view of this, women's statements about sexual

harassment—"He would always stand right on top of me"; "He was always staring at me"; "He'd always manage to rub against me"—are articulations of the way men use these gestures to assert dominance. In her article "The Politics of Touch" Henley says, "Some typical dominant gestures which may evoke submissive ones are staring directly at a person, pointing at a person and touching a person." She also noted that "Corresponding gestures of submission, all of them common to women, include lowering the eyes, shutting up or not even beginning to speak when pointed at, and cuddling to the touch."[10] Women stand up to these male assertions of dominance with extreme difficulty—or at the very least uneasily. They have been socialized to powerlessness—in Henley's words, to "docility and passivity."[11]

It is a matter of sex-role conditioning. The essential nature of women's and men's conditioning has been well documented in the last ten years, but its importance to this discussion warrants a brief restatement. Social psychologists Harriet Connolly and Judith Greenwald explain:

In our culture the importance of sex-role conditioning cannot be underestimated. In general, boys learn to be independent, to initiate action, to be task-oriented, rational, analytical. In contrast, girls are schooled in empathy, noncompetitiveness, dependency, nurturance, intuitiveness. These standards continue to provide the model for "normal" behavior and exert a powerful demand for conformity throughout adult life.

Female passivity is further encouraged by social confusion. Because men possess the right of sexual initiative, the communication of power and dominance by men is generally discounted as mere sexual interest. Nevertheless, as Henley has explained, "Even those who put forward a sexual explanation for males' touching of females have to admit that there is at least a status overlay: female factory workers, secretaries, students, servants and waitresses are often unwillingly felt or pinched but women of higher status (e.g. 'boss ladies,' 'first ladies,' and 'ladies' in general) aren't."[21]

That sex is hardly the real meaning of much male behavior at work is further indicated by testing the results. A recent study of female response to touching by male co-workers showed that the female respondents were "unattracted and unaroused." Catherine Radecki, a graduate student at the University of Delaware, conducted the study among forty women at three different worksites. As a result of her research she concluded the "women were somewhat disgusted, unaroused, unexcited, turned off, insulted, not attracted by or disliked the experience of men at work touching them."[13]

Whether it results from unsolicited demands for sex as a condition of working, or from the pressure of unsolicited daily intimidation, sexual harassment is described by Connolly and Greenwald as including the following elements:

Structurally, both types of actions usually are initiated by someone with power against someone with lesser power, not the other way around. In a word, they are nonreciprocal. The second structural similarity is the element of coercion, that is, it is either stated or implied there will be negative consequences if the woman refuses to acquiesce and/or comply. These actions function to assert superior power. As a result the consequences for the victims are much the same. All sexual harassment is a stressful experience and ego functioning may well be seriously impaired. The victim is violated either physically or psychologically and she experiences a loss of autonomy and control.

Because sexual harassment is an assertion of male power that undermines the autonomy and personhood of female workers, the generalized expressions of dominance must be condemned and eradicated, by both men and women, certainly no less vigorously than specific demands for sex.

36

Says Henley: "Men should become conscious of their tactual interaction with women especially, and guard against using touch to assert authority . . . women similarly have a responsibility to themselves to refuse to accept tactual assertion of authority—they should remove their hands from the grasp of men who hold them too long and remove men's hands from their person when such a touch is unsolicited and unwanted. . . ."[14]

HOW WIDESPREAD IS IT?

The phenomenon of sexual harassment is pervasive throughout the workplace in our society. With respect to employment policies alone, a 1960 National Office Management Association study of 2000 firms revealed close to 30 percent give "serious consideration" to sex appeal in the hiring of receptionists, switchboard operators, secretaries, and stenographers.[15] Moreover, as of 1976 this figure is probably low, according to acting chief of the Equal Employment Opportunity Commission's Decisions Division, Tom Cosentino, who has explained, "Employers won't admit to such discrimination."[16] Leslie Wolfe of the U.S. Civil Rights Commission's Women's Rights Office comments, "It's definitely a big problem . . . the problem is absolutely pervasive. Everyone knows at least a dozen people who've been discriminated against in this way."[17]

Indicative of the extensive nature of the problem is the country's single largest employer, the federal government. News accounts of the abuse here are widespread. Even more damaging, sexual harassment is practiced in the very agencies charged with enforcing sex discrimination. The Equal Employment Opportunity Commission, the country's main enforcement agency against sex discrimination in employment under Title VII, has been the subject of two criminal investigations as a result of audits of its thirty-two field offices. According to a 1976

37

story in *The Wall Street Journal,* the reports were secretly ordered "in response to rumors alleging staff misconduct."[18] Sexual harassment was never contained among the criminal investigations' formal charges—probably because, as one unidentified lawyer in the *Journal* article put it, the reports are "hearsay." No one at the EEOC has ever publicly commented on this hearsay either, but the report of one source, who has refused to be named, who read the audits maintains they indicated a high level of sexual harassment within many of the EEOC regional offices. In the meantime the EEOC has continued to build up a backlog of sex-discrimination cases. The processing of all EEOC cases today, including those involving sexual harassment, is conservatively estimated at three years.

If allegations of sexual harassment have remained informal against the EEOC, however, the charges have become formalized in relation to other government agencies. Diane Williams, a black professional in the Community Relations Bureau of the Justice Department, successfully prosecuted a suit against a high-ranking Justice official after alleging the abuse was "common practice" within the agency. Madeline Leon Salas De Vila also won her sexual harassment suit against three officials of the Cooperative Development Agency in Puerto Rico; Paulette Barnes has won $18,000 in back pay and attorney fees from the U. S. Environmental Protection Agency, after her job was eliminated when she rejected her boss's sexual advances; and in New York City, according to a *Daily News* report, "several New York based officials of the U.S. Department of Health, Education and Welfare are under investigation on charges of misusing federal funds, granting jobs in return for sex and going on unauthorized pleasure junkets."[19] The *News* added that one hundred top administrators were being questioned and the investigation was confirmed by Robert O'Connell, HEW's Regional Director for Public Affairs.

As bad as conditions are for federal employees, con-

ditions for working women in the private sector are often worse. Recent studies of sexual harassment—to date
a series of unrelated, separate surveys of working women
—have all elicited a dangerously high rate of incidence of
this abuse. Sexual harassment has also turned up in older
surveys of working women, but investigators seemed to
have dismissed it as inconsequential.

An example is found in *Women View Their Working
World,* which was published in 1963 by the Hogg Foundation for Mental Health. In this study, 107 members
of four clubs of the Texas Federation of Business and
Professional Women were queried as to some of their
basic concerns at work. Sexual harassment emerged in
two separate categories: as "fresh men" creating problems at work, and in comparisons between men and
women in authority positions, the respondents stated
"Women bosses are never wolves."[20] These comments
were duly reported in the book, but completely over-
looked in the overall evaluation of the report. After a
decade of activism by the women's movement, statements
like this were no longer so easily dismissed.

In May 1975 the Women's Section of the Human
Affairs Program at Cornell University distributed the first
questionnaire ever devoted solely to the topic of sexual
harassment. The behavior was defined as: "Any repeated
and unwanted sexual comments, looks, suggestions or
physical contact that you find objectionable or offensive
and causes you discomfort on your job." Among those
women queried were women who attended a speakout on
sexual harassment in Ithaca, New York, and women members of a Civil Service Employees Association in Binghamton, New York, who were not unduly familiar with
sexual harassment on the job. There were 155 responses
in all, and although they did not constitute a random
sample of the population, the results were startling:

- 92 percent listed sexual harassment as a serious
  problem

- 70 percent personally experienced some form of harassment
- 56 percent of these reported physical harassment

It occurred among all job categories, ages, marital statuses, and pay ranges.

In January 1976 *Redbook* magazine published a questionnaire on this topic. More than 9000 women responded; over 92 percent reported sexual harassment as a problem; a majority described it as serious. Nine out of ten of the respondents reported they had personally experienced one or more forms of unwanted sexual attentions on the job.[21]

At about the same time, the Ad Hoc Group on Equal Rights for Women was conducting its own study among members of the United Nations Secretariat. This questionnaire was designed to obtain information about sex discrimination in general, but a question about "sexual pressures (overt or subtle)" was included. There was speculation, in fact, that the response to this question may have caused the eventual confiscation of the questionnaire, since, according to a Reuters dispatch, "several of the respondents let down their hair." The San Francisco *Chronicle* headlined the story UN QUASHES INFORMAL SEX PROBE.[22] The UN denied any reason for the confiscation other than that the questionnaire was not the work of an officially authorized group. Before the questionnaire was confiscated, 875 staff members of the United Nations had responded; 73 percent were women, and more than half of them reported they had personally experienced or were aware that such pressures existed in the UN.

According to the Ad Hoc Group's report, the specific job situations which resulted in the "unprofessional conduct" were in promotion (62 percent of all those women who named cases), recruitment (13 percent), obtaining a permanent contract (11 percent), and transfer and going on missions (7 percent each). The survey showed that only about a third of the staff members dared complain about their experiences, and several who did said they were made to pay a penalty for exposing such practices. "One woman said she was forced to transfer; another that she was given no challenging work assignments following the incident, and a third said that she was denied a promotion which was due her." Sixty-four percent of the women who reported sexual pressures lodged no protest at all. Many of them cited the reason as a "lack of proper channels." Others were reported to have said "It would be useless to protest," "It would have jeopardized my career," and "It would have been very hard to prove." One woman professional wrote: "To whom could I protest? It was my boss who was putting me in that situation in the first place!"[23]

HOW DO WOMEN REACT?

According to both the UN survey and the Cornell questionnaire, most women respond to sexual harassment by quitting their jobs, although not necessarily right away. Among the 70 percent who personally experienced sexual harassment in response to the Cornell questionnaire, 9 percent quit immediately and another 2 percent asked for a transfer; but 23 percent first ignored it and another 13 percent pretended not to notice. One twenty-five-year-old secretary who was kissed by a client wrote on her questionnaire, "I was frustrated but couldn't speak up. I got a nervous stomach from anger. Of course, I sounded off loud, but to some friends away from work. At work I just pretended it didn't happen." Apparently, the hope is, if left alone, maybe the harassment will just go away; but according to the results of the Cornell questionnaire it didn't go away at all. *In fact, 75 percent of the time that the harassment was ignored it eventually worsened and about one-fourth of the women who ignored it were eventually hit with on-the-job penalties for*

41

not responding. It is apparently during this period, when the coercion is getting worse or the situation has begun to escalate, that many women give up and quit. A woman who worked as a woodworker for a Tompkins County, New York lumber company wrote on her questionnaire, "I felt humiliated, incompetent. I was unable to do my job. I finally quit.'"

Most women in the Cornell study were unwilling to use internal channels such as grievance procedures because they almost universally believed nothing would be done. That belief may be based on experience, for of those (12 percent) who did complain through channels, nothing was done in over half the cases. Other women reported that they didn't complain because they feared ridicule or were anxious about repercussions. Their fears are often realistic. A former waitress at an ice-cream shop in Cortland, New York, wrote on her questionnaire that she complained about harassment by male customers to her female shift supervisor. As a result, she said: (1) Nothing was done; (2) She was demoted; (3) She was eventually fired; and (4) A negative report was placed in her personnel file.

While these studies indicate clearly that a large number of working women respond to sexual harassment by quitting, they do not indicate that in any given group of women who are sexually harassed a smaller percentage will comply or submit and some will hold on until they are fired. There is, in addition, another relatively small group of women who will be pleased by the harassment. This is borne out by the Cornell survey, in which of the 100 working women who experienced the abuse, 90 reported being "angry" or "upset" while 10 reported they were "flattered." This discrepancy raises a major question about female perceptions of sexual pressures: Why is it that only a small minority is pleased while the overwhelming majority is not?

To sexually harass a woman at work is to base an encounter on her sex role in circumstances where her role

42

of worker is the appropriate focus. When a woman expects her working role to be respected, she will object to sexual harassment, which is behavior based on her sex role. However, when she does not expect this respect or dismisses it in favor of her sex role, she may welcome the harassment as reinforcement of her success. Fortunately, the large majority of working women have absorbed the American ideal of ability and achievement as the only measure of merit at work.

Economic need, the structure of the workplace, and female sex-role conditioning are critical factors in the way women respond to sexual harassment. Because assertions of male dominance are socially sanctioned, because men normally hold higher rank at work, because work is a source of income, and because society trains women to be "nice," few women object to male invasiveness unless it is profoundly disturbing. However, when there are overt threats to job security coupled with requests for kissing, petting, fellatio, and intercourse, working women are faced with a somewhat insoluble dilemma. They want work but they also want, and deserve, freedom of choice in sexual intimacy.

To make a decision women must weigh in the balance economic necessity, prospects for other jobs, a good recommendation rather than a poor one, the chances of being fired, the attitudes of husband, friends, lover, or parents, interest in the job and rate of pay, the number of times the abuse has been experienced and countless other factors. Usually, after weighing each of these variables, a woman will decide to quit. This decision is basically compatible with her sex-role conditioning, since it permits escape without a scene and, no less important, promises the best chance of obtaining future work.

She will tend not to complain and not to use grievance procedures because of the male domination of work and the practical reality of pitting her word against that of her boss or some other high-ranking male authority. Additionally, she fears public exposure of the matter will

43

result in her being blamed, being branded as a trouble-maker, and thus being unable to find future work. Future work is the key here. The goal is to get out with her reputation as both worker and woman intact. Influencing this decision, of course, is the fact that women predominate in most of the low-level, dead-end jobs, so that it will seem that transferring from one such job to another involves relatively little economic injury. For those women more attached to their jobs because their positions are at the professional level, involve an accumulation of a high level of seniority, are better-paying than the general run of female jobs, or are important in a career progression, quitting is much more difficult; but all indications are that these women, by and large, also quit when faced with severe harassment.

As a result, it is not uncommon to find working women who have left two, three, and even five or more jobs over their working career because of sexual harassment. It is also not uncommon, however, to find women severely penalized economically as a result of job-quitting. This is particularly true in our present economic climate, which almost guarantees that many women will be unable to find comparable employment, will be unable to obtain unemployment benefits as a result of having quit and will therefore be unable to economically maintain themselves. They will become ensnared in a cycle of downward mobility which could end in welfare or an eventual return to a job at less pay to the point of insufficiency in a market that now promises no other options.

There are no absolute figures available on the numbers of working women who quit their jobs because of sexual harassment. More research here is essential. Nevertheless, a reasonable deduction can be made from present information that female job turnover for this reason is uncommonly high. This is reported by the studies mentioned and is reinforced by interviews. Over and over, working women said not only that they quit but also that they were advised to quit. Leaving, in fact, is practically the only "thinkable" option for nearly every woman experiencing difficulties on her job because it is the prevailing social advice.

This only underscores the importance of the personal variables previously outlined. Those with fewer options will be pressured into submitting or holding on until fired. In terms of market and economic options (although these two are always influenced by personal factors), sexual harassment will weigh hardest on teenagers and older women, female heads of families, minority women, poor or uneducated single, divorced or widowed women, homely women, and working wives whose husbands' income is below $5000 per year.

The quitting–submitting–getting-fired dynamic is the predominant response of working women to sexual harassment. However, many women would choose to redress the situation. This is not readily evident by the scant number of women who complain. Nevertheless, it should be recalled that in both the Cornell and the UN questionnaire, when women did complain they were often punished for doing so. This is the kind of information that travels quickly on the grapevine. That this discourages others and that more women would complain if not frightened of retaliation is obvious. Twice the number of women who complained about superiors (12%) complained to their peers (25%). The reason: their coworkers couldn't fire them, nor could they apply job sanctions. (When women complained to co-workers, according to the Cornell Study, the behavior frequently stopped; many of the women interviewed also stated that this approach proved effective. However, this tactic was not successful if the aggressor could borrow authority from his relationship with a supervisor or boss, when the woman held a "man's" job, or when there was an economic motivation for the harassment.)

Opportunities for redress without the threat of retaliation are critical if women are to respond to the abuse any way other than by personal sacrifice. This recourse should be obtainable on the job. At present, however, working women have virtually no protective labor organizations, male unions generally do not treat the problem seriously, and internal grievance procedures have proved more hostile than friendly. Outside the job, though, the situation has begun to change. The new equal opportunity laws have increased the possibilities of lawsuits and of intervention of civil rights agencies. As yet, this option is being exercised by a relatively small minority of women.

This is the result of our social climate. Sexual harassment has been a source of hidden injury; society has either disbelieved or trivialized the damage. Unemployment compensation is not available to those workers who leave their jobs without good cause, and sexual harassment has never been so designated officially. Often when a woman quits, only to discover she can find neither a comparable job nor collect unemployment benefits, she will focus on her own act of leaving rather than the acute discomfort that forced her out. Society has permitted her no alternative to blaming her own behavior. Consequently, many women come to feel they should have handled it better or that somehow it was their fault. One woman wrote on her Cornell questionnaire, "I thought it was my problem." Female socialization adds to the difficulty. It is extremely hard for many women unequivocally to condemn the man who harassed them sexually. On their Cornell questionnaires one woman said, "I felt honor-bound not to publicly embarrass him," another "I did not want to get him in trouble."

In the present social climate women are often cast in an unfavorable light for even raising the issue. For all these reasons formal complaints by women are still relatively rare in relation to the extent of the problem. In Kentucky, Galen Martin, Director of the State Human Rights Commission, has said he knows the complaints his office receives are "just the tip of the iceberg."[24] This is frequently echoed. Jeannine Dowling, Director of Public Information for the New York State Human Rights Commission, reported her office received sixty complaints of sexual harassment during the first nine months of 1976, commenting, "I'd say those sixty are just the tip of a huge iceberg."[25] The Illinois Human Relations Director, Connie Seals, has said, "Women seem more anxious to complain but they are afraid to report sexual harassment for the same reason they are afraid to report rape. Women fear they won't be believed."[26]

Women are fired for resisting sexual harassment. There are no hard statistics as to how many women are punished in this way. Women are loath to cite harassment in exit interviews, and most employers have no inclination to elicit the information. However, all information from court cases, interviews, and the questionnaires mentioned indicates that proportionally about as many are fired as will submit to actual sex relations for their job. This number is much smaller than the number of women who quit, but the significance of this group is greater than their actual numbers. It is these women who prove that the job-loss for refusing to respond to sexual pressure is real. Their example swells the ranks of the quits. Retaliation on the job can be swift. Faced with dismissal or having to submit, quitting seems the only realistic way out.

Outside redress is usually sought only after either having been fired or having to quit. Redress requires time (and savings) that are often needed for the search for a new job. In addition, women feel that their chances of winning are slight. Frequently, the sexually coercive behavior itself remains a matter between the woman and her harasser. It is her word against his. (Women fear other female witnesses will be viewed with suspicion, that male witnesses will not testify, and also discount factors such as their previously excellent work record.) Further-

47

more, even raising the issue will evoke the specter of slander and libel lawsuits against them. Not surprisingly, the majority of women do nothing.

Clearly, women will continue to pursue personal solutions until they feel the social climate changes as follows: by condemning the abuse, rather than the objection; by acceptance of the damage as real, rather than trivial; by ceasing to presume women's accusations to be gratuitous and false; by recognizing the enormous effort it takes for working women to overcome their socialization to passivity in order for them to complain; and by insuring that slander and libel laws be fairly applied. In addition, the slander and libel laws must also be made available to those women whose previous employers knowingly distort employment reports to the women's prospective employers.

Until then, women will remain locked into a posture of defending themselves both psychically and physically at the expense of their jobs or they will defend their jobs at the expense of their wellbeing. New laws will go only so far in correcting this. No society can convince its victims through statutes alone that justice will be served.

3
The Historical Imperative

The patriarchy has perpetuated itself through insuring the subordination of female labor by endlessly maintaining and adapting its systems of hierarchical control. Before capitalism, for example, men controlled the work of women and children in the family. The emergence of capitalism, however, threatened this base of control by instituting a "free" market in labor. Capitalism, writes economist Heidi Hartmann, "threatened to bring all women and children into the labor force and hence to destroy the family and the basis of the power of men over women (i.e., the control over their labor power in the family)."[1]

The critical question remains: if capitalism would have equalized laborers in the marketplace, regardless of sex, why are women still in an inferior position at work today? There are a score of possible answers, but more and more evidence has begun to identify the most important factor as job segregation by sex. Hartmann writes:

Job segregation . . . is the primary mechanism in capitalist society that maintains the superiority of men over women because it enforces lower wages for women in the labor market. Low wages keep women dependent on men because they encourage women to marry. Married women must perform domestic chores for their husbands. Men benefit, then, from both higher wages and the domestic division of labor. This domestic division of labor, in turn, acts to weaken women's position in the labor market. Thus, the hierarchical domestic

49

division of labor is perpetuated by the labor market and vice versa.[2]

From the beginning, women entered wage-labor handicapped by the patriarchy that influenced capitalist development. Male dominance was already beginning to express itself in some sex-ordered jobs, with women's work offering lower pay, demanding less skill, and involving less exercise of authority or control. However, male workers soon effectively turned a trend into an iron-clad tradition. Hartmann explains:

"Men acted to enforce job segregation in the labor market; they utilized trade union associations and strengthened the domestic division of labor which required women to do housework, child care and related chores."[3]

MODERN MALE CONTROL OF FEMALE LABOR

Originally, in England, the rise of capitalism required little adjustment in the prevailing male methods of control, since the early factories utilized a family industrial system. Men could hire their own children for assistants, and whole families were often employed by the same factory for the length of the same day. When technological change made this system obsolete around 1840, male factory workers began to switch their demands of the preceding two decades from continuing the family system to limiting work for children. According to Neil Smelser, the effect of the subsequent child labor laws was that parents began to have difficulty with child care. The remedy then proposed by male workers and a majority of the upper and middle classes was to remove women from the factories.[4] Frederick Engels described the concerns about women workers that readily facilitated the auspiciousness of this remedy; "incapacity as housekeepers, neglect of home and children; indifference, actual dislike to family life . . . the crowding out of men from employment . . . husbands supported by their wives and children."[5]

It is about this period in English history that one finds male workers beginning to drive women out of industry, chiefly by means of trade unions. This prompted Engels to refer to these unions as elite organizations of grown-up men interested solely in their own benefits and not in benefits for workers who happened to be women or children. Hartmann explains:

"That male workers viewed the employment of women as a threat to their jobs is not surprising, given an economic system where competition among workers was characteristic. That women were paid lower wages exacerbated the threat. But why their response was to attempt to exclude women rather than to organize them is explained, not by capitalism, but by patriarchal relations between men and women: men wanted to assure that women would continue to perform the appropriate tasks at home."[6]

Needless to say, the male unions were successful in creating the widespread idea that women belonged at home and men's wages therefore should be increased since they should be paid on a family basis. Because men were never able to force women out of the labor market entirely, however, union policy eventually adapted by evolving a strategy of confining women to women's jobs. This was accomplished by denying them training. In 1891 Sidney Webb, in the Webb–Rathbone–Fawcett–Edgeworth series of articles in the British *Economic Journal* justified women's lower wages on the ground that women rarely did the same grade of work as men, but he also admitted that the male unions were intransigent in permitting women to gain equal skills.[7]

The full effect of this policy crystallized at the end of World War I, when—as is usual in time of war—more women had worked and performed many jobs normally reserved for men. Women consequently expected better employment prospects. Millicent Fawcett wrote in 1918 that equal pay for equal work was now possible. She reasoned that the integration of females throughout the entire work force would demand this equality of pay if men's wages were not to be undercut. The only obstacles in the path of this realization were male unions and social customs, she said, since they both led to an overcrowding in women's jobs—a condition which, of course, deflated women's wages.[8] In 1922, F. Y. Edgeworth formalized Fawcett's observations into an overcrowding model. Job segregation by sex, he said, produces a surplus in the supply of workers in the female sector so that male wages are raised while female wages are lowered. Edgeworth explained: "The pressure of male trade unions appears to be largely responsible for that crowding of women into comparatively few occupations, which is universally recognized as a main factor in the depression of their wages."[9]

We have, then, as early as 1922, a depiction of the effect of male policy in forcing female workers into "women's jobs," as well as a clear indication of the way men adapted their techniques of hierarchical regulation to ensure their continued control of female labor.

American workingmen never entertained the idea of excluding women from the work force totally, since American capitalism frequently turned to female labor power. This is a pattern throughout American economic history that has continued to the present, with the post-World War II expansion of female employment.

In many cases female employment opportunities have been the consequence of a field being abandoned by men who forced women out of more skilled jobs while simultaneously apportioning them occupations of only the most monotonous and dead-end nature. Job segregation then lowered women's wages even in those few skilled occupations which became associated with women. One example is public-school teaching, where wages became notoriously low.[10] Clerical work too offers a good illus-

52

tration of this process. When the increased demand for these workers first appeared, there simply were not enough males with a high school education equal to the need; but, even more, the subdivision of the tasks and the introduction of machines had changed the job structure. Hartmann writes this "reduced its attractiveness to men—with expansion the jobs became dead-end ones—while for women the opportunities compared favorably with their opportunities elsewhere."[11]

Much of the literature of the late nineteenth century tied this changing sex composition of jobs to technological factors and biological sex differences, but the role of unions and male workers cannot be denied. Edith Abbott indicates the way male workers enforced the sex composition of jobs in an incident that involved mule spinners, a machine traditionally operated by males in the textile industry. According to Abbott, a woman had learned to run "the mule" in Lawrence, Massachusetts, and then she moved to Waltham when "mules" were introduced there. The woman apparently had to leave, however, because (according to a male operative), "The men made unpleasant remarks and it was too hard for her, being the only woman."[12] As Hartmann writes, "Social pressures were powerful mechanisms of enforcement."[13]

American trade union policy also maintained job segregation by turning the British program of exclusion into one of limited participation. The form for this was "protective" legislation for female workers. The policy of the Cigarmakers International Union is a good example of the way this strategy evolved. In 1878, twenty years after the union had publicly stopped excluding females, according to Elizabeth Baker, a Baltimore local wrote Adolf Strasser, the Cigarmakers' president, "We have combatted from its incipiency the movement of the introduction of female labor in any capacity whatever, be it bunch maker, roller or what not."[14] One year later, according to Andrews and Bliss, Strasser himself would say, "We cannot drive the females out of the trade, but we can restrict their daily quota of labor through factory laws: No girl under 18 should be employed more than eight hours per day; all overwork should be prohibited. . . ."[15]

This kind of attitude has been interpreted by many as a justified hostility to unskilled labor rather than as a hostility to women per se but, as Hartmann writes, "Male unions denied women skills while they offered them to young boys.[16] The American unions were as determined in this policy as were their British counterparts. In printing, for example, women had been typesetters from Colonial times; it was a skilled trade that required no heavy work. However, they were eventually driven out by the National Typographical Union, which in 1854 declared it would not "encourage by its act the employment of female compositors."[17] As a result women were forced to learn what they could in nonunion shops or as strikebreakers. In fact, Susan B. Anthony was refused a seat at the annual National Labor Convention of 1869 on the grounds she had encouraged women to serve as scabs. (As Gail Falk has explained, Anthony freely admitted she had so encouraged women compositors. Her actions, she said, were the direct result of union policy because women could learn the trade no other way.)[18]

Male unionists discouraged women in more ways than just union policy. In 1870 the National Typographical Union agreed to charter a woman's local in New York City, but union men would not support the fledgling local and it died before the end of eight years. In the words of Augusta Lewis, its president, "It is the general opinion of female compositors that they are more justly treated by what is termed "rat" foremen, printers, and employers than they are by union men."[19]

The printers' union was no isolated exception in the mainstream of American union attitudes; if anything, this union was a trend-setter. This is evident in Edith Abbott's 1910 statement that "Officers of other trade unions frequently refer to the policy of the printers as an example of the way in which trade union control may be successful in checking or preventing the employment of women."[20] The typographical union, incidentally, backed equal pay for equal work; it was the means by which men protected their own wage scale, since, as Hartmann writes, "Women who had fewer skills could not demand, and expect to receive, equal wages."[21]

As long as barring women could place them in a position to strike-break, the overall male union strategy had to continue its efforts to cripple the competitive market power of female labor. The drive for "protective" legislation began to gather momentum. Eventually it gained wide popular support, and by 1908 the Supreme Court upheld a maximum-hours law for women. This decision was a major victory for male workers. Even though it wasn't long before there was a similar decision about men, this was never followed—as it was in relation to women—by a flurry of state maximum-hours laws. Hartmann explains, "Unions did not support protective legislation for men, although they continued to do so for women. Protective legislation, rather than organization, was the preferred strategy for women."[22] As a result, female competition against men was successfully curtailed and the maintenance of job segregation further assured.

There are many who argue that this particular impact of "protective" legislation is overrated, since narrow coverage and inadequate enforcement softened its effect. However, this ignores the fact that wherever male unions had a foothold they could now conjure up the specter of the law to deny women opportunities. In many occupations where long hours and night work were essential, as in printing, women were successfully excluded. Hartmann writes, "While the law may have protected women in the 'sweated' trades, women who were beginning to get established in 'men's jobs' were turned back."[23] The devastating impact of the laws on women's overall employment cannot be discounted. As Ann C. Hill has explained, they confirmed women's "alien"[24] status as a worker.

Attacks on this alienation of women from work outside the home are receiving a relatively popular reception at present. This change is the result of two influences occurring back to back. The first is that business has had a big stake in encouraging non-working segments of the female population to meet the rising demand in the service sector, a traditionally female field. The second is the curtain that still hides the on-going role of male workers in hamstringing female competition and in isolating women inside a female job ghetto. Nearly a century has passed since the results of this male stratagem were first noted, and yet the flawed motto of "equal pay for equal work" has become the renewed rallying cry for improving women's working conditions. Equal work *and* equal pay is more to the point. Even so, this still ignores the importance of male sexual harassment. Its influence on the sex composition of jobs was noted earlier in this chapter. This is a significant aspect of male practice, but it is one that will be dealt with in the present period. Historically, sexual harassment has had an effect that can no longer be countenanced today.

A HISTORY OF SEXUAL HARASSMENT

Sexual harassment of working women accompanied the new methods developed to control female labor with the rise of capitalism. The historical record is unofficial, a patchwork pieced together from letters, recorded conversations, interviews, women's writings, and newspaper articles that often mentioned the abuse only incidentally. It is nevertheless clear enough. The practice of sexual harassment throughout much of the nineteenth and early twentieth centuries contributed to the premature deaths of an incalculably large number of working women.

Understanding the full past impact of sexual harassment requires a reminder about the Victorian era. This was the golden age of the double standard in sex relations. All attitudes of public morality weighed hard on women. Elisha Bartlett, M.D., made this patently clear in his 1841 article, "A Vindication of the Character and Condition of the Females Employed in the Lowell Mills. . . ."[25] In this article on conditions of factory morality Bartlett declared: "It is only by maintaining an unsullied and unimpeachable character that a girl can retain her situation in the mill, and when dismissed for any impropriety from one establishment, there is no possibility of her getting a place in any of the others. . . ." It would be hard to find a situation more ripe for exploitation when the mere imputation of bad conduct from any mill authority could literally drive a woman out of town. In addition, the climate of the times made it extremely difficult for a woman accused of sexual wrongdoing to clear herself, since mere accusation tended to smear her reputation irrevocably.

Illustrative of this is the report of a trial in an 1846 issue of the *Voice of Industry,* a magazine of the Lowell Female Labor Reform Association.[26] According to the paper a "lady" who had worked for the Middlesex Corporation under an overseer named Snow "left his employ or was dismissed 'irregularly' . . . and he is charged with having circulated slanderous reports relative to her character to prevent her obtaining work elsewhere." There had been two previous trials. In the first Snow was fined five hundred dollars and costs; in the second the jury could not agree, "though ten were in favor of his conviction." In this, the third trial, the case was decided against the woman.

"It is important," the article concluded, "to break up the infamous conspiracy of the agents in this place to libel the characters of all who are turned out of their employment or leave irregularly that they may deprive them of work in other factories and drive them out of the city."

57

Subsistence wages contributed to the mortal danger sexual harassment posed for these early working women. Most female wage-earners barely eked out the necessities of life from their weekly earnings. In the face of this economic reality and the prevailing moral code, the sexual advance was disastrous. To refuse invariably resulted in retaliation, which commonly ended in either a decrease in present wages or losing the job altogether, the sure road to starvation. At the same time, to accept was sure damnation; after this marriage was out of the question and future employment was also forbidden. Prostitution was the only remaining option. As a result of widespread sexual harassment, many former working women swelled the ranks of prostitutes into numbers which have never been equaled throughout American history. The phenomenon was much lamented in the press of the time. There was less sighing, however, over the venereal disease that regularly killed these women within two or three years.[27]

Sexual harassment (before the arrival of cheap immigrant labor) was somewhat affected by the periodic push-pull between capitalism and man's patriarchal imperative. The early manufacturers, concerned with attracting and insuring a ready supply of domestic labor, strove to appear above reproach. The Lowell Manufacturing Company in 1836 stated that it would not "continue to employ any person who shall be wanting in proper respect to the females employed by the company."[28] However, with the arrival of cheap foreign labor the abuse became endemic. Manufacturers no longer cared either to make the effort to restrain their managers or even to give the appearance of doing so.

Upton Sinclair's searing exposé *The Jungle* (1905) portrayed the struggle for survival by the Lithuanian peasants Jurgis Rudkus and his wife Ona in Chicago's giant meat-packing industry. The book caused a sensation, although not for the pervasive sexual harassment it unsparingly revealed; this was a given. Sinclair explains that Ona was subject to sexual abuse at her job and that "she would not have stayed a day, but for starvation, and as it was she was never sure that she could stay the next day."

But there was no place a girl could go in Packing-town, [Sinclair continued] if she was particular about things of this sort; there was no place in it where a prostitute could not get along better than a decent girl. Here was a population, low-class and mostly foreign, hanging always on the verge of starvation, and dependent for its opportunities of life upon the whim of men every bit as brutal and unscrupulous as the oldtime slave drivers; under such circumstances immorality was exactly as inevitable, and as prevalent, as it was under the system of chattel slavery. Things that were quite unspeakable went on there in the packing houses all the time, and were taken for granted by everybody; only they did not show, as in the old slavery times, because there was no difference in color between master and slave.[29]

The sexual exploitation described in *The Jungle* was an accurate reflection of a daily reality. It was not a reality of general concern (except to the victims) and it never became a popular cause. But the consequences were a matter of life and death well into the twentieth century. Andrew J. Cawley of the Bronx attests to this in a letter he wrote to the wife of William Sulzer, the governor of New York. It was dated January 5, 1913, and written to Mrs. Sulzer a few days after her husband's inaugural in the hope she would exert influence on the new governor to get Mrs. Cawley out of jail. "I can't understand why the man who wronged her is at liberty," Cawley wrote. "His wife was alive when this happened and my wife says he asked her to come to his office in reference to getting employment in the health department. It was while there that he locked the door and attacked her which was not right. . . ." At other points in the letter Cawley had explained that they had one young daughter, that his wife was pregnant, and that he was unemployed. There is no way to know if the Sulzers intervened.[30]

59

The Practice Against White Women

In 1887 a remarkable woman journalist, Helen Campbell, investigated the circumstances of working women and published the results in a book titled *Prisoners of Poverty*. About the authenticity of her information Campbell wrote it was "based upon minutest personal research . . . it is a photograph from life; and the various characters, whether employers or employed, were all registered in case corroboration were needed."[31] Although Campbell had never heard the words *sexual harassment,* the practice turned up repeatedly.

When they could, working women sometimes aided one another in the face of such coercion, as exemplified by the story of Rose Haggerty, who was protected in her first work at home by an older woman who would daily pick up each of their sewing bundles, assuming the additional burden of delivering Haggerty's to her. Campbell explained this was so "the agent had no opportunity to follow out what had now and then been his method, and hint to the girl that her pretty face entitled her to concessions that would be best made in a private interview."[32]

This is Campbell's description of the prevailing employment practices: "The swarming crowd of applicants are absolutely at the mercy of the manager or foreman, who, unless there is a sudden pressure of work, makes the selections according to fancy, youth and any gleam of prettiness being unfailing recommendations. There are many firms of which this could not be said with any justice. There are many more in which it is the law, tacitly laid down, but none the less a fact. . . ."[33]

A woman known only as a Mrs. W. is reported saying, "So far I've kept decent; I came of decent folks; but it's no fault of many a man that I've worked for that I can say so still. I've had to leave three places because they wouldn't let me alone, and I stay where I am now because they're quiet respectable people, and no outrageousness. . . ."[34]

"The True Story of Lotte Bauer" follows a young German girl's losing efforts to keep her wages at survival; about midway through this struggle, Campbell wrote:

by January her ten and twelve hours' work brought her but six dollars instead of the eight or nine she had always earned. The foreman she hated made everything as difficult as possible. Though the bundle came ready from the cutting-room he had managed more than once to slip out some essential piece, and thus lessened her week's wages, no price being paid where a garment was returned unfinished. He had often done this where girls had refused his advances, yet it was impossible to make complaints. The great house on Canal Street left these matters entirely with him and regarded complaint as mere blackmailing. . . .[35]

Aside from manufacturing work, the largest field for women at this time was domestic service, where conditions of sexual harassment were the same if not worse. Campbell recorded the following bitter story from a discussion among sweatshop workers:

Do you know what come to my girl . . . I put her with a lady that wanted a waitress and said she'd train her well. She'd three boarders in the house, and all gentlemen to look at, and one that's in a bank to-day he did his best to turn her head on the sly, and when he found he couldn't one Sunday when she was alone in the house and none to hear or help, he had his will. The mistress turned her off the hour she heard it, for Nettie went to her when she came home. Such things don't happen unless the girl is to blame, she said. "Never show your shameless face here again." Nettie came home to me kind of dazed, and she stayed dazed till she went to a hospital and a baby was born dead, and she dead herself a week after. It's over an' over that that thing happens . . . I'll warn every girl to keep to herself an' learn a trade, an' not run the risk she'll run if she goes out to service.[36]

Risk or not, many women could only earn money by entering this field. Louisa May Alcott, who wrote *Little*

Women, began her writing career with newspaper articles, the theme of one of these early pieces being "How I Went Out to Service." It is a description of sexual harassment by the Reverend Josephus, a thirty-five-year-old bachelor, who first lavished "tender blandishments" and then, when rejected, only the ugliest and dirtiest of work. Alcott quit the post, writing that her heart had "suffered many of the trials that wound deeply yet cannot be told."[37] Whether they could be told or not, the trials of sexual harassment in domestic service were rampant. As a result of her investigations into conditions in this field Campbell wrote:

"Household service has become synonymous with the worst degradation that comes to woman. Women who have been in service, and remained in it contentedly until marriage, unite in saying that things have so changed that only here and there is a young girl safe, and that domestic service is the cover for more licentiousness than can be found in any other trade in which women are at work."[38]

In addition to manufacturing work and domestic service, a working woman of the time might have sought employment in the newer occupations of shop girl and waitress, but if she hoped by these routes to bypass sexual harassment she was bound to be frustrated; the hazards persisted. From one of Campbell's interviews:

"I was at H——'s, for six months, and there you have to ask a man for leave every time it is necessary to go upstairs (to the ladies' room) and half the time he would look and laugh with the other clerks. I'd rather be where there are all women. They're hard on you sometimes, but they don't use foul language and insult you when you can't help yourself."[39]

Campbell commented: "Many sensitive and shrinking girls have brought on severe illnesses arising solely from dread of running this gauntlet."[40]

Waitresses were prey to other hazards. A 1907 issue of *McClure's Magazine* includes "The Diary of An Amateur Waitress" by Maud Younger, who recounted the way a regular waitress advised her to get customers. "Oh, you must jolly your customers along. Sometimes I give him a whack. The boss likes us to be fresh with the customers."[41]

The Practice Against Black Women

The history of sexual harassment toward black working women begins with slavery, when the pattern for exploitative sex with black women first evolved. Gerda Lerner writes in *Black Women in White America:* "Their free availability as sex objects to any white man was enshrined in tradition, upheld by the laws forbidding intermarriage, enforced by terror against black men and women and, though frowned upon by white community opinion, tolerated both in its clandestine and open manifestations."[42] When slavery ended this pattern was perpetuated in both the North and South through sexual harassment of black women on the job.

In a 1912 issue of *The Independent* a black nurse published "More Slavery at the South," in which she wrote of this firsthand:

I remember very well the first and last work place from which I was dismissed. I lost my place because I refused to let the madam's husband kiss me. He must have been accustomed to undue familiarity with his servants, or else he took it as a matter of course, because without any love-making at all, soon after I was installed as cook, he walked up to me, threw his arms around me, and was in the act of kissing me, when I demanded to know what he meant, and shoved him away. I was young then, and newly married, and didn't know then what has been a burden to my mind and heart ever since; that a colored woman's virtue in this part of the country has no protection. I at once went home, and told my husband about it. When my husband went to the man who had insulted me, the man cursed him, and slapped him, and—had him arrested! The police judge fined my husband $25. I was present at the hearing, and testified on oath to the insult offered me. The white man, of course, denied the charge. The

63

old judge looked up and said: "This court will never take the word of a nigger against the word of a white man."[43]

Conditions in the North were as terrible, only different; there the black woman was excluded from all but the most menial labor and sexually victimized by dishonest employment agencies, agencies that pushed her more and more into odd jobs and "disorderly houses." In a 1905 issue of *Charities and the Commons,* Frances A. Kellor, general director of the Inter-Municipal Committee on Household Research, described the employment-agency traffic in black women workers:

These green Southern girls are collected in the South by white agents and shipped North, assured that good places exist. They are charged $19.50 for transportation which costs $7: they sign a contract to work one or two months without pay; they agree to send their baggage to the employment agency, which can keep it if they do not pay at the end of sixty days; a runner meets them at the docks and often robs them of their small savings; they are taken to a lodging-house —often the agency—where men and women, colored and white, habitués of disorderly houses, intemperate and good are all lodged together. There is no protection at the docks or at the stations. The new arrival does not meet one person outside of those under the influence of this agent. When a girl without baggage, $20 in debt, and a total stranger in the city, is sent to a disorderly place, upon threats or promises, can she be said to be anything more than a slave?[44]

Kellor, in typical Victorian fashion, begs the real issue. Jane Addams in *A New Conscience and an Ancient Evil* did not. According to Brownlee and Brownlee, she was among the first to show that these "agencies" were "often found to be associated with pimps . . . arranged lodging in a house owned by a pimp, and thereby provided a means to ease young women into prostitution. Facilitating the exploitation was the reluctance of courts to give credit to the testimony of black women when it was given against white men."[45]

The Cover-up

On August 20, 1890, Mrs. Alexander Bremmer, a deputy factory inspector, read a paper to a convention of her peers on the usefulness of female inspectors, citing certain "immoralities" that existed in some of New York's factories. She immediately collided with New York's Chief of Factory Inspectors, James Connolly, who vehemently denied her allegations, forbidding her to talk to the press and demanding her resignation. In the controversy that ensued it was Connolly's alleged involvement with the Tammany machine and Mrs. Bremmer's job that became the contested issues rather than the sexual harassment inside the factories.[46]

Of course, Connolly's response could have been predicted. There simply was no other public position. Over and over again both government and private agencies sponsored and then published investigations and reports that either whitewashed or denied the problem. The public accepted their conclusions as fact and these "facts" became even further elevated in the public mind by virtue of having been produced by prominent business establishments. Howard B. Woolston, Ph.D., in the first volume of *Prostitution in the United States,* as late as 1921 denied the existence of sexual harassment based on a 1915 department-store investigation that was paid for by fourteen prominent retail houses. He wrote:

It has sometimes been stated that work in stores and factories has a demoralizing effect upon young women who are thrown into intimate contact with employers and customers who may have evil designs upon them . . . but "investigators" found that exceedingly few of the many stories related could be traced to an extensive basis in fact . . . immoral employers and employees might be found in any large establishment.[47]

65

Here and there a little-noted report acknowledging the abuse would appear and then slip into complete obscurity unless it suited the purpose of controlling female labor. One of these appeared in Detroit as early as 1866. It issued a finding that "much of the prostitution which curses the city is the loathsome fruit of the depravity which dates its commencement at the tobacco factories."[48] Unfortunately and against logic, this investigation by the Committee of the Eight-Hour League and Trades Assembly was also used by the unions as proof of their program of "protective" legislation for women.

The first female organizer for the International Ladies Garment Union (ILGU), Pauline Newman, severed her connection with the union in 1911, just two years after beginning, because they wanted to pay her less than the male organizers. *She also complained of sexual harassment.* In an angry letter to her friend Rose Schneiderman, she commented on the women selected to replace her, saying, "Well they too are not bad looking, and one is rather liberal with her body. That is more than enough for Dyche."[49] (John Dyche was the union's executive secretary.)

Within a few months of this letter, though, Newman was back with the ILGU; she could find for herself no other acceptable option. Her good friend Schneiderman worked for the Women's Trade Union League (WTUL), a woman's movement group whose goal was to aid working women. Since the League also provided working women with organizing help—help simultaneously denied them by the very unions they were struggling to join—Schneiderman made a different choice. However, her conflicts between male socialism and feminism were the same as Newman's. Although they believed in women's rights and fought for them most of their lives, they were alienated by the middle- and upper-class majority of the women's movement and their heavy emphasis on women rather than class oppression. In the end they and nearly all other female organizers of the day opted for the male left, a

66

decision that seriously shortchanged all work-related feminist issues. Sexual harassment was no exception. Caught in the tug-of-war between priorities, it was finally deliberately ignored in lieu of the "larger issues" of socialist reform. Newman's approach was typical, as Alice Kessler Harris explains:

She thought it bad strategy to raise issues of morality when they threatened to interfere with negotiations over wages and hours. It may have been true, she argued, that a factory owner's son and his superintendent had taken liberties with female employees: "There is not a factory today where the same immoral conditions [do] not exist. . . . This to my mind can be done away with by educating the girls instead of attacking the company."[50]

The male left and the accompanying socialist attitudes, of which Newman's statement is typical, not only guaranteed that sexual harassment would victimize millions of working women for decades to come but added to the problem by trivializing it. The growth of this approach was facilitated by a decline in feminist influence on working women, the result of increasing feminist focus on obtaining the vote and of a sudden male union militancy against middle-class women's "interference" with the workers.[51] The unions, fearing the impact of feminists on working women, insured the split by portraying feminists as opposed to labor's cause.

There was in this whole period only one voice which, had it been heeded, might have redirected history. That voice was Emma Goldman's. Her thinking bored straight to the core of woman oppression: sexual exploitation. Having once perceived this to be society's major weapon against women, she went on to stump the country preaching her doctrine of sexual emancipation. Despite jail and rejection she never swerved from her belief that female liberation would only begin when women's sexual exploitation ceased. Among the competing philosophies of the day this

67

view was the only one that could admit to sexual harassment of women at work as a serious problem. Goldman not only adjudged this to be true, but placed the blame where it belonged—in society's hands. In her classic essay "The Traffic in Women" she wrote: *"Nowhere is woman treated according to the merit of her work, but rather as a sex. It is therefore almost inevitable that she should pay for her right to exist, to keep a position in whatever line with sex favors. . . ."*[52]

Emma Goldman has been vindicated by history—and in no areas is that more obvious than in the sexual harassment of women at work; her words are as true now as they were seventy years ago. We will have gained little beyond understanding her prophetic vision, however, if we do not also go back and reclaim the anonymous and unnumbered women who have perished because of sexual harassment. The nature of the coercion has always been to deny the reality of their deaths, to say that women asked for their suffering or, at best, only suffered the terrible common plight of their times. The record is quite different. Thousands of women expired either because they could not be coerced into cooperating with male dominance at work or because they submitted, only to be hounded into an ignominious oblivion. These women died from male supremacy, their lives sacrificed to the male control of female labor in a war now unremembered by male history.

4

The Contemporary
Economic Influence

Sexual harassment is much too widespread to be viewed as random rather than representative of male mistreatment of working women. It results in a pattern of female job loss. Sexual harassment accordingly has a marked negative influence on women's labor-market behavior.

The first of these major influences is discernible in the reasons for women's higher rate of unemployment. In 1974 women's unemployment exceeded that of men by about one-third. Women's rate also remained higher when education and skills were great, although normally these factors will contribute to less unemployment. According to the Women's Bureau, the higher female rate is significantly affected by women's movement into and out of jobs. The Bureau explains, "This type of mobility is much more likely to be accompanied by unemployment than is intra-labor force mobility [movement within the labor force] which is more common among men than women. . . . In the latter case a considerable amount of shopping for a new job can be done while one is still employed."[1]

The significance of women's entry and re-entry into the labor force is considerable. This movement accounted for 1.7 percentage points of the 4.6 percent unemployment rate for adult women, but only 0.7 of the 3.6 percentage rate for adult men. Without women's higher entry–re-entry rate, men's and women's unemployment would have been the same at 2.9 percent.[2]

A comparison of men's and women's unemployment also shows a higher proportion of the female rate as a result of leaving their jobs but a lower proportion as a result of losing them. This is particularly true for young women, especially teenagers, whose unemployment rate in 1974 was 14 percent for girls between sixteen and seventeen and nearly 12 percent for those between eighteen and nineteen years of age.[3]

Traditionally, the reasons for this entrance–re-entrance phenomenon both among teenagers and all female workers have excluded sexual harassment. For teenagers, the factors usually cited include schooling, marriage, part-time or seasonal work, and geographic mobility; while for all working women the reasons usually include all of these factors as well as the presence of children.[4] Nevertheless, the evidence of vast female quits in reaction to the extensive practice of male aggression predicate a case that the abuse is greatly boosting female unemployment. Further evidence of this is also indicated by the even greater degree of leaving jobs by teenage girls, who suffer so much sexual harassment it is virtually symptomatic of their employment conditions.

In the same way that the influence of sexual harassment can be inferred to contribute to higher female unemployment, its influence can also be contributed to women's lower rates of continuous employment. In January 1973 employed women averaged only 2.8 years of continuous service with the same employer, while men averaged 4.6 years.[5] The negative impact as a result of this is serious. Nontransferrable fringe benefits, seniority rights, and on-the-job training, for instance, are only a few of the advantages that accrue to employees as a result of longer continuous service. The aggression also thwarts a good employment record. In addition, absentee rates for women tend to be higher than those for men, and absenteeism, according to the women I interviewed, frequently served as a temporary female coping mechanism.

Because of the way women's harassment-induced job turnover contributes to these aspects of female employment, this area requires considerably more study. In addition, the whole subject of female job turnover is a sensitive one. For years many have believed that business held it aloft only to deny women opportunities, and in reaction women's advocates have sought to minimize its difference in comparison to men. This attitude is evidenced by the 1975 *Handbook on Women Workers,* which acknowledges that some studies do indicate a higher turnover rate for women but then argues that overall comparisons are unfair.[6]

The problem, however, won't go away. Jean Hayman in a 1973 issue of *Harvard Business Review* wrote that management's effort to provide opportunities to women are dampened by concern "over a purportedly high turnover rate for females—especially in the post college age group."[7] Juanita Kreps confirms this attitude: "Employers have cited other reasons for their failure to hire women: they have higher absentee rates and are in and out of the labor force more frequently."[8] In view of the impact of sexual harassment on working women, one has to consider that business may not be completely hedging. Female job turnover as a result of this abuse is serious. However, business cannot continue to blame women for higher female turnover when management consistently promotes men over women and then provides no redress for women when that authority is abused. Women's advocates have much to gain by scrapping their past posture of underplaying the whole issue of female turnover and replacing it with detailed research. This is particularly true in the present period of federally mandated female integration of male jobs when female quits as a result of sexual harassment will create a serious backslide.

The financial damage to working women as a result of male sexual harassment is devastating. In the first place, a female worker will have the economic penalty of a

71

lost salary in the period between her present employment and her next job. This is always damaging, although the degree will depend upon the woman's skills, education, and general "employability." Even skill, however, is no cause for optimism. It frequently will do little to offset the cycle of downward mobility that the quit will trigger either by the lack of comparable employment or none at all. Prolonged unemployment, particularly when no employment benefits are forthcoming, as is often the case, frequently ends in welfare or in severely overloading the financial resources of the immediate family.

It therefore cannot be emphasized enough that almost all women who work today do so because of real economic need. This has always been true of the 23 percent who are single and the 19 percent who are widowed, divorced, or separated, but it is also true of the labor market's most recent entrants, wives and mothers. In 1974, 23 percent of this group's husbands had incomes below $7000.[9] Working wives in white families in 1972 accounted for nearly one-fourth of total family income, and black wives accounted for one-third of total mean black family income. Moreover, in 1973 12 percent of all American families were headed by a woman, and yet the following year a quarter of a million of these women were unemployed. Their rate of unemployment was nearly two-thirds that of men family heads in husband/wife families.[10] The loss of female income due to unemployment as a result of sexual harassment spells poverty not only for the great majority of working women but for many of their families as well.

Low female wages are also partially the result of male sexual harassment. Male aggressiveness at work reinforces female subordination, which helps to maintain man's hierarchic control—virtually all positions of authority. This control simultaneously permits a level of sexual harassment of working women that renders them insecure by causing a perpetual job rotation of a significant percentage of the total group. At the same time, female efforts

72

to enter male occupations are thwarted by this abuse. This insures the maintenance of job segregation, the source of women's unequal wage scale.

Female earnings are outrageously poor compared to those of men. Overall in 1973 women averaged only one-third the yearly income of men. Women employed full-time, year-round earned an average of $6488. That is barely 57 percent of the $11,468 enjoyed by their male counterparts.[11] The future looks no brighter. As the divorce rate continues to climb and the economy continues to shift to a service orientation with a concomitant shrinkage of employment in goods and production, more and more women will find work increasingly critical to their own and their families' economic survival.

Meanwhile, depressed female earnings are already the cause of serious concern. *In 1974, one out of eight families was headed by a woman. More than one-third of these families, including one-half the families headed by minority women, lived in poverty.*[12] The problem is so serious that Robert Stein, an economist for the federal government, has labeled it "One of the most important domestic problems facing the Nation."[13] These families, which are increasing dramatically, now comprise the largest growing proportion of poverty in the United States. By extension, one also has to consider that male-headed families dependent upon female income (and that number is now substantial) are also penalized by depressed female wages.

Depression of female earning power reinforces the domestic division of labor, which in turn reinforces job segregation, which in its own turn reinforces depressed female wages. The dismantling of job segregation would go a long way toward turning this around. Without sex segregation of the labor force, women's wages would be on a par with men's. As a result of this wage parity women would no longer be financially dependent upon marriage; and without marriage necessitated by female

73

survival, the domestic division of labor might no doubt become equalized.

Occupational equality is a major goal of Affirmative Action. Unfortunately, it has been a goal in a campaign to raise female wages and opportunities without an adequate analysis of the means by which men have traditionally controlled female labor. And so, male sexual harassment—which insures the maintenance of job segregation by sex—has gone largely unchallenged.

Sexual harassment's critical role in the maintenance of job segregation and its contribution to female unemployment comprise two directly negative influences on female earning power; but it also depresses women's wages in still a third way. Age, particularly after about thirty; a homely appearance; a poor or working class background; minority status; and the financial inability to dress in style all comprise a female liability to both employability and earning power in a job market dictated to by male hierarchical control. Very simply, women who do not stand up to men's prevailing sexual standard of attractiveness are often economically penalized. The financial damage is real and extensive. Older women with skills and experience far beyond their junior counterparts are standardly unemployable, or when hired are often paid far less than a twenty-year-old just starting out. Correspondingly, women with skills and experience who also happen to fall into any other category of liability are regularly paid less than their more attractive co-workers.[14]

The economy is changing. Nearly all the increase in employment between now and 1980 will be accounted for by the service sector, which will employ twice as many people as the rest of the economy.[15] Despite this phenomenal expansion in the traditional women's sector, job segregation within this area is keeping women down. According to *Exploitation From 9 to 5,* "In 1971 over 60% of female white-collar workers (more than one-third of all employed women) worked in clerical jobs. Yet almost

70% of all male white-collar workers (28% of the male workforce) were in either the professional and technical or the managerial category."[16] It might be hoped that integration of women into other occupations would offset this imbalance; and, of course, it is true that since 1960 women have been entering the skilled trades at a faster rate than men. Thus in 1970 there were twice as many women in these trades as in 1960,[17] but as *Exploitation From 9 to 5* explains:

This total is less than 2 percent of the total female labor force. Men also have the highest-status, highest-paying blue-collar jobs. Only 8 percent of women blue-collar workers (1.3 percent of employed women) were craftsmen or foremen in 1971. Yet over 43 percent of the men in this group (20 percent of the male labor force) were categorized as craftsmen and foremen. Data collected by the EEOC indicate even in industries where women represent a large proportion of operatives, they may be excluded from craft jobs. For example, in Cleveland, over 60 percent of the operatives, but only one percent of the craftsmen were women. Similarly, in the electronics industry of that city 57 percent of the operatives, but just three percent of the craftsmen, were women.[18]

The overall trend is clear. Men are extending their control of female labor by monopolizing the technical, managerial, and professional occupations in the service sector, despite this area's incredible expansion in female employment; while simultaneously maintaining their already-established management of production as well as their monopoly of the skilled trades, extending it even to the fastest-growing and newest, such as electronics. In addition, economic factors could exacerbate this trend. Nancy Smith Barrett warns that "if high levels of unemployment continue, there will inevitably be more and more bumping of inexperienced and unskilled workers on the part of the skilled and potentially trainable . . . the result could be a movement of men into previously female jobs,

75

forcing many women to choose between being unemployed or dropping out of the labor force."[19]

This could happen even without the continuation of our present unemployment levels. As employment in the goods and production sector of the economy continues to shrink, men will inevitably cast an eye at female occupations, particularly the more lucrative; and there is some evidence that this movement is already under way. Howard Wilensky writes that "women have entered low-status men's occupations (bookkeeper, bank teller) but do not control them, while men have entered and are gaining control of the more attractive female occupations (secondary school teaching, social work, librarianship, hospital and perhaps nursing administration)."[20] More worrisome still, expansion in the service sector increases the inevitability of automation whereby many clerical and semi-skilled manual jobs may be wiped out. This could eventually reduce the number of working women in this sphere while reinsuring that men, through their monopoly of all the non-technologically replaceable occupations, would become even more dominant.

We are now in an economic transition period. By the end of it, if women's present employment levels stabilize or increase, we will, in all probability, have shifted from a society where men have continued to rule through the male-dominated, primarily female-serviced family to one where men will perpetuate their rule through a male-dominated, female-serviced economy. Moreover, homework for women will not disappear. Although the expansion of capitalism itself will facilitate a more thorough weakening of home commitments in favor of stronger work commitments, men will attempt to weather this societal transition by emphasizing women's domestic duties and practicing sexual harassment on the job. This will insure the continuation of job segregation. Eventually there may actually be strong support for easily accessible daycare, but most men will not accept heavy duty in the home.

Despite the whole package of interventions devised over the last ten years to end sex discrimination, women stand little chance of preventing a scenario along the preceding outline unless they also put an end to sexual harassment.

5
Sexual Harassment in Nontraditional Jobs

The advent of Title VII in July 1965 unleashed a campaign of correcting sex discrimination aimed almost exclusively at employers. But employer policies are just one facet of the job segregation problem. These policies are just one facet of the job segregation problem. These policies are, in part, simply a reflection of the unremitting refusal of men to work alongside women as equals (let alone as superiors).

In *Developing Women's Potential* Edwin C. Lewis has written: "It is so difficult to say just why men are so strongly opposed to working women. Traditionally, they expect all women to be like their mothers and the odds are great that their mothers were housewives. Regrettably, it also is likely that many men view the potential invasion of the labor market by women, and particularly the invasion of their own male-dominated occupations, as a threat. Just what is being threatened is not clear, but such a fear undoubtedly exists."[1]

This is a common attitude. Male opposition to female workers is often readily acknowledged while the reasons for this opposition are couched in either the most outlandish Freudian psychology or as "irrational." As a result it is frequently presumed that contact between the sexes on the job will melt this male opposition, since it is widely believed that mingling will soon dispel male prejudice. This approach to the problem is at the very least naïve. There can be little question that men have a great deal to lose by an integration of females in the labor market, and men know it.

For evidence of this one need look no further than the four most common reasons men give for their opposition to female workers: that women lower their wages, that women will take their jobs, that women belong in the home, and that women have no business trying to compete with men. With the exception of lowered wages, each of these reasons is either a rationalization or a justification for the status quo. A fear of lowered wages, meanwhile, is simply a case of the chickens coming home to roost. By creating and struggling to maintain job segregation, men have insured that women's wages will be lower than their own; consequently an influx of women into a previously all-male occupation does raise the specter of lowered wages. It often portends as well a tipping of that occupation, which is to say that because wages are reduced men are subsequently less inclined to pursue the field and the occupation eventually goes heavily female. The only solution is an end of job segregation, and until then men can fear a lowering of their wages, but they cannot justify their opposition to female workers on this ground when they are themselves responsible.

The naïve belief that male opposition to female workers will eventually disappear from a sexual intermingling of occupations, as is now required by law, is best replaced by a more realistic assessment of the ways men, despite this forced entry, will attempt to insure their domination and the continuation of job segregation. We don't have far to look. Sexual harassment is regarded as an acceptable means of control so available that it frequently is described as just "part of the job."

This is not to say that sexual harrassment is a male plot per se, only that men have evolved a code of behavior that ritualizes unsolicited and nonreciprocal aggression at work and their use of this code functions to insure dominance..The code also permits individual men to remain ignorant of the impact of their behavior. According to social psychologist Harriet Connolly, "People most often do certain things or behave in certain ways because of norms, because it is just the way one behaves." The code provides the license for normalizing behavior, which in effect is coercion. Men may or may not recognize this, but they routinize their aggression, by presuming the right of sexual favors—including sex itself—and by their acting as if all working women are sexual prey. This behavior will insure a sex-segregated job market.

ALL-MALE FIELDS

The much-publicized female integration of the previously all-male field of police patrol work demonstrates that an intermingling of the sexes will not necessarily bring about a decrease in male prejudice but rather an increase in male sexual harassment. In the early 70s the Washington, D.C., Police Department was considered a pioneer in female integration. Not only had the department hired 200 policewomen, triple the normal number, but it had also begun the largest model program of employing women on uniformed patrol around the clock. Patricia Marshall in a 1972 issue of *Manpower* reasoned that since the D.C. "experiment" was perhaps the largest in the country it seemed likely the program would have a major effect on policewomen everywhere. Marshall was optimistic the policewomen would increase; she noted that all preliminary accounts indicated the women were performing with "professionalism, poise and courage."[2] It wasn't long, however, before this model program was awash in charges of rampant sexual harassment.

The revelation of the abuse first became public knowledge in two separate articles by Jane Seaberry and Alfred Lewis that appeared in the Washington *Post* in October 1975. Just three years after Marshall's hopeful predictions the *Post* articles contained charges by D.C.

policewomen that they were being coerced to have sex in exchange for better assignments. Police Officer Peggy A. Jackson was reported as saying, "You've got to make love to get a day off or make love to get a good beat."[3] According to the article, at least a dozen other policewomen said they had experienced sexual harassment but few of them wanted to be quoted by name. Two of the department's three Equal Employment Opportunity officers said they had heard about harassment of women officers, and one of these officials (who also refused to be named) reported, "We've had two women come down here and say they've had pressure on them."[4] He explained there was little his office could do without an official complaint and that the women wouldn't sign because they said they were afraid of retaliation by their superiors.

Penny Bolden, another District officer, recalled an experience when her male partner swung their squad car into a Washington park, subsequently requesting that she have sex with him, and then warning her that she had better not say a word about it. Bolden commented, "If he had put his hands on me I would have shot him."[5] Bolden's experience was not unique. By the time the articles appeared about half of the District's 333 policewomen had been assigned to patrol duty, and Seaberry and Lewis reported that of this number the policewomen they interviewed estimated about half had probably been sexually harassed. They said the harassment complained of most frequently consisted of male officers—many of whom outrank the women—punishing policewomen who wouldn't submit to sexual advances and rewarding those who did with better treatment and assignments.[6]

The Washington police chief, Maurice J. Cullinane, responded to the policewomen's allegations by labelling them "unsubstantiated innuendo and back-alley gossip."[7] He also said that there were official avenues open to air such grievances; and, as if the policewomen had never said they were too frightened to complain, he dismissed their allegations on the ground that to date there were no official complaints. The Washington *Post* went on to interview some fifteen policemen about the problem. Although most said they wouldn't talk for fear of being fired, there was one seven-year man, Sergeant M. L. Clark, who did say, "I won't say it hasn't happened. Just because a man's wearing a sergeant's badge I wouldn't put it past him. Sometimes a man will say something to a woman officer, I know that happens. But as far as an official using that against her, I'm going to waive judgment on that."[8]

About one year after the Washington allegations of sexual harassment, the powerful commanders of America's largest police and sheriff departments, known as "The Major City Chiefs," convened at the FBI training academy in Quantico, Virginia. Phil McCombs of the Washington *Post* was there and reported a "joking" session by the chiefs in relation to their female employees. As carried in the San Francisco *Chronicle,* the discussion went:

"Hi," said the smiling, attractive FBI trainee as she walked by in her drab, green starched fatigues.

"Wow," said one of the police chiefs as she passed.

"I was born 40 years too early," said Indianapolis Chief Gene Gallagher.

"If there had always been policewomen," added Seattle Chief Bob Hanson, "I wouldn't have just celebrated my 32nd anniversary."

"If you put two women together [in a squad car], they fight," said Dallas Chief Dan Byrd. "If you put male and female together, they fornicate."

"One of the most destructive things in police work is male-female partners, as far as breakups of families go," said FBI man Ed Tully.[9]

Basically, what is being said here is that women should not be working with men. The hostility to female co-workers is concealed by implying that sex is inevitable and by transforming the desire to force women out of police work into a more legitimate worry about the future of American families.

The chiefs seem unaware that their own attitude is hostile to women; the female trainee was immediately transformed from a potential colleague into a vagina, hence an object for comments and jokes and an excuse for a discussion of a menace of sex (women) in their ranks.

There are many women who have come to understand this attitude from their own hard experience. J.J., a former Washington D.C. policewoman, has requested that her real name not be used in the interest of future police work, an occupation that has been a goal since childhood. She was terminated from the D.C. Police Department in the spring of 1976 for insubordination, for filing a false report of rape against another police officer, and for possessing a personality unsuitable to law enforcement. While a policewoman, J.J., who is a dedicated young woman, had earned three commendations: a general commendation that went to all officers, a second one for noteworthy performance in pursuit of duties, and a third one for setting a record as to the highest number of arrests in the shortest period of time in one of the divisions. She has filed with the D.C. Office of Human Rights and with the EEOC a discrimination suit charging sexual harassment from male officers from the onset of her job.

J.J. had applied unsuccessfully at six police departments immediately after high school before the District police force promised her a job if she could lose eighty pounds. She did. However, her long-awaited life of cadet policewoman was not what she had expected. "Right away, I was getting grabbed at." When one fellow officer bullied her into letting him visit her apartment he tried to force sex and she had to pull his own gun on him to get him to leave.

J.J. eventually began dating one policeman but sexual harassment from other officers did not diminish. "It's like these other guys just didn't see me basically with one guy." A quarrel over whether or not she should quit the police force after another policewoman was killed in the line of duty ended this relationship after two months. J.J. subsequently went to bed with a police lieutenant. "It was then that I got real worried whether I'd ever get to be a police officer. The men talk a lot about being out with a policewoman and, then, after a woman does go to bed with one or two guys, or even if she is just rumored to, they transfer her out so she can't get seniority anyplace. Every place you go, too, they start badgering you all over again."

In part J.J. blamed her own naïveté for getting herself into a game that she didn't understand. She had never even dated in high school; now she was supposed to be everyone's playmate. Largely in response to threats of overtime, lousy schedules, no promotion, and the worst beats, J.J. began to sleep around. "I didn't think I could get to be a police officer without putting out, but then it was like impossible. . . . I had this reputation. It felt like dominoes. I hit the first one and every one fell in succession."

The pressure only worsened once she left probation and finally put on her badge. She had determined when that happened to say "no more," but she was penalized by a foot patrol in a rough neighborhood. When one superior officer continually demanded sex, J.J. got herself transferred to another division, where she worked as a decoy prostitute. Although she made a good record there she was summarily transferred back to her former department.

J.J. had barely returned when the same superior officer repeated his demand for sex. Two nights later she was suspended for telling him "to quit fucking with me." Relieved of her gun and badge, she was sent home and ordered to go to the department psychiatrist. He told her she was fine; her badge but not her gun was returned and she was assigned to a station house. Then she was ordered to see the psychiatrist again:

"This time he says, 'You screwed your way through a

lot of policemen.' He didn't say, 'A lot of policemen screwed their way through you.' I just said what's that got to do with that guy? And he says, 'Well, you're just not acceptable.' I didn't argue with him about that. I just didn't argue."

J.J. was ordered to visit two other psychiatrists. "They come up with this report that I'm a self-something-something-something-something." Independently, she visited a psychiatrist of her own choosing at Walter Reed, who declared her to be "a rational, mature young lady."

Throughout this period J.J. was indefinitely suspended and working at clerical duty only. "It was the part about not knowing and waiting that hurt me the most and to have these people know what they were doing, it was too much; it was like a big snake just squeezing me until I finally would suffocate." The uncertainty and fear were aggravated by the hostility of many male officers. "A lot of guys are hollering at me, 'You'll get fired!' I'd go home at night and cry and cry and cry. I started drinking and I couldn't sleep."

J.J. also found herself incessantly comparing her own record to those of many male officers. It didn't help:

"I still had to go to court on some of my cases and then I'd see other police officers in their uniforms and I'd go, 'He stole, that one over there smokes grass; that's real violations of the criminal code, but they're still in uniform. What did I do so bad?' "

It was in this atmosphere of general hostility that J.J. was apparently befriended by a male officer. "He seemed sympathetic. I was really shocked but grateful." J.J. accepted an offer to go drinking. It ended in rape:

"I just felt like that's the last son-of-a-bitch that's going to do that to me. I filed a report. But, then, after I sobered up, I withdrew it. I thought I'm not going to let this scum go to court although he deserves worse. It's like I told a girlfriend, I just couldn't go through with it. They'll bring in so much about me; I just can't put myself any more on the stand than I am now."

J.J. withdrew the report. "They said, 'Fine, we'll drop it.' " However, she was soon charged administratively with filing a false report of rape. "I've never had a chance to appeal that. It's like they won't charge me criminally because they know a good lawyer would tear it apart. They couldn't make it stick just like I probably couldn't have made the rape stick."

J.J. requested two weeks' leave. "Do you believe I had never used any of my sick leave; I had three-hundred-some hours sick leave. The psychiatrist said, 'Why don't you resign, wouldn't that be easier?' I said, 'Oh, no. I'm going to fight to the end.' " That day, however, was not far off. It took place in the hospital where J.J. was recovering from a coma, the result of one too many sleeping pills, and pneumonia. "I'm right there in the hospital bed and two officers who aren't even from my section come in and say, 'You've been terminated; Chief signed it.' "

When J.J. applied for unemployment the Washington Police Department contested the initial decision in her favor, asserting that she had been fired for misconduct. A second hearing, however, at which both sides of the case presented testimony was also decided in favor of J.J. The victory was bittersweet: J.J. is presently employed as a security guard, but she still wants to be a cop.

"It was just the old double standard. The guys could do it, they could sleep around, force themselves even; but not a woman. Oh, no, that's downright terrible. Women are always subject to this, they are always going to be the one to blame; a guy can do no wrong. It's like I'm the one who led all these poor men astray. It's such hogwash. The double standard prevails over everything in the police department, and they'll always get rid of the woman because everybody knows police work is a man's job.

"I wasn't judged on the merits of an officer. I remember one police sergeant who said, 'I'd give anything to have you in my section because I know you're a good officer. I'm not going to proposition you and you're not going to proposition me. You do something wrong, I'll burn you; if you do something right, I'll praise you.' I could have made out in his section."

The following is an excerpt from an evaluation of J.J.'s psychological functioning by Dr. Irene S. Vogel, a clinical psychologist who extensively examined J.J. at her request:

—is a 21-year-old female with no known history of psychopathology. She first came to see me on April 26, 1976, after having been told that she might be released from the Washington, D.C. police force. She was obviously upset at the possibility of being terminated and expressed a great desire to do whatever was necessary to keep her job. She expressed the opinion that much of her difficulty stemmed from her off duty behavior. This behavior was similar to the behavior of her fellow officers; however, there seemed to be an acceptance of behavior in male officers which was not allowed for in female officers. At the time I first interviewed her she appeared frank and honest and highly motivated to retain her position on the police force.

She returned for psychological evaluation on May 6, 7, and 8, a few days after her discharge from —— Hospital. She was given a battery of intelligence and personality tests including the Wechsler Adult Intelligence Scale, the Rotter Incomplete Sentence Blank, the Minnesota Multiphasic Personality Inventory, the Rorschach Inkblots, the Thematic Apperception Test and the Holtman Inkblot Test. In addition to the above tests she was clinically interviewed for 2 hours in 2 separate segments.

. . . In summary, I do not believe that there is anything in the profile to warrant ——'s dismissal from the police force.

As it was with police work, women's entrance into the traditionally male domain of horseracing was accompanied by tremendous publicity. Like the policewomen, females began entering the field in the early 70s, about seven years after Title VII became the law of the land,

and by the late 70s, a period of about three years, the charges of sexual harassment were everywhere. In May 1976 Associated Press reporter Linda Fillmore wrote:

"Women jockeys say their lives are not easy. Instead of encouragement or a genuine break, they get rapped and sneered at. They're told there's one way to make it to the top, baby, and if you deliver you might make it and if you don't what are you doing hanging around a place like this, anyway."[10]

One month later female jockeys had found their own spokeswoman in jockey Donna Hillman. Announcing her premature retirement in an article that appeared in the *Sun-Sentinel* in Pompano Beach, Florida, she declared, "If you don't cooperate sexually, you don't get the mounts —it's that simple." She described the track as a "hookers' paradise," and said she was definitely ending her career because no female jockey could succeed without submitting to sex with trainers and others. Hillman, who was the leading percentage rider at Delaware Park in 1972 and Atlantic City in 1973, added, "If I were a man I'd be a leading rider today. I would have all the shots in the world, I'd never have run into the problem. Ninety percent of racing is a good mount. It's the good mounts that make a name for a rider. You wouldn't believe the bums I've ridden. Impossible horses no one else would touch."[11]

Jockey Sally Look is another casualty of sexual harassment. At twenty-six, after five years in the racing business, Look is shopping for a new career, one that will allow her to work alone. "The whole sexual squeeze-play in racing took a lot of sting out of me. . . . It's like I've turned to butter inside and I just don't want to have to fight any more."

Look began her career in racing because she "just always loved horses." She left Bennington College— where she had spent a great deal of her time hanging around the nearby race track—to learn the business at a horse farm in New Jersey which was owned by a friend of her father. She subsequently attended a training center in Florida, where she worked at exercising hunters, hacking and breaking yearlings. After this, her first job was with the trainer for her father's friend, a conservative man who never abused his position. Look had heard countless stories and jokes about other female jockeys, however, and she suspected that at some point she would be sexually harassed. It didn't take long. The abuse started after her early apprenticeship:

"Racing is a very macho business. It's very male-oriented and there's lots of money involved. It's a ruthless sport, so, of course, women are blackballed to begin with; but it's more than that. It's like most of the men just don't know how to think of women except in one way: you fuck them. Ultimately, there were only a couple of people in whom this feeling did not emerge. I got into riding for the challenge. It looked like I could do what I like to do best and also have a career. I worked hard and I didn't screw around. I was dedicated. I exercised and ran and when I was in training I stuck by the rules. And then I was just treated like a half-assed silly chick. It really hurt."

Look frequently found she would ride well against a male apprentice who would perform terribly, yet he would still get the mount. "Then the trainer would say, 'You treat me nice, I'll see you get some first-time starters.' It made me feel awful. That's not what you want to hear when you're running two hours a day and lifting weights. You want him to say, 'I know you've got strong hands and your horses don't run away with you and you're going to be a good jockey.'" Look stuck it out through rough horses, green horses, horses that would try to bump her, and eventually she began to get some decent mounts and win a little. "Then a cocky little male apprentice came along and that was the end of Sally. All I can say is I wasn't up to fighting a war."

Today Look is not without some anger toward other women: "There were just enough girls who'd go along with it to jeopardize me professionally. This sexual harassment exists because of men, but some women aren't helping because every time a woman yields she perpetuates the whole thing."

MOSTLY MALE FIELDS

In addition to the recent drive to integrate previously all-male fields, women have also over the last decade renewed their efforts to expand both their numbers and their authority in many of the heretofore mostly-male fields. Among these preserves there is none more male·than art, which is simply another way of saying that within all the occupations in this field men have never permitted women either to go very far or, by male standards, to count for very much. These two characteristics of the art world, in fact, are greatly intertwined. Explaining a contemporary manifestation of this connection, Elizabeth C. Baker in *Art and Sexual Politics* wrote:

"While it is no longer difficult for a woman to train to be an artist, one has only to look around to realize that genuine obstacles stand in the way of her further pursuit of a serious career . . . The problem of how an artist is to make money when work isn't selling has always been a knotty one. However, in recent years various kinds of flexible teaching appointments which pay comparatively well and may occupy only a part of the year, or grants of various sorts have started to fill the gap. Women artists have not received a reasonable share of these jobs or these grants. . . . Most of the fifty-percent-plus female art students now in the schools, if they end up making a living by teaching—and many of them do find their jobs at the high-school level or below . . . In addition, they are often hired in a peripheral capacity, perhaps as a last-minute fill-in, often not given full pay or tenure."[12]

Again with the help of federally-mandated equal opportunity and the ferment of the women's movement that encouraged women artists to publicize their unequal representation in art-related jobs, women began to both seek and demand their fair share of this institutional bounty. It has been slow going. Male resistance, not just from employers but from male faculty, sometimes in spite of employers, has been implacable. In many cases entry has been slowed by sexual harassment. For those who do get jobs sexual harassment also remains the long-range problem.

Juno [a pseudonym] is a tall, Nordic-looking woman in her middle twenties. She is a highly talented sculptor skilled in foundry, welding, wood- and stone-carving who recently obtained a Master of Fine Arts in Sculpture with an eye to supporting both herself and her art by teaching in this field. Sexual harassment forced her off her very first job which—indicative of her talent—was as a replacement for the art department chairman of a well-known Minnesota college. The chairman, who was to leave on sabbatical, was still on campus. When Juno began work he immediately began a pattern of forcing his attentions. After a series of incidents the man interrupted a lecture to escort her to his office where he physically detained her against her will for five hours. During this time he both physically and verbally demanded sex, acting as if all her rejections, demands to leave and repeated expressions of acute discomfort were actually coy suggestions that he persist. Finally, the man released her.

"I had no witness. There was no evidence to take to the administration. I had no legal case. I went to see my graduate advisor at the University of Minnesota and she said, 'Don't rock the boat. He's tenured; he can't be fired. It will only hurt you. You'll never get a good recommendation.'

"I just left and kept my mouth shut. People have told me about other jobs and I investigated some of them. Two of the jobs I was offered were only available because the women before me had been sexually harassed. The abuse is incredible. They are just going to sexually abuse us until we drop out of the competition."

We have, as a culture, become inured to a mistreatment of women. The daily male invasion of female space combined with a ritualized appropriation of the female body by men at work is perceived as normal. However, it isn't always only one major act of violence that forces women out of these jobs; almost as often it is a series of less explicit but no less undermining experiences. These violations, particularly for women who enter nontraditional jobs, are frequently abetted by prejudice, disrespect, contempt, and even misguided concern for the woman at the expense of the worker. One example of this latter attitudes often goes: It's a big mistake for you to work at a man's job, how will you ever get a man to marry you? All these attitudes, it should also be noted, are frequently shared by both sexes with regard to any female who has dared to cross the sex line on occupational labor.

As of May 1975 women comprised 4 percent of the nation's total drafting and design workforce.[13] Despite the fact that this field is growing rapidly it is not expanding the opportunities for women. Barbara Anger, a former draftswoman in New York State, explains in the following incident why she quit the field:

It was National Secretaries Week. I was a draftswoman but this guy needed a secretary to go out to lunch with him and I was one of the women there so he asked me. I said, "No, I don't want to go. I'd just rather work." He's an old man who used to own the company and even though he sold it he has some sort of psychological influence on everybody. So the secretaries came to me and said, "Come on, he's an old man, do it, do it, do it." And somebody else came to me and said, "Do it." So I said, "Okay, I'll go out with you." And he said, "But you'll have to wear a dress." You see I never wore a dress to work and I said, "No, I won't wear one." Finally, he said, "Okay, you can come even if you don't wear a dress." And I figured, well, I won that battle, maybe I will wear a dress. So I wore a dress, which was a big mistake because everybody said, "Why don't you dress like that every day, Barbara? You look so good. It really helps you."

So I went to lunch with this guy and I got there and of course he pumped me with lots of drinks. I figured, well, it's okay to have a few drinks, but as soon as I had one drink he wanted to touch my breast. He wasn't even subtle about it at all. He just said, "What do you think about those things under your clothes? My, could I touch them?" This is in a restaurant! And I'm going, "Will you please leave me alone. Take your hand off my leg." Finally, it got to the point where I said, "Fuck you!" And he was amazed that a young woman should say "Fuck you."

I had to go from there back to work to get my car and to finish the day and in the car he was all over me. I got back to work and I said, "Okay, it's all over with, I'm going back to work." He came into my office and hung around and every chance he'd get he'd try to kiss me. He thought because he'd given me this lunch he deserved a kiss. I refused to kiss him and from that day on I never spoke to him. Everybody in the office kept saying, "Why aren't you nicer to him? I mean this poor fellow." Poor fellow!

TRAINING

Sexual harassment not only reinforces female job segregation by forcing women out of nontraditional jobs, it also forces women out of on-the-job training for these occupations. Pamela Ann Roby, Associate Professor of Sociology at the University of California at Santa Cruz, writes:

Despite the vastly increased sums spent on vocational education during the late 'sixties and early 'seventies and despite the national legislation which reaffirmed women's right to equal education opportunity . . . thousands of female students are barred from sex-segregated vocation education school and classes and most others are actively discouraged, or not encouraged to take courses leading to the higher paying jobs which have been traditionally stereotyped as "male."[14]

93

Recent federal legislation bars sex discrimination in the allocation and use of federal funds for training, but what effect this will have remains to be seen.

Men also generally exclude women from apprenticeships, the oldest organized form of skill-training, through unions which hold a near monopoly on approximately all 300,000 apprenticeships in the skilled trades. Fewer than one percent were women in 1973.[15] In view of this the Women's Bureau has reasoned, "it is apparent women are using a variety of other routes to become craft workers."[16]

This is undoubtedly true, and these "other routes" are usually on-the-job training, but this is precisely where sexual harassment is a nearly foolproof deterrent to women since there isn't even a program administration to which a woman might apply for redress. Moreover, a woman who attempts to learn a trade this way is highly motivated. This attribute is rewarded in male workers, but in female workers it only ignites male aggression. Men frequently decide they will only share trade skills with women in exchange for sex. The result is that the temptation to make this exchange presents for many women an insoluble dilemma; even if they win they lose.

The cases that follow are representative, and reinforce the conclusion that for every woman who submits there are scores more who either cannot or will not. Of course, male coercion remains the problem; both groups of women are equally victimized. From the outset, the innate longing for learning and achievement is ravaged.

Dawn Holden's first job was as a clerk; she was sixteen and still attending high school in Washington, D.C.; she is now twenty-six and presently employed as an administrative assistant with the American Bankers Association. According to sex-segregated job standards this would appear to indicate a reasonable success, but for Holden it is just the opposite. Her real interest has always been in graphics. She tried to pursue this trade with jobs that offered training until one of these resulted in an EEOC suit that alleges discrimination in hiring, promotion, and wages and that there were overt sexual demands.

Holden had been working as a free-lance. The new position was full-time, offered more training and steady money. She was delighted, especially since she had recently moved into a new house with friends who had a young baby. They had all been out of work and Larry, the baby's father, was also hired as a trainee. Her first day on the job, Holden was impressed by the owner's skills and his demonstrations of new methods, although she also had to watch him incessantly sexually harass other women employees—particularly a former topless dancer. "He never said a nice word about her work. He'd just cut her down and humiliate her and then he'd feel her up all the time she was trying to work. He also demanded sex. I don't know how she stood it except I do know she didn't want to be a topless dancer."

On the second day the middle-aged boss continued to demonstrate new techniques to Holden, assigning her more advanced jobs, but he also began to harangue her with sexual monologues. Holden recalled he would say things like "I've interviewed two hundred people the last three weeks and I told the women to take off their clothes. I said if they wanted the job they could prove it." Holden would shrug her shoulders. Late in the third day, however, after patiently working with her and helping her the man demanded sex. She was given fifteen minutes to appear in his office willingly; if she did he promised to continue the training and in six months or a year she could write her own ticket. If she didn't she and Larry were both fired. Holden was appalled. Confused and crying, she sought the counsel of a male friend at work who advised her she should put out if she really wanted the job because "that's the real world." He also advised that if she was smart she could manipulate the man and come out the "winner." Further confused, she finally decided to go to the man's office and reason with him.

I'd been a feminist for years and I'd been hassled before and I convinced myself I could handle it [she said]. I got there though and I just fell apart. I really wanted that job. He made a drink and then basically said take off your clothes and lie down and I did it. I didn't know it then but the one thing I really learned from him was what it is like to be a whore, to be a total prostitute to do it for money. I hated him.

At home Holden couldn't stop crying. Her friends assured her it would be all right if she quit. Only her woman therapist, the following morning, advised she get a lawyer. But by then it was nearly time to go back to work.

I was really torn between whether I could do it for six months and use him or whether I would allow it to eat at me, destroy me. I didn't want to give up graphics but I didn't want to destroy myself for it. What happened was I couldn't get any legal help and I just didn't go in. That was a Friday and I didn't go in on Monday. Larry did and was told we were fired. What followed was a pretty bad period. It was six weeks before I got another job and most of that time I was really miserable, no energy, no confidence, no self-esteem. I had just given up what I wanted to do and was getting forced back into looking for a job I didn't want.

Holden eventually found a lawyer, but because she had submitted to sex he advised her to find other women who would verify the owner's pattern of sexual harassment. Corroboration was no problem. Holden quickly found eight women besides herself who agreed to testify. She said, "You could just see the pattern. The less skill a woman had, the less essential her job, so the heavier the hassle; hence the range was anywhere from yes, I've seen it happen; yes, he's made comments to me; yes, he demanded sex but so far I've held him off to yes, I've given in. I was the only one in this last category, but only two of the women from the time I started were still working there. Six had already quit. Now they have all quit."

Holden, like many others, has since despaired that her harasser will ever be brought to justice. "People in graphics move around a lot. My witnesses keep vanishing. They won't stay interested forever. It's rotten. You get a hassle like this and you finally get it together to do something and then you get a stupid little piece of paper from the EEOC saying, 'We have your file made. This is your number. There is a two-year backlog; in two years we will open your file.' " Society's tacit permission of this backlog at the EEOC has communicated to Dawn Holden that there is little hope for her. "I'm okay on the surface, but I'd be making a lot more money if I was in graphics. It still comes up in my mind, I think it always will. It's what I really wanted. Of course, I can't go back defenseless again, but there's nothing. Nobody helps."

Cheryl Senna lives in a small, run-down house on several acres which she gardens in upstate New York. She fixes the house in exchange for lowered rent. Seeing her dress often in coveralls and second-hand sneakers, many people are surprised to learn that she is a skilled film-maker whose talent has earned her two separate government grants. Film, in fact, was Senna's one ambition until pursuit of a film career in New York City was stonewalled by incessant sexual harassment in both filmmaking and other jobs. This is her own description of the last six months in her short-lived career:

The kinds of jobs I'd previously gotten to support the film-making, especially waitressing, had always involved me being harassed so much sexually that I finally decided to drive a taxicab. I made myself deliberately unattractive and I thought this way I'd get left alone. It didn't make any difference. I got constantly harassed, constantly bothered. The conversa-

97

tion would always start, "Oh, you're a woman cab driver. What're you doing that for, why don't you come home with me!"

So again, because I drove the cab at night and worked on films during the day, both things going on simultaneously was real heavy for me because men don't want to deal with a woman filmmaker except in one way. That makes it real hard to learn more things and you can't get any experience. It's, like, in connection with one of my grants I'd come into contact with this director, he was very important, and I really wanted to get a permanent job with him. He was going to be making a film. He really needed people and I watched all the men around with no more experience than me getting jobs. He never paid much attention to me at all and then one day he pulled me aside and said, "You know the only way you're going to make it in the film world is if you sleep with me."

Later on I was interviewing with this director of a small film company and he offered me the job of production manager. I was ecstatic. It was a real break because it was a very well-paying job and, although it wasn't exactly where I wanted to go, if I got the job I knew I'd really have a place to go from. I really wanted that job. Before I actually had the job, though, he starts asking me out for cocktails.

Finally, after a few of these sessions he got down to the script and the job responsibilities. He says, "Look, we should really spend a long time together to talk about this. I've got a house in the Poconos, why don't we go up there for the weekend?" I said, "I don't know. I don't really think I could do that." He told me to think about it and then he called me up. Out loud I said, "I don't know, I don't know." But inside my head was *I want that job*. I was considering it; I really was considering it. I didn't want to sleep with him, but he was holding it over my head and I was willing right then to sleep with him in order to get the job.

I finally came to my senses. He called me back and I said, "No. I just can't do it." Of course, that was the end of the job. I left New York City after that. I was real flipped between the taxicab driving and the idea that I even thought about getting a job this way. I'd just really had it. I haven't been able to do anything about film ever since then either, because every time I think about that kind of pressure I just can't handle it.

ACADEMIC PREPARATION

Women are often blocked by sexual harassment from obtaining the academic degrees without which there can be no entry into the majority of professional occupations. Women were 38 percent of all students in colleges and universities in 1963 and 40 percent in 1967; yet in the 1970–1971 school year they accounted for only 14 percent of all doctorates and only 6.3 percent of all "first professional" degrees (those requiring six or more years of higher education).[17] In addressing herself to the small proportion of women doctorates, Juanita Kreps has commented:

"Differences in attrition rates of men and women graduate students have been explained in various ways: lack of interest and dedication on the part of women; interruption of study by marriage and child-bearing; reluctance of graduate schools to grant fellowship support to women; admissions policies that strongly favor male candidates, particularly after the M.A. degree."[18]

It is time we recognize that what has been judged female disinterest or lack of dedication is often the effect of sexual harassment. Sexual abuse is, in fact, so widespread in higher education that school administrators should have made this connection some time ago. In 1974 female students at San Diego State University organized an "A for a Lay Day" workshop. In 1977 a survey by Donna J. Benson of 290 University of California at Berkeley female graduate students reported that one in five had received some form of "sexual attention" from male teachers.[19] Also in 1977, a group of women students and one male professor filed a class-action suit against Yale University charging that the administration's "fail-

99

ure to combat sexual harassment of female undergraduates and its refusal to institute mechanisms and procedures to address complaints and make investigations of such harassment interferes with the educational process and denies equal opportunity in education."[20] One year before the Yale suit, the University of Delaware Commission on the Status of Women—recognizing that the problem was no more prevalent at Delaware than in other academic institutions—nonetheless began efforts to bring the University of Delaware into a position which would both oppose the abuse and provide safeguards against its practice.

In attempting to secure these ends the commission, comprised of a heterogeneous group ranging in ages from the early 20's to mid–50's, held several planning meetings. The following excerpts from one of these sessions document the experiences and observations that underlie the members' concern about the abuse in academic settings in general, particularly at the undergraduate and graduate level, and with regard to the difficulty in providing an adequate grievance procedure in a male-dominated academic setting. The group, all women, included a graduate student, an associate professor, an assistant professor, an administrator, and a member of the Commission on the Status of Women. The names of speakers have been withheld to protect confidences that were shared.

The most interesting thing about the discussion of this at the Commission was the way the people readily acknowledged the problem. They know it's real.

It was the same thing at the President's dinner. He invited deans, cabinet people who were vice-presidential level and representatives from groups like the faculty center. When sexual harassment came up all kinds of people started offering up examples.

All of us knew sexual harassment existed but women won't talk because they think everyone will think they invited it.

Women also don't report it because we still have to act like the male ego is our responsibility. I know of one student, a feminist, and that's why she didn't report it. She said she didn't turn him in because to turn a man down sexually is *the* putdown and she was frightened what kind of retaliation she'd get.

One part of the trouble is how hard it is if you have any kind of style. This woman in medical school with my husband could wear the most plain thing by anyone's standards and yet everyone would say, "What are you doing here? Can you really do this stuff?" She had a lot of trouble—with patients too. It's a great shame. She purposely tried to dress down all the time.

Also, just try and dress presentably to defend your master's thesis or something. The men wear suits, they don't come in jeans; but if you put on a dress, half the men students make four million comments. They say things like "I see how you're getting your degree." And these are people that work side by side with you year after year. It's not a joke either, they make these comments very seriously.

People also assume that's how you got where you work. It's like, "Oh, boy, we sure know how you got your Ph.D."

Yeah, but the trouble is that says a lot about the people who think they might award Ph.D.'s on that basis.

They're telling their own values.

The point is, that is their values. I got one job because I was attractive to the dean of that department. [This was not at the University of Delaware.] He liked any age as long as they were attractive and he was notorious for sexually harassing women all the time. He was finally gotten rid of, but not for that reason. I actually had a pretty rough time. . . .

"I know all the sexual statements that are repeatedly made in class drive the total female graduates down."

I'm concerned because I think that sexual harassment vitally affects working and studying and besides that, it does enter into the academic arena in decisions about all kinds of things, and that is completely unacceptable as far as I'm concerned.

I guess it's time I admitted how I became interested in the whole thing. I was sexually harassed as an undergraduate. The man who did it was the Chairman of the Economics Department [this was at another school], very nationally known reputation and everything. He was a teacher for a class and I'd gone to lunch with him and afterwards he took another road and started masturbating and asking me sexual things. I found out later he had done the same kinds of things with other girls I knew, but we just kind of all shared this guilt. Like I felt guilty that I had gone to lunch because maybe I should have known better. I never did anything but I kept thinking what if this had happened to someone more emotional than I was or more naïve. It's like right now I could name three different girls who are getting explicit propositions from people with real power over them. It's a serious threat. There needs to be some kind of outside force intervening so people feel free to bring their grievances somewhere. Without that it's very hard to stand up.

I know, if this is occurring, if there are overtures being made, it's usually from people right over you who control all the power; whether your master's proposal is going to be accepted, how well you are doing on your comprehensives. After all, they are the people who are reading them. These are the people that you have for the majority of your classes, they hold your career in their hands. So you can complain about sexual overtures but then because of their rank they can find some way to get rid of you for a million or more reasons; it can be as simple as just undermining your performance. It can just get all mixed together and it's no longer clear what's happening to you.

102

We talked about that in some previous meetings with the President, but it always leads right back to the inevitable question, "Where is the documentation?"

Yes, and it is always coming down to somebody's word, doesn't it? Because it's like rape, there aren't any witnesses and also in many situations one person who's being harassed doesn't know that there are six others and couldn't get together with those other six.

The problem is clearly protection and adequate grievance procedures. We are fortunate in having a President who's concerned. For example, there's the way he handled that off-campus affirmative action consultant who sexually pressured a woman faculty member. He refused to let him consult for the University again. Of course, that was handled quietly and informally. It can't always be handled that way, especially in view of the whole question of a university structure in the hands of a majority male faculty, especially tenured faculty.

The point is that formal protection is essential on campus because there are vested interests against taking the side of the woman.

The whole problem really is that we have no structure that's safe for the complainant to complain in. The normal grievance procedure is terrible, very simply because some faculty members are on the student grievance committee so that when the student does go to complain she can find that sitting on that very committee is either the person himself or his three best friends.

There's got to be a clearing house, like a women's committee or an ombudswoman, where women can take up the case and fight it on behalf of the students and the student remains anonymous.

Yes. Having a woman isn't an ironclad insurance that it will be properly treated, but hearing complaints has got to be taken out of the hands of men. Just as we are having policewomen in rape cases and so forth. I think that principle needs to be established.

I don't care what procedure we come up with. It all involves risks. It's like there's this chap and we all know perfectly well that this is going on, but who's going to put themselves on the line?

I think another thing that's going to help the problem is just our visibility. If this is something starting to be discussed in departments. If it's brought up at faculty meetings. . . .

I'll go that even one better and say why shouldn't the same thing also be announced in all classes? And there you are sitting there thinking, and I thought I was the only one. I'll tell you if I had been sitting there at age nineteen when that S.O.B. with the one glass eye went after me and I heard in my class that this was going on, that would have just blown my mind. I mean that would have helped me so. Just to know I wasn't alone.

The preceding comments are neither exceptional nor limited to any one institution or geographical area. Sexual harassment is pervasive in American colleges and universities. This pervasiveness, combined with lack of adequate procedures for complaint, virtually assures that a certain percentage of female graduate students will be victimized by this abuse.

As in other work or work-related situations, many women leave school because of an explicit demand for sex, because of accumulated sexually harassing experiences, or some combination thereof. In almost every case the decision is impulsive. Either she will flee immediately or eventually break from the pressure like a rubber band; in either case these are life-changing decisions made without adequate preparation. At the point the impulse to quit becomes irresistible, it is frequently because it appears to be the only way to save both autonomy and career. Unfortunately, this is often completely untrue with regard to career.

Sharon (a pseudonym) traveled from Albany for the Ithaca Speak-Out on Sexual Harassment. This event occurred at the close of the 1974–1975 academic year; however, Sharon, a graduate student working on a mas-

104

ter's thesis in criminal justice the preceding fall, was no longer attending college.

As long as I can remember I have wanted to be a lawyer, and especially a judge. I thought I'd acquaint myself with the criminal justice system by getting a master's degree first in criminal justice and then going on for a law degree. I don't really know how to say it, but I got cornered in a professor's office three weeks into the term. I had an assistantship. I didn't know what to do. It seemed like I could go along with him and get A's or if I didn't I could work my head off and not get A's, get nothing better than a C, maybe just a C if I was lucky.

What I did was quit. It's one of the hardest things I've ever done in my life. I lost a lot of self-respect because I'm not a quitter. I've never done anything like that but I have to live with it. My family didn't understand, a lot of people don't understand. [Crying from here on.] And now I have to put it on law school applications and it's hard for women to get into law school, and that's just going to make it a whole lot harder.

The decision posed by the demand for sex from a professor in graduate school is frequently no less life-changing when the student, believing that her career will be irremediably harmed by a decision to quit, decides to submit. Moreover, it should be noted that when men use their professorial power to extort sex from a female student, the exchange only guarantees a female student that she will be judged by her performance, not that her performance will be inflated. The performance meanwhile is inevitably impaired by the emotional stress of prolonged sexual intimacy exacted through fear and coercion.

Diane [a pseudonym] is a twenty-eight-year-old assistant professor of psychology at an undergraduate college in New York state; she relocated there from a major Ivy-league university after uninterruptedly completing a successful Ph.D. candidacy. This accomplishment, however,

105

is tinged with an ineffable sadness, and there is as well the nagging sense that the acute personal hardship behind the achievement is still affecting her career.

At the time Diane applied for graduate school, the pattern of sexual intimidation that would follow was begun in several ways. The first was that the chairman of the department discouraged her application, advising her to apply elsewhere, and the second was that her husband was already attending the same school. "He was always treated much more seriously and I was always viewed as just more or less an appendage." Diane persevered. She executed some independent work for one of the psychology professors; he spoke in favor of her admittance, and she was eventually accepted as a Ph.D. candidate. Her new faculty advisor, however, was a young man who soon began complaining to Diane about his marriage difficulties.

He cried and so forth and I responded as if he were my friend. It was the wrong thing to do; he was soon making real advances. I was utterly repulsed but I was terrified to say no. He just had too much authority over me. It was absolute. It was even more than the authority that a boss has over you in a job, it has parental aspects to it because this whole graduate experience is an apprenticeship system. You get attached to a guy, they were all guys—there were only two women in the department and neither of them took graduate students—so there was no possibility of getting away from men. There was never the thought that you could go to one of them to help out against another. It was a solid bloc.

Diane spent a great deal of time trying to think of ways to get out of the situation, but thoughts of refusing always ended with the conclusion she would have to leave school.

It was like gambling, I guess, and it was gambling with something that I wasn't prepared to gamble with. It always seemed at the time that I would rather be sexually exploited than risk my whole career. You see, nobody else really knows that much about what you're doing academically. The whole way they judge you is by what your advisor says to them at coffee and over lunch and so forth. Everything depends on his opinion and I thought if I get him pissed off at a personal level he's going to communicate negativity about me to the others. I knew I couldn't overcome that because I'd seen it happen before, and once you get a reputation for not being a good student they don't ever give you a chance to perform otherwise. I also remember the chairman walking into the common room and banging his fist down on the table and saying, "If I had my way there would never be women in this laboratory, women don't belong in a laboratory." We were marginal there to begin with. We all knew we were just being tolerated, that was it.

Diane remained in this situation for the first two years of graduate school, until the end of her master's work, when she finally found a reason to switch advisors without creating any waves. As soon as the switch was made she ended the sex with her former advisor. Diane now finds her behavior to have been an error, but she also feels it would have been extremely difficult for her to have behaved any other way short of quitting. "I don't know how to say it, but women, more than men, are brought up not to argue, not to fight, not to conflict and not to confront but always be a nice little girl. Going along with this harassment is just an extension of that, of always being polite even when someone is insulting you. But the truth is, the personal price of that was far too high —although I didn't know that until I already paid it."

Diane's tendency to blame herself for cooperating with her advisor's sexual advances is typical of many victims of sexual harassment. This is the result of male-biased social values: women are encouraged to stress their own culpability, discouraged from claiming the full impact of sexual coercion. It is not enough to say that women tend to blame themselves. Until society comprehends and condemns the pervasive extent of male coercion there is little a woman can do.

Power implies the ability to wield coercive force. The burden of guilt, then, should rest with the party of power, not with its recipient. It was not her responsibility to explore his intentions, but rather his responsibility to allay her fears. Until women are free to reject such demands without risk, men cannot absolve themselves of the consequences of their power. The man who robs a woman at gunpoint cannot defend himself on the ground he didn't realize she would think he might shoot.

COLLEGE TEACHING

The most popular profession for educated women is teaching, although a relatively small proportion of all women who teach hold college or university posts. These positions are better-paying; they comprise the cream of the profession and are often dominated by men who frequently sexually harass women out of the competition.

Sociologist Diedre Silverman sought her first college teaching post at a job fair for members of her discipline at a large hotel. She was, at that time, pregnant but not advertising it for fear of chasing off prospective employers. This continued until an incident with a man who taught at a college with the only job opening anywhere near her home.

As we were speaking he leaned over and dropped his hotel room key in my lap. There were a whole bunch of people around us at the time; they were all people I'd gone to school with who'd been in my classes, and I really didn't know what to do so I handed the key back to him. He dropped the key in my lap again and I sort of thrust it back at him and this time, when he dropped the key in my lap again, he really sort of threw it and said, "What's wrong?"

I didn't know what to say; I'm not too good in this kind of situation and so I said probably the dumbest thing, which was "I'm married." He said, "What difference does that make?" I saw then he was married too, so then I said, "Well, I'm just really not interested in you." And he said, "That's because you haven't gotten to know me yet." Finally—and I was really desperate by this time because I really didn't want him to know I was pregnant—I blurted out, "I'm five and a half months pregnant!" He drew back and he said, "Five and a half months? *Five* and a half months?" And with that he disappeared. Okay. That's a really funny story, but there's a dark side to it. To this man my interest in his college was an opportunity for rather crude sexual advances which humiliated me in front of my classmates and professors, and I consequently had to give up a possible job and the only chance I had to stay in an area I loved.

One woman among those present for the discussion at the University of Delaware revealed her own experience. The incident occurred at her first teaching post long before her present job, but she still had never before dared talk about it:

"I hadn't been teaching that long when the dean of my college was all over me for sex. He was terribly insistent and I repeatedly refused. The next thing I know he suspended me from teaching; of course, he gave all sorts of other reasons. I couldn't believe what was happening. Can you imagine when the dean is saying all these terrible things?" Attempts to be reinstated utilizing procedures for this purpose within the university were of no avail. She finally had to apply for help from the American Association of University Professors and eventually she was reinstated. "Yes, I won, but it was after an interminable battle and that bastard jeopardized my whole career and the real reasons never came out; it was all fought over other issues, It isn't something I talk about either, because it really is like a black mark on my professional record. Even if you win it presents a terrible image."

A second incident raised in the course of the discussion concerned a woman who had worked at the University of Delaware. She was not a teacher but had been hired for a top administrative job:

Here she was a Ph.D. and a woman with all kinds of strengths who also happens to be exceptionally attractive. All her colleagues were men and they just never gave her a chance because they thought she had been brought in to be the playmate of the man who hired her. It wasn't true at all, but she never could establish her credibility as a person. She finally confronted one of the men because, although she was the official channel, they wouldn't come to her about things. He just said they thought she was only there for sex. She said that was completely false and he just said, "Well, you do lead us to that conclusion. You dress real nice and you have a very seductive voice." She eventually got a bad evaluation. The whole thing just kept her from doing her job well, because they wouldn't deal with her, and then she was criticized for not being up on things when there was not any other way to be up on them than to be told. She finally left.

In 1974 women were 27 percent of college and university faculty staff; however, they are increasingly comprising proportionally less of the professorial ranks and more of the instructor level. Compared to 1959–1960, when women were 29 percent of the instructors, 45 percent of these jobs were held by women in 1973–1974. Also during this same period, despite a 10 percent growth in their overall numbers, women declined from 10 percent of full professors to 9 percent and from 17.5 percent of associate professors to only 15.2 percent.[21] Sexual harassment, both subtle and explicit, is partly responsible.

THE PROFESSIONS

It has long been held that working women in general comprise a large proportion of all those persons employed in the professional fields. This confuses the large numbers of women segregated as teachers, nurses, librarians, and social workers with integration in a broad range of professional occupations. Women are less than 2 percent of the engineers, 4 percent of the dentists, 5 percent of the lawyers, 9 percent of the physicians, 10 percent of the scientists, 18 percent of all salaried managers, officials, and administrators, and only about 21 percent of all professionals outside the fields of education and health.[22] The majority of the professions unmistakably constitute nontraditional job areas for women. The role of sexual harassment in the maintenance of this status quo is significant, although the widespread incidence of the abuse has been rarely acknowledged, and certainly not publicized.

The professional woman has been viewed as a class apart, a cut above the mass of working women, an exception. She has in some cases fostered this attitude herself in the vain hope of forestalling her sexual exploitation, but it has been to no avail. All this popular perception bred was a failed strategy for stopping the abuse and a convenient cover for harassers to hide behind. Today that cloak of being "above it all" has been pulled aside.

Professional women have been among the first to seek redress of their grievances from the courts. Virginia Morgheim of Anchorage, Alaska, is one example. In the fall of 1975 she was employed in the news department of a local television station. "I felt it was an extremely promising position, but [as she alleged in her complaint] over a period of weeks the station manager made a series of sexual advances to me that included touching and kissing." She rebuffed them and within a few weeks was fired. She adds that the corporation that owned the television station never gave her an opportunity to explain the situation but relied instead on the termination recommendation of her "assailant." Ginny Morgheim, a happily married mother, went on to file suit for over one million dollars in damages, charging a broken contract that resulted in damage to her career as a broadcast journalist, intentional infliction that led to her being fired, clear state and federal discrimination in being fired for not giving sexual favors, abridgement of her right to privacy as guaranteed in the Alaska constitution, and negligence on the part of the corporation for not looking into the problem to discover the truth.

Her fight is shared by many other professional women presently embroiled in the struggle to work free of sex-based intimidation. In Puerto Rico, Madeline Leon Salas de Vila sued three officials of the Cooperative Development Agency where she worked as a financial analyst, charging sexual harassment by her immediate supervisor followed by collusion from officials above him subsequently to deny her due process on the job. She won $70,000. Another professional, Diane Williams, has won the most celebrated sexual-harassment case to date. In a Title VII suit against the Justice Department the court awarded her $23,000, which included $17,000 in back pay—although, as she makes very clear, a financial settlement can never completely repair the damage of sexual harassment:

"I wasn't completely satisfied with the decision, primarily because the judge did not reinstate me to the federal government let alone to the justice Department and the Community Relations Service, and I didn't get a promotion to a grade level comparable to where I would have been by now, so that I'm about $2100 a year below what I should be making after all this time."

Williams is a black woman with a graceful manner and stately good looks. The Justice Department hired her in January 1972 as a public-information aide; she was twenty-three and recently divorced, with an infant son to support. Shortly after her hiring the Justice Department's Public Information Officer, Harvey Brinson, her immediate supervisor, who is also black, began to make sexual advances. She rejected these advances and managed to maintain a good working relationship for several months, when the demands escalated; after she continued to reject these overtures the harassment began in earnest, resulting in her termination. In her suit Williams alleged that sexual harassment was "the pattern and practice in the agency":

There were a lot of things which happened while I was there which I just didn't think was job-related so I chose not to participate. [But it was not so much that Diane Williams was the only person being asked to participate in this kind of conduct as it was that this was a widespread practice.] It was something that had been accepted because it was known that some young women in the agency frequently got their promotions because they were cooperating with their boss or somebody the boss liked. I just happened to believe that my professional skills and my initiative were enough to get the job done and should be recognized on that basis.

On May 9, 1972, Brinson sent Williams a Mothers Day card that said, "Seldom a day goes by without a loving thought of you." It was signed *Harvey*. It marked a turning point, according to Williams, who says that her refusals after this card were often followed by Brinson coming into her office declaring, "If it comes to a showdown between you and me, you would be the loser because I am the Director's boy!" A few months later Williams, who at this time had earned the rank of public information assistant, making her the second-ranking professional in the Public Information Office, was terminated with twenty-five minutes' notice on a Friday afternoon. Her own attempts to remedy the situation through internal procedures had been unsuccessful when the dismissal occurred and she had just found a lawyer and filed a formal complaint with the EEOC; there never had been a hearing. It was thirteen months before her next comparable position and she barely managed in between on a low-paying part-time job.

It had a very traumatic effect on me. I found it embarrassing; I was humiliated and very demoralized. I had never been fired, I'd never even known anybody who had been fired. I felt, God, this is the end. You're fired on a Friday; you don't have anyplace to go on Monday except to look through the want-ads on Sunday and start pounding the pavement. Nobody had taken into consideration whether I would be able to get another job, especially after they had said such terrible things about me [the Justice Department had placed in her personnel file a notation that she was fired for making a false, malicious, and slanderous statement], or whether I had any money saved, or how I was going to pay the rent, or how was I going to buy food—whether I had to go on welfare or stand in the unemployment line. Nobody took that into consideration. It was so ironic too because this is the government agency that is supposed to be enforcing the nation's civil rights laws.

Unlike the majority of sexual harassment victims, Williams, who is presently employed as a writer and editor for the University Research Corporation in Chevy Chase, Maryland, was considerably helped by her parents and a support group of other female complainants against the Justice Department; she had also found outstanding legal counsel who needed no convincing that sexual harassment is a major obstacle to female employment. However, it was still difficult to overcome the pernicious effect of the harassment:

It took a long time to come to grips with the actual facts as I knew them to be and that was that I hadn't done anything wrong, and then I was very much embarrassed to discuss the issues involved in the case. And the fact that this was a black man who had done this to me, I felt embarrassed on that account. You just feel a lot the way sexual assault victims feel. You're the victim but you're the one who's fired or being harassed or you didn't get the job training or you've had to quit. It's demoralizing, and there is this inescapable feeling of being responsible because you *are* being punished. It finally came to the point where I had to realize I was the complainant, not the defendant.

The number of women who work as managers or administrators is less than one-third that of men. Even this figure is misleadingly high if thought of in terms of broad authority. In 1973 one out of five women employed in these jobs was either self-employed or an unpaid family worker; the large majority of the rest were concentrated in restaurants and apparel and accessory stores.[23] Women do not hold similar jobs in large businesses and corporations, and of the number who do it is almost unheard of to have come up from the clerical pool. However, that is precisely how Carmita Wood, a forty-four-year-old mother of four, after twenty-seven years of uninterrupted work, was promoted in 1971 to the post of administrative assistant in one of Cornell University's major laboratories.

Less than one year after assuming her new duties Wood was driven out by a pattern of sexual harassment from an extremely well-placed Cornell official. The New York State Unemployment Board denied her unemployment compensation and circumstances militated against an EEOC lawsuit. Carmita Wood refused to throw away a lifetime of work quietly; she went on to expose the abuse by talking about her own case and making herself an example. This decision caused her to be one of the early voices in bringing this issue to public consciousness, but the controversy created as a result of this stand cost her dearly. Job possibilities dwindled to zero. Her children were ridiculed at school, the result of parental attitudes suspicious of any woman who would talk publicly about sex. Although her family has lived in Ithaca for generations, Carmita Wood eventually had to leave. The description of her harassment is by attorney Ellen Yackin, who prepared her appeal for the New York State Unemployment Commission:

When she left her job Carmita had been an outstanding employee who had been working in one of Cornell's laboratories since 1966. She had been promoted in 1971 to the job of Administrative Assistant, the first woman to hold such a post. At this time she became the second woman ever admitted to the Ithaca Management Club and in the glow of all this new-found status and security she felt it was "safe" to take out a $10,000 loan to remodel her home in Ludlowville.

It wasn't long after her promotion, however, that she moved into a new office which brought her into closer proximity with an extremely high-up Cornell official. He found reasons to visit her office at least once a day. This became a matter of concern to her as almost all her previous contacts with him had resulted in repeated, unwanted touching.

The repeated visits of this man to Ms. Wood's office now involved more of the same treatment and became an intolerable source of tension and emotional stress. He would make her feel exceedingly uncomfortable by making sexual gestures, he would often lean against her, immobilizing her between his own body and the chair and desk. He would never look her in the eye but would instead move his eyes up and down her body below the neck. He would also stand with his hands in his pockets as if rubbing his genitals. These actions were persistent throughout the whole time they worked in this proximity.

Carmita complained about his behavior, both towards herself and other women, to her supervisor on several different occasions, but his response was that they "were very capable women." He further suggested that "they try not to get into these situations." Beyond this, Carmita consciously avoided the man as much as she could, to the point of using the stairs instead of the elevator because she knew of at least one instance in which he had molested a woman in the elevator. She also made a point of wearing slacks in order to avoid the man's staring at her legs and she also told her secretary that she didn't want to be alone with him. Finally, she made a consistent effort to transfer away from the situation; however none of these attempts were successful.

There finally occurred an incident at a Christmas party which she attended because it was part of her job to supervise all social functions for the laboratory. At one point the man asked her to dance; she refused several times because of her past experiences and because she was managing the party. He insisted, however, and yanking her arm he pulled her forcibly onto the dance floor, where he then shoved his

116

hands under her sweater and vest, pushing them up and exposing her back and rubbing her bare skin. Ms. Wood was embarrassed and later said, "I felt I was publicly humiliated," but she didn't want to make a scene in public so she didn't push him away until he released her at the end of the dance. There were witnesses to this incident, including her supervisor and her secretary; the supervisor again failed to do anything about the situation.

She intensified efforts to obtain a transfer but was frustrated. Finally, unable to cope with her building emotional and physical distress and desperately not wanting to come into contact with this man again, Carmita resigned from her job, although she was fully conscious of the current economic recession and the great risk she was incurring in leaving. Her position was a substantial one and had she stayed there two weeks longer she would have been eligible for a raise.

She stayed in the area looking for another job. Unable finally to find an acceptable job, she applied for unemployment insurance. She was denied insurance benefits because her reasons for leaving her job were termed merely "personal" and "non-compelling."

Between 1960 and 1970 employment of women lawyers rose to a total of 12,000, a doubling of their numbers; however, women are still less than 5 percent of all lawyers,[24] and sexual harassment is strongly affecting female participation in this field. Sadie (a pseudonym) is an attorney for a major federal agency. "Sexual harassment just makes the whole point of equal opportunity for women meaningless." This attitude is the result of experiences that began with her first job as a lawyer nearly three years ago at an eastern regional office of the federal agency she will soon be leaving—partially because of sexusl harassment, although she is not fleeing and has taken pains to insure she leaves for a better job. (This is not true of many other female lawyers.)

When I was first hired there was only one other female professional on the staff. To describe my office as a male fraternity is to say the least of it; I found out when I got there

117

that she only got hired because Washington put the pressure on. There had been other women but they all had left. The men would say they left for better-paying jobs but I'm convinced it was the sexual harassment.

It's like when I first went to work there, the office lunch ritual was unbelievable. The men would do nothing except gross-out women. The language was not to be believed. I expressed my displeasure and explained how destructive it was; I stopped going when they wouldn't stop. Then about one month later two more women were hired. They got the lunch treatment and one day when a man walked by in real tight pants one of these women exclaimed, "Wow, look at that basket!" She was just retaliating and trying to show them, but the men went crazy. They couldn't see it at all and came down on her real hard for being unladylike. She left after a year and I'm sure one of the reasons was this sex thing.

Sadie objected to the general sexual harassment, but there were explicit sexual gestures from the director that combined with this to create what she describes as "an atmosphere of general abuse":

One time I was doing some writing of cases for the director's signature. He called me in to tell me how great one was and then he leaned over and passionately tried to kiss me. I screamed and shouted, "No, stop." Well, he tried to explain that he just wanted to show me his approval and I asked if he showed his approval that way to the man who had been doing the same kind of work. He said, "No, he has a mustache." I said, "Well, from now on just think of me as having a mustache." It always got down to the fact I was a woman. He just never could see me as a professional.

As soon as two more women came on staff Sadie joined them in an effort to force the director to stop his harassing behavior by confronting him publicly and telling him to take his hands off. Their efforts were consistently attacked, however, by the majority of the sixteen male attorneys:

There were three men who stayed neutral and one who actually tried to make him stop but the rest defended him violently. They all called me up to say he was an old man —he was fifty-four—and he couldn't help it and I was going hard on him. It's interesting too, the one man who kept hammering away at the director to get him to stop didn't do it because he supported us, he just didn't want the director to get caught. He'd go in and say, "This is going to be the downfall of your career. Washington can stand you being a racist and sexist, but not a dirty old man. One of these days one of these girls is going to complain to Washington." That eventually did happen. Washington did call up about a complaint about him but that's all. They didn't care.

Sadie's experiences have led her to believe that men endorse sexual harassment of women even after they understand it is a serious problem:

"We explained and argued and struggled to get those men to see what it did to us both as women and as professionals. But the whole time I was there it just never changed. Even when more of them began to agree that it was disgusting, even began to admit that it meant we didn't get treated as professionals, then, all they did was play on it. In an office like mine those men are just waiting for you not to be able to handle yourself, they want you to fail and I'm convinced this is one way they are trying to insure that happens."

Doris Asantewa is a black woman and the single mother of a four-year-old daughter; she was fired from her last job as associate director of a national social welfare organization because of sexual harassment. At twenty-seven, she holds both a B.A. and an M.A. in business administration as well as an M.A. in library science; however, she is presently preparing to leave San Francisco for New York City in the hope of better job opportunities and by that route to get off welfare. Asantewa appropriately rounds out this exploration of sexual harassment toward professional women. Her experience tragically illustrates not only that credentials do not protect a woman from this abuse, but also that the lack of recourse is no better and that the financial injury is no less for the professional than for the nonprofessional.

The sexual harassment of Doris Asantewa began shortly after she relocated from Los Angeles to San Francisco to assume her new job as an administrative advisor for all the organization's field operations:

"I was concerned. The executive director hired only women and he fired them very quickly. I was there eight months and in eight months he had eight secretaries, all of whom left very bitter. Sexual advances were a lot of it. That's why, though, I never believed he was really sexually interested in me. It happened to so many women I just didn't give it any special importance. He pinched, you know, and I got the finger up and down the spine. I just totally ignored it. I was a little concerned, as I say, but I just thought I could handle it by an attitude of disdain and indifference."

The harassment continued in this fashion for about six months, and then while on a business trip to Portland for a conference the executive director asked to spend the night in her room. Asantewa flatly refused. Almost as soon as this occurred the director no longer approved her job performance. "It was just all over from that moment on." Asantewa sought help from a member of the personnel committee, a vice-president for one of San Francisco's bigger banks, who said he knew the man had a reputation for liking women. "That wasn't all. He then said, 'Of course, you have a child and you are a woman so it's quite possible that many men will take the attitude that you're available.' And that was it. I knew I had no recourse."

Shortly after this Asantewa received her six-month job evaluation, although it was about one month past due and she had at this point remained on probation longer than the required period.

"It said nothing about my technical performance at all. Everything was about the way I related to my boss:

that I seemed afraid of him, that I didn't relate to him, that I should meet him more frequently, that I didn't correspond with him, that I didn't talk to him enough. I wrote him a reply protesting that it was all about him rather than about my performance and I was immediately fired. He just told me to get out and pick up my final check."

Asantewa went to the American Civil Liberties Union to see if her civil rights had been violated because, although as long as she was on probation she could be fired at any time, her probation had extended past the time limit.

"They shot me right into this other black woman. She had just been appointed to the national board of my organization. She's on a lot of boards, but all she said was you've been fired now, it's too late. You didn't cover your ass, you should have made the proper moves at the right time. In other words, it's your own fault cause you got fucked over, so now, just live with it and don't rock the boat any more. I'm pretty sure she just didn't want to get involved. My boss is this nationally recognized black human rights figure. He's about fifty-seven and he's always getting these awards for civic service and social welfare awards. Who wants to mess with that?"

The emotional and financial repercussions of harassment and job loss were substantial; they were also long-lasting. Although her salary had been about $18,000 per year, she had nothing saved, mostly for job-related reasons that included the move from Los Angeles, for which she had never been reimbursed; enormous monthly child-care expenditures because of so many night meetings; commuting expenses from Foster City, where she had first settled; and finally, four days before the firing, a second move into San Francisco in order to be closer to the job.

"I really didn't have a cent. I got unemployment. He didn't contest that, but then I just couldn't get another job. I sent my résumé to at least twenty-five places. I couldn't live on unemployment. We'd also moved into a slum. I couldn't afford anything better, but the conditions were terrible. It was incredibly depressing. I finally stopped paying rent after about five months and so I managed food and phone and child care while I kept looking for work. It was a disaster. The unemployment ran out and I had to take welfare. I still can't believe it. It all makes me very bitter."

Asantewa is not optimistic about her next job:

"It wasn't that this was the first experience of this that I've had. I'm a strong woman and I've tried very strongly to make my way in the world as a woman but this happened constantly. I've always ignored it. I even developed a habit of de-emphasizing my looks. But it didn't help, really. It's a continuous kind of aggression. I thought as I got older that it would diminish, but that was unrealistic. I just ran into older and older men."

It may be argued that Doris Asantewa's long-term unemployment was exacerbated by the fact she was black and that to propose her experience as representative is misleading. Unquestionably, race was a factor (race invariably affects black women's employment), but at the professional level this is not nearly the problem that it is for black female employment in general. Asantewa's experience is representative because the problem ultimately rests not with women's race or age or appearance but with a professional labor market controlled by men who are hostile to women's employment at the professional level.

The male sexual harassment of women in nontraditional jobs is a serious threat to affirmative action and all hope of a sexually integrated job market. Even when sexual harassment does not succeed in driving women out of training and jobs, it inevitably damages their career potential, undermines their self-esteem, siphons energy away from job performance, and creates serious, extended obstacles to motivation and ambition.

The psychological damage to working women in nontraditional job areas as a result of this abuse is almost incalculable; moreover it is a constant even though its expression will vary from woman to woman, although depression because of internalized rage appears to be a shared reaction. We have only just begun to comprehend the problem. We cannot yet begin to map the full extent of the damage.

6
Sexual Harassment
in Traditional Jobs

The function of sexual harassment in nontraditional jobs is to keep women out; its function in the traditional female job sector is to keep women down. Because working women throughout these job categories are often subject to continuous male sexual aggression in one form or another, the abuse influences both their prospects and their continued employment opportunities.

At the generalized level of the aggression, female powerlessness and submission are continually reinforced. Because of female job segregation work in the female sector is dead-end and low-paying, but the constant humiliation and violation inflicted by this aggression cause women's work to be triply unrewarding. Sexual harassment thus reinforces the attractiveness of marriage and/or staying at home when financially feasible. Men are also ensuring that despite the promise of equality inherent in modern work females will remain in their own eyes, in the eyes of men, and in reality subordinate.

Female solidarity that might lead to change in this situation is also effectively undermined. Sadie, the female attorney in the preceding chapter, observed in her office that sexual harassment created enormous competition among the nonprofessional female workers:

"The atmosphere in that place was terrible. There was this feeling among the older women who he never paid any attention to that this lack of interest was hurting their advancement. The younger women hated the harassment, but it started this competition between the younger women and the older women."

Further competition among female workers because of sexual harassment occurs at the hiring stage of female employment, when divisions among women according to class, age, appearance, and race are deeply aggravated by male sexual standards. These standards economically penalize all those women workers who are not young, white, attractive, and middle-class. Finally, sexual harassment promotes still a third source of female on-the-job competition when some women cooperate and others do not. The animosity and mistrust among female workers because of all of these harassment-inspired competitions is pervasive in traditional female employment, and unity in this atmosphere is hardly even conceptualized.

The weakness of women's employment is also exacerbated by this abuse. Female rejection of sexual harassment, which ends in firings and "quits," creates a large number of continuously rotating workers throughout the female sector. This aggravates the oversupply in ready labor, promoting greater job insecurity; but—even more important—it helps to effectively forestall all hope of higher wages. Longer job tenure is also a prerequisite to more widespread and forceful demands for better working conditions, including training, advancement, and raises.

Turnover in women's jobs had traditionally been chalked up to female dissatisfaction with the dead-end nature of the work or to nonmarket influences such as marriage, children, and change of husband's job location. However, because of the high incidence of job terminations due to this abuse as well as the contribution it makes to female job dissatisfaction, these assumptions have to be readjusted. The readjustment, moreover, will have to rank sexual harassment as a primary cause.

Understanding sexual harassment's role in the weakening of women's employment position is also increasingly critical. The phenomenal growth in the number of women working outside the home has made inroads in the previously abundant female labor supply. In addition, the female work force now approximates the composition of all females in the population, and this has brought a new consciousness that all kinds of women will spend many more years in the work force. As a result women's extreme exploitation is now less acceptable on the ground that this is only a temporary condition until marriage. However, job tenure will still provide an important prerequisite for change and sexual harassment, which will keep pace with the growth of working women, will continue to maintain its treadmill effect of keeping women moving from job to job while conditions remain the same.

HIRING POLICIES

Throughout women's work, particularly all public-contact employment (including waitress work and virtually all office occupations) sexual harassment has been institutionalized through discriminatory hiring policies that screen applicants first for sex appeal, regardless of skills and qualifications. In a job market controlled primarily by white men whose sexual standards are largely the result of racist social values, minority-race women are handicapped. Statistics bear this out. In 1973 less than one-fourth of minority-race women were in clerical jobs as compared with 36 percent of white women. They also comprised less than 6 percent of all secretaries and only 14 percent of all typists. Only 2.5 percent of minority-race women were employed as sales workers, 5 percent below the number of white women.[1]

Catherine Ettlinger, in a 1976 *Washington Newsworks* article entitled "The Beauty Queen Syndrome," wrote:

One of the most blatant cases of a company's discriminatory practices is the D.C. branch of the Bank of America. It's a

126

small office and when there's a need for a secretary, office manager Carol Willingham usually works through an employment agency. She used Albers a few months ago and placed her order with Susan Collins. Collins said that unless the applicants were in their early twenties, pretty and Caucasian, they wouldn't get past Willingham, who screens applicants for her boss. . . .[2]

Attractive appearance is another major element in male standards when employing women, regardless of the job, and employment possibilities for the physically handicapped are accordingly obstructed.

In 1943 Lena Ross was forty-four years old. A blind resident of Boston whose work experience included a shoe factory, a chocolate factory, and a large Boston department store, she had until recently been employed for the last six years with the WPA Braille project. When that job ended she eventually obtained a new position with the Holtzer-Cabot Electric Company as an assembler of parts in generators; after only five days at this new job, however, John R. Millon, the placement agent for the Boston Division of the Blind (who had arranged this last job) informed her she was through. Ross later sent Millon a letter inquiring why he had not better defended her and asking him:

"Just consider for a moment. Suppose you had started to work for the Division of the Blind. And the understanding of your employment was to give you a fair and sufficient opportunity to find jobs for blind people—say about five or six months. And suppose that at the end of two weeks you were kicked out unceremoniously. The explanations given to you were that your trouser legs were too short and your sleeves too long, and that your mustache was not of the right color. . . . How would you feel?"

Millon had previously informed Lena Ross and her brother that the company had dismissed her for "personal" reasons. He had refused further explanation until pushed by her brother, when he finally declared, "Well, if you want to really know the truth I will tell you straight from the shoulder. You were unsatisfactory because of your personal appearance. . . ." Lena Ross defended herself in the letter, saying, "I cannot understand . . . I had worn my best and cleanest dresses and the only comment any of the girls had made was that I was dressed too well for the job as it was greasy work. . . ."[3]

It is often argued that men are also discriminated against on the basis of their appearance, but as Betty S. Murphy, head of the National Labor Relations Board, has pointed out, "The unattractive woman is affected more than the unattractive man by virtue of the type of job she applies for."[4] This is another way of saying that male standards of sex appeal and attractiveness in women are virtually an occupational requirement for many women's jobs. It is often a requirement that overrides all others.

A Middle Eastern embassy in Washington, D.C., recently advertised for an administrative secretarial position asking for someone with good secretarial skills, proficiency in at least one other language, and a background in economics and political sciences. Ettlinger wrote that according to one employment agency counselor who was involved with this opening, "At least 30 well-groomed applicants—most typing over 80 words a minute, fluent in three foreign languages and with strong politically oriented backgrounds tried to get the job." None of these women was hired; instead, the successful applicant typed only forty-five words per minute, spoke only English, and possessed a degree in fine arts. Ettlinger explained: "Her chief qualification, according to the personnel counselor: 'She was a beautiful girl with a gorgeous blond mane of hair and a nice big bosom.' "[5]

Thousands upon thousands of working women experience this daily. Skills, training, experience, and motivation all take a back seat to attractiveness—and on this kind of a scale it isn't a question of grooming and a neat appearance but of physical endowment that frequently determines employment possibilities in the female job market, although as Ettlinger commented: "There are no signs saying . . . Ugly women are not employed by this company."[6] Homely women frequently find themselves wondering if they aren't too handicapped in this kind of a market to earn a living at all. In reality they must forever resign themselves to jobs that involve little public contact and be grateful in general that they are permitted to work at the jobs other women don't want.

Ellen (a pseudonym) is presently employed taking care of children. She says, "Right now I do child care not only because I feel I am skilled in working with kids, but also because of the harassment I have felt on many jobs." The harassment Ellen is referring to has frequently but not exclusively had to do with her appearance. Ellen is not unattractive. At twenty-eight she dresses acceptably. However, she is also not what would be called a "looker." This has sidetracked her employment over the last ten years, seriously affecting her possibilities.

Job interviews were always terrible experiences for me. Personal appearance is a very important criterion in getting a job, and it was always clear to me that this judgment extended beyond neatness and tidiness. When I applied for a job as a waitress, I got a job at a truck stop for small wages and hardly any tips. The more lucrative waitress jobs were not open to me. For the better-paying office work the want-ads clearly said they wanted an "attractive girl." When I was working my way through school and desperately needed the money to support myself I applied for a job as a library assistant; the man who interviewed me had a reputation for hiring mostly beautiful women; he put my application aside. I did eventually get the job because a friend of mine worked there and she signed me up for the last available hours. I ended up working there for over four years and when we were eventually rated on our performance I was given an outstanding rating.

Throughout my whole working experience I don't think I was ever allowed to forget that this male sexual standard was being applied.

Last year I was working for a temporary agency. I'm considered a highly skilled worker; I type 80 words a minute

129

and have experience. However, the men who want a "temporary girl" frequently expect an added decoration in their office. I remember one time when I showed up for work as a receptionist/typist for the manager of a symphony; he was obviously disappointed as he looked me over. He ignored me and made me feel very out of place in his office for a few days and then sent me home saying that he decided he did not need a temporary worker after all.

Although sexual harassment seriously depressed Ellen's employment opportunities, she was not exempt from overt, explicit harassment once she did find work:

When I was a switchboard operator, we kept our headphones in a closet. The male supervisor would follow me in and pinch me. When I was a waitress, virtually all my customers were men and they would make remarks like 'Let's lie down and do it here, baby,' and follow me into the back room to feel me up and down. A co-worker at the library would corner me and try to kiss me when we were alone in the elevator. I felt anger, but it was a confused anger. I felt insulted and degraded but it was very difficult for me to deal with because I didn't want to admit that I wasn't attractive. I didn't want to offend the men, they had too much power over me.

Opportunities for employment, even in jobs which are traditionally assigned to women, are distributed according to male sexual standards at hiring. This influences which groups of women will receive higher salaries. In 1973 the median salary in the clerical field was about $6500; among female operatives (usually factory and/or machine operators) the median income was about $5350, and for women service workers about $4600. Private household workers averaged $2069.[7] Male hiring practices based on sex appeal and a standard of sexual attractiveness have tended to exclude minority-race women from the clerical occupations, forcing them into less-paid occupations. More than one-sixth of all minority-race women were operatives, compared to one-eighth of all white women; about 38 percent of all minority race women were service workers—that was nearly twice the proportion of white women—and 27 percent of them were household workers, four and one-half times the percentage of white women in this occupation. Not surprisingly, minority-race women in this same year earned only 88 percent of the median salary earned by white women.[8] The Women's Bureau notes that the gap between minority-race women and whites in clerical jobs has been narrowing in recent years,[9] but this does not necessarily indicate that their salaries are or ever will be at parity so long as male sexual harassment dictates who gets what job. Minority-race women are still consistently denied nearly all the receptionist and secretarial positions and most other jobs that require public contact—and these are the better-paying jobs.

There are no statistics for lower-class, overweight, homely, and physically handicapped women, but from experience, it is not unreasonable to assume that their discrimination within clerical work parallels that of minority race women. As a result, their lack of employment opportunities are probably comparable.

The male sex standard in hiring—which the acting head of the EEOC, Tom Cosentino, describes as a "real problem"[10]—requires the active help of employment agencies from coast to coast. Each day they flood the country's newspapers with advertisements for female workers. These ads invariably use modifiers like pert, snappy, very good, attractive, pretty, and they all precede that all-important word: *appearance*.

OLDER WORKING WOMEN

Employment-agency ads will never use the word *young* because discrimination on the basis of age is now illegal, but the requirement of youth in women's work is an unwritten law. Mary Kathleen Benet writes in *The*

131

Secretarial Ghetto, "Adults of both sexes are now included in the office but mainly women between 16 and 30 and men between 25 and 65.[11] If they stay in the workforce all women are harmed by aging in a job market controlled by men free to exercise their preference for young sex partners and sex symbols. This is no less true for attractive white women who although once preferred are just as scathed eventually by male sexual harassment. The economic spin-off of this dynamic is substantial." In describing the "myth of the sexy secretary," Benet wrote:

"First of all it keeps the secretaries young. This keeps pay raises and overt discontent to a minimum. . . . Older women are made to feel superfluous and out of place and their firing or persecution is justified on the grounds that the men like working with younger women, or that the atmosphere of the typing pool is so young and gay it's a shame to spoil it. Just at the point where an older woman may feel she's ready for the promotion and the raise she has worked so long for, she suddenly becomes an embarrassment to the management and is shunted into a backwater. . . ."[12]

The abuse also influences the high unemployment level of older women when compared to men of the same age. Not only are they less employable as age increases but they are also deemed unemployable at a much earlier age. While women and men in 1974 had comparable unemployment levels until twenty-four, at twenty-five to thirty-four women experienced about a 1-percent-higher rate and after thirty-four for the next ten years their rate was nearly twice that for men of the same age. After forty-five their rate remained consistently higher.[13] It can also be assumed that these rates, particularly after about thirty-five, would be still higher if they included all those women who had just given up hope of finding a job.

In explaining this "discouraged worker syndrome," a 1974 article in *Industrial Gerontology* said that many middle-aged and older women fall into the category because they frequently feel employers prefer younger women. The article added that "the reality and significance of such preferences are often difficult to document,"[14] but Women Office Workers of New York City recently proved they exist to a profound degree. After conducting an investigation of the major Manhattan employment agencies, this female workers' rights group issued a well-documented research report that blasted "the widespread continuing discrimination against older women."[15] The group subsequently filed age- and sex-discrimination complaints with the New York State Division of Human Rights against Snelling and Snelling, Cosmopolitan Girl, Key, Kellogg, Aavis, and the New York State Employment Service.

The WOW investigation successfully exposed the cooperation of employment agencies with age discrimination by male employers through a telephone survey of 100 agencies, which all accepted the following discriminatory job order:

I want a girl who is college educated, has pizazz, young, maybe 25. . . . I need someone who looks good, a young girl, a sharp dresser. . . . She should be under 25, say 20 to 25 years old.[16]

A sample of ten agencies was then compiled and they were visited by a team of two women "checkers"; they had equal skills, training, and background although one was fifty years old with twenty years of office-work experience and the other woman was young with only six years' experience. Among other abuses, the investigation showed: the older woman always entered an agency first, but the younger woman was frequently interviewed before her; the younger woman spent one hour, the older woman spent two or three; two agencies flatly told the older woman there were no jobs at the same time the young woman was referred to several; two other agencies referred the older woman to the low-paying jobs while the younger

133

woman was referred to the better-paying ones; and one agency told the older woman they might be able to help her but only if she would pay her own fee.

One employment-agency job counselor quoted in the WOW report said:

Employers want to have young, cute things around them. I know they are not supposed to discriminate, that's the law. But face it, we understand what they want after a while when we send over a lot of prospective employees. It's an unwritten agreement. I'm not supposed to say this, but that's the way it is.[17]

The repercussions of this kind of sexual harassment of the older woman worker are serious and far-reaching. It lowers wages; employers only pay for a maximum of five years' office work experience. After that, experience signals advancing age, so that very early in her office career a secretary will peak at the top salary—which is currently about $10,500. After that she will not only never go any higher, she will also watch that "top" hacked back with any move she makes in the ensuing years.[18] It is an impossible situation.

This situation is particularly serious since more middle-aged and older women are working than ever before. Prior to World War I the typical woman worker was young and unmarried; today she is thirty-six years old and married. More than half of all women thirty-five to fifty-four years of age and 42 percent between fifty-five and sixty-four are workers.[19] These figures have leveled off in recent years, but the problem of unemployment and deflated wages due to age remains severe. Meanwhile the male standard in hiring continues to ignore the mounting evidence that older women workers excel their younger counterparts in better turnover rates, better attendance records, better productivity over the long haul, and better safety records. However, this should not be interpreted to mean that older women are less subject than younger women to sexual harassment once they are on the job. On the contrary, it may even be that their vulnerability in the job market contributes to their attractiveness as victims.

Genvieve [a pseudonym] is sixty years old. She is perky, petite, and fashionable, but after she left her last job because of sexual harassment all she has encountered is hostility:

"I haven't had a job since. I'm registered with thirty agencies and I haven't had one referral in seven months. I feel like I'm being punished. Age, age, always my age. I walk into an employment agency and all they do is attack and criticize. It's like trying to climb out of a hole. I don't know what I'm going to do. I won't have unemployment a whole lot longer."

Genvieve has been working since 1935, when she started out as a secretary/stenographer in New Bedford, Massachusetts, where her parents settled after emigrating from England. "I've never married and so I've never stopped since then, couldn't afford to." She relocated in New York City after a few years to go to business school; eventually unhappy with secretarial work, she continued to work at these jobs by day and at night she attended the New York School of Finance to become an account executive. At the end of three years she had successfully completed courses in security analysis, portfolio management, money and credit principles. She felt what she had learned was adequate and she applied to an investment banking firm where she explained her goals. Genvieve took the job under the impression she would have a chance to work as more than a secretary but that promise was unfulfilled, something that would continue to be the case in many other jobs.

"I left there after fourteen months because of being run all over the place and because they kept me at the most menial level of my capabilities. Since then and since all my training I've had a succession of positions which haven't begun to offer me full recognition. My mother

135

was very ill and my income was essential so I persisted in these sorts of jobs."

Genvieve eventually gave up the idea of ever achieving an account-executive position and after her mother died, thinking opportunities might be better outside investment banking, she decided to go the "temporary route" in search of new work experience and possibly a better job based on proven performance. For five years, from 1965 to 1970, Genvieve worked as a temp but permanent positions were like the pot of gold at the end of the rainbow.

"There were some outstanding recommendations, but they always turned me down at personnel. Age, mostly. ITT precluded me from getting a job in 1970. At the interview the woman said, 'How old are you?' I said 'I'm fifty-two.' She said she couldn't do anything for me. I sued through the State Division of Human Rights and I won. I got $3240. I still didn't get the job."

Genvieve eventually went to New York University's Testing and Advisement Center, where she tested in the top 97 percent of her age group, with written and oral intelligence into the ninety-fourth percentile; they recommended a supervisory or junior management position in education, medicine, or the foundations. Genvieve decided to try it. "I assumed I could enter as a secretary and use that as an entry vehicle, but I couldn't get a job." Genvieve spent all of 1970 unemployed although she job-hunted incessantly. A secretarial position finally materialized but the firm soon went out of business; and then, after spending another five months out of work, Genvieve accepted her last job in July 1974.

"In the first interview Mr. S., who was fifty-four, sat in front of me; he was sitting at the end of the table handling his penis. I tried to pretend that nothing happened. He offered me the job but I turned it down."

About two weeks later Genvieve still hadn't found a job, so she checked to see if the job was still open. As it turned out, the man had hired another woman, although he had already fired her, and Genvieve got the job, but only after agreeing to a salary of $185; he had been paying $235. The sexual harassment began on the second day, when dictation involved her new boss sitting alongside her and rubbing his leg against hers. "I moved away, but his leg just kept coming over and over. I thought I'd fall off the chair." The following day the Executive Vice-President, who was forty-eight, played with himself as Genvieve delivered the mail. "I ran back to my desk and collapsed, but I said nothing as I couldn't figure out what prompted it." Genvieve eventually determined the politic way to handle the entire situation was to complain to her boss about the other man's behavior. "He answered me by saying the only reason any man would behave like that is because you're probably no good and have been through the gutter. Those are his exact words. I was so shocked the only thing I could think was that he knew I was single. Nothing changed; about a fortnight later he was standing across from me and he suddenly started playing with himself."

About a week later Genvieve demanded to be allowed to do her job in a reasonable atmosphere:

At the end of that day he walked up and said in this terrible voice and spitefully, "There she is, Rosie the Riveter, the Instant Retriever, the maid from the modest background." I stood right up to him this time and shot right back, "I may be a nobody, but I know the difference between right and wrong." Well, that did it. His eyes practically bugged out of his head and that's when the vendetta really started. He got extremely abusive; there was no aspect of my work that he didn't attack. The sexual incidents stopped, except he seemed determined now to prove I was just a stupid steno. I'm absolutely convinced that all the other abuse, the whole vendetta that followed had to do with objecting to those sexual performances in the office.

Genvieve stayed on the job a total of eighteen months, but eventually she quit. "None of this sits very easy with me. I feel like I have to be careful not to come across as some neurotic misfit woman, but I want to make it absolutely clear that those sexual gestures were not involuntary. They were deliberate and they were terribly intimidating. I can't say how done in I've felt by the whole thing. I keep thinking: Is this what I get after forty years?"

JOB-HUNTING

For many women, job interviews often turn into wrestling matches, and securing jobs often depends upon a willingness to engage in sex. These interviews constitute a brutal male communication of man's dominance at work, and women are intimidated. Ivonne Elias said, "I left that place and I felt like shit. I just felt like why bother. It was a horrible experience and it was terribly degrading." Elias is thirty-four; she is a recent arrival from Puerto Rico and these remarks are the residue from her first job interview in New York City.

Elias had been referred by a friend in the U.S. Civil Service to the personnel manager of a well-known credit company; however, at the interview, the man not only refused to look at her résumé but he also refused to discuss the job opening with his own company. Instead he touted an executive-secretary job for a friend, although he also said it would depend on how liberal she was. When the man explained this Elias said it sounded like a job for a prostitute and she wasn't interested. At this the man finally looked over her résumé; excusing himself a short time later, he left, ostensibly to talk to his manager. He returned to say the manager was busy and would call her. Elias has never heard a word.

"I still feel very embarrassed at the situation. It was especially hard at the time to have to explain to people who cared about me. I knew it would hurt them and that made it hurt even worse. I felt so helpless. I just wanted to be able to do something. It was a great injustice; I needed that job. I remember too that it made me look at myself. I'm big-breasted and he commented a couple of times: 'Why is a good-looking girl like you interested in an office job?' I just thought perhaps I was doing something. It's like the whole thing just puts a doubt in you and it stays with you for a while."

Both the content of these feelings and the order of their progression is significant. Before questioning her own behavior, Elias endured a humiliation followed by a profound helplessness because her attacker could not be punished. This feeling of powerlessness is perhaps the prime response engendered by the abuse of working women, although it frequently registers as self-blame. Women do know when they are being violated without provocation, an expression of power to which the natural response is a defense. Without a socially approved framework within which they can claim and assert their own power, however, many women either suppress or quickly dismiss the realization of such a desire. Self-blame follows.

Joan Handel was sexually harassed during a job interview with an older, well-known civil libertarian at Cornell University. Handel, who has always been interested in social work, was desperate for a job, and overjoyed to find that this one would involve counseling law clients. Because of this she never questioned that the man seemed unconcerned with her office skills, focusing instead on her attitude and asking if it would upset her to deal with prostitutes, or people who weren't married and were living together. For more than an hour Handel fielded questions of this sort, repeatedly declaring that none of these things would upset her; the man finally seemed satisfied and it appeared she had the position. Upon leaving, he held her coat and she turned her back. At that moment the man shoved his hand under her sweater, groping her breasts and asking if that upset her.

"I felt dumb, horrified, unbelievably naïve. He had no right, but I thought I should have seen it coming and I ran home crying." Handel subsequently confided in friends who urged her to report it, particularly as she had been referred by a woman-run job service who would continue to send other women to this man. "I was afraid. I felt like who would believe me. I didn't do a thing, I didn't even tell the job service." Handel's fear that she wouldn't be believed was subsequently realized. "I finally talked about it last year in my woman's group but one woman said 'I know him; he's a great liberal and he just couldn't do that. I don't believe you.' That's exactly what I had been afraid of. It made me frustrated and angry because, goddamn it, it did happen."

THE REVOLVING-DOOR ATTITUDE

The incessant sexual harassment symptomatic of female labor has much more of a negative influence on women's attitudes toward work than is realized—even more of an impact, perhaps, than the knowledge that their employment is low-paid, monotonous, dead-end, or backbreaking. This sexual degradation often accounts for the revolving door attitude regarding jobs which has become a way of life.

Cindy Pullano is twenty-four and single. Having worked primarily in factories in upstate New York, she says, "Mostly it's affected my attitude. I guess you could say it's made me bitter. All I know is I won't go to work in a factory again, never, I don't care if I have to be unemployed the rest of my life. I've hit 'em all, all the factories around here at one time or another and it happens all over." Pullano was fired after six months from her last factory job for using the public telephone. She says it was for standing up to sexual harassment.

I did pick and cut—I looked through a microscope and picked out excess copper and blister out of the copper layers. It was a dirty place and the fumes were enough to kill you

140

but I'm used to that, I mean it's like a sweatshop really and it's terrible but everything was all right except that the vice-president of the company was a pig. He just harassed all the girls. He was constantly embracing you or trying to embrace you or he'd come up and whisper things in your ear. He did it to all of us, I was no exception. It's like my sister got the job there before me. "Hey, Boobs," he'd say, which embarrassed her in front of other people. He had little nicknames for all the girls. One girl he called Crisco, fat in the can, and he was always making these gross obscene remarks. He'd been known to have affairs with different girls that worked there at different times and from what I'd heard he'd been fired ten years ago from another job for fooling around.

Two separate times he came by my work station to say, "Hey, Cindy, want to go in the back room and fuck?" I'd say get lost or ignore him. What I really wanted to do was kick him but I didn't want to lose my job. He said things to my sister too. He'd say, "Hey, Cheryl, why don't you come to my office and I'll give you an interview." There was nobody you could go to 'cause even the people over us were afraid to lose their jobs. But I started complaining about the guy to the other girls. I couldn't help it, I just felt like there was something we oughta be able to do. Bam! I got fired.

After that my sister called me up crying and real upset about the things this guy was saying to her now. You know, there was no heat in that place in the winter, you'd sit there with your coat on and the temperature's below zero. On top of that he was just too much. I also got denied unemployment 'cause he fired me. I've had no income for the past six months and it's all because of him. Somebody finally told me about the human rights commission and I filed a complaint. I don't think it's really gonna help me very much, but this guy should be stopped. I mean 'cause he's still doing it, he's still harassing the girls down there and they won't do anything 'cause they're afraid of losing their jobs. My sister was the only one who'd sign a statement.

I just wanna do something. It's happened to me before other places where I've worked. It just doesn't happen to me, it happens to everybody.

I don't know. There's just no reason for it. We shouldn't have to put up with it. I'm an employee, not a plaything.

They treat you like a toy and you don't go along and Bam—fired. I know it happens all over. I've worked department stores, same thing. I'd still like to get into an office, whether that would be any better or not I don't know, but factories, never. I won't go near them. I don't care if I was collecting unemployment and they sent me there. I wouldn't go 'cause that's where the worst of it goes on.

THE PATTERN OF MALE RETRIBUTION

Another pattern of sexual harassment in the female sector is a form of retribution exacted by rejected male suitors. This harassment is almost invariably conducted by a man of authority in the workplace at the conclusion of a mutual relationship with a female subordinate when she has been the one to end the relationship. This form of harassment is common and occurs throughout all the traditional occupations. It also usually works out that the woman loses her job, often by firing, more often by quitting, and sometimes (very rarely) through a transfer. Kate Harps, a secretary at Cornell University who bicycles to work and studies Arabic on the side, managed a transfer in these circumstances. "I was very lucky, there just aren't that many jobs. What I think is terrible is the way it always ends up that the woman has to leave. This man is still in his job and nobody—nobody ever suggested that maybe he should leave the office if he could find another job."

Harps' job difficulty began after she dated her boss and then decided she didn't want to see him any more. "Suddenly, everything I did was wrong. My typing was bad, I didn't wear the right things to work, I was thirty seconds late getting back from lunch." If she went to lunch with him once in a while "things went much more smoothly," so at first she did that until she felt dishonest and stopped. The harassment worsened. The last straw occurred when her new boyfriend, who would occasionally come by the office to take her to lunch or to give her a ride home, was not allowed in the office any more; in fact,

142

according to a note she received, he wasn't supposed to come anywhere near the building. "I went over my boss' head to his boss, but he just said, 'Gee, this is the first I've heard of it,' which is silly, because he knew what was going on all the time. Nobody cared about the abuse of power that was going on. It was like nobody dared to say he was wrong, so all that ever happened was that they blamed the situation on us both. Only I was the one who had to leave."

The unwillingness to either condemn or punish the male harasser in this situation is typical. Harps was lucky to stay with the institution under these circumstances; most women soon find themselves without any job at all. There is an old injunction for working women, often found in women's magazines, that goes: "Don't play where you work!" This bit of advice is grounded in a knowledge of the syndrome of male retribution. The only trouble is that some *mutual* attraction is inevitable and it is useless in the face of this reality to keep telling women not to become involved. It would be much more appropriate to condemn this abuse of male power and to advise women to be prepared to defend themselves from this harassment when the interest fades. This is especially true since a woman doesn't always have to end the relationship for the abuse to occur. Sometimes when an affair just fades away or on some occasions when the man has ended the relationship, he will harass the woman simply to remove her as a reminder of the involvement or because he wants to make room for new possibilities.

WAITRESS WORK

Waitresses and related service workers who depend on men not only for employment but also for tips and good will are exposed to a double jeopardy in sexual abuse. Nowhere more than in waitressing have women been pressured to appear "easy" and available. An obvious indication of this is the revealing costumes demanded by many establishments so that the female worker is forced to work half-naked (sometimes in air-conditioned lounges), providing a sexually provocative image that invites abuse.

There is no reason that a waitress has to smile "pretty," has to flirt with male customers, cannot tell an offensive male to quit abusing her, has to accept sexual insults, obscene jokes, pinches, slaps on the rear, and a promiscuous mauling by men of every description who have the price of a cup of coffee. No reason save one—sexual harassment. The excuse given: it's good for business. So was the fourteen-hour day. Business has survived abolition of that practice; it would survive as well the end of this gratuitous abuse of women.

Abolition of this practice, however, would be a serious blow to the maintenance of female submission and male control of female labor. In 1973 more than one million women worked as waitresses—the second largest single group of service workers—but the Women's Bureau in a survey of eighty-four occupations ranked waitress ninth in the amount of annual openings. This was attributed to high turnover,[20] a direct correlative of sexual harassment. Work conditions are no harder in several other female occupations, but the turnover in this field outstrips all the others—as does the concentration of male sexual abuse. Meanwhile, high turnover keeps discontent to a minimum and keeps wages low.

Among the recent annual 86,000 openings in this field is the place once held by Connie Korbel. At the time of her harassment Korbel was divorced with children to feed and support checks that didn't arrive without going to court. Money was a big problem. In addition to her full-time office job she started waitressing part time at the invitation of a man who had once been a steady customer at a former waitress job.

"He'd always been a gentleman, very friendly. I also knew his wife. They had a family restaurant and when I arranged my hours she was tickled to death to have me."

144

Korbel was also going to school part-time in the evenings. "My hours were set for Friday and Saturday night; it was a rough schedule to keep. My oldest daughter had to stay home and babysit, so, really, it was like we were all working."

The first Friday night the man made a pass. "I'm used to that game; I just shrugged my shoulders and said that's not what I'm here for. I'm sorry, you know, like we always do." Korbel was relieved when Saturday passed without incident; however, the following Friday he again approached her and she again refused. This became the routine on Friday, and with each rejection the man became more antagonistic. "It got more difficult just to pass it off. I'd get sick to my stomach, I'd get headaches, and customers noticed a difference in me."

As time passed the man became less subtle and he took to retaliating for the rejections by making snide remarks about Korbel in front of customers. He also would hold her check back, forcing Korbel to come into his office after everyone had left. One night after he tried to force her onto a sofa she swung on him; the next week the man turned outwardly abusive, shouting at her and barking orders. Korbel quit on the spot, but not before she told him off in front of customers.

"It was the first time in my life I'd ever done that, and it felt great. Now, I'm not a woman's libber. I've got nothing against wearing short skirts and I'm not one of the braless crew, but when I went back there to pick up the paycheck I had coming I got it from his wife. She was just as friendly and nice as ever and that woman knew, she knew what I had been through and many, many women before me and more to follow. I don't want my girls who'll be working one of these days to go through that and I don't want them to be like that woman either."

The rejection of a boss' demand for sexual subservience is frequently penalized by loss of a job; a similar rejection addressed to a male customer will often result in loss of the tip. However, this is only one form of male-customer punishment. The incalculable hostility that is triggered when a woman asserts her independent worker role over the submissive female sex role can and will express itself in any number of threatening ways. One example of this is afforded by Janet Ostreich, a twenty-three-year-old resident of northern California who has worked since she was sixteen, mostly as a waitress:

One day I was pouring a cup of coffee from the urn which is right out in front and a man came up to the urn to get his own coffee. As he was doing that he reached around me and started rubbing my back. I said, "Let's cut it out." He said, "I was just feeling the fruit." I said, "Not this fruit." That was all, no need to get heavy about it. The next moment he turned around and he started yelling at me and calling me a bitch. He was cursing me out in front of everybody and saying, "Well, I just bumped into you and the next time I bump into you I'll spill this coffee all over you." I was going, "Whoa!" I started shaking real bad and I had to go in the back. I was in tears by the end because he was this big man and I was intimidated. It was really awful. For the next two weeks I started to shake every time that man walked in because I was just waiting for him to do something else.

Sue Terwilliger is seventeen. She has just finished a stint as a waitress at Woolworth's, where the injury from having to act available has come home to her with tremendous impact.

The whole trip of it is hustling. It's no sleaze joint or anything, it's Woolworth's and you get a lot of families, but I guess there were around thirty or so regular men who behaved in ways I found offensive. I couldn't tell them off, though, because either I wouldn't get their tips or they'd complain and my boss would get on my ass.

There's this one guy, for example, and depending on his mood he'll either leave you nothing or leave you a dollar or two dollars. So a lot of times I've been nice to him just 'cause I want the money. It's a strange feeling because inside

146

I'm thinking absolute daggers at him, but outside I'm just smiling and saying yes. Then I take his money and put it in my pocket. If I saw him on the street I'd tell him to eat shit and so in some ways I think he's a sucker but in other ways I know I am because I'm pretending. Some days I feel on top of it, but other days to behave nice to this slimy guy really gets to me.

At first I didn't understand that acting like this was part of the job. It just slowly dawned on me that you have to be nice, especially to men. If you flirt with them they keep coming back, and that's what the boss wants. My boss is a woman and I don't think she expects you to sleep with every customer that comes in but she does expect you to hustle the customer, get him to come back.

I wouldn't even dream of objecting to her about it. I like her and respect her and she just says that hustling men is part of the job and she does it as part of the job and she considers that you should too. If I tried to say anything she would just say, "Well, how does it hurt you to do that? All you have to do is talk nice."

I talk to my friends about it a lot. I never talk to anyone at work about it, basically for job-security reasons. I'm sure they think about it some of the time, but they've basically accepted it and for me to bring it up again, I think it would cause real resentment on their part if they have come to accept it as necessary.

Sometimes when I just laugh it off or ignore it or I play the game and flirt a little, I'll find little things happening. I make more mistakes, I break things. It's all subconscious, but I don't want men treating me like I'm a piece of shit and there's no way I can deny those feelings.

I also find myself doing terrible things to them in my head. I see myself throwing food at them, I swear at them, I put daggers through them. It's incredible. I imagine seeing them on the street and telling them what I really think of them, especially once I quit this job.

It's not like men do so many direct physical things, but there are always these really strong sexual advances and sexual remarks and just the way they look at you is terrible, it's a terrible feeling. The thing is: all by itself I could handle it, if

147

I just could tell them off. That's what bothers me the most, not rejecting it, because they have no right and when I can't say so it just destroys some part of me.

THE YOUNG WORKING WOMAN

Sue Terwilliger is typical of thousands of young girls who are being taught by male sexual harassment in all its forms that women are subordinate at work. Most teenagers who work have to do so and usually, although not always, the younger the girl, the greater the need. The majority begin this new step with some excitement. This optimism is completely divorced from the menial labor to which their sex and age confine them because it stems from the idea of work for wages; this is the true mark of an adult in our society. After only one or two jobs, however, the excitement has been so violated that it is frequently difficult to find a remaining vestige. Instead there is only the knowledge that the female worker is inevitably compromised into a position of subordination vis-à-vis men, that this accompanies all labor no matter how numbing, and that while work has provided wages it has also proved a whole new area of terror.

Denise De Cesare grew up in an Italian neighborhood on Long Island, where at fifteen she went to work in the local bakery as a salesgirl:

"A friend of mine has worked there before me and the son of one of the owners had attacked her in the basement, so she had really warned me about what to watch out for. I felt sorry for her because she was so afraid for months after it happened that if anybody came up behind her, she'd jump. He had sent her into the basement—the son had—and then he followed her and leaped on her from behind. She was really terrified; it was downstairs and nobody could hear you. Luckily, two other guys came down just then and pulled him away from her."

De Cesare had been hired during the school year, but

it wasn't long before summer vacation and the son, home from college, was back in the bakery:

I was pulling the rolls out of the tray and he asked me to go downstairs, but I said no because I remembered what happened to my friend. The next thing I know he came up behind me and kind of turned me around. I still had the roll tray in my hand, and the most amazing thing was his father was watching the whole thing. He was on the telephone in the back and he could see everything. The son was groping at me and grabbing my shoulders and trying to take the tray away and pushing me towards the back. I was screaming for the father to tell him to stop but he just stood there with the phone in his hand, watching.

I wasn't thinking of rape, it was just him groping on me. It frightened me. I was also confused because his father was right there watching and other people were around and I kept thinking nothing could really happen. But it was. He was doing it and then I thought maybe it could happen, maybe it can happen like this. Finally another man who worked there told him to cut it out and pulled him away.

I was crying and shaking, but I walked up to the father and said, "Your son needs a leash." Then I walked out. I was a nervous wreck. I was trying to figure out what to do but I just went right home and told my family. I was terrifically embarrassed. My older brother, especially, wanted to do something but I was too embarrassed. I think my parents understood that and they just didn't know what to do. It was like even if they told him off he'd just get another girl, another sucker like me who needed the job. It's funny about the embarrassment; I don't think it would embarrass me now [she is twenty-one], but at the time it was just a natural feeling. It came natural and I didn't question it. I guess maybe it was because sex and things at that point in my life were really taboo.

Carol got her first job in New York City at sixteen; it was a summer job as a model in a showroom. "I had lied and said I was nineteen and that I had all this other experience with other manufacturers on Broadway.

149

I just bullshitted my way through and the guy took me. I was thrilled because I thought I was hot shit. I thought work was terrific, the summer was going well, I was making good money and it was a big ego trip." However, before the job was over Carol was terrified into learning her place:

It was two or three weeks before I was going back to high school. I was showing the new fall line to my boss, who was this really big man, he was about six feet, four inches and weighed about 260. My dressing room was a small room adjacent to his office and I came out wearing a couple of the dresses and then I went back in. I was in the middle of changing and I had on my bra and my underwear when he came into my room, charging at me. He pinned me against the wall and started ripping my clothes off. He was slobbering all over me, and there was nothing I could do. I was absolutely petrified. I tried to fight him and I was kicking him but he was really hurting me. He just kept going for maybe a minute, two minutes—it seemed like hours. When it was over I was practically naked, bruised, and sopping wet from his saliva. He stepped back, like a couple of feet, looking me up and down, and then he said, "You know, Carol, if I really wanted to do something to you, there's nothing you could do to stop me." With that he walked out.

I couldn't believe it. It was so true and just the fact that he knew that it was true, that he really could have raped me if he had wanted to, made me absolutely sick. I didn't know how to respond. I decided I was just going to ignore it. I figured nothing worse than this was going to happen now. I only had two weeks and I thought that if I quit and made some sort of complaint—I thought about the Better Business Bureau, I thought about telling my father, who's a lawyer—but I really felt like no one would believe me. It was just so bizarre. The whole powerlessness got to me a lot. I went from feeling way, way up there to just zero.

Even one experience can completely undermine a woman's motivation to work; two experiences only multiply the damage, frequently locking early quits into a lifelong pattern of leaving jobs. This only ensures female subordination at work, the very expression of which women are trying to escape. In Carol's case it also only took a second incident to show her the ultimate meaning of the behavior. "I guess I just never thought it would make me quit my job. I just feel like it's at the point where I can't take it any more. They make it impossible to work except on their terms." Carol is only twenty years old. The last incident involved nothing physical, but it did involve an explicit demand for sex from a manager at a well-known motor inn.

Denise De Cesare's second experience involved a physical confrontation. Like Carol's, her harasser also was the manager of a restaurant in a chain, this one known for its ice cream flavors. In fact, the confrontation occurred in the cooler:

We had gone in there for cartons of ice cream and he piled two on me when suddenly he jumps in front of me. It was like I was cornered in the refrigerator part and he's smiling at me with his yellow teeth and then he starts throwing his hands all around hollering, "Now I've got you cornered. Now I've got you." I was outraged. It was making me sick just to look at him.

I said, "Look, buster, my knees are free and I'm going to send your balls flying right around your neck if you don't leave me alone." I was furious and all of a sudden he jumps back. It's like he realized I really meant it, that I really would fight him. So I just went flying out of the cooler. I held out another week. The other manager was a woman, she was a good friend and I didn't want to hurt her by just leaving. She knew he propositioned a lot of waitresses and bugged them. I wasn't the first, so she wasn't surprised. She was even on the borderline of leaving. It was just something that really affected a lot of people. I mean he was the general manager. He just had all the power.

So just like the bakery, I up and left. I've been in and out of a lot of jobs now and it's the kind of thing where if these people are going to give me a hard time, it's definitely not worth it; I'll just up and leave. I walk into a job now and

151

I more or less just put it out there that I'm here to do the job and I'm going to do it good but if you bug me, if you harass me, I'm gone. I can always find another job like this and maybe run across nicer people to work for.

Carol and Denise are not exceptional other than perhaps that only two experiences of sexual harassment may be below the average for the young female worker; the male sexual harassment of this age group is very high. Sexual inexperience, economic necessity, and a high rate of unemployment contribute to the prevalence. Upstate New Yorker Mary Moon, for example, was sexually harassed from thirteen to nineteen on every single job at which necessity forced her to work:

When I was a girl my mother had a bakery, that was how we could make ends meet, if you could call it that. We lived in a farmhouse; half the house was the bakery; and it seemed like sooner or later everybody on our road needed work, so off and on different people within a two-mile radius would work in the bakery with me. I was thirteen, and even though they were frequently the fathers of my girlfriends they wanted to put the make on me. At that time I had no idea what sexuality even was. I was very embarrassed. I've repressed most of it. It was too scary and awful. That lasted for two years.

Then when I was fifteen the bakery went bankrupt. I had to get other work, so I went out to a new motel that had been built and I got a job as a chambermaid. It was about sixty hours a week and no overtime and I was constantly sexually harassed by male customers. I worked there for about a year, and at least once a week I would be cleaning the room and a man would pretend to check it and then he'd offer me ten dollars or something like that to stay. I would get extremely upset. I couldn't tell my parents because I was too embarrassed, but it's all I thought about from the moment I left work till I went back again. It's like I didn't quite know what was going on, that's why it was so cruel—because I was too young to even know what sexuality was.

When I was seventeen I left that job and I got a job in a

factory. I had the same things happening to me. I was still very naïve. When I was eighteen I got a job at the racetrack walking thoroughbreds early in the morning, around five in the morning, and also after the races. The same things happened to me over and over again from the groom who worked there. That lasted until I was nineteen. I just don't have the words to tell you how awful it all was. I hated work. The whole thing still makes me really upset.

Unemployment for young girls runs about three times as high as that for all working women.[21] This virtually assures a high incidence of sexual harassment as men capitalize on the vulnerability of job-seekers and the insecurity of job-holders. This high unemployment rate, however, is also a symptom of this abuse. Fast turnover in industries utilizing the labor of large numbers of young females has already been discussed; the prevalence of sexual harassment is also well known. This is particularly true of the fast-food industry, which (roughly-estimated) employs nearly a quarter-million young girls. The connection in this industry between sexual harassment and turnover is spelled out in this excerpt from a letter by forty-nine-year-old F.L. Wright of Wilmington, Delaware:

I recently resigned from a growing Fast Food establishment. One of my reasons was the working conditions. As an assistant manager I saw this [sexual harassment] going on all the time. We hired mostly high school girls and boys and the girls would talk to me all the time about what other managers would do or try to do. I might add I was raised to respect womanhood. I tried talking to other managers, some married, but it was a joke to them, always saying the girls could quit if they didn't like it.

Harassment of young ladies is very strong in fast foods. . . .

Meg (a pseudonym) first went to work for a famous hamburger chain:

"I was only sixteen but I had already graduated from

high school and my mother said either you get out of here and support yourself totally or else I'll charge you $40 rent and you can work somewhere. I just desperately wanted the job; well, not the job, but the money. For the first three months it was really neat. I had my job and I was making money and I got along with everybody pretty good."

After this the general manager accused Meg of being stuck-up. She had been avoiding him because she neither liked nor trusted him but, frightened that he might fire her, she stopped the avoidance routine. As soon as she did the manager raised her hourly wages from $2.10 to $2.35 and hour; he also began approaching her sexually.

One day he pinched my ass. I got all red in the face and I didn't know how to handle it. I just tried to level with him as best I could and I said really clear I didn't want him to touch me again, that it made me uptight. He just didn't care.

The next awful thing was that in front of a whole bunch of other women working there he announced in this loud voice that he had this dream that he made love to me. All the other women started snickering. I got the impression they thought I was getting it on with him or something, but to make it worse he kept it up.

He would also hang around me and help me do things, which a manager never did. Like he'd help me wrap hamburgers and he'd stand real close and press against me. I hated it but it made the other women resentful. When I first got the raise I was so happy I told everybody, but then all this other shit started and a lot of the women got really burned up. They wouldn't help me any more and it was real uncomfortable. I wanted out real bad but I didn't think I could get another job.

It got where I really hated him. After a while his face looked like a monster to me. At work I was constantly pissed off. Every time he'd walk by I'd have these little fantasies of pushing him away or telling him off. I'd fantasize about smashing his face. I'd also have long involved conversations at night about what I'd say to him the next day. Of course, I wouldn't really do it.

I thought about complaining to management, but it was

154

useless. We had an area supervisor come in and he had the evil eyes too. I'm sure most of them were into it or into looking the other way because I tried to talk to the other manager at our store but he wouldn't talk to me, he just pretended it didn't happen.

Meg didn't last much longer; she quit within a matter of weeks and, as she feared, it was a long time before her next job. "I don't think I've ever had a more miserable time in my life. I just wish to God working women would get together."

Male customers in fast foods often add to the problem. Louisa, seventeen and desperate for a job, worked illegally for a New York state delicatessen that served beer. She was unceasingly sexually harassed by male students from the surrounding colleges. "They'd laugh at me, make fun of me, just be totally obnoxious. I just said, 'This job makes me uptight and I'm going to quit.' Now I'm housecleaning because I think working with the public means that I'm going to be harassed by men sexually, that the whole way they think of me is about my body. It's scary because as a young woman looking out, I do want to work."

The unemployment rate for minority-race girls is more than twice that of white girls;[22] obviously their problems with sexual harassment are doubly compounded—jobs are scarcer and their vulnerability is even greater. In addition, the particular fact of color complicates the problem of sexual inexperience. Liza (a pseudonym) is a recent graduate of Cornell University. She was sexually harassed in the course of successive summer jobs while home from school in Atlanta, Georgia. In each situation she was the only black person. "I thought I was being harassed because I was a black woman and they thought that was my role."

The first experience occurred the summer of her freshman year, when she worked as a telephone solicitor for a land-development corporation. There were six men:

"They would all come and kind of snuggle up to you in the name of telling you how to use the telephone and things like that. One man stood so close to me that you could feel his penis poking you in the leg. The room was full of people and they just sat there like nothing was going on. I was immature and I didn't say anything because I was kind of waiting for the other people to come to my rescue. They just went about their work, you know, like this was the way things were, so I thought, well, maybe I'm imagining all this."

When one man forced himself on the pretext of showing her work that in reality needed no explaining, Liza finally said, "Why don't you knock it off?" The man played dumb, accusing her of an overactive imagination. Liza backed off, especially since she had seen him doing the same things to the other women. "They didn't seem to object; it made me feel crazy." The man continued. One day he slapped her on the behind. "I just didn't know what to do because I'd told him and he didn't stop, so I just didn't go back. I didn't talk to anybody. All the women were white. They were also older and this was their real job for the rest of their lives, while I was just an outsider. I think now that's why they didn't object, but at the time it just didn't dawn on me. I just thought it was because I was black. I lasted a month."

The following summer Liza worked for a company selling home development courses, the only job she could scare up after a month of hunting, and she didn't want to give it up even after the branch manager began sexually harassing her. At first it was the same thing. "He would insist on sitting next to you and then he'd press and rub against you, pushing his thigh into yours." Later he would call her into his office and sit on his couch demanding that she sit next to him. "The next thing is he would then put his hand in his pants and sit there and handle himself till he came." This time Liza did talk to one of the other phone solicitors, who confirmed he did the same thing to her; however, she didn't object. "I guess

156

I just felt that nobody was really peeved but me about that kind of thing, and maybe it did bother her but she wouldn't admit it. There was nothing you could do so I just left the job again."

The issue of race again prevented Liza from making more of a fuss:

In Atlanta it was really segregated when I was growing up. The schools were black, the stores you shopped in were black. I saw white people on television and that was it. Maybe I'd see one on the bus. I just felt, you know, that when I finally got a job and was working among white people that it happened because white men think that black women are whores. It's like if you're black you fit into two categories: if you're fat and dark-skinned you're a mammy; all other black women are whores. I'm sure I had feelings like that before I could talk, it was something that was accepted as true. So I was afraid of talking to the white women because I thought they would think the only reason I thought that way was because I was black. It was impossible with those kinds of feelings to say or do anything. Now I feel that it's more that I'm a woman, because when I look back on the situation that I was in, you know, it was happening to all the women.

The financial damage to Liza as a result of these experiences was immediate; the psychological harm has been long-term:

At first all I could see was that it was hurting me at school. I went to Cornell on financial aid, and you're expected to earn a certain amount of money over the summer. I would come back to school with no money and then I would end up working over the year to try and make up some of the money. It took time away from studying. It's also still affecting me, though. It's like on my job now, sometimes they say I'm not smiling enough, but it's because I find that, you know, the stone face has a better chance. I'm also conscious of the way I dress. I always feel like I should put on a nun's habit to go to work. It also affects my job performance, because

157

where as a guy might bend over and pick up something that he dropped, I don't because I might draw attention to myself.

The young girl who refuses to appear or act in conformity with social norms about appropriate female attire and behavior will almost invariably be sexually harassed on the job. Suzanne Brink went to work at thirteen, left home at fifteen, and at sixteen was expelled from high school because of a lesbian romance. After early jobs in upstate New York vineyards, Brink landed a chef-assistant's job at a large resort hotel but she was eventually laid off: "My boss didn't think women should smoke or wear slacks." Her next job was in a pizza parlor:

I was hired to make the pizzas and I'd make them up front where everybody could see. I was kinda heavy-set, then, and the creepy guy that hired me, who was about fifty and no joy to look at, was always giving me shit about being fat. He would say, "I'm gonna put you out back because you can cook but you don't look so good." I'd also have to go in the back to mix the sauces and he would come back there and taunt me about having big breasts; but I was so broke that I wasn't in a position to quit—an old story.

One evening I was working at the front counter and he came up behind me and grabbed my breasts saying something about their size in front of a whole line full of customers. I was blown away I was so embarrassed, but then when it didn't stop I was furious. Without thinking I turned around and grabbed his balls, saying they were big too. He got real angry and went in the back room. Later he threatened to fire me on the spot. He didn't, though, because he couldn't replace me so easy.

After that he would avoid me and he wouldn't talk to me except to take potshots at me when people were in earshot; it didn't matter, workers or customers. I couldn't stand it. It also made me sick the way he treated the other women. He'd feel them up and abuse them and push them around. They really needed the money, so they'd just try and laugh it off. He threatened to fire them all the time. He even short-changed me on my next paycheck, which was my last paycheck. I was going to talk to the Labor Board or something, but I was so angry I just walked out.

My next job was as a night cook in a nursing home. I wore a dress but then I switched to a chef's uniform, which is much more practical. When it's on a man it's okay, but if it's on a woman men don't like it. I saw the administrator about once a week, and when he saw the uniform he sent word through the supervisor to take it off. Then a few days later the administrator came down to the kitchen just as I was going from the stockroom carrying a fifty-pound bag of potatoes and two number ten cans of vegetables. It was a lot of weight, and there's a law in New York that a woman can only carry forty pounds or something. Anyways, I was walking through and I saw him start to bawl me out and then change his mind when he realized he'd have to help carry it. Right after that while I'm in hearing distance he tells the supervisor that he doesn't approve of the way I walk, that it isn't ladylike.

Brink is presently unemployed. She draws continually and dreams of art school. "I could do it if I could find a chef's job because it pays good, but they keep me out because I'm a woman and I'm different. I've just turned eighteen, but in terms of work I feel like a forty-five-year-old washed-out woman."

The sexual harassment of young females extends to all jobs, regardless of whether or not they involve wages. Each year, for example, a few of Maryland's brightest high school seniors who show an interest in civics are selected to serve as pages at the Maryland General Assembly in Annapolis. The purpose of this program is to give students practical, on-the-job experience of government; in 1976, however, it turned out that this practical experience for the female pages primarily involved a big dose of sexual harassment. Eighteen-year-old Sara Arthur from Lutherville was involved with the program that year:

Secret service, legislators, state troopers, it didn't matter, they all did it. One trooper was always saying very loudly that he thought I was good-looking and he was always staring at me in a way that bothered me. I felt the same kind of staring from the delegates. One night I was stationed at the door in back and this one delegate got obnoxious. Finally, he said, "At twelve o'clock my friend's going to drop his drawers and all you virgins better turn your heads." Another time a delegate grabbed a page and turned to another delegate, saying, "Do you think I could be arrested on the floor of the legislature for rape?"

A few of the delegates were quite insinuating. There were about five who were real hard-core and who were more or less taking advantage of the situation, but the others didn't stop them.

The situation reached a crisis when Sara's roommate accepted a ride home from one of the delegates, who turned into a side street and began to force his attentions.

Luckily, Mrs. Connelly, the coordinator for the pages, had seen my roommate get in his car and she followed them. When she saw the car parked she told him to take her right home. My roommate said the man screamed at her to keep quiet. She was really shaken up and scared, but a group of us went to Mrs. Connelly. She talked to the Speaker, who reprimanded the delegate. It didn't stop him. The same day he gave my roommate his card with a note for her to write him because he wanted to make amends. It was so phony, he asked her not to put her return address on the envelope.

The female pages were angered all over again but eventually decided they wouldn't do anything else. "We were afraid and we weren't sure we had the right to be upset. They were higher up, they were important people for us. It was so hard in the face of that to know that sometimes they would call us just to see us walk down the aisle. The women delegates didn't do that to the boys. I just couldn't believe some of those men had gotten elected. I wouldn't work in government now for anything."

Sexual harassment of female workers in traditional jobs constitutes a successful coercion that ensures the maintenance of male control at work. This emerges clearly in an examination of the broad patterns of aggression and their overall effects. However, the full impact of this behavior is probably best comprehended by the experiences of the young female worker. Harassment of them, like that of all working women, is obviously both a cause and an effect of their position in the labor market. Their reactions to flee the aggression because of their powerlessness zeros right in on the origins of working women's lifelong, self-defeating market-behavior patterns. The overwhelming devastation is often best articulated at this age, when they have not yet become desensitized and do not yet accept it as "part of the job." They also further articulate an overwhelming sense of loss when they see older women role models accept it, or become resigned to it. Their initial interest in work is transformed by pain or fear into hopelessness. The pattern of female submission thus begins at an early age.

PART TWO

It is better to have a system that abets justice to people
who have been denied recourse for a long time;
I have never been persuaded by the argument
that because you promote recourse it will be abused.

—Aileen Hernandez
Original Commissioner
Equal Opportunity Employment Commission

7
The Law:
Civil Remedies

Working women have sought legal redress from sexual harassment on the job since early 1974 in nearly every imaginable form of civil legal action; this includes unemployment hearings, private suits, human rights complaints, and federal-law suits brought under Title VII jurisdiction. These actions comprise a broad legal front that has begun to move the whole question of the illegality of male sexual aggression and coercion of women at work into the nation's courts.

At the federal level the battle is poised on the issue of whether sexual harassment is bona fide sex discrimination and can be prosecuted under Title VII; decisions have gone both ways, there are at least three cases under appeal, and the issue could go all the way to the Supreme Court for a final decision. In the meantime, private suits are being filed under the aegis of a variety of legal sanctions; human rights commissions are fighting harassment as a violation of civil rights; and unemployment boards in numerous states are arbitrating the question whether women have a right to be compensated because of unemployment due to harassment. Cases in all these areas are being both won and lost, still more are pending, and even more are currently being filed.

In the matter of unemployment insurance, the specific question at issue is whether or not sexual harassment qualifies as good cause for a woman to leave her job. All the states demand that this requirement be met before a worker who voluntarily leaves her job can collect benefits. State laws vary in their definition of "good cause." There is, of course, no state that has a specific provision against sexual harassment. However, according to Laura Perlman, a member of the Manpower Administration, women have begun to lobby for new interpretations of the good-cause proviso by asking unemployment insurance administrators to make judgments about employer attitudes and practices that women consider unfair enough to make them quit their jobs."[1]

Harold Kasper, Director of the Unemployment Insurance Division of the New York State Department of Labor, has said that sexual harassment is "good cause for leaving a job," adding, "If true we would pay benefits without question. But it's one of the toughest cases to handle. It's a question of credibility. Where we would have witnesses, we would tend, without question, to throw the case to the claimant."[2] Despite this statement, though, and despite the fact that she did have witnesses, Carmita Wood's request for unemployment compensation from New York state was denied. The reason given was that her first application listed the reason for leaving her job as personal. Although she later appealed the decision carefully explaining her humiliation, embarrassment, and fear of being accused of libel and presented an outstanding work record and the sworn testimony of three witnesses to the sexual harassment she had experienced—the New York State board never reversed its decision that she did not have a good cause.

At the same time the New York case was being denied, a similar claim in California was being upheld. In that case a San Jose woman applied for unemployment benefits, asserting she had been forced to quit her job because of a history of sexual misconduct on the part of her boss. He had, she said, in addition to making sexual advances continually, made crude, vulgar, and sexist remarks to her, and told his friends and male customers

166

she would be willing to comply with their sexual requests if the price was right. The California Unemployment Insurance Board first denied unemployment benefits because the "claimant voluntarily left her employment without good cause." Indicative of the attitude behind that decision, a male referee had asked the claimant whether she didn't think that "today's modern world requires that females in business and industry have a little tougher attitude towards life in general."[3]

Rina Rosenberg, Director of the Commission on Women for Santa Clara County, to whom the complainant then applied for help, said, "That is a remark clearly displaying the referee's lack of sensitivity towards women." She wrote a letter to the Sacramento Appeals Board and the board reversed the previous ruling, holding that "the relationship between the claimant and her employer had ramifications for exceeding the normal employer-employee relationship . . . at a given point in time it became impossible for the claimant to endure the situation any longer." The Appeals Board subsequently ruled "the claimant had a compelling reason for leaving work and, therefore, is not disqualified for benefits."[4]

Concerning the important question of whether or not women can collect unemployment insurance when they are forced to leave their jobs because of sexual harassment, the emerging trend is that they can, if they carefully document their case and can successfully overcome the bias of male referees. Thousands of claims will nevertheless have to be filed before a working woman can rest assured that her unemployment claim of "good cause" due to sexual harassment will become just as valid as poor ventilation and inadequate lighting are now.

Human rights commissions are state or city government agencies charged with enforcing human rights acts which ban discrimination on the basis of race, sex, national origin, and religion (and sometimes age and physical handicaps). They are enforcement agencies empowered to bring opposing parties together in an effort at reconcilia-

167

tion; and, depending upon the state or city charter, they can also be empowered to prosecute alleged violators. Countless numbers of working women have used these agencies to put forward their complaints about sexual harassment at work, and there is no area in the country today that does not have some such complaint in progress.

The largest award to date was won by Barbara Taibi in April 1978 after the New York State Human Rights Commission effected a $10,000 settlement with the Monsanto Textiles Company. Taibi, a former secretary in the advertising department, had charged Monsanto with sexual harassment that included derogatory remarks, sexual innuendos and sexual advances. Upon signing the finding of probable cause in favor of Taibi, Werner H. Kramarsky, the New York State Commissioner for Human Rights, commented, "Sexual harassment is a violation of a women's right to equal working conditions. The assertion of that right will be enforced by this agency."

Another of these complaints, and perhaps the most sensational, was filed with the Minnesota Department of Human Rights on April 1, 1975, by Marti Borneman against the Bloomington, Minnesota, Chief of Police, James Brekken. Bloomington is the third largest city in Minnesota and the complaint eventually involved the highest levels of city government. As a result it caused a furor among the city's 80,000 citizens. The controversy continued for months.

Borneman, a twenty-seven-year-old police clerk, initially filed the complaint because "the Chief wanted me to go out with him and he wouldn't take no for an answer." She said that when she continued to reject these advances a pattern of harassment began in December 1974, "when a printout on sick leave was required of me. One Captain asked me why I was sick so much; he said, 'The Chief wants to know.'" According to Borneman, "they began to pick my work apart," but it wasn't until March 1975 that the harassment became quite overt. She said, "On March twenty-sixth another female police clerk asked me to transfer. She also wanted to know why it mattered so much who touched me. I talked to another Captain and he said, 'Marti, quit your job and move out of Bloomington. The man is sick and once you are on his list, he'll never leave you alone.' "

On the day she signed the complaint, Borneman said, "One of the Sergeants bent over and pushed his buttocks into me so I was pushed against the wall. Later I got my first obscene phone call. The man calling said, 'Marti, if you won't f—k the chief, how about f—king me?' "

Borneman said the harassment not only continued but got worse after the complaint. "On April fourteenth City Manager Pidgeon walked into the lunchroom and called me a frog. The same day one police officer called me a nigger. I remember one officer going by and saying, 'You know, Marti, if women weren't so good at screwin' there'd be a bounty on their heads.' " Borneman feels strongly that all the harassment she experienced (thirty-seven separate incidents) was because of the chief: "Brekken is a pro at it. If he wants you harassed he can get anybody in the department to help. And, let's face it, when the top man in the police department says do something, you usually do it." Borneman added that she thought things were done to "whip up people's feelings" against her. "An example of that," she said, "was the way hundreds of copies of articles with City Manager Pidgeon saying the charges were unfounded were distributed in everyone's mailbox."

City Manager John Pidgeon has refused to comment. In July, when he transferred Borneman out of the Police Department, he said she was no longer doing her work in the department and that she was negatively affecting the work of others there.

Police Chief Brekken, who is forty-four and separated, has been with the department twenty-one years and has been chief since 1972. He said, "The Borneman complaint is a vicious lie. The reports in the paper are inaccurate; it's nothing but character assassination. There is no hard evidence for any of the allegations she made." When asked about Borneman's charges of repeated harassment, he said, "It's all her imagination." Brekken is contemptuous of the Human Rights Commission because "it accepts probable cause and not hard facts. If I, as a police officer, could accept that my job would be a lot easier." Brekken also said that under Minnesota law the charge Borneman made against him is illegal because it can't be made against an individual, only an employer. He pointed out that in his situation the employer is the city of Bloomington and City Manager John Pidgeon and "that's why the City Manager conducted an investigation which found nothing—it found no basis for her accusations."

The actual chronology of events precipitated by the complaint is as follows. Borneman filed her complaint with the Minnesota Department of Human Rights alleging that she had been subjected to harassment and threats of discharge because she refused the sexual advances of Police Chief James Brekken on April 1, 1975. On April 23 and 24 City Manager John Pidgeon held closed hearings attended by himself, Brekken, Borneman, and their respective lawyers; on April 28 he ruled Borneman's complaint unfounded.

On May 19 the Minnesota Human Rights Department ruled "probable cause" that Brekken had committed "unfair discriminatory practices" against Borneman and Brekken was given sixty days in which to initiate a conciliation conference before a complaint would be issued. On July 7 the Human Rights Commission complaint was amended to add Bloomington's Mayor, City Manager, and City Council members as defendants; the human rights officials explained that when a settlement is reached, city officials must implement it.

Three days later Bloomington's Mayor Robert Benedict announced he would ask the City Council to suspend

Brekken with pay until the end of the conciliation procedures with the Human Rights Commission. He said he would also seek a re-examination of the City Manager's investigation. On the following day the City Manager notified Borneman she would be transferred at the end of one week to the Parks and Recreation Department. Borneman immediately filed a second complaint with the Human Rights Department alleging reprisal for her first complaint.

On July 14 the President of the Bloomington Police Officers' Association presented the City Council with a letter supporting the Mayor's motion to suspend Brekken and to re-examine the City Manager's investigation of the Borneman complaint. The Council rejected the motion to suspend the Chief and tabled the motion to re-examine the investigation.

On July 21 city and state officials met for a second round of conciliation sessions. The City Manager did not attend.

On August 5 the Human Rights Commission turned the complaint over to the State Attorney General after city officials failed to participate "satisfactorily" in conciliation "despite repeated extensions of the deadline." A commission spokesman said a full public hearing would be scheduled in a matter of months and at that time the attorney general's office would represent Borneman and the state. The hearing would be presided over by an officer to be appointed by the Human Rights Commission with authority similar to that of a trial judge. The hearing officer also has the authority to award a maximum of $500 in punitive damages and require Brekken to write a letter of apology or sign an agreement to discontinue the probable harassment. The state was reported to be seeking the maximum in damages and a letter of apology.

In late August the City of Bloomington sued the Human Rights Commission to dismiss charges against Brekken because the Commission did not make investigative material available to the city. The suit further alleged that the complaint was not within the state commission's jurisdiction.

The Human Rights Commission has announced it will appeal any adverse decision from the Hennepin County District Court, where the case is presently pending.

If the countersuit by the City of Bloomington fails to persuade the court of its claims, Marti Borneman will eventually have the solace of seeing her alleged harasser prosecuted by the state and of knowing that the full authority of the government of Minnesota is behind her, advancing her cause to the limit of the law. This is exactly what Borneman wants. She has frequently said, "I don't care about money. I'm not after that. What I want is justice, simple justice and that's all."

Many victims of sexual harassment want the same thing, but there are some who feel that the only way this can be fully achieved is for punitive damages to be paid as a result of injuries from having either quit or been fired from their jobs, with all the attendant consequences: financial loss, destroyed reputation, physical distress, and/or unemployable status.

This redress via private suits can follow a variety of legal strategies and can be brought under a wide variety of legal sanctions. Two examples of these kinds of cases are mentioned in the chapter on professional women. Virginia Morgheim is seeking a million dollars in damages to her career as a broadcast journalist as a result of a broken contract and Madeline Leon Salas de Vila has won $70,000—$20,000 in actual damages and $50,000 in punitive damages—as a result of a jury verdict that she was, in fact, denied due process on her job at the San Juan, Puerto Rico, Cooperative Development Agency.

A third case had been won by Olga Monge against the Beebe Rubber Company of New Hampshire. Monge, a married mother of three, was a schoolteacher in Costa Rica before immigrating to the United States in 1964. About a year later she moved to New Hampshire, where

172

she attended college evenings in order to teach in America, and where, on September 1968, in order to meet college expenses, she began working at wages of $1.84 per hour on a conversion machine at the Beebe Rubber Company. At the time of her hiring, she was allegedly told that if she worked well she would get better jobs with better pay. And she was also employed in a union shop, so that she joined the union as required, becoming subject to union rules including seniority.

After three months without incident Monge applied to fill an opening on a press machine at $2.79 per hour. She testified that her foreman told her that if she wanted the job she would have to be "nice."[5] She got the job and testified that the foreman then asked her to go out with him, which she refused to do. The machine was subsequently shut down, and she was placed on a lower-paying machine at $1.99 per hour. At the same time she had all overtime removed, although no one else did, and she was informed that if she needed overtime she could clean the washrooms and sweep the floors. She did this and testified that the foreman ridiculed her as she performed these tasks. Shortly after this the foreman fired her (at 2 A.M.). After complaining to the union she was reinstated with a warning.

Subsequent to the foreman's advances, Monge testified that the personnel manager had visited her at home about some annoying telephone calls she was receiving. In the course of their conversation he reportedly told her he knew her foreman used his position to force his attentions on the female employees under his authority and he asked her "not to make trouble."[6]

Soon after this Monge entered the hospital for an operation. After returning to work she had a relapse and was found unconscious in the women's room and was taken to the hospital. The company records show her hospitalized for the next four days, including August 8. Nothing is shown in these records regarding the next two days, but they do show her absent on August 11, 12, and

173

13 without having called in. On August 13, 1969, the personnel manager sent her a letter stating that since she failed to report for work for three consecutive days without notification to the company, she was "deemed a voluntary quit,"[7] although there was evidence both from the foreman and the plaintiff that she did in fact call in on Sunday, August 10, to report that she was still sick.

Monge sued for breach of an employment contract. Trial by jury resulted in a verdict for her in the amount of $2500 in actual damages and damages due to mental suffering. The verdict was upheld on appeal, the judgment of the court holding that "a termination by the employer of a contract of employment at will which is motivated by bad faith or malice or based on retaliation is not in the best interest of the economic system or the public good and constitutes a breach of the employment contract. . . . The foreman's overtures and the capricious firing at 2 A.M., the seeming manipulation of job assignments, and the apparent connivance of the personnel manager in this course of events all support the jury's conclusion that the dismissal was maliciously motivated."[8] However, the appeal did result in a cutting of the settlement to about $1500 in actual damages, on the grounds that the rest of the settlement was attributable to mental suffering and such damages are not generally recoverable in a contract action.

It should be clear from the preceding that one must assess each case individually, review the appropriate channels available to redress the grievances, and then adopt a legal strategy which best matches the hoped-for results. In Olga Monge's case a contract action did not best suit the desired ends. If she had, in fact, started out to seek punitive damages for mental suffering in addition to actual damages as a result of the discrimination she experienced, a private lawsuit still would have been the best option provided it pursued or combined a legal sanction more easily affording punitive damages. If, however, she had been interested only in recovering money based on actual damages and in rectifying the situation, she might have chosen a third option that could have resulted in the same $2500 sum.

This third option is the relatively new legal course, which can be pursued under the terms of the 1964 Civil Rights Act and which sits midway between the two extremes of the generally minimal, carefully proscribed intervention of human rights agencies and the private lawsuit that seeks punitive damages. Popularly called Title VII after that section of the act which prohibits employment discrimination on the basis of sex, this legal course permits a victim of sex discrimination to win back wages —the amount of money she would have earned if she had not been discriminated against dating from two years prior to filing charges up to the end of her successful lawsuit. It also permits her to sue for reinstatement.

The Title VII statute is the farthest-reaching law in the area of employment discrimination on the basis of sex and, accordingly, holds the greatest potential for forcing change in employment practices. The act has already brought about a new realization regarding job discrimination, as evidenced by the following excerpt from a discussion at a 1970 Senate Committee:

In 1964, employment discrimination tended to be viewed as a series of isolated and distinguishable events, for the most part due to ill-will on the part of some identifiable individual or organization. It was thought that a scheme that stressed conciliation rather than compulsory process would be most appropriate for the resolution of this essentially "human" problem, and that litigation would be necessary only on an occasional basis in the event of determined recalcitrance. This view has not been borne out by experience.

Employment discrimination, as viewed today, is a far more complex and pervasive phenomenon. Experts familiar with the subject generally describe the problem in terms of "systems" and "effects" rather than simply intentional wrongs . . . In short, the problem is one whose resolution in many instances requires not only expert assistance, but also the technical perception that a problem exists in the first place, and that the system complained of is unlawful.[9]

Susan C. Ross explains in *The Rights of Women: An American Civil Liberties Handbook,* that this new realization of job discrimination is the result of three key concepts that developed under Title VII: the class effects of job discrimination, the necessity to challenge sex segregation, and the neutral-rule doctrine.[10] The class effects concept is the strategy behind class actions. Discrimination is a problem by definition affecting large numbers of a class: women. The concept, then, encourages fighting policies rather than individual decisions, with the end result that a great deal of pressure can be applied on employers to change the present job situation.

The second concept, that of fighting sex segregation, is simply the result of an emerging consciousness that this is the primary manifestation of employment bias. It matters little, for instance, to argue for equal pay for equal work when the reality is that most women don't do the work men do because they are systematically segregated into lower-paying "women's" jobs.

The final concept is often called by lawyers the neutral-rule doctrine because it refers to any employment policy which may appear neutral but which in fact adversely affects employment opportunities of women or of a minority group. In other words, it is the effect, not the intention, of the policy that is discriminatory.

It is important to understand these concepts to grasp the legal questions presently snarling a broad use of Title VII in the area of sexual harassment of working women, although this situation is beginning to improve. In July, 1977, the United States District Court of Appeals in Washington, D.C. held that proven sexual harassment comes under the protection of Title VII. As a result, Paulette G. Barnes, who charged her job with the U.S. Environmental Protection Agency was abolished when she refused sex with her boss, has received $18,000 in back pay and attorney fees from an out-of-court settlement negotiated by her attorney, Linda Singer.[11] Similarly, in April, 1978, U.S. District Court Judge Sherman G. Finesilver found the Johns-Manville Corporation guilty of sex discrimination after a former employee, Mrs. Mary Heelan, was fired when she refused sex with her boss.[12]

However there are at the present time an additional four widely reported cases of sexual harassment invoking Title VII. All have been under appeal, three as a result of decisions against the women. In order of their chronological appearance on the legal scene these cases are: Jane Corne, Geneva De Vane v. Bausch & Lomb, Inc. and Leon Price; Diane Williams v. William Saxbe, *et al;* Margaret Miller v. Bank of America; and Adrienne E. Tomkins v. Public Service Electric and Gas Co. and Herbert D. Reppin.

Jane Corne and Geneva De Vane of Tucson, Arizona, who are former clerical employees of Bausch & Lomb under Leon Price's supervision, filed their Title VII complaint alleging sex discrimination in employment due to repeated unsolicited and unwelcome sexual advances from Price, to the point where their employment conditions became so onerous that they were forced to resign. They alleged that the supervisor's sexual advances were directed to other female employees and that cooperation with Price's allegedly illegal activities resulted in favored employment.[13] They claimed the advances constituted a condition of employment that discriminated by sex in violation of Title VII because putting a male in a supervisory position over female employees, where the supervisor persistently takes unsolicited and unwelcome sexual liberties with the female employees, results in the creation of a sex-discriminatory condition and a limitation that tends to deprive the women of equal employment opportunities.

Bausch & Lomb and Price moved to dismiss the complaint, arguing the women failed to prove a claim within the scope of Title VII. The issue was also raised that the women had not exhausted state remedies, which is required before Title VII action can proceed. The EEOC, the enforcement agency for Title VII, filed an amicus curiae (friend of the court) brief in opposition to the company and the supervisor's motion to dismiss.

United States District Court Judge William C. Frey held the main focus of the women's suit to be the issue of sexual harassment as discrimination under Title VII and subsequently ruled that it was not, arguing:

Nothing in the complaint alleges . . . that the conduct complained of was company directed policy . . . Mr. Price's conduct appears to be nothing more than a personal proclivity, peculiarity or mannerism. By his alleged sexual advances, Mr. Price was satisfying a personal urge. Certainly, no employer policy is here involved. . . .

It would be ludicrous to hold that the sort of activity involved here was contemplated by the Act because to do so would mean that if the conduct complained of was directed equally to males there would be no basis for suit. Also, an outgrowth of holding such activity to be actionable under Title VII would be a potential federal lawsuit every time any employee made amorous or sexually oriented advances toward another. The only sure way an employer could avoid such charges would be to have employees who were asexual.[14]

Corne and De Vane appealed Judge Frey's decision in May 1975. The appellant's brief filed by attorney Heather Sigworth argues: "The language of Title VII is sufficiently broad to define a male supervisor's unsolicited sexual advances to a female subordinate as an unlawful employment practice." She cites the act itself to the effect that it reads:

"It shall be an unlawful employment practice for an employer to . . . *discriminate against any individual* with respect to his . . . *conditions* . . . of employment *because* of such individual's . . . sex . . . or to limit, segregate or classify his employees . . . in any way which would deprive *or tend to deprive* any individual of employment opportunities *or otherwise adversely*

affect his status as an employee, because of such individual's
... sex" [Emphasis is hers].

It is difficult to see [Sigworth continues] why putting a
male in a supervisory position over female employees, where the
male supervisor persistently takes unsolicited and unwelcome
sexual liberties with the female employees as a matter of
course is not the creation of a sex discriminatory employment condition, and a limitation that tends to deprive the
women of employment opportunities. The women are limited
to the choice of putting up with being manhandled, or being
out of work. Presumably Defendant is not contending that it
places women in supervisory positions over men, and permits
the women to make sexual advances, all in order to avoid
discriminating because of sex.

Congress, in forbidding employers to discriminate against
individuals because of their sex, intended to eliminate virtually all forms of discrimination against women. . . . And, as
the court in *Sprogis v. United Air Lines, Inc.* . . . put it, Title
VII subjects to scrutiny all "irrational impediments to job
opportunities and enjoyment which have plagued women in
the past." It is hard to imagine a more irrational or un-
warranted condition of employment than that alleged in this
case. Women employees, in order to be productive workers,
must be allowed to enjoy their employment, as men do, free
of unsolicited verbal and physical sexual advances directed
toward them simply because of their sex. And, as Plaintiffs
contend, the choice between frequent unsolicited sexual advances and being unemployed has a significant and clearly un-
warranted effect on employment opportunities. Congress in
enacting Title VII clearly intended to prevent the toleration
of such sexually motivated conduct from being a term and
condition of employment. For if Title VII does not provide
such elementary protection against sexually motivated conduct,
its promise to women is virtually without meaning.

It is irrelevant that the prohibited acts are not a policy of
a defendant corporation if they are engaged in by their supervisor. The Company is, of course, responsible for insuring
that those whom it places in authority do not utilize the
power they are thus granted to discriminate in violation of
Title VII. . . .

It is understandable that many of the cases decided under

Title VII involve company-wide policies rather than complaints against individual agents of employers. Such cases are simpler to prove (from a Plaintiff's point of view), affect larger numbers of employees, and therefore involve larger damages. It does not follow, as the District Court states in its opinion, that a discriminatory act must be pursuant to a company policy in order to constitute an unlawful employment practice. The EEOC routinely finds reasonable cause to believe that unlawful discrimination has occurred when the act complained of expresses simply isolated prejudice. See, e.g., EEOC Decision No. 72-1301 (March 8, 1972) [employee terminated for writing a book expressing religious views distasteful to his employer—unlawful religious discrimination]; EEOC Decision No. 71-2613 [district sales manager's refusal to hire female because of her husband's illness when male salesmen employed have sick wives—unlawful sex discrimination]. The courts have agreed that when supervisor's discretionary decisions rather than policy result in discrimination, the discrimination is unlawful. See, e.g., *Baxter v. Savannah Sugar Refining Corp.*, 8F.E.P.84 (5th Cir. 1974) [blacks excluded from management on supervisor's discretion]; *Leisner v. New York Telephone Co.*, 5 F.E.P. 733 (S.D.N.Y. 1973) [females excluded from management on supervisory discretion]. . . .

In summary: both the language of Title VII, and the cases interpreting it, make clear that a condition of employment that in fact discriminates by sex, and which presents a fairly serious impediment to equal employment opportunity is a violation of the Act. Such is the situation where a male supervisor directs unwanted sexual attentions at female employees with such frequency that they become an onerous condition of employment.[15]

On April 20, 1976, United States District Court Judge Charles R. Richey of Washington, D.C., ruled that sexual harassment was a violation of Title VII, and for the first time a female victim of sexual harassment was successful in winning a complaint against her harasser and his employer under the statue. Diane Williams, a Public

Information Officer in the Community Relations Service of the Justice Department, as we have seen, filed her Title VII complaint alleging sex discrimination in employment because she said she had rejected the sexual advances of her supervisor, Harvey Brinson, and that Brinson subsequently engaged in a continuing pattern and practice of harassment and humiliation that resulted in her termination.[16]

The defendants, the then Attorney General of the United States, William Saxbe, and the Director of the CRS of the Department of Justice, Harvey Brinson, moved to dismiss on the grounds that the complaint was not sex discrimination as defined by Title VII. Their argument contained two major points: (1) No sex discrimination occurred because anyone, not just women, can be made subject to "carnal demands" and (2) the case was not the result of employer policy but rather an isolated personal incident which should not be the concern of the courts. The defendants also included in their analysis the argument that sexual harassment was akin to other sexual classifications, like hair length for men, having only an insignificant effect on employment opportunities.

In handing down his opinion Judge Richey categorically answered each argument put forth by the defendants. In rejecting the "anyone can be made subject to sexual demands" arguments he found that sex discrimination under Title VII "does not require that the discriminatory policy or practice depend upon a characteristic peculiar to one of the genders. That a rule, regulation, practice or policy is applied on the basis of gender is alone sufficient for a finding of sex discrimination."[17] In this instance, he argued, the fact was that the plaintiff's supervisor created an "artificial barrier to employment which was placed before one gender and not the other, despite the fact that both genders were similarly situated."[18]

Richey based his decision, in part, on *Phillips v.*

Martin Marietta Corp., in which the Supreme Court, "while vacating the decision of the Fifth Circuit, accepted the Fifth Circuit's finding that there was discrimination even though it was not based upon a characteristic peculiar to one gender." (The Fifth Circuit had held that a policy which allowed the hiring of men who had preschool children for certain positions, but not allowing the hiring of women with preschool children for the same position, was sex discrimination in violation of Title VII.)

He also cited *Sprogis v. United Air Lines Inc.*, which concerned a no-marriage rule providing that stewardesses had to be unmarried when hired and remain unmarried under penalty of discharge. Richey argued, "The no-marriage rule could have been applied to men as well as women, since both are capable of marriage. The criteria of marriage can also not be said to be a characteristic peculiar to one of the genders. Nevertheless, the court held that the rule resulted in sex discrimination in violation of Title VII. . . . The court found it sufficient that the rule was applied to women and not to men, despite the fact that they were similarly situated."[19]

In answering the defendant's argument that the Williams case was not the result of an employer policy but rather an isolated incident, Richey ruled: ". . . if this was a policy or practice of plaintiff's supervisor, then it was the agency's policy or practice. . . ."[20] In response to another of the defendant's arguments—that the courts would become embroiled in sorting out the social life of the employees of the numerous federal agencies—he argued: ". . . the decision of the Court that plaintiff has stated a cause of action under Title VII will not have the feared result defendants urge. What the statute is concerned with is not interpersonal disputes between employees."[21] As in this instance, he said, the case reveals the "statutory prohibition" of a discriminatory imposition of employment by the supervisor of an office or agency.

Finally, in the matter of the defendant's argument

that sexual harassment is insignificant, Richey ruled: "Assuming Title VII permits a weighing of the effect of a particular policy or regulation, this Court could not find the instant policy or practice to have an insignificant effect."[22]

The conclusion of Judge Richey's decision reads: "Retaliatory actions of a male supervisor taken because a female employee declined his sexual advances, constitutes sex discrimination within the definitional parameters of Title VII of the Civil Rights Act of 1964."[23] He then went on to uphold a finding by a Justice Department Hearing Examiner that Harvey Brinson and hence the Justice Department had so discriminated against their former employee Diane Williams. The government has appealed the decision.

Four months later, as if the Williams decision had never occurred, United States District Court Judge Spencer Williams, in trying a case similar to Diane Williams', defined the issue to be "whether Title VII was intended to hold an employer liable for what is essentially the isolated and unauthorized sex misconduct of one employee to another."[24] He went on to rule that it was not. Margaret Miller, a black NCR operator, had filed a Title VII claim of sex discrimination against her former employer, Bank of America, alleging her white male operations supervisor at the bank promised her a better job if she would be sexually "cooperative" and caused her dismissal when she refused.[25]

The Bank of America moved to dismiss on the grounds that a supervisor's sexual advances are not a violation of Title VII. It cited the *Corne* case "as the sole authority on the issue" and then argued that under that decision the "only possible genuine issue of material fact which could be tried is whether the Bank had a policy of condoning, supporting or allowing such sexual advances."[26] The Bank then introduced evidence of an Employer Relations Department that was established to investigate employee complaints, including those of sexual advances, to the effect that the Bank did not have an employer policy fostering such behavior.

Judge Williams completely concurred. In his opinion the *Corne* case was the authority. He noted the decision in Williams v. Saxbe but completely disregarded its ruling that a case alleging a practice of a supervisor's advances to female employees was, if true, in effect employer policy and hence required a factual determination. Margaret Miller did allege this to be her supervisor's practice and she did introduce evidence from another female employee that she also had witnessed this practice, but Williams ruled this allegation irrelevant, choosing to accept the Bank's stated employer policy. He further found that the Bank could not be held culpable for its supervisor's conduct because the plaintiff failed to bring the matter to the Bank's attention by means of an internal grievance. This judgment completely ignores the fact that the plaintiff was summarily fired. Judge Williams goes on to concur with *Corne* that it is "ludicrous" to hold that sexual harassment was contemplated by Title VII and adds his own philosophical musings to the effect that:

it would not be difficult to foresee a federal challenge based on alleged sex-motivated considerations of the complainant's superior in every case of a lost promotion, transfer, demotion or dismissal. And who is to say what degree of sexual cooperation would found a Title VII claim? It is conceivable, under plaintiff's theory, that flirtations of the smallest order would give rise to liability. The attraction of males to females and females to males is a natural sex phenomenon and it is probable that this attraction plays at least a subtle part in most personnel decisions. Such being the case, it would seem wise for the Courts to refrain from delving into these matters short of specific factual allegations describing an employer policy which in its application imposes or permits a consistent, as distinguished from isolated, sex-biased discrimination on a definable employee group.[27]

184

Margaret Miller is appealing the decision.

The last case to be noted here is that of Adrienne Tomkins v. Public Service Electric & Gas and Herbert D. Reppin; Tomkins is seeking compensatory and punitive damages and equitable relief via a legal strategy that seeks to proceed under the authority of Title VII. Tomkins, a former office worker for the Newark, New Jersey, offices of PSE&G alleges that after she became eligible for a promotion to secretary her supervisor, Herbert Reppin, requested she lunch with him to discuss her prospects with the firm. At that time she alleges he made sexual advances and that she was detained by him against her will through economic threats and physical force. She also alleges her complaints to the company about the incident resulted in a transfer to a less desirable position in the company, and retaliation against her in the form of disciplinary layoffs, threats of demotion, salary cuts, and eventual termination.[28] In sum, Tomkins' complaint alleges sex discrimination under Title VII because of her superior's sexual advances coupled with his threats of reprisal and the company's subsequent retaliation and ultimate termination because of her complaints.

The defendants moved to dismiss on the now-familiar grounds that the complaint was not actionable under Title VII.

The lawsuit itself raised two issues—the sexual harassment and the conduct of an employer after a complaint of such harassment—to be determined as sex discrimination within the meaning of Title VII. United States District Court Judge Herbert J. Stern responded to both issues in his opinion.

On the first issue he ruled in company with *Corne* and *Miller,* completely ignoring *Williams.* A reading of his opinion on this issue is instructive:

Title VII was enacted in order to remove those artificial barriers to full employment which are based upon unjust and

185

long-encrusted prejudice. Its aim is to make careers open to talents irrespective of race or sex. It is not intended to provide a federal tort remedy for what amounts to physical attack motivated by sexual desire on the part of a supervisor and which happened to occur in a corporate corridor rather than a back alley. In this instance the supervisor was male and the employee was female. But no immutable principle of psychology compels this alignment of parties. The gender lines might as easily have been reversed, or even not crossed at all. While sexual desire animated the parties, or at least one of them, the gender of each is incidental to the claim of abuse. Similarly, the pleadings in this case aver that the supervisor's advances were spurned. Had they been accepted, however, and plaintiff thereby preferred, could co-workers be heard to complain in federal court as well?

The abuse of authority by supervisors of either sex for personal purposes is an unhappy and recurrent feature of our social experience. . . . The EEOC [amicus curiae] urges that a contrary decision would not open the floodgates to litigation. The Commission argues that only sexual advances from a superior to a subordinate under the cloak of the superior's authority would be actionable under Title VII, and then only if such a practice contributed to an employment-related decision. But plaintiff's theory rests on the proposition, with which this Court concurs, that the power inherent in a position of authority is necessarily coercive. And, as the representative of the EEOC candidly conceded in oral argument, every sexual advance made by a supervisor would be made under the apparent cloak of that authority. Any subordinate knows that the boss is the boss whether a file folder or a dinner is at issue.

. . . If the plaintiff's view were to prevail, no superior could, prudently, attempt to open a social dialogue with any subordinate of either sex. An invitation to dinner could become an invitation to a federal lawsuit if a once harmonious relationship turned sour at some later time. And if an inebriated approach by a supervisor to a subordinate at the office Christmas party could form the basis of a federal lawsuit for sex discrimination if a promotion or a raise is later denied to the subordinate, we would need 4,000 federal trial judges instead of some 400.[29]

On the second issue Judge Stern ruled that "When a female employee registers a complaint of sexual abuse and the company chooses to fire her rather than investigate, the corporate response may constitute discrimination based on sex. In brief, it may reflect a conscious choice to favor the male employee over the female complainant on the ground that a male's services are more valuable than a female's. Such a preferential practice may violate the act even though the grievance procedures do not by their terms implicate characteristics peculiar to either gender. . . . Plaintiff must be permitted her day in Court on this issue."[30]

He accordingly granted the defendant's (Herbert D. Reppin's) motion to dismiss while denying the same motion to PSE&G. Adrienne Tomkins appealed the decision.

These four cases—two from the East, one from the Southwest, and one from the far West; two by black women and two by white women; three by clerical workers and one from a professional woman—have one common complaint: the loss of work due to sexual harassment by a male superior. Over and over the attitude "ludicrous" is applied to their arguments. The doctrine of the manifest destiny of male sexual aggression is also everywhere apparent, although it is couched in a seeming neutrality. Examples include Judge Frey's opinion in *Corne* that "an outgrowth of holding such activity [sexual harassment] to be actionable under Title VII would be a potential federal lawsuit every time *any* employee made amorous or sexually oriented advances . . ." or Judge Williams' argument in *Miller* that "flirtations of the smallest order would give rise to liability" or Judge Stern's reasoning that "no superior could, prudently, attempt to open a social dialogue with any subordinate of either sex."

The judges' arguments are pure obfuscation accomplished by translating sexual harassment into *all* amorous activity at work, by masking superior male authority at work as belonging to "either sex" that can be applied to "any employee," and by asserting that because sex is inevitable this doesn't have a thing to do with employer policy. In this light, the judges' comments are nothing less than gratuitous and irrelevant philosophical comments upholding the right of men to initiate sex and a fear that women will somehow storm the barricades if sexual harassment were to become actionable under Title VII. Moreover, their rationalizations are plainly indefensible alongside the arguments of the complainants:

1. Sexual harassment is not synonymous with all sexual activity any more than rape is synonymous with intercourse.

2. Liability is not widespread, but limited to supervisors who abuse the power granted them by their employers.

3. Either sex could theoretically engage in sexual harassment, but given the fact that the vast majority of managers, foremen, supervisors, and bosses in this country are males, the practice is a discriminatory one by men on their female subordinates.

4. Employer responsibility is not limited to formal policy statements by the company, but also includes what is actually done in its name. In addition, employers are responsible for the systematic exclusion of women from positions of authority. It is this policy which in the first place lays the ground for the practice of sexual harassment of female subordinates.

The pattern of pro-and-con decisions concerning sexual harassment is similar to a number of other issues within the scope of Title VII, which is only a ten-year-old field of law. In the past, when the courts of appeals have divided, resolution has only come from the Supreme Court; the issue of sexual harassment will probably go the same course. In assessing the outcome, John J. Pemberton Jr. says:

The objective criteria of defining employment discrimination is with an eye to the realities of the society. The Act is designed to get at any discrimination or differential treatment that distinguishes between members of the two sexes. Clearly, in an industrial setting in which men tend to be the supervisors this practice of sexual harassment tends to have a disparate impact. If you had a situation where women were mostly supervisors and you coupled that with a physical dominance on the part of women then the shoe might be on the other foot. But these things all get tested in terms of how they actually work. The very neutral requirement of a high school diploma, for example, is struck down because fewer blacks than whites have high school diplomas. Fewer females than males are supervisors and it really is as simple as that.

Pemberton, a professor of law at the University of San Francisco who was formerly with the EEOC, specializes in employment discrimination. In comparing the present decisions he ranks Richey's decisions as more convincing, explaining that the rationale used by the other judges to excuse supervisor misconduct is unique to sexual harassment. "The supervisor who uses racial epithets or who harasses minority employees in non-sexual ways or who discharges an employee in this context, these acts always result in the employer being held responsible."

"I just don't see how it can stand up," he adds. "In fact, that defense, that the employer is not responsible for supervisor-related, employment-related conduct is quite extraordinary in the Title VII context because the supervisor was hired to supervise and he was the employee's contact with the employer, his word was the employer's word as far as the employee's responsibilities were concerned."

This opinion by the former Executive Director of the New York American Civil Liberties Union has recently been borne out by the courts. The Court of Appeals for the third circuit has reversed the decision by Judge

189

Stern in the Tompkins case finding that sexual harassment is a valid cause of action under Title VII and it remanded the case to the District Court for trial on the merits.

Pemberton also rates the Richey decision as superior because it does not countenance the fear that affirmative findings of sexual harassment under Title VII will open a floodgate of litigation. "The fear is just not realistic given the fact the plaintiff carries the burden of proof." In terms of this burden, moreover, Pemberton counsels that victims will always do well to avail themselves of whatever grievance procedures are available: "Of course, all employees and women particularly don't believe they'll get a fair shake at these proceedings. Still, they should go through the motions. This makes the violation more clearly the intention of the employer if those remedies don't work. Also, it is relatively easier to convince the court that the grievance procedure has been unfair to the employee."

While the issue of sexual harassment under Title VII is winding its way through the courts, present attempts at redress under this statute continue. Although the EEOC has a three-year backlog in cases, in most instances you can pursue your case with a private lawyer after 180 days following filing. Efforts are hampered at this point, however, by a scarcity of willing lawyers. Some attorneys will take Title VII cases on a contingency basis, which means that they will take their legal fee from a portion of your earnings if your suit is successful. Title VII also allows the court to award attorney's fees, which is even better. Still, there are relatively too few attorneys willing to meet the demand, particularly when the case involves sexual harassment. For the present, feminist law firms and the EEOC (which maintains a list of Title VII lawyers) are among the practical routes to pursue. A long-range solution requires more lawyers to take these cases. Pemberton believes this will occur when there are "a lot more women lawyers who will understand this problem and take it seriously." Widespread legal redress may, thus, ultimately depend on a weakening of female job segregation, the same male division of the labor pool that sexual harassment helps to maintain.

8
Employers

The employer's role in the sexual harassment of working women is inescapable. In the first place, employers are responsible for promoting men over women. This provides men with the economic authority to practice coercion. Employers frequently further their complicity by turning a blind eye to the resulting widespread sexual harassment by their male managers. In addition, they may be complicitous by expecting these same male managers to conform to an unwritten policy of hiring only attractive and/or sexually compliant women. And, finally, if and when complaints of abuse are brought to the employer's attention, they may all too often harbor the harasser at the expense of the harassed to protect the company's name.

Sexist hiring policies are often overt. Robert Fitch, a former personnel analyst for Alameda County in Oakland, California, says, "As soon as I began working there my immediate supervisor told me whenever possible to hire an attractive [woman], a pretty one over an unattractive one." Many policies demand not only physical appeal but sexual complaisance as well. Employment services around the country, although off the record, are reporting these kinds of demands by prospective employers.

One personnel counselor, interviewed by Pat Michaels in a local San Francisco newspaper, refused to permit her name to be used because it might jeopardize her own employment opportunities. She had just quit her job with an agency in California. She said, "I was just a procurer, I wasn't a personnel administrator." She said the game now is to demand skills as well as sexual willingness. "They want a girl who not only will go out on dates with the customers for no overtime, but also one who types a hundred words a minute and takes seventy at shorthand." The personnel administrator went on to say that it was ironic, but as these demands have increased the wages for these workers have diminished. "A girl with typing and shorthand capability could get as much as $700 a month a year ago; today, the employers are more and more demanding promiscuous girls and the average salary is down to $450 a month."[1]

Some corporations and businesses are also turning to the underground press to recruit "swinging" female workers, the word *swinging* acting as a code word for sexually compliant. For this same news article Michaels did a spot check of the underground press in northern California. A University of California Ph.D. advertised: "I am offering a job to a female as a receptionist, who must be open-minded and a swinging chick. I am an advisor and counselor. She must be able to take messages, answer telephone with light typing from 18 to 26 years of age." Another ad said, "Swinging office gal wanted to answer phone. Some typing some phone." And there was this one: "Young lawyer seeks sharp young girl. The office is casual, friendly and relaxed. We work hard when it's time for work. We play hard the rest of the time. It's no place for nuns or prudes. Free thinking and liberal ways are a must."[2]

Rae (a psyeudonym) is a woman who has directly experienced the ways in which management may act to protect a supervisory male accused of harassment:

I used to work as a clerk at Cornell University. My boss was always sliding past me and putting his hand on my behind or he'd come into my office and put his arms around me while I was sitting at my desk. I'd say "Don't," but it just never sank in. Finally one day, he put his hand on my behind and I drew a line around myself and I said, "Anything inside this circle is mine. Don't touch it." He just laughed. When a girlfriend told him how nasty it was and that didn't bother him either, I decided to try and find another job.

One day I brought some different clothes into work to change into for an interview. Shortly before I had to leave, I put my bra on, which I didn't usually wear to work, and he came over and started snapping it. That made me boil. I was still mad when I came back to work after the interview, which was terrible, and when he asked me to do some work I said I was too busy. I did it, of course, I was just blowing off steam. Besides, I'd seen lots of the men that I work with do the same thing only much worse, using filthy language and yelling and screaming, and he always took it.

The next day he handed me a letter that had gone into my personnel file telling anybody who read my file that I was not what he would consider a really good worker . . . that I disobeyed rules . . . and if I ever disobeyed again I would be fired immediately. I got really angry because I'd worked with the man for two and a half years and put up with all his shit and all of a sudden I was no good. So I went to personnel. I asked them to please take the letter out of my file.

They said, "Well we're sorry but we can't do that. Anything that goes into your file stays there unless you want to file a grievance."

So I said, "Okay, I guess I'll have to file a grievance." The man I spoke to said the conversation I was having with him was completely confidential. "Well, in that case," I said, "I'll tell you some of the shit that goes on in my office." I told him about my boss putting his hands all over me and snapping my bra.

He said, "You know what you're saying is very serious."

I said, "Listen, I'm not going to press charges. I'm not going to make it public. I just want to let you know that something's going on that shouldn't be."

When I came back to work the next week, my boss wouldn't come inside my office. Then personnel called me and told me to come down, they wanted to speak to me. I saw the same man again.

He said, "If you so much as breathe a word of this to anyone you will be sued for slander or libel. So I would watch who you talk to and what you say." (That's why I won't tell you my name.) He said, "We are willing to offer you a compromise. We'll take that letter out of your file and give you four months to find another job at the University with our assistance, and then, if you don't find a job within the four months you'll have to resign."

There was a very heavy job freeze going on at the time and it didn't look like I was going to be able to find another job. As it was I resigned before the four months were up even though I didn't find a job. My boss was so threatening about bringing a libel suit against me that I'm still afraid to talk about the whole thing.

Cornell University's Director of Personnel, D. K. Willers, commented, "If, and I say if, we had someone who came to us with a complaint about [sexual harassment] we would advise them to use the grievance procedure." When asked if there had been any complaints to his office, Willers said, "Some newspapers say so, but all I know is what I read in the paper."

In disputes between employees it has long been known that management will tend to favor the man over the woman. Cases involving sexual harassment are no exception. On May 26, 1975, Sheila Cosgrove, a cocktail waitress for Host International of San Francisco, wrote a detailed memo to Michael Olivera, an assistant general manager with the corporation, outlining the problem in her own words, and restating the outcome of a meeting they had held a few days earlier:

After consulting with my attorney, I requested this meeting since I felt it was now necessary to present to the management of Host International what has been a growing concern of mine for more than two and one-half years. I feel that this is a problem which Host management needs to be made aware of due to its sensitive position as holder of a concession contract at the San Francisco International Airport and a holder of a state liquor license.

195

I explained to you that my problem involves ——, a bartender of the Lounge where I am employed as a cocktail waitress. I presented to you a series of incidences involving communication between —— and myself starting two and one-half years ago and continuing to the present. Initially, —— approached me, insisting on my cooperation with him in private sexual acts. Also, he urged me to work for him as one of several prostitutes. I declined both offers. Since then, I have been subjected to repeated harassment by ——.

In the last month, I have been in communication with other women similarly employed as cocktail waitresses as well as employees of other airport concessions. These women have related to me incidences in which they also were approached by ——.

At our meeting, I expressed concern over —— and his dealings with the public in the Host Airport concession.

I explained to you my concern that as a result of my problems with —— that I might be transferred to a less desirable shift or even terminated due to ——'s considerable influence with Host's management.

You gave me your assurance that you would immediatly check into this situation and "get it straightened out." You also indicated that you would speak to Mr. Garrett, the General Manager.

I am looking forward to the resolution of this problem.

On June 4, 1975, Tom Pope, a supervisor for Host International, informed Cosgrove that her shift was being changed to 5 P.M. to 1 A.M. and would henceforth be all night work. The shift was readily acknowledged to be less desirable and Cosgrove assumed that women with less seniority than herself would probably be allowed to take her old shift, a more desirable one. A spokesman for Host International who refused to be quoted by name explained:

We conducted an investigation to the best of our ability. We interviewed the employees involved. Nothing could be substantiated. The more we dug into it the less clear-cut it seemed. There seemed to be some bitter personal confrontation between them. We decided to reschedule Sheila simply because it's easier to reschedule cocktail waitresses than male personnel. It was just a case of it being more expedient for us to relocate the waitress. I'm not going to say how fair it is because there's only one thing that's important, and that is the company reserves the prerogative to relocate its employees as it sees fit.

Some employers profess all the best intentions in the world and they sincerely mean it. However, they are so deeply steeped in the right of male prerogatives they are virtually oblivious to the sexual harassment of their female employees. These same presumptions will then compound the problem by keeping subordinates from expressing an opposite point of view. It is the very broadcasting of these presumptions through manners, perceptions, and jokes that act on women like injunctions against speaking up. Then men will deny there are any problems because they've never been told about them.

Hubbard Broadcasting in St. Paul–Minneapolis employs about 250 people, two-thirds as many men as women, in its television operation and two radio stations. The President and General Manager, Stanley S. Hubbard, is forty-two, blond and slightly balding; pictures of his children adorn his desk. "So you're the sex-in-the-office girl," he said while he leaned back in his swivel chair. "There isn't any problem here. There's really no problem —or if there is, I'm not aware of it."

At that moment an adolescent girl walked in to leave some papers on Hubbard's desk. "Now, here's a very sexy girl," he bellowed, staring at her. Blushing, she looked away. "Oh, c'mon now," Hubbard boomed, "isn't that what you're always telling me?" She shrugged, averting her eyes. It was a few more moments before the girl darted from the office. Hubbard was shaking his head and laughing very loudly. It never once occurred to him that he was engaging in sexual harassment, and a few min-

197

utes later he told me he was unequivocally opposed to any such practices.

When asked how he would respond to a woman who complained of sexual harassment by one of his male employees, Hubbard said, "I'd fire his butt out of here. Listen, when you're a boss you have a responsibility to treat people fairly and not abuse the power of your position." Later he added, "You know, some women dress so that people will look at their breasts." And still later he added, "A man has to earn a living, you know. Most women don't—they can get married and be taken care of."

Kay Greaser is married and has short dark hair and brown eyes. She's been at Hubbard Broadcasting nine years and in that time has worked her way up the ladder into an executive position. "There's a great big mound of sexual harassment confronting any woman in business," she said, "and as you move up it grows. It's been a lot of mental strain." Asked for an example, she said, "Several years ago I was given the opportunity to be a promotion manager and I decided to see how the other male managers would feel about it and if they would support me. Do you know, one of the managers tried to use the situation! He made an outright proposition along the lines of okay, I'll support you, if you do something for me." Greaser said she never mentioned the incident to a soul. "It's just not the kind of thing you talk about, and I'm a pretty private person anyway."

Greaser did recall one time when she complained, "although I didn't mean to. There was this new man who I was training and he just would not keep his hands off me. I complained to the secretary to a manager and she told her boss. Her boss said something to the manager and I know he said something to the guy, because one day he just stopped. I mean he never touched me again." She smiled. "They're pretty good people here, really."

Norm Page is a television air-time salesman. When asked if he thought there was any sexual harassment at

Hubbard he replied, "It's seventeen below outside. You gotta do something to keep warm out here."

Jan Murphy, a terminal computer operator, said, "I just try and dodge these things. Of course, it doesn't always work." Several women are standing around as we were talking and they begin to tease her. "Why don't you tell her about 'Horny' ——?" Jan looked annoyed; her face fell. "Oh, him," she said. "He's disgusting." Many other heads nodded.

"Horny" is middle-aged, married, with children. He is a salesman. When asked about sexual harassment at Hubbard he said he didn't see enough of it to think it was of a serious nature, adding, "I think a person who does this is a little bit distorted. He isn't the obscene phone-caller, but that type." When informed of his nickname he practically shouted: "They're misinterpreting things. I'm not putting the harassment on anybody. They are interpreting a friendly attitude in the wrong manner. An outgoing person conveys that attitude, that's all; it doesn't mean anything.

Brian Zoccola, the Traffic Manager, believes if you're a woman, you can't be nice: "I was friendly to two news photographers and the next thing I knew one of them grabbed me around the waist and pressed himself into me real hard. I screamed, 'What are you doing?' and you know what he said? 'I'm getting married so I gotta get it while I can.' I'm cold and aloof now. It confines you from really getting to know people, but I don't want to take the chance."

Zoccola nodded that this doesn't always work, however. She said that there was one TV director in particular who was always touching her. "I didn't know what to do and it was really getting to me. My younger brother finally told me to just do it right back." Zoccola said it took her a while to work up to it but that finally that day came. "He did his number going by me in the lunch line and I went right up and goosed him as hard as I could. At the same time I hollered, 'That's the mushiest stuff.

199

You really are built like a marshmallow.' Everybody just howled with laughter and that guy has never come near me again."

Zoccola is typical of nearly all the women at Hubbard—she would rather deal with it herself than take it to management. There is one man, however, a member of management, about whom none of them even try to pretend they know what to do. He has no nickname and is described by many of the women as "a gross man who uses his power." All the women, in fact, had been trying to help his most recent secretary. About this woman's harassment, Zoccola said, "It was impossible working conditions. I would have quit. He was calling her at home and climbing all over her on the job. I don't know how she stood it." This secretary, it turns out, finally did quit. Jan Murphy explained, "We backed her all the way. We told her to get out. It was just real bad." But it is clear from this that not one woman dreamed of recommending that the woman take her complaint to management.

The man in question is in his middle years and handsome. He's married, with children, and holds down a top job. His attitude at first was expansive: "I've been in business for many years as a manager and I think it is generally known that this does happen. I do recall instances of girls saying, 'He's a pincher, he's a grabber.' I think it's my job as a manager to try and discourage untoward advances. Of course, you always have to ask yourself, why does someone complain? Has there been a barter arrangement? It takes two to tango. Maybe, today, people dance alone, I don't know. I do know I would feel terrible at the end of the day if I thought I had abused the innate power of my position."

Imagine my surprise, then, when instead of feeling bad at being told about his reputation, this aging executive nimbly leaped to close the door, locked it, and then whirled around to face me, demanding, "You are not leaving here until you tell me who you've talked to." A curious sort of face-off ensued.

"The whole thing is completely ridiculous," he later declared. "I don't consider myself harassing. This is a business office, of course, it's not as rigid as a galley ship. Some people just resent authority. I got along fine with my last secretary; she left of her own free will."

As with other problems of working women, it is often stated that employer policies on sexual harassment will improve when more women become managers. We are such a long way from female integration in management that at best this is futuristic. The notion is misguided on other grounds as well. Managers implement policy, they do not make it. Moreover, it is economics—not people—that normally determines the policy that will be followed. This is well illustrated by Levi-Strauss attorney Cassandra Flipper, who explains the history of Levi-Strauss policy about sexual harassment:

Levi-Strauss makes pants. Traditionally, women have been involved in that task. In the fifties, when we began to grow outside of California, our management was aware that we had the stigma of men exploiting women sexually. Whether that was based on exhaustive factual data or myth I don't know, but when we began to recruit women in smaller communities it had to be dealt with. It became well-established practice that management-level staff shouldn't have any social contact in the plants; it seemed the best way. Those terms have been strictly enforced and a number of men have been dismissed for fraternizing.

Here in San Francisco, at headquarters, the company's policy is very different. The economic incentive to see that it doesn't happen just doesn't exist because the company doesn't lack for women. . . . So we don't have a strict rule, like in the plants.

Flipper, a former Equal Employment Opportunity manager with Levi-Strauss before her present job as counsel, has recently been involved with a case of sexual harassment. She is frank in admitting she took a middle road despite the fact that the woman who complained of punitive job pressure for rejecting her manager's advances was supported by a second woman who confirmed the manager had made sexual advances. "I decided the best thing was the manager should be reprimanded and the woman should be transferred." The woman was subsequently relocated to a comparable secretarial position and an improvement notice by her former manager was wiped out.

The woman, Gay Garcia, never wanted to move, was not interested in being tracked into another secretarial job because she wanted to move up in merchandising, an ambition the transfer effectively ended, and very much resented management's response to the situation. Flipper is still confused. "She kept talking about justice a lot. I was interested in a practical solution and my priority was getting her out of the situation and making up a plausible cover story. We did ask her not to discuss what happened." On November 11, 1975, Garcia was dismissed by her new manager. She has since charged in an EEOC and California Fair Employment Practices' lawsuit that she was terminated as retribution for talking about her sexual harassment.

It is interesting to note that the manager in question was considered effective at his job. Before her decision Flipper had also already ascertained that "on the corporate side of things in a first offense of this nature a manager would probably only be reprimanded."

Employer policies on sexual harassment are not likely to improve without pressure, either through legislation *which is enforced,* or, better still, by determined female employees organizing to protect their rights. Of course, the best way to insure the most complete protection would be a joint effort.

9
Unions

The mainstream of the American labor movement was fueled at birth by a desire to maintain the male domination of female labor; the very heartbeat of this movement's unions is male rights. They are consequently a great enemy of the working woman, and it is only wishful thinking to believe this could be otherwise, despite much union rhetoric to the contrary. This rhetoric stresses unity and equality for all workers and, when pressed about the painful truth about the status of women, the unions will cry foul on the ground that employers are the root of all women's problems while anyone who says differently is antilabor, an enemy of the people. The rhetoric has been believed by many.

The facts are: only one out of eight working women is in a union—less than 22 percent of all women who work outside the home;[1] as the number of employed women continues to grow, the ratio of female union members is shrinking—from 15 percent in 1952 to only 10.3 percent in 1970.[2] Unions relentlessly discriminate against their female members' needs for equal hiring practices, seniority, equal pay, nondiscriminatory promotions, daycare, maternity leave and social insurance; continue to enforce rigid exclusion in training and segregation in jobs; deny protection from sexual harassment; will not promote more than token female leadership and steadfastly blame their refusal to organize the millions of women in the female job ghetto—the most exploited, underpaid sector of the work force—on women's "unorganizability."[3] The AFL–CIO endorses the Equal Rights Amendment and the propaganda grows, but only silence greets labor's dogged pursuit of seniority rule and seniority systems, which ruthlessly perpetuate sex discrimination and present a crucial obstacle in the path of equality.

Indicative of the extent to which the labor rhetoric has been believed, in fiscal 1972 the EEOC received a total of 419 complaints against union practices compared to 9056 against employers. *Exploitation from 9 to 5* reports: ". . . women do not think of filing complaints against unions for a number of reasons; one, the prevailing social belief that unions are the worker's friend and that to make a complaint against the union is a form of scabbing; two, a failure to see the union's role in the perpetuation of discrimination on the job; three, a lack of information about Title VII's applicability to unions . . ."[4]

Although this latter option would mean little to the millions of working women outside unions altogether—a number that now overshadows all those in the entire labor movement[5]—it could mean a great deal to those women inside unions. But Title VII pressure from militant union women activated by the women's movement into a new self-consciousness about discrimination will be a long time coming. Energy for change has been somewhat strong-armed into internal struggle rather than external force. This is manifested in an encouraging of women's caucuses and committees at the local, district, and state level of union activity, which has satisfied many union women although the overall effect is questionable. At the 1975 AFL–CIO national convention, for example, there were innumerable calls for a new commitment to women's rights. The Executive Council endorsed the general idea and then filled four vacancies on its all-male, thirty-three-member Executive Board with four new men.[6] In addition, there is the Coalition of Labor Union Women

(C.L.U.W.), which, although verbally committed to the cause of working women, has also precluded all but internal struggle. This can only succeed by virtue of male acquiescence, a doubtful prospect. It is no doubt the recognition of this that is behind the suspicion that this organization, if not itself a male-inspired creation, is a front for considerable behind-the-scenes male manipulation.

In the meantime, Title VII pressure languishes. This is not for lack of interest in some quarters of the EEOC, where Herbert Hammerman and Marvin Rugoff, Special Assistants to the Director of Compliance, have detailed what they believe would be required of unions to protect themselves from Title VII suits—this program would cover sexual harassment. It calls for "a combination of affirmative action, in which unions take initiative to discover and change discriminatory patterns, and a revised grievance arbitration procedure adapted to the requirements of Title VII."[7] It sounds simple, but Hammerman and Rugoff in the April 1976 issue of *Monthly Labor Review* leave few illusions about the obstacles:

First, of course, the leadership must commit itself to the effort. Next, it must resolve major problems of implementation with respect to politics, priorities, and resources. Politically, the program must be sold to the locals. Clearly, there are difficulties in convincing locals to push for better opportunities for minorities, when often they will be at the expense of the white male workers who are a majority of those voting for union officials. Priorities are a problem in that, to the extent the union wins bargaining concessions for minorities, the benefits may well come out of what could have been won for other workers. Finally, the resources needed for staff will not be inconsiderable.[8]

Despite the formidable roadblocks, efforts in behalf of women have been begun by dedicated individuals within the United Auto Workers; the International Union of Electrical, Radio and Machine Workers; The Newspaper

205

Guild; and the International Woodworkers, who are pioneering a special equal employment opportunity grievance procedure. Another union, the American Federation of State, County and Municipal Employees, has executed a survey of all its state councils and locals to determine the number of women active in union affairs. This survey was also meant to serve as a subtle pressure on local leadership.[9] Indicative of what unions could accomplish if they had the will, this effort accidentally sparked an amazing fight by one of the locals against the sexual harassment by foremen of female employees.

AFSCME Local 1585 represents all the nonexempt employees at Michigan State University—approximately 1100 service and nonskilled maintenance workers, about half of whom are women. In 1976 a new chief steward began investigating persistent rumors of sexual harassment of female employees in the custodial department. Two female janitors subsequently agreed to sign statements about the sexual demands one foreman had made on them. A survey of all the female janitors was then executed; this resulted in a carefully researched report of serious, extended sexual abuse within the department as a whole. The union decided to act. It went directly to the university's campus labor relations board, where it presented both the signed statements and the report with a demand for reform that included the removal from any position of authority of one foreman in particular.

The AFSCME local never intended to take on such a crusade. The rumors about sexual harassment in the custodial department had been around for a long time; only a series of apparently unrelated events appear to have made its involvement possible. These events included, as a result of the national survey, the formation of a minorities committee, which only women attended; an incident of severe harassment; the election of an idealistic chief steward; and, finally, the hiring of an outside feminist to write up the sexual harassment questionnaire. The people brought together by each of these events didn't necessarily like or even trust one another, but they nonetheless combined to force this seemingly unexceptional local to face up to the real needs of half its members.

The local's office in Lansing, Michigan, is squeezed into three small rooms. There are folding chairs, an American flag, and an enormous bulletin board which is virtually empty save for a few giant glossies advertising Red Wing safety shoes. The chief steward, Roy Barr, is a huge man with an air of perpetual worry. He welcomed me with a handshake. Richard Kennedy, the president, looked on. Both men are in their forties; their pants have cuffs and their hair is short; they are obviously ill at ease. Kennedy, who started out as an animal caretaker, has worked his way up over a long history with the local. Barr is relatively new, although he is a veteran of many other unions including the Hod Carriers, the Teamsters, and the UAW, where he was a shop steward.

When the rumors first surfaced at what Kennedy calls the antidiscrimination committee, he said "I wasn't too concerned. I just didn't think it was that big a deal. Employees get upset a lot. I thought we had more rumor than substance." After the investigation by Barr, however, Kennedy recalled, "I found out I was wrong. We do have a serious problem. It's especially serious because the people who are having these problems probably won't come to you. They are suffering in silence. If you've got rumors, you've got to take a look at it."

Barr's investigation began with getting names from the committee and talking to the women janitors firsthand. He said, "I could see right away what was happening was not right. However, I could also see it was highly sensitive. I talked to a lawyer, who said we should get signed statements. We still can't get more than two. It's there but the women won't sign. They just don't want any more hassle and they're frightened of repercussions. They don't want their names associated with sexual acts. They don't want their husbands to know because they're afraid they'll try to hurt the supervisors. One woman who has signed is very influenced by her husband and he's constantly telling her she's going to get fired or sued or something. Many of these women can't read or write too well; they are afraid if they try it will just backfire on them."

Barr is also quite clear that his own sex was an obstacle in gaining the women's confidence. "They didn't come to us; remember, we had to go to them and then that we were men, it was really difficult. They just didn't trust us." It was partly for this reason that Barr was inclined to include a woman at a later stage of the investigation. This stage developed as the two men began to look for a way the union could correct the foremen's abusive treatment of the female janitors. Their plan eventually involved bypassing the regular grievance procedure. Barr explained, "There are five different steps in our regular grievance procedure, and that would have meant a lot of people would know the identities of the people involved. It seemed like that would be bad for the women and bad for the union. In a case like this discretion is important." Kennedy added, "I didn't know what our liability would be if we had to use names."

The two men consequently decided to go directly to the university campus labor relations board, but before taking this step they wanted better documentation of the problem among the female janitors. Barr explained, "In this particular department there are transfers for all kinds of reasons. Women say they want to be closer to a bus line or one wants a building with an elevator or reasons such as that, and it was difficult to pin down who had left for sexual advances." This is how they hit on the idea of a questionnaire to help determine the extent of the problem, and Barr enlisted the aid of a local feminist who compiled it.

Kennedy said, "The results of that made it absolutely without question. There are at least three of the seven supervisors in that department who are clearly doing things that they shouldn't, but there is one guy who is really, really a problem. He is the one we are focusing on." Barr added, "We don't want to destroy the guy, we just don't want him supervising our people."

Roy Barr, who has been the prime mover behind the union's stand, has two regrets:

"I think you've got to have a woman in an official capacity in on this kind of thing from the beginning. The women's committee also wasn't too helpful. There was one woman who had made a statement about sexual harassment in 1974, that long ago, but the committee didn't do anything. The problem was one woman on that committee wanted to be Queen of the May. She was jealous of her position. She had the group go to personnel and pursued it there; of course they didn't get anywhere. I don't know why they didn't try and use the union."

Mary Walker is head of the Women's Committee. Originally from Chicago, where she worked as a packer with Jergen's Lotion, she has worked for the MSU custodial department at various jobs and for the last five years has been a swimming pool operator. Her small house sits in an area of Lansing that resembles a bombed-out battlefield, strewn with craters from the last flood. Walker greeted me at the back door and then settled us down with a pack of doughnuts and some instant coffee for a thorough briefing:

About the discrimination committee:

I always had a lot of mouth and I always enjoy meetin' different peoples. I called womens on the telephone. I was always slippin' around places, talkin' to the womens, gettin' them to come to a meetin' because they was refusin' to give the womens to the jobs they was qualified for. If you was a brown-nose you got the job. Always givin' it to the hometown boys. If we got enough people to look into things, the things might change.

About the rumors:

We always go to the union. At the time there was twenty-four womens was supposed to have met. In 1973 we had one

209

lady out there who was workin' for one foreman who any girl wears a dress turns him on and if she don't give in to him she works so many days and then she's fired. This girl didn't tell me, but she told someone else and the other party told me. I thought it was lousy. I went and talked to the steward and he said to find out how long she worked and when she left and where she lives. The steward say, "There's not very much we can do about a situation like this." I thought it was his place to find out the information he wanted. I can't pull her file but he could. He make me very mad. I went to a friend at personnel but she say to go back, to take it to the president of the union. The president was very busy and had no time. So then I went to the day steward, Roy Barr. He said he'd try to pressure the union to do somethin' about it.

About the problem:

In some cases men have been sayin' if you love me I get you a better job. Of course, if it's seniority job and you only been there six months you shouldn't have the job. Husbands are goin' to know somethin' is wrong. We have about three foremen out there that has been confronted by the husbands. We had to try and force the foremens to give one women a foreman's job. They didn't want her 'cause she is older and not so pretty and didn't play along.

If you don't play along they say you a surly type person. They don't really go for that. There's one guy who likes girls to be nice to him and if they aren't he put the lie on them. He'll report them to foreman about their job. If you don't know to call the union you can get fired. I believe a lot of the womens goes along with things 'cause they think they should.

One time one white guy go into the office to complain about favoritism. He'd seen what was goin' on, that some girls is havin' it really easy because they been nice to the foreman. The foreman got real nasty. He say if he didn't shut his mouth and mind his own business the nigger gonna get his job. He had gone in to complain about treatment of a black girl he worked with. Afterward he turned really cruel and mean. He got scared they'd get rid of him and he just changed. The foreman he complained to is now a general foreman.

About the acceptance of sexual harassment:

I was always under the impression when I first got hired if you didn't play with the mens, if you didn't go out with them, you didn't get a good job. That's what I was told.

This is the way I found out what was goin' on. A maid asked me if I knew any peoples who was goin' out. She started namin' names of ladies, then she say do I know such-and-such a foreman. I say, "Wow." She say you should learn the score around this place. You will learn if you go with a foreman you okay but if you don't you gonna get fired. Then another lady tell me the same story. I was transferred to another department and they tell me the same things. Then I say, "Wow," what you all do if you is married already? So then they tell me about a foreman who was confronted with two womens' husbands, the same year. One night one husband was lookin' for him and they didn't even let him go on his route.

About her own struggle against it:

There was one time this one woman was goin' along with a foreman. She was young and childish but she got thirteen kids. He was really nasty to all of us. She started flirtin' around with him, thinkin' she'd get it easier on the job. We filed a grievance on him for liftin' weight. She got mad and say, "Why did you go to union office on him, you wreckin' overtime and you only bumpin' me. I wanna do the job." They try to get me to drop the grievance. I say as long as I stay black I'm gonna do the grievance. She really couldn't do the job either, but because she was smilin' all the time she was gonna get help.

About her escape:

I didn't want no one messin' with me. Real quick I got a relationship with the union steward. That wasn't all of it,

211

but I did go with him a little bit for job reasons. Now that's over ain't no one gonna bother me 'cause they know I go to the union. I want more womens to use it. The union don't help so good all the time. Sometimes I don't even see notice of meetins'. You got to talk to people. You got to make it work. Me and my committee is helpin'. Now womens feel they got a place to go to. Most people now is takin' it into consideration.

About the abuse:

I think this sexual harassment is rotten. I think it's one of the worst things on earth that a person would have to do. I think it's terrible you have to make love or put out or screw just to keep a low-down dirty job. You workin' for yourself. I can do without work if I had some other way of livin', you know, but myself if I had to feel up to some guy I might wind up on welfare. I mean, how many times you wanna have to do that?

The questionnaire distributed by the union defined sexual harassment in categories ranging from "leering, suggestive looks, insults and innuendos" to "subtle or out-and-out threats to a job or working conditions if one didn't cooperate with sexual demands." It was distributed to seventy-seven (80 percent) of the ninety-six female custodians. The questionnaires were unsigned and no names were requested, but respondents were asked to specify their shift and building so that names of the seven foremen could be readily identified. When the results were compiled, 73 percent of the women reported sexual harassment to be a problem that should be remedied and four foremen were identified as engaging in harassment. Of these four there was one who had harassed nine separate women, several to the point of outright physical force. The other three foremen had respectively intimidated three, two, and one women, for a grand total of fifteen victims who could be traced to specific foremen. There were four more reports of harassment, but three failed to identify their building and shift while one reported harassment from an earlier foreman whom she didn't name. In all, then, a full one-quarter of the custodial women were being harassed by at least half or more of their foremen.[10]

Joan Nelson of Lansing is a woman's counselor on rape, a teacher of self-defense for women, and a recent social science graduate of Michigan State University. It is largely by her efforts that the twenty-five-page report on sexual harassment (which corresponds totally with all previous studies) came into being. This was only accomplished by many long hours of meeting with groups of the female janitors.

Nelson explained, I asked them to meet me at the union office because a significant number of women in that department can't read because of being Latino or poor black and white women with little education:

Twenty-six women out of the ninety-six total actually met with me. We then talked to women at work on their breaks, at lunch, whenever we could. We continued to do this for about three weeks and that brought the total of interviews to seventy-seven women. Some women did it on their own. Some I helped to understand the questions. The nineteen women we didn't contact were on various kinds of leave: sick, maternity, and military. The twenty-six women who came the first time was a tremendous turnout. It seemed indicative that the women felt strongly about sexual harassment, because even five or six at a meeting is really phenomenal. Apathy is really high in the union. It also seemed to indicate that the women's committee had probably been supportive. The majority of that first group was black.

In Nelson's experience almost all the women were surprised the union was taking an interest and they believed nothing would come of it. She also observed that because she expressed a receptive attitude they would eventually feel free to express both anger and frustration. "They were never really punitive. By far the largest category of options they would choose was to remove the man

213

from a supervisor's position but not go beyond that." Nelson also found the women as a group to be anxiety-ridden. "They were really frightened. Most of them feared talking at all because it could result in a scandal for the university and they thought they would be the ones to pay. That they'd be transferred or fired. I just can't say how many women also feared they'd be blamed. An amazing number were also terrified of what their husbands would do, not only to the men but to them. Often they were deathly afraid of their husbands."

Hilly [a pseudonym] is a slender, soft-spoken young woman in her twenties who is married and has one child whom she adores. Five years ago she began working in the custodial department; this experience had led to her signing one of the two written statements despite both her husband and mother-in-law's vigorous protests—they think she is "acting like a fool."At her house in the suburbs a few hours before she was due at work, she was tense, unsmiling. "My husband doesn't know I let you come out here. He'd be furious. I know he cares about me. He just feels nothing will be done. I guess I've just got to take a chance."

Hilly had worked in the custodial department for three years without a problem until she was transferred. One week later her new foreman requested she leave her regular building and drive with him over to another building, where he locked the two of them inside. Subsequently escorting her into a basement room with a couch he invited her to relax and have intercourse. This request occurred about 10 P.M.; her shift lasted until 1 A.M.; throughout most of that time the foreman pursued her around the floors of the empty building. Repeated requests that he stop were ignored, until finally at 12:30 P.M. he agreed to unlock the doors and drive her back to work.

Hilly talked to no one about what had happened. Two days later she was in the museum with another female janitor when the foreman showed up and told the second

214

woman to go home sick. "I got her alone and I begged her not to go 'cause I knew what he was up to. She said she wasn't sick but she thought she should go. When she left she said she was sorry." The foreman returned later and forced himself physically. "I was real scared but I got free of him and I took off running. I could hear him walking around in the building trying to find me." Eventually Hilly thought she heard him leave and she stopped hiding, but he quickly reappeared, lunging at her. "I screamed, then I hollered I'd report him." Running away again, she darted into the telephone office. "The supervisor there asked me what was wrong and I told her. She said it didn't surprise her because she knew of his reputation. I talked to her the rest of the night. She said I could come in there and hide if he kept it up."

The foreman showed up again a week later. He told Hilly she was a sad case, that he just wanted to help her, then he left. After this Hilly arranged to come to work with her fifteen-year-old brother; the foreman would see her brother and leave. This continued until one night the two of them were playing cards on her break when the brother left to use the john. The foreman immediately slipped into the room and closed the door. "He was really upset. I got mad and I found my brother and I found Dolores [a pseudonym], the lady I work with. I said I just had to get away from that foreman. Dolores said she'd go tell my old foreman, because he had once said if I ever had any trouble to get in touch with him."

Hilly's former supervisor showed up immediately. When she told him the problem, however, he thought it was funny. He also encouraged her to keep quiet. "He told me to call the general supervisor, who transfers people, and tell him I was afraid of the snakes up on the third floor of the museum." Following the foreman's advice, she was promised a transfer but only in one or two weeks. The foreman renewed his attacks and Hilly finally told the general supervisor the real reason. She was immediately transferred. This was not the end of her trouble.

The transfer placed her under the supervision of one of the man's friends, who continuously complained about her work; this culminated in an attempt to have her fired. Hilly kept her job, but only as the result of a third transfer at the request of the union.

Throughout most of the trauma Hilly could hardly think beyond the fact she needed her job. Her daughter has a disease that requires a doctor's care monthly. Her husband works as a utility man. "I just have to keep my job. We're barely keeping our heads above water now. So all I could think was that if I talked I'd get fired for being a troublemaker. I also couldn't tell my husband because I knew he'd try and kill the foreman. I just didn't know where to turn. I didn't trust the union. My girlfriend was all I had and all we could think of was trying to get witnesses."

After the reaction of her former foreman when she finally did talk, Hilly also felt all her fears had been well-founded. "He made me feel so little. He acted like it was all my fault. I got scared all over again. I was really desperate when I finally told the general supervisor the truth. Of course, afterward, I realized by the way he didn't ask any questions that he must have already known about him." After the first transfer Hilly felt she could no longer keep the situation from her husband. Once more her worst fears were confirmed. "He told me he'd take care of it. He said he'd kill him. I had a terrible time convincing him not to do something like that."

Hilly's attitude about the union is a mixture of amazement and cynicism. Her only previous experience with the union was a complete bust. After a fall on company property that soon required that her tailbone be removed, the company refused to pay for the operation and the union never pressed her claim. Hilly hired her own lawyer. "I won, but it was no thanks to the union. That's why I was shocked when they got involved. Roy Barr is wonderful; I just wish there were more union officials like him. I'm glad the union's involved, of course,

216

but I can't help thinking they might not follow it through."

Seeing it through and standing up for her rights has not been easy for Hilly. After bucking the opposition of both her husband and her mother-in-law, who feel she is uselessly jeopardizing her job, she has been sorely disappointed by a lack of support from other women. "It's so hard. Many of the women have gone all the way with that foreman. They are completely compromised. They didn't want to, but now they won't do anything. I don't want to jeopardize my job either, but I do want to stop that man. There was one woman who even went on the ten-o'clock shift to get away from him. I'd like to feel like I had some power behind me. It's just me and my girlfriend."

According to union sources, the Michigan State University Campus Labor Relations Board turned the sexual harassment report over to the general supervisor, who called a meeting of all the foremen involved. What happened at that meeting is not known. About two weeks later the CLRB informed the union president, Richard Kennedy, by letter that there was "not enough evidence" to take any action. They advised any future course follow the regular grievance procedures. Kennedy sent a letter to a reputedly liberal member of the University's Board of Trustees to which there has to date been no response. On December 1, 1976, Roy Barr resigned his post. A short time later Guy Munger, one of the foremen in the custodial department, committed suicide. He left a note for the general supervisor, but the contents have never been made public. As of this writing Hilly is in grievance about her harassment.

10
Men

There will always be plenty of dumb bunnies
who are willing to do all
the dull drudgery in every office and factory.
Don't *you* do it!
See to it that you always bring your employer
the charm of your personality,
the maddening effect of your beauty,
and the inspiration of a romance with you.

—Harford Powel
Good Jobs for Girls[1]

In *Male Chauvinism: How It Works* Michael Korda has
set himself the unprecedented task, for a male (to para-
phrase his preface), of talking about the ways men discriminate against women at work by exploring all the
reasons men feel, think, and behave that way and by en-
tertaining alternatives to this system of making special
demands on women while simultaneously rewarding them
with lower pay, fewer opportunities, and thinly veiled
contempt. In commenting on sex in the office, Korda
writes:

"In office affairs, as in the politics of the Seraglio,
women are always in the wrong. When a man makes a fool
of himself over a girl twenty years his junior, the odds are

that *she* will be fired in the final reckoning, unless the management of the company was looking for an excuse to fire the man anyway. The 'double standard' lives on, indeed flourishes."[2]

A little later he pointedly comments on men's expectations toward female employees:

"It is difficult enough for a woman to work in a world run by men without having to reflect back to men their own fantasies about her; yet women are constantly placed in the uncomfortable position of providing a passive audience before which men can project their chosen roles in the sexual drama of their lives. Men impose upon women the demands of their imaginations, making them, in their minds, as captive as was poor 'O.' . . ."[3]

This is a reference to *The Story of O,* a modern French classic of pornography, from which he quotes: "You are here to serve your masters. During the day, you will perform whatever domestic duties are assigned to you. . . . Nothing more difficult than that. But at the first sign from anyone you will drop whatever you are doing and ready yourself for what is really your one and only duty: to lend yourself."[4]

Korda concludes:

"Of course, the office is not 'O's' house of torture in any physical sense (though a lady of my acquaintance claims to have been raped on the mahogany table of the empty boardroom of a major corporation by a senior executive of the company who had invited her in to talk about her future), but men often behave as if they thought it were."[5]

This view of male behavior at work is reinforced by another contemporary male author, Marc Feigen–Fasteau. In *The Male Machine* Fasteau writes, "For men to play their roles, women have to play theirs or be kept in them. This is true in every area where men and women interact, but most of all at work."[6]

Specifically, on the subject of sex, Fasteau believes that unless a woman carefully represses all hint of

219

sexuality "the male sexual idea of 'nameless, cooperative and uncritical' women will not permit men to take anything but her sexuality seriously." He writes further:

A man working with an attractive woman may view every encounter, no matter how businesslike in purpose, as sexually charged. The obligation to make at least a perfunctory pass is reinforced by the predominant view of sexual attractiveness as a relatively impersonal matter of physical assets—one woman with good breasts and nice legs is more of less interchangeable with any other. Men don't actually come on seriously to every attractive woman they work with, but they do expect a show of ritual, ego-satisfying flirtation. And when they have the power, as with a subordinate, they often insist on it, viewing it as part of her job. This byplay is especially manageable with a secretary: If she doesn't play the game, or when an affair goes sour, she can be fired or transferred with no more explanation than that a "personality conflict" has developed.[7]

This is something new. The male mind-set behind the male code of sexual aggression at work is finally under assault from men themselves, and it is doubtful it will ever fully recover. However, unlike Korda and Fasteau, most men have not concluded that these kinds of male expectations and behavior are irrevocably wrong. Rather, they are in a state of shock.

According to Aileen Hernandez, this is the impact of equal opportunity. Hernandez served as an original commissioner for the EEOC and for the past ten years has acted as an urban affairs consultant for business, labor, government, and private groups on programs for utilizing the talents of minority groups and women. She says, "Men are not sure what they should do. They're getting signals of reverse or stop short. They are very uncertain.

"Men need liberation to deal with it. With women, if you don't give in to sex on the job you must be a lesbian, but the reverse is that the man who doesn't engage in it

220

must have a sexual problem. This absolutely has to be challenged. They've had it their own way and now the changes are threatening their egos. When they lose jobs to women, men have to deal with the fact that they lost to a low-status individual; the male fraternity and men accordingly feel obligated to do something. They fall back on sex. They have barred women by exploiting the issue of sexuality. Look how women have been blocked from some of the male-only, high-paid career opportunities such as the fire department because of the arguments, mostly by men, that no man and woman can work together without sexual involvement be it voluntary or involuntary."

Hernandez, through her own consulting firm, has pioneered affirmative action agreements and a broadening of management development through training programs to firms such as United Air Lines; Sears, Roebuck and Company; and Standard Oil of California. Before many of these programs Hernandez has lately preinterviewed the prospective trainees on their attitudes. For this purpose she has a standard questionnaire that now includes a true–false question on sexual harassment; the exact wording is "Women frequently complain that they lose opportunities for promotion because they resist unwanted sexual advances by male bosses."

A major national company's high-level executives, 121 in all, were recently preinterviewed. A full one-fourth of these men answered the question on sexual harassment affirmatively. This percentage would have been still higher, according to Hernandez, because some of the men later told her they had only answered negatively because they didn't think women complained about it.

Of course, the most interesting question about these results remains unanswered. Were the men who answered affirmatively referring to their own experience, their friends', or their company's, or were they acknowledging the problem even while continuing to hold it at arm's length? (In all probability they were doing the latter. Men see sexual harassment as someone else's behavior problem.)

Their attitudes about sexual harassment in general also seem to depend a great deal on whether or not they have been forced to become involved with the abuse in some personal way. Bill Korbel, a twenty-nine-year-old senior electronics technician in upstate New York, says, "I'd like to bury some of them—the guys who do stuff like this." His attitude is the result of an experience several years ago when Connie, his wife, was severely harassed by the owner of a restaurant where she was working a second job as a waitress. The two weren't married yet and the money she was earning on this second job, since she had two small children from an earlier marriage, was important to their future; she asked him not to interfere. Korbel says of that period, "It made me damned uncomfortable, but the extent that I could do anything was limited. I just tried to make sure I was there when she got out of work."

Korbel's direct experience of his own helplessness in the situation has led to an understanding that the problem must be publicly exposed. He says, "The more it comes to light, the more limitation will be placed upon the employer. He'll have to be a lot more responsible." Korbel, however, also feels that men's attitudes are in part responsible. He says many women don't want to bring it up because they are afraid "they'll get a stigma or reputation," and he thinks they are right.

He also thinks they would be punished "right in the home," because men would tend to blame their wives: "There are some men who think that nobody's gonna go near their wife unless she invites it. These are the same men, of course, who'll do it to a woman themselves. I think a lot of them would have their ego in the way. Men have got their own double standard, and that is an incredible barrier in the way of understanding what's really happening. It's like, for men, accountability is just a one-way street."

Korbel's opinion is based, in part, on a recent experience at his own place of business when a woman that he knows and describes as "a really hard worker, very competent" got a raise. He said she had been seeking the raise for a long time but then, when it finally came through, she missed work for a few days and when she returned she was badly bruised. Korbel says, "Her husband beat her up, he didn't believe she'd get that much of a raise without putting out."

Men also generally do not like other men who take the woman's side. Although this is happening more frequently, this kind of moral commitment to women's rights from a male may be treated by other men with suspicion, ridicule, and disdain. Michael Hausfeld, the thirty-year-old attorney for Diane Williams in her successful suit against the Justice Department, has experienced this first-hand. Hausfeld says, "Even though there has been a big reaction to this case because it is so important to women's equal employment opportunities, the only reaction of my colleagues has been to laugh. Everybody seemed to say, 'Why'd you do it?' It's kind of a joke and there's a lot of skepticism. I remember one comment from a fellow attorney was, 'You're cramping my style.' Another colleague said, 'You've ruined my office.' "

Hausfeld is personally undismayed, explaining, "I just keep telling them we took this case because it is serious." Professionally, however, he is concerned:

"What we have now is a situation where women are finally being hired, either by choice or by force through a court order, but the truth is they're being placed in a situation that can almost be more horrible than not being hired at all. You've got an abuse of the power of the purse combined with the fact that the employer has almost complete control over your future. . . . It's an extremely serious situation where people really take advantage of the

223

fact that they have. That they are the haves and the have-nots want in."

Hausfeld is optimistic that this will change, but "not overnight," and believes this is the promise of Title VII —that by court orders society can begin to play a role in changing people's attitudes. "At least," he says, "it will force them to recognize they can no longer continue in the traditional modes when it denies people an equal footing in employment opportunities." What's really operating here, he explains, is "an historical stereotype that a man is superior to a female. Consequently, when a female does work for a male she has to provide these other consider-ations, be grateful she has the job and understand that to keep it she's got to keep her man happy."

Hausfeld says, "That's going to take time to dispel. Court orders saying these women are right, that they don't have to submit to this any longer is a beginning; and, then, hopefully with time, people's ideas and concepts will change." This is the real reason he says the attitudes of his colleagues bother him. There have to be lawyers to take the cases, to break the ground. Even here, he concedes, however, "It's going to take a while."

Sol Rosen was Colleen Gardner's attorney in the Washington sex scandals (see Chapter 12). His experien-ces parallel Hausfeld's, although the abuse in his case wasn't just confined to colleagues. Rosen, moreover, was not inclined to respond politely. The abuse affected him on a much more personal level and he felt honor-bound to give as good as he got. This led, he says, to the point where "I actually came close to a couple of fights, fist-fights, with different policemen." The forty-year-old at-torney represented Gardner, a personal friend, out of the belief that sexual harassment is a serious problem, partly because it is hard for women to talk about, and because "it took a hell of a lot of courage for Colleen to come forward." Rosen felt Gardner should have been praised and encouraged and he was consequently appalled at the male abuse:

224

"People say these things out of their own smallness, but it got to be pretty embarrassing. Every guy just seemed to feel he had a license to make cracks. 'Are you getting paid in trade?' 'How's the whore you're representing?' Things like that. I just couldn't stand it and I have a big mouth, so I'd tell them where to go."

Rosen says the abuse has diminished, although it still happens. "Just last week I was in court and this guy said, 'How about fixing me up with your client?'" Rosen, however, is least concerned about his own abuse. "What sickens me most," he says, "is the way I know Colleen's been hurt. She was really abused. I don't regard myself as one of these—a woman's libber per se—but I do believe in human dignity."

On any Monday through Friday there are hundreds of men at work who will become aware of the fact that a female co-worker is being sexually harassed. The majority will find this either humorous or a matter of indifference. Occasionally, however, it will get through that the woman cannot dismiss it so easily. Bob [a pseudonym] is a thirty-year-old liberal who works in the Los Angeles office of a national newspaper. He says, "I probably make sexual comments about women in the office. I don't think there is anyone who doesn't make comments like that on women. It seems like a natural thing to me."

About two years ago, however, the newspaper hired a young girl to work as a receptionist for a supervisor whom he describes as someone "everyone knew made advances whenever he got a few drinks in him." He says of the girl, "I liked her very much. She was a nice person. After a few months the girl left giving her primary reason to be the supervisor's unwanted and repeated sexual advances, although just before leaving she confided in Bob, that it was getting to the point she couldn't take it anymore. He says:

"I agree with her it would be a good reason to quit. His antics were a joke to everyone in the office. It was rather interesting, though, that what everyone in the office took as buffoonish behavior was to the person to whom it was directed a rather scary experience."

Most men cannot rise about their internalized belief in female submission. Bill Moffat is a tall, skinny truck-driver for C & J Drive-Aways in Lansing, Michigan. He thinks sexual harassment is a problem although it's primarily the woman's responsibility because "the way society is, the man is the aggressor and it's up to the woman to put a stop to it." Moffat thinks that if women would just act outgoing and friendly a lot of the problem would disappear, because "most men are real nervous about the various women they have to deal with in the work setting." He explains further:

"If the woman acts friendly, then you can feel like you kinda conquered something and everything's okay. But if she's quiet and withdrawn you can find it difficult to approach the woman and a big problem develops."

Moffat thinks most men are nervous with women because you "never know what to expect from them." He gives such reasons as menopause and various "nervous types." Men are more understandable to him, and the problem, the way he sees it, is the way men get their egos damaged when women don't "handle them right." He says he's worked in several automobile factories and observed this constantly:

"The girl isn't friendly or she's uppity or the foreman puts the make on the girl and she doesn't know how to put a stop to it; the foreman just gives her all the heavy work and makes her life miserable. He'll harass her over a million things, in every way he knows."

When this happens, though, Moffat doesn't think it's too difficult to deal with because the woman can just ask for a transfer. He says, "The way the laws have been changed, it's all for the women now." Moffat explains that he first noticed the effects of these laws in 1969, when men and women started doing more of the same work and there was more association. He says there was also more sexual harassment, explaining, "The men don't know quite what to do with the women and there's a huge resentment. They're worried about their jobs disappearing. Man's pride of family support is suffering a lot."

Moffat occasionally acknowledges the effect of sexual harassment on women. There was a time when he worked in an all-male factory—except for one woman who had been there before the war. She was, he says, the meanest woman he ever met but adds, "the truth is she had been harassed so much she just got mean in self-defense." The abuse was constant, but he recalled a particular incident when one man turned to another saying, "I wouldn't screw her with your dick!" Moffat shudders, saying, "I was real embarrassed. I know I wouldn't want to work under those insults."

Even as he acknowledges how hard it must have been for this woman, however, Moffat is quick to defend the men's behavior:

"Society was arranged to protect the woman. The guys only get their hackles up when she steps out of that arrangement. She loses respect as a woman. They don't feel she's entitled to respect for her femininity."

Ultimately, then, Moffat concludes it is just a simple question of a better understanding between men and women about male gestures of dominance and assertion. He puts it this way:

"A woman comes in and a guy comes up and puts his arm around her and says, 'Hey, come on in.' What would you think? Is he being friendly or is he making a pass? It's something women gotta get used to. Personally, I don't see anything against it. A lot of line men are just trying to be friendly. The way the woman responds is the key. The guy'll say 'Miss' or 'Mrs.' It's up to her."

Moffat very well understands that what he's describing is implicitly unequal; walking me out to my car, he adds a postscript: "If they'd teach it in school. If they'd say, 'Hey, that's a girl, so what!' But they don't. They say, 'That's a girl, don't hit her.' That's where it begins, that's where the difference begins."

An expression of oppression in a patriarchy designed for the benefit of white heterosexual men often finds its counterpart among other oppressed groups. Although minority men, by virtue of the fact that they are male, will themselves victimize women on occasion, they are in a position to make connections. Sometimes the breakthrough occurs; a minority male will begin to get a clear line on the abuse by seeing the parallels. When this happens his disgust knows no bounds. His outrage, in fact, becomes the greatest of which men are capable very simply because he comes the closest to understanding how it feels; correspondingly, his solutions for it will be among the most radical.

Lewis Merrick, Coordinator for Special Programs for the Oregon State System of Higher Education, is a black man in his thirties who's spent a great deal of his life analyzing his own oppression and working for change. Always seeking the core of problems, Merrick believes that, with respect to sexual harassment, "Women are expected to conform to a certain kind of physical proximity and that is the trap because it means men are always in control." Merrick adds that he thinks women are frequently seduced into thinking they can control these expectations, but he cautions, "Men have worked twenty-four hours a day to design these hustles and in the face of that the little moral defenses that women can muster against it are just nothing." Merrick believes that women's whole future at work depends on coming to grips with this.

"For women in general I think their possibilities are limited to the degree that they will entertain the thought, that they have to pretend to entertain the thought. Once they accept the basic assumptions it's just a no-win situation. Women should resist it out of hand because

228

there's no way they can win. If they protest too much they're trite."

Merrick says that female protest is even part of the game because men always turn women's protests to their own advantage. "Men in their cowardice will always cop a plea. They will always say when a woman protests (the behavior, not the assumption), 'Oh, I didn't know you'd get so upset.' They imply that women are too sensitive, can't take a joke." He says, "It's like white people are always touching my kids' hair and I hate it, but if I protest too much I'm the one who looks trite." Merrick has observed that women frequently don't even bother responding "because there's no dialogue that doesn't make them look foolish."

On the other hand, Merrick has also observed that women can't win by going along with it either. He says, "It's like damned if you do and damned if you don't. If you do, you are still the submissive one; he's got all the cards." Merrick finds this is true even if the woman is the nominal superior, because she could never penalize him for the simple reason that he's the male. He concludes: "The simple truth is once a woman becomes vaginally related she abrogates all rights—all employee rights—whereas a man never loses those rights."

Mario Cesar Romero, Special Arts Project Director at Cayman Gallery in Soho, is gay. This sexual orientation has afforded him an outsider's view of female sexual harassment. From that vantage he says, "Men use their power to abuse women like they were so much cattle." Romero thinks he's been aware of sexual harassment since he first started working at about sixteen. He says the abuse has always been common, but that lately "it has gotten terrible" within the poverty programs for Puerto Ricans in New York.

"I've actually seen some of these macho guys who are in positions of power because they've got the jobs to dole out feel women up and insult them and handle

229

them. I've seen girls rebuff this and lose the jobs and I've seen them give in because they just had to get the job."

Romero describes sexual harassment as "runaway machismo," a function of the way "the male chauvinist is very insecure and takes advantage of any situation in which he has power." He feels the abuse is especially hard on Latin women, since it simply reinforces the way they have always been put "in a secondary position, objectified and subject to male rule." Romero is pessimistic about stopping sexual harassment because he believes those who have the power won't easily yield it.

Men frequently attempt to avoid the whole question of male sexual abuse of women on the job by saying that it happens to them too. Their harassment, they say, is that women will try to use them sexually to get ahead or obtain some advantage, and they will ask: Isn't that corrupt, isn't that immoral and isn't that the same thing? The answer is no. What men are experiencing is a symptom of their own abuse. The sexual harassment of working women is so universal that many women merely attempt to influence what they perceive to be the inevitable. Eradicate male abuse of female working conditions and you will eradicate this symptom; and, to this end, men who feel so oppressed by female overtures might strike directly at the problem by lending their own weight behind skill, not sex, as the standard measure of merit. With anything less men merely participate in the problem by virtue of a hypocrisy that absolves them of blame, removes it to the woman, and leaves it all up to the "other guy" who is down the hall, around the corner, and up the stairs.

To equate a symptom of abuse as equal to the abuse itself is a fallacy. Sexual harassment is the use of coercion, force, or intimidation by using rank within the work hierarchy or through social status which accords superior value to men and which men protect through bonding. When a female attempts to trade sex for favors, there simply is no harassment (coercion) involved, rather an attempt to strike a bargain. This clearly admits no possibility of penalties on the male if he fails to agree. For the man, it is a virtual no-loss situation.

There is of course the theoretical possibility that a man could be harassed by a woman on the job if he were in a subordinate position. This version of the possibilities is virtually nonexistent in my investigations and research, a function of the fact that women are scarce in positions of power and also seemed by training and motivation not so inclined, but I did find a man who was sexually approached in relation to a better job by a female in a position to help this effort. Mathew is a six-footer, dark-complexioned, a good looker. The proposition occurred when he was twenty-three, while he was in the Army and wanted to get out of serving as a typist for an older boss named Teresa. He made some inquiries and a short time later a friend of Teresa's named Gladys approached him. She was an assistant to a ranking officer and initiated a conversation about his job. He expressed dissatisfaction, saying that he thought he really belonged in her office because he was classified as a personnel specialist. Mathew says:

"She said, 'Let's talk about it.' She seemed like she could maybe do something. So we went for coffee. I said, 'So you think you can get me into personnel?' She said, 'No, I'm not sure. I'd have to talk to the officer in charge.' She then started asking me about my personal life. She asked if I had any hobbies. I said I played the piano and she said, 'Oh, I do too! I have a piano in my house. I'd love to hear you play. I'd also like to go to bed with you.'"

Mathew said he was definitely interested in getting the job, "but not that way," and that he was embarrassed and declined the offer. He says, "She turned right off and her face went blank. She said, 'I have to get back to work.' And that was the last I ever talked with her." Later, however, the workload increased on the typing job almost "tenfold" and the pressure became relentless. This is the way he handled the problem:

"I finally just blew up. I went into my office and I threw all my papers around, just heaved them, and I went straight to my superior officer and said, 'Get me the hell out of here. Teresa's just like an old maid.' "

Mathew was immediately transferred. He says now that he thinks some of the pressure was because of Gladys, but "I didn't get scared or anything like that."

There could be no better example of male bonding and male status at work. Sexual harassment is not a problem for men, it is rather a male problem; and, needless to say, if women could handle it as Mathew did, there would be no issue.

11
Social Coercion I:
The Casting Couch

"The casting couch" is a cliché about working women that contributes to the popular myth that women respond positively to male sexual harassment. ABC Records Vice-President Herb Belkin says: "The availability of people with mutual interests means no one gets forced. All the people who participate are adults. I could tell you fifty stories and they'd all be the same, a chick comes in with a guitar and may go down on the producer before, during or after."

Belkin also says, "Of course this availability leads to a result where a woman who is not inclined to participate may have a harder time getting doors opened after she knocks." For Belkin, however, this is merely a side effect in a tough business, the result of the interplay of a free market where people with mutual interests find each other. That this "free" market is controlled by men who make the rules to which females are expected either to conform or get out is not part of the conceptualization. When asked, apparently for the first time, if this is a practice woman would prefer not to engage in, he says belligerently, *"I don't know*. Well, yes, that nice Catholic girl from Des Moines who thinks she can sing would really try in a different fashion."

Belkin is a victim of the casting-couch mentality, a pervasive mind-set in American culture that most women will do anything to get ahead. The cliché conveys the idea of a bargain is struck between two equally consenting parties. The imposition of sex on women subsequently becomes an acceptable working condition because they are agreeable, even happy to comply; sometimes they even ask for it.

Cynthia [a pseudonym] has always been interested in politics. After leaving the entertainment field she went into law. The result has been a successful career; she is presently employed by a large, well-respected firm whose practice includes many entertainment clients, some of them men for whom she has negotiated contracts.

Because competition in the entertainment field is so fierce, Cynthia says, "I suppose for women with talent it probably doesn't hurt to sleep with the right people." However, she emphasizes talent, explaining that no one will employ someone who can't act or who could hurt their own career in any way. In those cases where she has known a few actresses who have been helped by men with whom they are intimate, she believes this wasn't necessarily intended. Her primary observation about the fierce competition, moreover, is that it is a situation that most producers will exploit. Consequently, the woman who believes sex is an automatic prescription for success will meet with tragic consequences:

"I have often seen over the years women who weren't too bright or too talented *try* to sleep their way up and become a kind of laughing stock. It really infuriates me. They are just being used, led on, and then laughed at. And, of course, they're not quite clever enough to realize that the myth doesn't work."

These women, in Cynthia's experience, are only a small minority. The truth, she says, is that the large majority reject sex as an acceptable exchange for work because when the proposition is presented to most women, they will refuse.

I'm surprised more women won't choose this way. I think it's a credit to us, women, as people. It speaks well for our in-

234

tegrity. When you look at the needs—just economic needs —and how little we are given with which to compete. There is so much stacked against us; it's actually amazing. I think for women, generally, sex is a commodity in the true Adam Smith, Marxian sense, that its use value is much less important than its exchange value. It is the only thing society says we really have to offer. For all these reasons I'm really surprised.

Because of the stereotype of working women established by the casting couch cliché, many people are surprised. This is the terrible impact: it creates a vulnerability in working women, reducing their will to fight the imposition of sex on their working conditions. And, the majority of women who do resist are doubted or even ridiculed. The illusion that sexual harassment is neither widespread nor serious is thus maintained, further deterring the thousands of working women who desire to stand up for their right to work free of sexual coercion.

The attitudes of these women are much like those of actress Jennifer Lee.

We're working people. We should have our protection and our rights. When you're robbed you report it to the police, this should be treated the same way. For example, I went to this producer's office and he locked the door and turned off the lights. I was scared. He said, "You don't look anything like you did in *Esquire*. [*Esquire* magazine had just come out with an article on starlets, including Lee.] I didn't panic and I was strong. He was a coward, really. After an incident like that do you go home and kick and scream and call your father long distance? I mean what do you do? You deal with it intelligently and logically and you call up and report it to the authorities.

Lee is twenty-seven and exceedingly attractive, with brown eyes and long, dark hair. She arrived in Hollywood over a year ago after a period as a successful model and two years of study with Stella Adler. She has found

235

plenty of roles since then in both movies and television but there have also been plenty of lost parts and lots of abuse. She says, "I experienced sexual harassment all the time. Luckily, when I arrived here I wasn't straight off the bus from Cropseyville [her home town in New York]; I wasn't Miss Naïve."

Eventually, Lee started to stand up for herself. The first time involved a part in a film about country and western music, of which Lee is a devotee, and she spent several weeks composing an original song for the audition. At some point in the tryout, however, she realized the man had never intended their meeting to be more than an opening for a date, and when the request finally came, she confronted him: "You mean you're just asking me out? I can't believe this is happening. Is that all I'm here for?" The man said she was being naïve. Lee said her intentions were strictly professional, that this was the understanding of the interview, and that he was behaving extremely unprofessionally. He told her she was ridiculous and overreacting, although Lee thought she detected a new nervousness. A short time later the man called her and apologized. Lee said, "Of course, that's funny for a situation where I overreacted."

Although Lee's decision to confront the practice of sexual harassment began somewhat auspiciously, this did not continue to be the case. A few months after this experience she was again harassed. This time the director told her to come by his office to pick up a script and discuss the changes, but when she arrived he suddenly was too busy to talk, and he rescheduled the meeting for 6 P.M. at a local nightspot. As the day lengthened Lee developed a bad case of nerves, remembering that she had heard "talk about the guy" so she called her agent, Mark Harris. Lee recalls that Harris said, "Oh, c'mon, you can handle it. If anything happens it would get back to me in a minute. He wouldn't dare." Lee kept the appointment. The man talked at her nonstop, juxtaposing statements about how many women wanted the part with statements that he could see she would be "fabulous" for it. Eventually he seemed to convince himself that he should hire her. Then, over dinner, he gave her a little box saying, "This is our contract."

Lee opened the box to discover an inch-long silver pencil. "It was a piece of junk and you just knew he had seventy more in his bedroom drawer." She immediately asked to be driven to her car, a necessity since the man had earlier insisted on leaving the nightclub and driving in his car to a restaurant across town. At this point the man turned hostile. Lee mimics him:

"Hey, I thought it was going to be you and me and you were going to test. If you don't want a screen test, baby, that's okay too. I want somebody who's really going to commit to this film. [Lee heard him saying I want somebody who's going to fuck me], and if they can't commit to it, boy, there's just too much money at stake here."

The man continued his hostile, undermining attack until Lee finally lost her temper at him, yelling, "I'm an actress, this is business, we're not on some date." This seemed to prick the man's confidence, and when they at last reached the car she recalls him saying, "Hey, Jennifer, I didn't mean anything." Lee remembers jumping out of the car and crying all the way home. "That was one of the worst nights of my life."

The next day Lee called Harris at the Nina Blanchard Agency; he told her he would take care of it. Interested to know how and having a few ideas of her own, Lee took the pencil over to the agency with a request that they send it back to the director accompanied by a letter with copies to the Screen Actors Guild and herself. She wanted the letter to read: "Enclosed please find Jennifer Lee's contract, which she feels she cannot honor at this time."

The Nina Blanchard Agency has done nothing to this day. Lee says, "They don't want to do anything because they didn't want to make any waves. They had other clients they wanted in the film." Mark Harris was asked by *Women's Wear Daily* a short time after the incident why he didn't take the complaint to the Screen Actors Guild. The newspaper reported Harris as replying, "This is what life is all about." He also referred to the difficulty in pressing complaints and his "doubts whether a police force would lead to less crimes." Harris finally said he would take Lee's case to the Guild, "But not now. It's just a matter of timing."[1]

This is the way the social coercion works. The attitude is to let it slide; the man has the power and the woman doesn't. Lee was even warned by the agency that making a fuss could hurt her career. Nina Blanchard, the head of the agency, said: "She's talking about working when she's complained. It doesn't work that way. She cannot have it both ways. I'm not saying that what Jennifer is saying isn't right. I'm saying we're talking about reality and reality is there's nothing she can do about it. People just cannot afford to care."

Despite this attitude from her commercial representative, in a town where one's representative is critical, Lee has refused to remain silent. Although this does not mean she hasn't been scared. Socially coercive pressure is a kind of corrosive and one can hear its influence in her conversation:

Actually, I've wondered if I have hurt myself, my career. I wouldn't have done anything differently, though. It's ridiculous to worry about blacklisting. Talent and self-worth, that's the way you get ahead. I don't feel I'm a troublemaker. I think these people are. They take advantage and misrepresent and exploit situations. Of course, you do have to be careful about your behavior in terms of getting a bad reputation, like a troublemaker, but in something like this I won't stop making noise about it because it's wrong. It's just wrong. I want to be someone who likes herself and I won't turn my anger on myself any more.

I know it's a widespread myth that women get ahead like this, but I don't think that's true at all. I don't think Jane

Fonda has or Katharine Hepburn did or Glenda Jackson. All the actresses that I respect professionally, they haven't done that kind of thing. It doesn't mean you can't sleep with people you like, but that's a whole other thing. I also know Marilyn Monroe supposedly said when she signed her first Fox contract, "Oh, thank God, I don't have to suck any more cock!" They say she did a lot of sleeping around, but I don't really know that either. All I really know is that there are a lot of girls who come to this town who think they can make it that way. I'm sorry they think that and I'm sorry for us as women because it hurts us and it doesn't work.

Lee hasn't bought the myth, unlike many others who have—because, although they may not believe women ask for it, they do believe the economic situation leaves women with few options. The equation roughly goes: Jobs are so tight men will use their advantage for a little free sex; women are so desperate they are happy to comply. Martin Kasindorf writes:

"The surprising thing is not that variations of the old casting couch routine persist, but that in today's hungry climate any women bother to complain." He has used the plural because Jennifer Lee is not alone in standing up for her right to work free of male sexual coercion. The economic basis for the myth may be real to the degree that it acknowledges a tough job market, but the conclusion that because of it women will easily surrender their bodies is not. Among the 5000 female members of the Hollywood Screen Actors Guild, SAG, a large number have complained to the Guild about sexual harassment and have demanded protection. The Guild, not of its own accord, but rather because it was pushed by a sufficient number of these female members, began a low-profile study of the problem. Kasindorf writes:

Prodded by an undisclosed number of member complainants to take their gripes to the police, SAG (two-thirds male in membership) shrinks from doing so. SAG Assistant National Executive Secretary Harry Sloan recently pleaded to the

"Hollywood Reporter" that there are too many separate police jurisdictions involved, making cooperation between SAG and the cops a difficult logistical and organizational problem. Actually, there are studios, producers' offices or agencies in only three separate cities—Los Angeles, Beverly Hills and Culver City. The problem hardly seems insuperable. More probable is that the complaints themselves put the Guild on the hot seat. "If we were to keep records of complaints," squeaked Sloan, "even if we didn't mention names, we'd be involved in a serious constitutional problem." Sloan noted that cops have adopted a hands-off approach in the past, anyway. "Often police are dealing with reputations of significance and don't want to be put in a position of falsely accusing an individual," he said. "There's the problem of slander and libel as well as the motivation of the victim, who may be bearing a grudge or be disgruntled for some other reason."[2]

The Guild's attitude will not change this situation. Police frequently refuse to take the issue seriously, partly because they do not get complaints. Kasindorf quotes Les Zabel, head of the administrative vice unit of the Los Angeles Police Department as saying, "This sex-for-job thing—no complaints have been filed with us at all. I know actresses. They do their number with the producer on a film. That's the way they are."[3]

At every turn, the social coercion that promotes the practice in the first place will reinforce itself by saying women do not complain about it. When women do complain, however, they are disbelieved, their motives are impugned, and they are forced back into a posture of silence either by threats to their economic wellbeing or by the suppressive attitudes of men who dominate the socially legitimate resources of help—law enforcement agencies and unions. As in the case of the Guild, National Executive Secretary Chester Migden eventually authorized the following statement:

"The Screen Actors Guild is in the process of investigating the workability and feasibility of establishing

240

a strictly internal procedure whereby members have a comfortable way of voicing their infrequent complaints regarding the problem confidentially."[4]

About this statement Kasindorf comments, "If the shark in *Jaws* were as toothless as this possible solution, the picture would have flopped."[5] Migden's statement, moreover, cannot stand up to the testimony of actress Jessica Walter, a newly elected second national vice-president, who began her involvement with the union as a member of the Hollywood standing women's conference committee and who helped to found the Guild's morals committee. She says:

"We have had, I must say, we have had a lot of complaints. Now, I betcha it's sort of like rape—how many are reported as to how many actually happened; and I've got a feeling a lot more women are taken advantage of in this particular business than are ever talked about. That's why we decided we should have some kind of judicial committee or morals bureau to deal with it because we wanted to be able to use the power of the union. After all, that's where the union comes in handy. The strength of the Screen Actors Guild is enormous—you don't want to mess with them."

The attitude in Migden's statement is clearly suppressive, Walter's is not; an indication that the complaints had caused enough impact on people's normally coercive attitudes to allow the idea that sexual harassment was a serious problem and that the power of the union was the logical means to bring it under control. Migden, however, before the bureau had even been established, was much more interested in keeping the complainants under control; his statement first underplays the number of complaints and then does not even suggest that the union should do anything more than listen. Meanwhile, Walter (and she was not alone) wanted the union to act as a policeman, a role the committee did initially undertake, apparently with some success. She says:

"There was one particular casting director, I won't

mention his name. Once it was publicized that we actually had the morals committee, we got a lot of complaints about him and the committee went to see him. They also talked to his superiors and he was eventually fired."

Walter, an increasingly well-known actress who won an Emmy for her lead role as a female police chief, is also a witness to the way publicity will encourage more people to think about doing something. She explains:

"Somebody did call me personally. It was an actor who had read about the bureau and he said he knew a girl who was having trouble with a particular casting director. I guess this guy would make them read kissing scenes in the office and he would start kissing them and then if they didn't come through, they didn't get the job."

Walter referred the man to the committee. Since she hasn't been with the committee "for a long time," however, she doesn't know if the man did call—or if he did, how the complaint was handled. She says, "What the committee's doing now, I don't know."

The truth is, nobody knows, and the Guild doesn't offer much enlightenment. Kathleen Nolan, another originator of the women's committee who built a large following among SAG's female constituency and used it to launch herself into the prestigious Hollywood Guild presidency, refused to talk about the morals bureau. No other official will comment either, and Harry Sloan, the man who once made a statement, is no longer with them. Jennifer Lee says:

"I've heard that the morals committee doesn't exist anymore, and if that's true it's simply because they weren't doing anything. We have to have our protection . It would be awful if they just let it drop. It's so sad too, because there's so much they could do. You can alert people to a man who does this. You can also say to some man who persists that he can't use union people. That would stop them. Isn't that what they do other places; isn't that what unions do?"

The Guild has gone so far as to disenfranchise agents

for engaging in sexual harassment. Jessica Walter, who now sits on the National Guild Board, explains:

I don't know if it was handled confidentially or not, but we did get the guy who did it, that's the important thing. In Denver there was a guy, an agent, who was, you know, if you don't come through, you don't get the job. It's a small place, Denver, and there aren't that many jobs or whatever and complaints came from three or four people and we sued. We went first to the government to get his license. We got this guy's license disenfranchised. Then we got to governing forces there in Denver to not allow him to practice working as an agent in Denver. We got rid of this guy. This was within the last year. We also had a similar case in Florida a while back. After three or four interviews or whatever, he'd say if you didn't sleep with this person, you won't get the job and all this kind of stuff. He was actually working as a pimp, but we got him out of business too.

As these examples indicate, Lee is right: there is a great deal the Guild can do about the practice of sexual harassment. The only question is why they have used a vigorous exercise of power to expel abusive agents and do not oppose the practice so vigorously among directors and producers. The answer may simply be that all the Guild's officers and staff are actors themselves, as Cynthia explains: "They are too frightened. They don't want to alienate the studios. They aren't going to rap the people who can give them work." Nina Blanchard says, "They're show-business people, they have a pretty big stake in not making waves."

Blanchard is a tough female entrepreneur who borrowed money to open her own talent agency about six years ago. She has made it pay with an astute, shrewd ingenuity and today her well-known agency, which handles eighty-five models and actresses, has a reputation for handling only the most beautiful. Blanchard is also an advocate of women's rights, but when it comes to accepting financial responsibility for male sexual harassment she is

243

as hooked as almost anyone else into a posture of cooperation. When her clients are rejected for a part because they won't stand for sexual harassment (she has just recently had the experience of this occurring with seven different clients for the same lead in a major picture) Blanchard will do little more than go on record as opposed to the practice and then quietly withdraw. The attitude that this is just something you live with and those are the breaks prevails. The reality eludes her that she is being penalized by men who impose unfair employment practices on her clients while she loses out.

The unquestioning acceptance of female responsibility is so pervasive that when there is a limited awareness of the abuse in a particular industry or business women are expected and even trained to assume this responsibility. Blanchard, who is aware of the abuse, is a good example. Instead of encouraging women to report complaints to people other than to their agent, she teaches them how to "handle" it:

"The main thing the girls have to be taught when they first come in is if they legitimately want to hire them professionally, they don't ask for the home phone number. Most of the girls know how to handle themselves. They can handle it. You get a youngster who doesn't know any better, say, an eighteen-year-old who's never been out before, then you've got a problem."

The problem here is clearly sexual harassment. It is the assumption of this role by women and the coercive attitudes that everywhere reinforce it.

It should be noted that Nina Blanchard is one of the best agents in a business known for its exploitation and opportunism, and her own ethics and business practices are above reproach:

"When we sign a brand-new girl who's eighteen or nineteen, even if she's ready to go into film we won't let her. Not until she's a successful model, because then she's armored and she comes from a position of strength. I never thought about it before but I suppose I'm trying

244

to protect them a bit. Obviously, there's some feeling here in the back of my mind of giving the girl the best advantage so that she can't be pushed around or become some kind of easy prey."

Nina Blanchard never intended to cooperate with sexual harassment. Unfortunately, socially coercive practices thrive when people, both male and female, become oblivious to what they are doing, to their own participation.

Actress Suzanne Sommers says: "This girlfriend I have is just so dumb. This producer comes up to her and tells her she's exactly what he's been looking for to play this great part. He tells her he's going to take her to the executive producer but takes her instead to his apartment. This sounds so ludicrous, but she actually believed it. He then tells her that there's a love scene and they should start practicing for when the producer arrives and he gets her to put on a negligee because that would make it more realistic. Well, there was no part, there was no movie, and how do you blame the guy when she was so stupid as to go along with it?"

The problem isn't the woman's behavior but the man's. We have laws against con artists, those people who prey on other people's unfulfilled desires; these laws clearly place the burden of these frauds and deceptions on the perpetrator, since human vulnerability in no way excuses criminal actions.

Still, there are few people who would not refrain from condemning the women in the preceding story. Coercion is frequently less a question of what we think than it is a result of how we feel. We have been trained to feel that the woman is guilty. The myth of the casting couch is part of that conditioning with respect to working women. Hence our feelings focus on the woman's behavior rather than the man's. Never mind that the man lied, misrepresented himself, lured a woman somewhere under false pretenses, is in effect guilty of fraud. It is the woman's burden to prevent fraud, by seeing through it easily and getting out of it gracefully. Accordingly, the woman is guilty—guilty of being stupid.

The result is that men are free to identify with the man in the story. What else do you do with a stupid woman except take advantage of her? Women, moreover, are not free to identify with the woman in the story because to do so would mean they could be as easily had. They will condemn her, then, for failing in her duty to know better, because she allowed it to happen, because she didn't handle it right.

What many people (and even the victims) frequently fail to understand, is that it is not the women's response to harassment which is at fault, it is the male extortion. Suzanne Sommers' following comment is an illustration: "I, myself, never slept with anybody to get a job, but I think the way I've played the game is definitely a form of prostitution. I knew what I was doing, though; I made the value judgment that I really wanted to work. I allowed them to use my sexuality to achieve a certain level of success. I take the responsibility myself."

Sommers, who has recently married for the second time, for many years lived alone with her son, now eleven, whom she supported as both an actress and writer. She made this statement shortly before she was first signed for the ABC comedy series *Three's Company*. The series went on to become a success and Sommers has gone on to become a well-known star, but at the time of our interview the vivacious blond-haired and blue-eyed actress was just beginning to hope she could finally "be taken seriously" despite the fact that her career had begun eight years earlier. Sommers divides her career into two stages: the first, unsuccessful period lasted six years:

It was just all these quasi-modeling jobs and they were really humiliating. I remember one I had to walk around Market Street in San Francisco all dressed up in a squirrel outfit except that this squirrel had cleavage. I had to pass out nuts. On another one I got hired as a model for a convention—I never asked what I was going to do—I was just so happy to work. It was for a medical convention and I was in traction for three days with one leg up in the air. The hitch was I was dressed up with these tight sweaters and hot pants. That was during the hot pants craze.

Sommers also did a few modeling jobs that involved nudity, jobs that she remembers as "disturbing and embarrassing." One job, however, didn't always make the next one any easier:

"There was a time in my career when I was absolutely poverty-stricken, I mean I really needed the money, when you've got a kid to feed it's no joke; but I went on this one job and I went and undressed in the bathroom and I just stared at the door a long time and then I put all my clothes back on and walked out."

The turning point in Sommers' job opportunities occurred when she was signed as one of three regular female panelists for a television show called *Man-Trap*. The format of this show called for the panelists relentlessly to question a male celebrity guest regardless of what he might say. "It was this real strange parody of women's lib. The producer would actually stand in the wings holding a sign that said ATTACK." As if this stereotypical denigration of women's liberation weren't bad enough, to Sommers' chagrin the show was also interested in promoting other female stereotypes:

I don't know when I caught on, but I could suddenly feel I was supposed to be the dumb, sexy-pretty one. It's like I'd catch the male host and then, later, the other two women asking questions that sort of presumed I didn't have a brain in my head or that I would say something funny. Slowly, I became the brunt of dumb jokes. I was hurt but, then I learned to go along with it, to get laughs like that—and pretty soon I knew exactly how to play it like that. Then I started deliberately doing it. I wanted to work and I have hard practice pressures with a son to raise . . . so you sort of end up playing the game.

247

For most working women "playing the game" means submitting to the generalized male touching, commenting, or staring; in Sommers' case, however, it meant going along with acting the stereotype of the dumb blonde:

"It's like losing a sense or a piece of yourself because you are performing or conforming to what they want you to be, not necessarily who you are."

This assessment is partly the result of having gone on one TV show on twenty-four separate occasions, all to go along with what she describes as "their gimmick—a blond tootsie who laughs a lot, especially at herself, and who goes out and does the one-liners and makes the dumb, sexual jokes." After two years of this, however, Sommers came to understand the act would be impossible to maintain without seriously hurting herself:

"You just reach a point where you no longer respect yourself, when you've prostituted yourself to the point that you don't really know who you are. . . ."

Sommers subsequently asked that show to let her try it "straight." She didn't win the right to play the whole show "straight," but she did get a concession that she could read one of her poems.

For the first time Sommers received letters from women. "They all thought the poem was beautiful, but then they would say, 'I never expected that to come out of you.'" Sommers almost throws up her hands. She says, "That's really me, only I've been sold as something else." Her image was, however, harder to shed than she realized, as one experience demonstrates:

We were talking about parts of the body that feel terrific when they're touched which, of course, has nothing to do with my book, but makes for a good, nothing-terribly-too-deep talk show, and one male guest, while saying, 'I'd like to touch you,' stuck his hands right down the front of my dress and grabbed me. I was furious. But what I was really angry about is that he believed what was being presented. He really believed that's who I was.

All I know is I attract men and I attract men in a way

248

that I don't want to attract men. So therefore it's like Candice Bergen would never get put into the same category as myself because she has a validity about her just the way she carries herself; it's like you know she goes to China, you know she's a photographer and she's into many things. I don't have that look about me. I don't know how you obtain that look. I am what I am, this is what I've always been.

In the same way that Sommers assumes the blame for the way men have divided the world into "ladies" and all the others largely on the basis of class or biological distinctions (whether you get you hair done at Macy's or Bergdorf or have big breasts or small ones) she also assumes blame for the way men—the "they" who could hire—have penalized her sexually in exchange for work.

Suzanne Sommers had no control over the sexually exploitive conditions by which she could obtain work, but this has been obscured by a mythology that will only fault the woman because she went along. The coercion here is remarkable. Given the fact that she wanted to work, she had no choice, but it is made to appear as if she did—an illusion that even she has come to share when she says, "I wanted to work, I made the decision."

How much more accurate it would be to say, "I wanted to work. They told me how that would be possible. I had no choice." Sommers will also be seen by many people as that classic example of the woman who used her sex voluntarily.

This raises another dimension of the casting-couch myth. Because women are perceived as volunteers, it is also often claimed that women invented the idea of using sex as a method for getting ahead. Furthermore, it will be argued this is a logical female invention because men are so gullible, unsuspecting, and naïve that the behavior often works. In actuality the opposite is true; men impose this on women. Consider the following: The talent coordinator for that show, who first signed Suzanne Sommers, says, "When I first interviewed Suzanne for the

249

show, the pre-interview slot I had her in mind for was provocative blonde with fabricated conversation. She's worked out great." About the incident on the show, he adds: "Suzanne's dress was not especially provocative. Not at all. She is always in good taste. There just really was no reason for it." He is oblivious to the way the image imposed on her provoked the incident; Sommers, however, is not. She understood immediately that the male image that had been forced on her in exchange for work, one which also threatened her emotional wellbeing, was simply being accepted at face value. She also understood that this created a fusion between the false front and the real woman so that she wound up publicly pawed.

The identical situation also results when men daily stare at, comment upon, and touch women at work because they are creating an image of the sexually subservient female with parallel results; women are frequently assaulted or propositioned and then penalized because *they* ask for it. Men foist their own image on women, confusing it for the real thing, and then cannot understand why women are upset. Meanwhile, women, like Sommers, frequently fail to perceive the full effect of their "going along" until there is a blatant violation of what passes for normal male-female behavior on the job. Only a massive female refusal to "go along" and resolute complaint-making will end the pervasive power of the myth in both men and women. Until then, any woman who is sexually violated in exchange for work will be lost in the apathetic acceptance of ritualized coercion.

In the final analysis, then, all that is real about the myth of the casting couch is its intent, which is to hide male sexual coercion by saying women ask for it.

Meanwhile the myth obscures the reality of talent, hard work, discipline, and struggle that is the daily fare of thousands of working women. This is not to say that there aren't some women who, like many men, will succeed for the worst of reasons rather than the best, be they sexual or otherwise, and that there aren't mediocre women

250

holding down some good jobs. But the majority of women must work twice as hard as men to achieve a high degree of success or advancement, a fact that is not only obscured but deliberately falsified by the widespread belief that any successful woman has gotten there "on her back."

Nina Blanchard states: "Sleeping your way to the top is just a complete fabrication; it just absolutely doesn't happen that way. I would say over the years that I have never seen anyone make it by going to bed."

The reality of women and work is that they must constantly wage an uphill battle to prove themselves workers deserving of advancement on the basis of merit while bullied by men through a pervasive sexual harassment that denies their true value and imposes sexual complaisance. This is the true goal of sexual harassment, and keeping this goal well concealed by obscuring the behavior, distorting its meaning, and blaming it on women is the ultimate aim of the casting-couch cliché.

Finally it should be noted that the casting couch has become a universal American shorthand for excusing the sexual harassment of working women everywhere, not just in Hollywood or the entertainment industry. It was invoked in Washington during the 1976 sex scandals; it has been used to defend the practice among policemen; it will be attributed to waitresses as well as movie stars; and it is constantly, invariably applied to secretaries who, if and when they should ever complain, are tarred with the brush that they are trying to sleep their way up.

12
Social Coercion II:
Washington Sex Scandals

> "It wasn't something I chose to do.
> I needed a job."[1]
>
> ELIZABETH RAY

The social attitudes that aid and abet the male practice of sexual harassment reached their apex in the 1976 Washington sex scandals. These public exposures of the sexual exploitation of working women in the halls of Congress will forever be linked to the name Elizabeth Ray. Vilified by an unprecedented rush of public sentiment that swamped the print media, Ray became a symbol of the corrupt, ambitious female devoid of morals, a veritable canary in skirts, who deserved neither sympathy nor understanding. *Time* magazine variously compared her to "Typhoid Mary," described her as "a comely if shopworn blond," and reported she gave interviews "with promiscuous delight."[2] Richard Reeves in *New York* magazine wrote "Miss Ray is obviously the pits."[3] The Los Angeles *Times* headlined one story MISS RAY TIMED HER STORY TO BOOST BOOK.[4] The Washington *Star* editorialized, ". . . Elizabeth Ray turns back the clock."[5] Finally *Time,* almost at the end of the month-long flurry, would summarize the entire story as THE RIPPLES OF ELIZABETH RAY'S PROFITABLE TRUE-CONFESSIONS CAPER.[6]

The evidence of sexual harassment in Congress which

subsequently emerged in the course of the scandals was buried beneath Ray's public pillory. To review the pertinent information: Ray, a clerk-secretary, accused her employer, Representative Wayne Hays of Ohio, of having hired her exclusively for sex. Colleen Gardner, another House employee, accused her boss, Texas Representative John Young, of pressuring her and other women on his staff into providing him with sex in exchange for work. Melanie Hall, a third congressional staff member, also employed by Congressman Young, corroborated Gardner's accusations. The FBI interviewed another congressional staffer, a woman formerly employed by Hays (who has remained unnamed), who also alleged she got a job with Hays only after agreeing to have sex with him.

Young consistently declined to discuss his relationship to Colleen Gardner. According to an Associated Press dispatch, he said, "The only issue is whether the federal government got its money's worth. The law isn't interested in personal peccadilloes, as the Justice Department calls it, but only in whether the tax-payers are being cheated."[7] Young clearly knew whereof he spoke. Gardner had originally left Young's staff in 1973, telling unemployment officials she had left because of "sexual pressures." An inquiry at that time had resulted in her giving a statement to the U.S. Attorney's office. *The New York Times,* reporting sources familar with that investigation, said it had not resulted in any charges against Young because Gardner had been unable to supply any corroborative evidence.[8]

This time Gardner, who had returned to Young's employ after he called her up, invited her back, and agreed not to harass her sexually, did have proof. She offered tapes made of her sexual liaisons with Young and of conversations in Young's office attesting to an atmosphere of coercion. The Associated Press, whose reporters listened to a few of the tapes, said, "One tape, of a discussion between Mrs. Gardner and another woman, described how the other woman felt she was coerced into sexual acts with Young.

The other woman wept as she spoke."[9] An AP interview also reported Gardner as saying women staffers dreaded rotating assignments to work in Young's office on Saturdays because they would be frequently left alone in the office with him; according to the AP, Gardner said that Young called any of the young women assigned to this duty "Lucky Lulu."[10]

The second Young staffer, Melanie Hall, who corroborated Gardner's assertions, had also come forward. *The New York Times* reported: "Miss Hall, who left Mr. Young's office two months ago, said that last February 14, while she was the only secretary on duty in the office, Mr. Young made advances to her. Miss Hall, who is 23, said that the next week Mr. Young offered her a 'substantial' raise, which she declined, and that she left his staff shortly afterward."[11]

Gardner had also alleged her salary increases had been commensurate with Young's satisfaction with their sexual relationship. She reported her salary had begun at $8500 and over an on-off three-year period had been raised to nearly $26,000 when she quit.[12] However, just as three years earlier (in 1973), when Gardner first sought help, the Justice Department was not interested; again a lack of proof was cited. It was held that the tapes were not so much proof of coercion as merely testimony as to a sexual relationship. The question of salary increments hinging on Young's sexual satisfaction, the testimony of Melanie Hall (who had quit), and Hall's own testimony to a proposed pay raise being involved were ignored.

So was the idea that both Hays and Young, by possibly making sexual relations a condition of employment, may have been in violation of Title VII—Congress's own legislation against sex discrimination. However, a full public airing of this aspect would not have helped the Justice Department at all. They were just in the process of recovering from losing the Diane Williams case, in which she had charged that sexual relations in exchange for work was the practice of their own agency. Interestingly too,

254

Justice had defended itself on the ground it was not responsible for the "personal peccadilloes" of its employees, a phrase and a defense Young plucked right out of the mouth of the nation's top law-enforcement agency and regurgitated back to the nation as if the argument had not already lost its day in court.

Of course, Hays, Young, the Justice Department, and Congress had little to fear. Elizabeth Ray took the heat. How could anyone seriously talk about sexual harassment, about an abuse of working conditions, about unfair employment practices or an exploitation of female sexuality in relation to a self-acknowledged whore?

The unstated premise by which Ray's tarring and feathering commenced was that she chose to do it; and when Ray would say otherwise, which was often, she would merely be treated to a new round of hooting and jeering. This reaction is male supremacy wrapped in a rather indecent, hypocritical, and self-righteous mockery that is also illogical. Elizabeth Ray did not make the rules. Of what crime did she stand condemned, of taking a job by the terms accorded her? That's no crime in a nation where the large majority of workers neither like what they do nor the way they do it, although their responsibility is dismissed because they don't make the rules. Since when, then, is the player held responsible for the terms of the game? Is there nothing wrong with making sexual demands a condition of work—only in acquiescing to them?

This attitude, which Ray symbolized, subsequently precluded any serious discussion of sexual harassment. The subject was alternately abused, mocked, or readily dismissed in favor of the more "important" issues. Consequently, the media blitz remains a blazing contemporary catalogue of public attitudes about working women and sexual harassment; it is in the main a compendium of cynicism, trivialization, male moralizing, opportunism, and misogyny.

Indicative of the way the imposition of sex in exchange for work was taken for granted, Warren Weaver wrote in *The New York Times* that sexual infidelity was characteristic of Congress for a number of reasons, which included that "Congressional staff workers are under the absolute control of their employers."[13] Ann Pincus declared in the *Village Voice,* "It may be, as one wag put it, that getting Wayne L. Hays for a sex scandal is like getting Al Capone for tax evasion, but you take what you can get."[14]

David S. Broder wrote in the Washington *Post:* "Of course it is an affront to decency if the hiring policies of some congressional offices reflect the sexual appetites of the boss rather than the competence of the employees. But . . . these scandals, gamy as they may be, are tangential and trivial compared to the real abuses of power on Capitol Hill."[15] On the same day James A. Wechsler wrote in the New York *Post,* ". . . I admittedly care a lot more . . . about the intimacies of Congressmen with special-privilege lobbyists and their contempt for ethical practice than about who did what to Elizabeth Ray."[16]

Turning the "sex scandal" to its advantage, the New York *Daily News* featured a series on sex and politics; the third article appeared under the headline LBJ AND JFK: A KEEN EYE FOR A SKIRT. It was the now-familiar acceptance of sexual harassment in the guise of gossip and included the report of a former LBJ staffer who woke up in the middle of the night at his Texas ranch to find the President trying to get in bed with her. According to the article, "The girl sought, and received, a transfer to the State Department."[17] President Ford meanwhile was seeking to turn the scandals into a boost for re-election; after one such campaign speech the Washington *Star* headlined RIGHTEOUS FORD TELLS BAPTISTS, OFFICIALS MUST "SET EXAMPLE."[18]

This is not to say that no other viewpoint was expressed. Here and there a letter to the editor or an article did appear. Alexander Cockburn and James Ridgeway came close to the mark in the June 7 *Village Voice:*

The essence of the scandal over Congressman Hays' relationship with Elizabeth Ray—who claims that he fixed her up in a congressional job she was incompetent to perform, in return for her sexual favors—is that this woman had enough tenacity to speak out about a situation which has existed on Capitol Hill for many years, and which symbolizes the way in which women are used in the Congress, not just sexually but in terms of their labor.[19]

The two men went on to discuss the widespread nature of sexual harassment by stating that Hays is not an isolated case, that many members also have on their payrolls women who provide sexual services for their friends as well as themselves, that women are used as bargaining counters in legislative negotiations, and that "the success of a woman on Capitol Hill often depends on her looks and her acquiescence to sexual overtures."[20] They added that the practice has even been "blatantly advertised in the Washington papers" and related the story of a woman who answered an ad for a $4000-a-year typing job only to be told by the office interviewer, "observing she seemed like a nice woman who deserved better things," that all raises would involve her "consenting to activities she might not like."[21]

At the close of this line of argument, however, as if completely oblivious to its implications, Cockburn and Ridgeway switch to a posture of having raised the subject only to point up one more example of the way women are abused "in terms of their labor."[22] What follows is a brief recitation of women's admittedly inferior employment status as manifested in bad pay, overwork, the wide discrepancy between male and female job titles, and the lack of remedies for any of these abuses (as if Congress were the only place these outrageous conditions existed). They subsequently conclude, "But the sex scandals are indicative of a far more serious problem. The fact is that members of Congress have employed hun-

257

dreds and thousands of women in a state of economic servitude."[23]

Sally Quinn wrote in the October issue of *Redbook:* "But in Washington, D.C., power is everything and for many the only way to get a piece of it is by making compromises. . . . For women it is often a sexual compromise."[24]

We have here the beginning of an apology for the way women let men "take advantage" of them; it continues throughout and remains the article's basic theme. Quinn eventually acknowledges she doesn't like men who use women but concludes it is still the women's responsibility, hence women simply have to stand up for themselves better. She ends, "Until then . . . women will be the biggest losers of all. For in choosing to compromise our bodies, ultimately we compromise ourselves."[25] This overlooks the hard truth: there are many women who simply have no better options. It is a classic version of the "I raised myself by my own bootstraps—why can't you?" mentality.

Caryl Rivers wrote in a *New York Times* article in June: "For a woman, one with no connections and no particular expertise, there was no Way Up—with one exception. . . . Many of the women don't understand their true role in the game. They will be used while it is convenient and pleasurable for the powerful men to use them, and then they will be discarded, like used paper towels. . . ."[26] She goes on to say, however, "A man who cynically and habitually uses women, as some of our public officials do, is not a man who represents my interests."[27] It is just not a question of overall conditions for Rivers, rather simply of voting a few of the bad guys out of office. This is a classic liberal position and, as is readily apparent, although sympathetic it neither advances our understanding of sexual harassment nor promotes a solution.

The public reaction to the scandals was an unequal mixture of disbelief, moral outrage, and galloping cynicism. Louis Harris, in an article in the July 1 New York

Post, reported the latest Harris Survey "indicates clearly that the revelations in the Hays case triggered a rather deep-seated suspicion that affairs with paid staff members abound in the federal establishment in Washington, and also in the top echelons of big business."[28] The poll showed 47 percent of the American people felt Hays' behavior was typical of "many" members of Congress and 55 percent believed "many" businessmen behaved the same way.

Letters to the editor merely echoed all the familiar themes with new accents. Men, for example, were often most upset at the mishandling of male power. In the June 21 issue of *Time:* George Johnson of Wausau, Wisconsin, wrote: "Congressman Wayne Hays apparently never heard of the warning: 'Hell hath no fury like a woman scorned.' "[29] Lawrence M. Jacobson of Olympia, Washington, said: "I hope Congressman Hays can judge the motives of the Russians better than he figured the aspirations of Ms. Ray. My confidence in Congress has not been bolstered."[30] Money was frequently the focus, as in the June 28 *Newsweek* letter from Harold Willens: ". . . Hays makes us pay for his play—that's taxation without representation."[31]

As the letters, the articles, the whole barrage of public commentary quoted has indicated, the public awareness of sexual harassment is poor to nonexistent. Women are widely held to be culpable. Hays and Young were welcomed back to their home communities. Young was eventually re-elected to Congress in November by a nearly two-to-one margin. He is back in Washington, doing business at the same old stand. We like our public officials a cut above the rest of us, but men are men. Hays and Young both denied the misuse of public funds, and that was the only serious part; besides, Hays resigned, that's punishment enough! As for Young, few people back in Corpus Christi believed "that woman."

Sexual harassment will never be the "serious part" until all its elements are understood and the sum of the

259

coercion it exerts is both grasped and condemned. Female oppression at work is the result of nearly universal male power to hire and fire. Men control the means of economic survival. This control, however, is also used to coerce working women sexually. Institutionalized male power has thus created its own means of maintaining its superior position—by socially enlisting women's cooperation in their own sexual subservience and accomplishing this by rewarding them when they do and punishing them when they do not. Work, the ostensible equalizer, the location of women's hopes for equality, and the means to her economic independence is subsequently transformed into new enslavement. In the meantime, we condemn women as whores for being coerced, fail to acknowledge the daily economic hardship of thousands who refuse to yield, and deny help to those who seek it.

13
The Future

The sexual harassment of women at work arose out of man's need to maintain his control of female labor. This tactic of nonreciprocal aggression is a major element in the maintenance of job segregation by sex. It ensures that female wages stay low, weakens women's employment position by undermining female seniority, and keeps women divided so they are incapable of organizing to change their situation.

Working women, by and large, have succumbed to this male extortion by escaping sexual aggression at the expense of their jobs or by keeping their jobs at the expense of their self-respect. They have forfeited their independence and equality at work either way. Meanwhile, the pervasiveness of the aggression has taken a toll of women's drive and desire to work that is beyond calculation. Work itself is a precondition of women's liberation. However, instead of liberation, women find the promise of equality inherent in modern work canceled out by sexual harassment. The abuse maintains the age-old requirement of the Patriarchy: that woman shall serve man with her labor and pay for the right to do so with her body.

The obvious solution is a totally integrated work force with both sexes sharing equally in all jobs and all authority throughout the hierarchies of business power. This kind of change, however, will require nothing less than an alteration in the balance of power at work. This will have to be effected by women. There is only one way women can accomplish it: by unifying and organizing themselves into a cohesive force that will protect their rights at work as vigorously as men will fight to preserve the status quo. Organization is the key to ending sexual harassment. This necessity, however, is often obscured by concern at helping the victims. Assistance of this kind is an immediate necessity, but altering the balance of power at work is the only long-term solution. Working women deserve not just aid for their mistreatment but an end of the victimization altogether.

Significantly, present legal recourse can go part of the way toward accomplishing both tasks. Currently, perpetrators of harassment can be prosecuted under present criminal laws that pertain to sexual assault—rape, extortion, and solicitation for prostitution. These laws have been invoked rarely in cases involving sexual harassment primarily because work is viewed as a world unto itself—also because of social attitudes that have denied the serious nature of the behavior while simultaneously assuming both parties to be equally culpable (if, in fact, the woman wouldn't be viewed as more culpable). In view of our increased understanding of this type of aggression, however, there should be more pressure on law-enforcement officials to make arrests.

This effort can take advantage of the lobbying about rape that has already been done with police departments so that male attitudes, once an initial unfamiliarity with sexual harassment is overcome, may be expected to be more cooperative than ever before. Of course, widespread prosecution will continue to remain problematic. Male attitudes, despite improvement, still constitute a strong obstacle. Women's reluctance to seek redress from the police in the face of this hostility will also continue. Even so, the advantages of criminal prosecution (and this cannot be stressed enough) are well worth the trouble. Any significant increase in enforcement of these laws will act as a deterrent; the abuse has only flourished in part because it has been spared the stigma of criminal activity.

Civil legal remedies are frequently less immediate than criminal prosecution, and their usefulness as a real deterrent is questionable. But they often prove more beneficial to the female victim by redressing some of the financial harm that has attended her victimization. Of all the civil remedies available, Title VII of the 1964 Civil Rights Act offers the best chance for potential redress by providing remuneration for lost pay, legal fees, and the possibility of reinstatement on the job. As the chapter on legal recourse makes clear, however, male attitudes are serious obstacles to enforcement and future prosecution of this issue under Title VII remains in serious jeopardy. In addition, the present three-year backlog in EEOC cases presents another deterrent. Society's condoning of this lengthy time lag between injury and adjudication casts grave doubt as to the more-than-symbolic intent of the legislation.

Aside from legal redress, there is a third widely-advocated remedy—women simply must become more active. Assertiveness training programs for women at work have sprung up all around the country, generally for the best of motives—to counter women's socialization to submissiveness and to reinforce assertiveness. It is believed this will enhance women's success at work by better enabling them to handle their discrimination. This kind of training is effective only up to a point, however, and it would be a grave mistake to rely on this training to combat sexual harassment. In the first place, the problem is not women's behavior, and in the second place, the aggression succeeds largely because women have no recourse at work, not because they can't stand up to it.

About the best that can be said for this kind of "solution," then, is that in some situations, for some women, it may help them deal with it a little better. Sandra Driggs of Communications Perspectives in San Francisco says:

"Be smart. If you find yourself in job difficulties because of sexual pressures, take time to analyze the situation. Build your own case, get documentation. Put it in writing. Get memos. Try and develop a case of the way it is affecting your job evaluations and performance. Don't just behave as if he automatically has the upper hand. This comes under the general heading of 'Cover Your Ass.' "

All of the preceding indicates that, while some things can be done once the aggression has begun, this frequently will not prevent the end result of job loss. Law enforcement is punitive rather than preventive except in the sense that punishment is believed or hoped to be a deterrent. In the meantime, however, the extortion has succeeded. Only a completely inclusive solution to sexual harassment will ensure a future for women at work that is free of this abuse. Grievance procedures are at present completely inadequate. Women do not trust in-house avenues of employee redress, and for the most part this is grounded in accurate assessments of the range of male power that will be arrayed against them.

The hope of working women for a substantial change in the work environment has been evidenced in recent years by their efforts in demanding better working conditions. Grass-roots working women's organizations have sprung up all across the country and include: "Women Office Workers in New York City, 9–5 in Boston, Women Employed in Chicago, Women Organized for Employment in San Francisco, and Union W.A.G.E. in Oakland. They draw their members from among the mass of unorganized working women who have no other way to articulate their needs, voice their complaints, or channel their demands for change. They are hybrid groups, neither pure women's rights nor pure labor rights, but an amalgam of both evidencing women's great need for organizations that will advance their cause as *women* at *work*.

These groups represent significant progress; nevertheless they cannot supply the full solution. Women on the job, inside the workplace, must gather their collective strength.

Sexual harassment will be stopped when women finally take control of their own labor power via collective bargaining and striking to regain their rights.

This will be a long fight, but it is the inevitable future. The sexual harassment of women at work is an intolerable working condition that negatively affects everyone. It is as onerous to women as rape, and as important as abortion because it involves the right to control their own bodies. It is this *sine qua non* which is at the core of all three issues. Women's stamina, energy, and courage in the battles on rape and abortion have made recent history; because of sexual harassment they will change the face of modern work as well. It is only a question of time. Women are 40 percent of the work force now. This percentage is expected to grow, and these numbers alone bespeak a power base which only lacks organization to make itself felt. Humor has always played a large part in the cover-up of sexual harassment, but women will have the last laugh. The sexual harassment men have used to keep women subordinate will ultimately prove the issue by which working women will unite.

14
Eleven Ways to Fight
Sexual Harassment

1. Sexual harassment is Criminal Activity. Rape because it occurs in an office or factory is no less a crime than elsewhere in our society. The same holds true for sexual assault, abuse, misuse and physical violation. No less importantly, when a manager, boss, supervisor or foreman tells a woman she can't get a job or keep one without "putting out" sexually, he is soliciting for prostitution. All of these forms of sexual harassment are *already* outlawed by criminal statutes. Take your complaint to your local police department. Don't be timid. Demand your protection under the law. Prosecute your assailant.

2. Sexual Harassment on-the-job is Sex Discrimination. Because this abuse deprives women of the right to equal employment opportunity, you can seek justice and/or compensation under a variety of government enforcement agencies:

• The Equal Employment Opportunity Commission (EEOC) is the federal remedy. Within 180 days of filing a complaint with the EEOC you can obtain a lawyer (often on a contingency basis which means you pay nothing until the successful conclusion of your suit) and you can, if fired, sue for re-instatement to your job plus up to three years back-pay dating from the time of termination.

• Closer to home, your local city or state human rights agency is empowered to intervene in your behalf at any point you experience sexual harassment. This can be before or after you are either forced to quit your job and/or are fired. All it takes is a phone call to determine if you have a complaint. Don't wait! Act immediately. You have nothing to lose and it could save your job.

• Private suits are a third legal option. You can sue for damages as a result of the trauma of being coerced sexually on your job. Consult a lawyer.

3. You deserve Unemployment Compensation. A bill now pending in the New York State Legislature will make sexual harassment good cause for leaving a job; Wisconsin has already passed a similar statute. File your claim immediately. Fair and just economic compensation for sexual harassment that results in loss of employment is your right.

4. File a Grievance/Go to your Union. Internal grievance procedures and unions are your on-the-job remedies. Use them. Even if you feel they will not take your claim seriously or are prejudiced against your complaint, these channels must be pursued if you are serious about stopping sexual harassment. No court, for example, can rule in favor of a female complainant if she has not first exhausted all internal remedies.

5. Document Your Case. Your job is in jeopardy from the second the sexual harassment begins. Prepare yourself accordingly. Keep memos that detail the attacks. For example, "On such and such day and time, so and so came into my office, met me in the hall, cornered me in the elevator and he either/and-or said or did thus." You don't have to post these memos on the company bulletin board, but you should send them privately to someone else at work, preferably a superior. Now you have a record of the harassment. Combined with your good employment record this documentation can eventually save your job.

6. Take Direct Action. This is particularly successful with co-workers. State your discomfort, say "NO" immediately. If necessary, pinch back. Many men will stop

when faced by a determined woman who forcefully communicates that this behavior is intolerable.

7. Get Help from Women's Groups. The experience of sexual harassment at work is a serious trauma. Women's organizations including N.O.W. and a variety of local working women's organizations such as the Alliance Against Sexual Coercion in Boston, the Interfaith Project on Working Women in Philadelphia and Work Options for Women in Wichita, Kansas are on your side. You need their emotional/legal resources. Don't hesitate. If your town doesn't have a women's organization to deal with women's job problems—start one.

8. Use the Power of the Press. Never underestimate the value of adverse publicity. Go public. Expose the situation. Sexual harassment can only succeed in secrecy and public exposure is a great asset.

9. Female Solidarity on-the-job is a Powerful Weapon. Ask for help from your female co-workers. Give help without being asked. Become friends of the women with whom you work. The company and the harasser can always pick us off one-by-one. When we stand up together we have power—the power of unity in numbers. Just think, he can fire you, but he can't fire all ten of you in the office at the same time.

10. Organize. This is the *whole* solution. When women have organized to protect their rights on-the-job as vigorously as men have organized to protect theirs, the world of work for women will be transformed. This is the future. It won't be long before a national women's union or federation of unions of women will negotiate decent working conditions for all women who work for pay, but you can begin now. Form a women's committee, a women's caucus, a female rap group. You have nothing to lose and your job may depend on it.

11. In school. While it is not strictly on-the-job, female students in University and College graduate schools frequently are blocked by sexual harassment from obtain-

ing the degrees necessary to get skilled jobs. Because the abuse in this setting deprives women of the right to an equal education, students should file grievances against the offending professor as well as sue the institution under all the government statutes and agencies which prohibit sex discrimination in education.

Notes

Preface
1. Elizabeth M. Almquist, "Women in the Labor Force," *SIGNS: Journal of Women in Culture and Society*, Vol. 2, No. 4 (1977), pp. 843–844.

Introduction
1. Nancy Smith Barrett, "The Economy Ahead of Us," Women and the American Economy, edited by Juanita Kreps (Englewood Cliffs, N.J.: Prentice-Hall, 1976), p. 157.
2. Edward Gross, "Plus Can Change . . . ? The Sexual Structure of Occupations over Time," *Social Problems* (Fall 1968) p. 202.
3. Barrett, loc. cit.

Chapter Two
1. *Reader's Digest* (August 1970), p. 41.
2. *Reader's Digest* (October 1970), p. 52.
3. See *Women Office Workers Newsletter* (Sept.–Oct. 1975), available from Women Office Workers, 680 Lexington Ave., N.Y., N.Y. 10022.
4. Adrienne Rich, *Of Woman Born* (New York: Norton, 1976), p. 57.
5. Nancy M. Henley, "Power, Sex and Nonverbal Communication" in *Language and Sex,* edited by Barrie Thorne and Nancy Henley (Massachusetts: Newbury House Publishers, 1975), p. 184.
6. Erving Goffman, "The Nature of Deference and Demeanor," *American Anthropologist*, LVIII, 1956, pp. 473–502.
7. Michael Argyle, *Psychology of Interpersonal Behavior* (London: Cox and Wyman Ltd., 1967).
8. "Both physical closeness and staring seem to be perceived as warning signals in the confrontation sequences. . . ." George

Maclay and Humphry Knipe, The Dominant Man (New York: Delacorte, 1972), p. 58.

9. Henley, op. cit., p. 192.
10. Nancy M. Henley, "The Politics of Touch," *Radical Psychology*, edited by Phil Brown (New York: Harper, 1973), p. 423.
11. Henley, *Language and Sex*, p. 184.
12. Ibid., p. 192.
13. Catherine Radecki, "Differences in the Use of Dominance Gestures in an Occupational Setting by Sex and Status," mimeographed, University of Delaware, September 1976.
14. Henley, "The Politics of Touch," pp. 431–432.
15. Charles E. Ginder, "Factors of Sex in Office Employment," *Office Executive* (February 1961), p. 11.
16. Catherine Ettlinger, "The Beauty Queen Syndrome," *Washington Newsworks* (March 18–24, 1976).
17. Ibid.
18. Walter Mossberg, "Reports on EEOC Charge Incompetence and Corruption, Prompt Criminal Study," *Wall Street Journal*, April 22, 1976.
19. William Federici, "HEW Officials Here Being Probed," New York *Daily News*, January 21, 1977.
20. Glenn V. Ramsey, Bert Kruger Smith, and Bernice Milburn Moore, *Women View Their Working World* (Austin: University of Texas Press, 1963), pp. 12–33.
21. Redbook Magazine (November 1976), p. 149.
22. San Francisco *Chronicle*, July 11, 1975.
23. "Survey of Staff Attitudes on Sex Discrimination in the United Nations Secretariat: Analysis and Recommendations for Action," prepared by the Ad Hoc Group on Equal Rights for Women at the UN.
24. Irene Nolan, "Sex and the Working Woman—Harassment On-The-Job," The Louisville *Courier-Journal & Times*, November 16, 1975.
25. J. Brown, "Sexual Harassment Plagues Women on Job," *The Guardian*, New York, June 22, 1967.
26. Nolan, op. cit.

Chapter Three

1. Heidi Hartmann, "Capitalism, Patriarchy and Job Segregation by Sex," *Signs: Journal of Women in Culture and Society*, Vol. 1, No. 3 (Spring 1976), Part 2, pp. 138–139.
2. Ibid.
3. Ibid., p. 153.
4. Neil Smelser, *Social Change and the Industrial Revolution*

(Chicago: University of Chicago Press, 1959), chaps. 9–11, cited in Hartmann.

5. Frederick Engels, *The Condition of the Working Class in England in 1844* (London: George Allen & Unwin, 1892), p. 199, cited in Hartmann.

6. Hartmann, op. cit., p. 155.

7. Sidney Webb, "The Alleged Differences in the Wages Paid to Men and Women for Similar Work," *Economic Journal* 1, No. 4 (December 1891), pp. 639–658, cited in Hartmann.

8. Millicent G. Fawcett, "Equal Pay for Equal Work," *Economic Journal*, 28, No. 1 (March 1918), pp. 1–6, cited in Hartmann.

9. F. Y. Edgeworth, "Equal Pay to Men and Women for Equal Work," *Economic Journal*, 32, No. 4 (December 1922), p. 439, cited in Hartmann.

10. Hartmann, op. cit., p. 160.

11. Ibid., p. 161.

12. Edith Abbott, *Women in Industry* (New York: Arno Press, 1969), p. 92, cited in Hartmann.

13. Hartmann, op. cit., p. 161.

14. Elizabeth F. Baker, *Technology and Women's Work* (New York: Columbia University Press, 1964), p. 34, cited in Hartmann.

15. John B. Andrews and W. D. P. Bliss, "History of Women in Trade Unions" in *Report on Condition of Woman and Child Wage-Earners in the United States*, Vol. 10, printed by Government Printing Office, 1911, reprinted as *History of Women in Trade Unions* (New York: Arno Press, 1974), p. 69.

16. Hartmann, op. cit., p. 163.

17. Abbott, op. cit., pp. 252–253, cited in Hartmann.

18. Gail Falk, "Women and Unions: A Historical View," mimeographed, Yale Law School, published in shortened form in *Women's Rights Law Reporter*, 1 (Spring 1973), pp. 54–65, cited in Hartmann.

19. Eleanor Flexner, *Century of Struggle* (New York: Atheneum, 1970), p. 136, cited in Hartmann.

20. Abbott, op. cit., p. 260.

21. Hartmann, op. cit., p. 164.

22. Ibid., p. 165.

23. Ibid.

24. Ann C. Hill, "Protective Labor Legislation for Women: Its Origin and Effect," mimeographed, Yale Law School, 1970; published in part in Barbara A. Babcock, Ann E. Freeman, Eleanor H. Norton and Susan C. Ross, *Sex Discrimination and the Law: Causes and Remedies* (Boston: Little, Brown & Company, 1975), cited in Hartmann.

25. Elisha Bartlett, "A Vindication of the Character and Condition of the Females Employed in the Lowell Mills Against the Charges Contained in the Boston *Times* and the *Boston Quarterly Review*," orig. published Lowell, Massachusetts, 1841; reprinted in *Women of Lowell* (New York: Arno Press, 1974), p. 19.

26. *Voice of Industry,* Fitchburg, Massachusetts, September 18, 1846. Cornell University Industrial and Labor Relations Archives.

26. This is largely based on William Wallace Sanger, *History of Prostitution: Its Extent, Causes and Effects throughout the World* (New York: Harper, 1869), an official report to the Board of alms-house governors of New York City; Reginald Wright Kauffman, *The House of Bondage* (New York: Moffat, Yard and Company, 1910), a report of the special Grand Jury appointed in New York in January 1910 to investigate white slave traffic; and Havelock Ellis, *Sex in Relation to Society* (Philadelphia: F. A. Davis Company, 1910).

28. Helen Laura Sumner, "History of Women in Industry in the United States, 1910," in *Report on Condition of Woman and Child Wage-Earners in the United States,* Vol. 9, printed by Government Printing Office, 1911; reprinted as *History of Women in Industry in the United States* (New York: Arno Press, 1974), p. 98.

29. Upton Sinclair, *The Jungle,* orig. published 1905 (New York: New American Library, 1960), p. 109.

30. William Sulzer papers, 1890–1940. Department of Manuscripts and University Archives, Cornell University.

31. Helen Campbell, *Women Wage-Earners, Their Trades and Their Lives* (Boston: Roberts Brothers, 1887), reprinted as *Prisoners of Poverty* (Westport, Conn.: Greenwood Press, 1970, 1975), preface.

32. Ibid., p. 22.

33. Ibid., p. 35.

34. Ibid., p. 87.

35. Ibid., p. 97.

36. Ibid., pp. 135–136.

37. Louisa M. Alcott, "How I Went Out To Service," *The Independent,* New York, June 4,1874.

38. Campbell, op. cit., p. 234.

39. Ibid., p. 181.

40. Ibid., loc. cit.

41. Maud Younger, "The Diary of an Amateur Waitress," *McClure's Magazine,* 1907.

42. Gerda Lerner, *Black Women in White America* (New York: Random House, 1973), pp. 149–150.

43. Ibid., pp. 155–156.
44. Frances A. Kellor, "Southern Colored Girls in the North," *Charities and the Commons,* 1905.
45. Mary M. Brownlee and W. Elliott Brownlee, *Women in the American Economy* (New Haven: Yale University Press, 1976), p. 244.
46. Women Factory Inspectors of New York State, 1890–91, #2367 m, a collection of New York state newspaper clippings. Department of Manuscripts and University Archives, Cornell University.
47. Howard B. Woolston, *Prostitution in the United States,* Vol. 1 (New York: The Century Co., 1921), pp. 279–280.
48. Sumner, *History of Women in Industry,* p. 203.
49. Alice Kessler-Harris, "Organizing the Unorganizable: Three Jewish Women and Their Union," *Labor History,* Vol. 17, No. 1 (Winter 1976), p. 16.
50. Ibid.
51. Ibid., pp. 17–18.
52. Emma Goldman, "The Traffic in Women," reprinted in *Red Emma Speaks Selected Writings and Speeches by Emma Goldman,* compiled and edited by Alix Kates Shulman (New York: Random House Vintage Books, 1972), p. 145.

Chapter Four
1. Women's Bureau, *Handbook on Women Workers* (Washington, D.C., U.S. Government Printing Office, 1975), p. 67.
2. Ibid., p. 68.
3. Ibid.
4. Ibid.
5. Ibid., p. 61.
6. Ibid., p. 60.
7. Jean Hayman, "Progress for Women: Men Are Still More Equal," *Harvard Business Review,* September–October 1973.
8. Juanita Kreps, *Sex in the Marketplace: American Women at Work* (Baltimore: The Johns Hopkins University Press, 1971), p. 93.
9. Women's Bureau, "Why Women Work," U.S. Government Printing Office (July 1972), p. 1.
10. *Handbook on Women Workers,* pp. 70, 139, 140.
11. Ibid., p. 127.
12. Ibid., pp. 20, 139–142. See also *Exploitation from 9 to 5* (Lexington, Mass. D. C. Heath, 1975), p. 53.
13. Robert L. Stein, "The Economic Status of Families Headed by Women," *Monthly Labor Review* (December 1970), p. 3.
14. This is documented in the chapter on Sexual Harassment in Traditional Jobs.

15. Gilbert Burck, "Before long we keep hearing, work will practically wither away . . . No such luck," *Fortune Magazine* (March 1970).
16. *Exploitation from 9 to 5*, Report of the Twentieth Century Fund Task Force on Women and Employment, background paper by Adele Simmons, Ann Freeman, Margaret Dunkle, and Francine Blau, op. cit., p. 48.
17. Ibid., p. 48.
18. Ibid., pp. 48–49.
19. Barrett, *Women and the American Economy*, p. 158.
20. Howard L. Wilensky, "Women's Work: Economic Growth, Ideology, Structure," *Industrial Relations* (May 1968), p. 241.

Chapter Five
1. Edwin C. Lewis, *Developing Women's Potential* (Ames, Iowa: The Iowa State University Press, 1968), p. 113.
2. Patricia Marshall, *Manpower Magazine*, Vol. 4, No. 12 (December 1972), pp. 6–7.
3. Jane Seaberry, "They Don't Swing to Sex on the Beat," Washington *Post*, October 13, 1975.
4. Ibid.
5. Ibid.
6. Ibid.
7. Jane Seaberry and Alfred E. Lewis, "Police Sex Charge Called Back-Alley Gossip by Chief," Washington *Post*, October 15, 1975.
8. Ibid.
9. Phil McCombs, "Sex in the Squad Car," San Francisco *Examiner & Chronicle*, October 10, 1976.
10. Linda Fillmore, "Women's Work Around Track Is Never Done," Los Angeles *Times*, May 19, 1976.
11. Los Angeles *Times*, June 4, 1976.
12. Elizabeth C. Baker, "Sexual Art-Politics," *Art and Sexual Politics: Why have there been no great women artists?*, edited by Thomas B. Hess and Elizabeth C. Baker (New York: Macmillan Publishing Company, 1973), pp. 110–111.
13. Pamela Ann Roby, "Toward Full Equality: More Job Education For Women," mimeographed, Santa Cruz, University of California, May 1975, p. 14, subsequently published in *School Review*, Vol. 84, No. 2 (February 1976).
14. Ibid., p. 30
15. *Handbook on Women Workers*, p. 232.
16. Ibid.
17. Ibid., pp. 195–207.
18. Krebs, *Sex in the Marketplace*, p. 51.

19. Ralph Craib, "Sex and Women at UC Berkeley—2 Surveys," San Francisco *Chronicle*, July 22, 1977.
20. Karen Lindsey, "Sexual Harassment on the Job," *Ms.* Magazine, November 1977, p. 48.
21. *Handbook on Women Workers*, p. 151.
22. *Sex in the Marketplace*, pp. 47–48.
23. *Handbook on Women Workers*, p. 96.
24. Ibid., p. 93.

Chapter Six

1. *1975 Handbook on Women Workers*, p. 104.
2. Ettlinger, "The Beauty Queen Syndrome."
3. From a suit registered with the federal Fair Employment Practices Commission, 1943.
4. Ettlinger, op. cit.
5. Ibid.
6. Ibid.
7. *1975 Handbook on Women Workers*, p. 134.
8. Ibid., pp. 104, 135.
9. Ibid., p. 105.
10. Ettlinger, op. cit.
11. Mary Kathleen Benet, *The Secretarial Ghetto* (New York: McGraw-Hill, 1972), p. 49.
12. Ibid., p. 83.
13. *Handbook on Women Workers*, p. 64.
14. "Mature Women the New Labor Force," *Industrial Gerontology*, Spring 1974.
15. "Patterns of Sex and Age Discrimination as Practiced by New York City Employment Agencies: 1976," A Women Office Workers Research Project Report, Women Office Workers, NYC, p. 1.
16. Ibid., p. 10.
17. Ibid., p. 2.
18. Ibid., p. 8.
19. *Handbook on Women Workers*, pp. 12, 15.
20. Ibid., p. 273.
21. Ibid., p. 70.
22. Ibid., p. 71.

Chapter Seven

1. Laura Perlman, "Less Than Equal Protection Under the Law," *Woman-power* (November 1975), p. 32.
2. Enid Nemy, "Women Begin to Speak Out Against Sexual Harassment at Work," *The New York Times*, August 19, 1975, p. 38.
3. Joan Jackson, "Office Sex Upheld As Reason For Quitting Job," Minneapolis *Tribune*, November–December, 1975.

4. Zelah Scalf, "Bloomington Chief's Sex Case Passed On To State," Minneapolis *Star,* August 5, 1975.
5. Monge v. Beebe Rubber Co. [114 N.H. 130].
6. Ibid.
7. Ibid.
8. Ibid.
9. S. Rep. No. 91-1137, 91st Cong., 2d Sess. 15 (1970).
10. Susan C. Ross, *The Rights of Women, an American Civil Liberties Handbook* (New York: Avon Books, 1973), pp. 33–38.
11. Gloria Berger, "GS-5 Is Awarded $18,000 In Sexual Harassment Suit," Washington *Star,* March 1, 1978.
12. New York *Post,* April 4, 1978.
13. Corne and De Vane v. Bausch & Lomb, Inc., and Price; USCD Ariz., No. 74-173-TUC-WCF, March 14, 1975.
14. Ibid.
15. Appellants' opening brief, United States Court of Appeals For the Ninth Circuit, No. CCA 75-1857.
16. Diane R. Williams v. William B. Saxbe, et al., USCD District of Columbia, C.A. No. 74-186, April 20, 1976.
17. Ibid.
18. Ibid.
19. Ibid.
20. Ibid.
21. Ibid.
22. Ibid.
23. Ibid.
24. Margaret Miller v. Bank of America, USCD NCalif., No. C-75-2680 JW, Aug. 19,1976.
25. Ibid.
26. Ibid.
27. Ibid.
28. Adrienne E. Tomkins v. Public Service Electric & Gas Co., and Herbert D. Reppin, USCD New Jersey, C.A. No. 75-1673, November 22, 1976.
29. Ibid.
30. Ibid.

Chapter Eight
1. Pat Michaels, "Playgirls in the job market," San Francisco *Progress,* September 6, 1972, p. 14.
2. Ibid.

Chapter Nine
1. 1975 *Handbook on Women Workers,* p. 76.
2. Edna Raphael, "Working Women and Their Membership in

Labor Unions," *Monthly Labor Review* (May 1974), pp. 27–28.

3. See *Exploitation from 9 to 5*, pp. 115–126.
4. Ibid., p. 130.
5. Jo Ann Levine, "Trade-union women find feminism—and each other," *The Christian Science Monitor*, February 22, 1974.
6. William J. Eaton, "Women in labor movement make gains, but so slowly," Chicago *Daily News*, October 11–12, 1975.
7. Herbert Hammerman and Marvin Rugoff, "Unions and Title VII of the Civil Rights Act of 1964," *Monthly Labor Review* (April 1976), p. 35.
8. Ibid., p. 35.
9. Ibid., p. 36. See also *Exploitation from 9 to 5*, p. 124–125.
10. Joan Nelson, "Sexual Harassment at Michigan State University: Results of a study by AFSCME Local 1585 of women employees in the Custodial Department," mimeographed, April 1976.

Chapter Ten
1. Harford Powel, *Good Jobs for Good Girls* (New York: Vanguard, 1949), p. viii.
2. Michael Korda, *Male Chauvinism: How It Works* (New York: Random House, 1972), pp. 98–99.
3. Ibid.
4. Ibid.
5. Ibid., pp. 99–100.
6. Marc Feigen Fasteau, *The Male Machine* (New York: McGraw-Hill, 1974), p. 51.
7. Ibid., pp. 56–57. Quotations is from Benet, *The Secretarial Ghetto*, p. 74.

Chapter Eleven
1. *Women's Wear Daily*, February 10, 1976.
2. Martin Kasindorf, unpublished excerpt from an article for *Newsweek*.
3. *Newsweek*, August 18, 1975.
4. Kasindorf.
5. Ibid.

Chapter Twelve
1. New York *Post*, May 27, 1976.
2. *Time*, June 14 and June 2, 1976.
3. *New York*, June 14, 1976.
4. Los Angeles *Times*, June 13, 1976.
5. Washington *Star*, June 2, 1976.

6. *Time*, June 21, 1976.
7. Ithaca *Journal*, June 11, 1976.
8. *The New York Times*, June 11, 1976.
9. Ithaca *Journal*, June 14, 1976.
10. Ibid.
11. *The New York Times*, June 11, 1976.
12. Washington *Star*, June 13, 1976.
13. *The New York Times*, June 20, 1976.
14. *Village Voice*, June 14, 1976.
15. Washington *Post*, June 16, 1976.
16. New York *Post*, June 16, 1976.
17. New York *Daily News*, June 15, 1976.
18. Washington *Star*, June 16, 1976.
19. *Village Voice*, June 7, 1976.
20. Ibid.
21. Ibid.
22. Ibid.
23. Ibid.
24. Sally Quinn, "The Myth of the Sexy Congressmen," *Redbook*, October 1976, p. 96.
25. Ibid., p. 104.
26. *The New York Times*, June 8, 1976.
27. Ibid.
28. New York *Post*, July 1, 1976.
29. *Time*, June 21, 1976.
30. Ibid.
31. *Newsweek*, June 28, 1976.

Index

Abbott, Edith, 53, 54
Academic careers, 90–91, 98–111
Actresses, 234–51
Addams, Jane, 64
Ad Hoc Group on Equal Rights, 40, 42, 45
Adler, Stella, 235–36
Administrators, 111, 114–15
Affirmative Action, 73–74
Age, women's, and employability, 73–75, 113–38
 deflated wages, 134
Alcott, Louisa May, 61–62
Almquist, Elizabeth M., 11
American Association of University Professors, 109
American Civil Liberties Union, 121
Andrews, John B., 53
Anger, Barbara, 92–93
Anthony, Susan B., 54
Argyle, Michael, 34
Art and Sexual Politics (Baker), 90–91
Arthur, Sara, 160
Artists, 90–92
Asantewa, Doris, 119–23
Associated Press, 88, 251–52
Automation, and male dominance, 76
Autonomy, loss of, 35–36

Baker, Elizabeth C., 90–91
Baker, Elizabeth F., 53
Barnes, Paulette G., 38, 177
Barr, Roy, 207–09, 210, 217
Barrett, Nancy Smith, 15–16, 75–76
Bartlett, Elisha, 56–57
Bauer, Lotte, 61
"Beauty Queen Syndrome, The" (Ettlinger), 126
Belkin, Herb, 233–34
Benedict, Robert, 171
Benet, Mary Kathleen, 131–32
Benson, Donna J., 99
Berg, Jody, 13
Bergen, Candice, 249
Berle, Milton, 31–32
Black Women in White America (Lerner), 63
Blanchard, Nina, 237–38, 244–45

on casting couch cliché, 251
Bliss, W. D. P., 53
Bolden, Penny, 81
Borneman, Marti, 168–72
Breasts (*see* Bust)
Brekken, James, 168–72
Bremer, Mrs. Alexander, 65
Brink, Suzanne, 158–59
Brinson, Harvey, 112–13, 181, 183
British *Economic Journal*, 51
Broder, David S., 256
Brownlee, Mary M. and W. Elliott, 64
Bust, size of, 31, 32, 128–29, 138, 158, 249–50
Byrd, Dan, 82

California State Department of Labor, 28
California Unemployment Insurance Board, 167–68
Campbell, Helen, 60–62
Capitalism and the "free" market, historical, 49–68
 American, 52
 and cheap foreign labor, 58–59
 covering up, 64–68
 earlier history in England, 50–51
 enforced prostitution, 57–58, 64, 65
 lower wages for women, 49–50
 particular instances of harassment:
  black women, 63–64
  white women, 60–63
 trade unions, 50–56, 65–67
 (*See also* Job segregation; Labor market behavior; Trade unions)
Capone, Al, 256
Case histories:
 actress, 235–39, 246–51
 administrative assistant, 114–17, 166
 associate director in social welfare, 119–23
 broadcast journalist, 111–12, 172
 Mrs. Cawley of the Bronx, 59
 college student, 102, 105–06
 college teacher, 108–09
 dental receptionist, 21–22
 draftswoman, 92–93

factory worker, 140–42, 172–73, 276–77
filmmaker, 97–98
janitors, 212–17
job-hunting, 138–39
lawyer, 117–19
male on receiving end, 231–32
male retribution for rejection, 140–43
office worker, 184–85, 193–94
    older woman, 134–38
on-the-job trainees, 94–97
policewomen, 81, 83–87
public-information aide, 112–14
racing, 88–90
sculptor, 91–92
teenagers, 148–61
waitress, 22–29, 42, 143–48, 151, 153–55, 195–97
    double jeopardy, 143–44
(See also Legal redress)
"Casting couch" cliché, 233–36, 239, 246, 250–51
creates vulnerability, 235
Cawley, Andrew J., and wife, 59
Charities and the Commons, 64
Child care, 128
Cigarmakers, 53
Civil Rights Act of 1964, 16, 175, 183, 263–64
Civil Rights Commission (see U. S.)
Clark, M. L., 82
Clerical workers, 41, 75, 126, 130–131
Coalition of Labor Union Women (C.L.U.W.), 204–05
Cockburn, Alexander, 256–57
Collins, Susan, 127
Community Relations Bureau (Justice Department), 38, 112, 181
Connolly, Harriet, 35, 80
Connolly, James, 65
Consciousness-raising, on women and work, 11–13, 32, 48, 176, 204
Cooperative Development Agency (Puerto Rico), 38, 112, 172
Corne, Jane; Corne case, 177–78, 183–84, 185, 187
Cornell University, Human Affairs Program, 11–12, 39, 41–43, 45, 46
Cosentino, Tom, 37, 131

Cosgrove, Sheila, 195–96
Cullinane, Maurice J., 81
Culpability, sense of, 107, 246, 249–50

De Cesare, Denise, 148–49, 151
DeCrow, Karen, 12
Degrees, academic, 98–107
Dentists, 111
De Vane, Geneva, 177–78
Developing Women's Potential (Lewis), 78
Dial-a-Joke (New York Telephone), 31–32
"Diary of an Amateur Waitress, The" (Younger), 63
"Discouraged worker syndrome," 132–33
Domestic service, 61–62
Double standard, Victorian, 56–58
    persisting, 218–20, 223, 227–28, 246
Dougher, Patricia, 13
Dowling, Jeannine, 47
Draftswoman, 92–94
Driggs, Sandra, 263
Dyche, John, 66

Economic force and fear, 22, 43–44, 260
    penalities for job-quitting, 44
Economic need, and working women, 72–73
Edgeworth, F. Y., 52
Elias, Ivonne, 138–40
Employers, and sexual harassment, 192–202
    economic determination of policy, 202
    policy and management, 200–202
    professed good intentions, 197
    protecting accused males, 193–196, 199–201
    role inescapable, 192
    sexist hiring policies, 192–93
Employment agencies, and hiring practices, 131–34
Engels, Frederick, 50–51
Engineers, 111
Entertainment field, 233–51
    exploitation of the untalented, 234
    study of the problem, 238–44
    tough job market, 239

women not compliant, 234, 239–240

(*See also* Case histories)

Equal consent, myth of, 233–34

Equal Employment Opportunities Commission (EEOC), 37–39, 75, 84, 95, 97, 113, 115, 131, 163, 177, 180, 185–86, 189, 190–91, 201, 204, 205, 220, 263

Equal Pay Act of 1963, 16

Equal Rights Amendment, 204

Esquire magazine, 235

"Etiquette," as male dominance, 33–37

Ettlinger, Catherine, 126, 128

Executive Order Number Four, 16

Exploitation From 9 to 5, 74

complaints against unions, 204

Extortion, 22, 28–29, 34

Factory work, 59, 61, 130–31, 140–42

(*See also* Case histories)

Falk, Gail, 57

Fast-food industry, 152–55

Fawcett, Millicent, 51

Feigen-Fasteau, Marc, 219–20

Feminine passivity, 36

Feminist movement, success with women's jobs, 15–17

Fillmore, Linda, 88

Filmmaking, 97–99

Finesilver, Sherman G., 177

Fitch, Robert, 192

Flipper, Cassandra, 201–02

Flirtation, ritual, 220

Fonda, Jane, 238–39

Ford, Gerald, 256

"Free market" (*see* Capitalism)

Freudian psychologism, 78

Frey, William C., 178, 187

Gallagher, Gene, 82

Garcia, Gay, 202

Gardner, Colleen, 224–25, 251–52

Goffman, Erving, 34–35

Goldman, Emma, 67

Good Jobs for Good Girls (Powell), 218

Greaser, Kay, 198

Greenwald, Judith, 35–36

Gross, Edward, 16

Haggerty, Rose, 60

Hall, Melanie, 251–52

Hamilton, Richard, 21–23, 27–29

understanding of sexual harassment, 29

Hammerman, Herbert, 205

Handbook on Women Workers, 71

Handel, Joan, 139

Hanson, Bob, 82

Harassment, sexual (*see* Sexual)

Harps, Kate, 142–43

Harris, Alice Kessler, 67

Harris, Louis, 259

Harris, Mark, 236, 238

Hartmann, Heidi, 49–50, 51, 53, 55–56

Harvard Business Review, 71

Hausfeld, Michael, 223–24

Hayman, Jean, 71

Hays, Wayne, 251–57, 259

Heelan, Mary, 177

Henley, Nancy, 34, 35, 37

Hepburn, Katharine, 239

Hernandez, Aileen, 163, 220–21

HEW (*See* U.S. Department of Health, Education and Welfare)

Hill, Ann C., 56

Hillman, Donna, 88

Hiring policies (*see* Sexual attractiveness)

Hodgson, Lorraine, 13

Hogg Foundation for Mental Health, 39

Holden, Dawn, 94–97

"Hollywood Reporter," 240

Horseracing, women in (*see* Jockeys)

Household workers, 131

"How I Went Out to Service" (Alcott), 61–62

Hubbard, Stanley S.; Hubbard Broadcasting, 197–200

Human rights commissions, 168, 170–72

Humor, and oppressed people, 31

Illinois Human Relations Director, 47

Independent, The, 63

Industrial Gerontology, 132

Initiative, human importance of, 13

Inter-Municipal Committee on Household Research, 64

282

International Ladies Garment Union (ILGU), 66
Ithaca Speak-Out on Sexual Harassment, 104

Jackson, Glenda, 239
Jackson, Peggy A., 81
Jacobson, Lawrence M., 259
Jaws, 241
Job-hunting, and sexual harassment, 138–39
Job interview transcript, 23–27
Job-quitting, economic penalties, 44
Jobs, women forced out of, 29, 42–48
Job segregation, 14, 49–60, 179, 190
 capitalist mechanism against women, 49–50
 denial of training, 51
 effort of World Wars, 51–53
 enforces lower wages for women, 49–50, 51–53, 74, 79, 124, 261
 service sector, 56, 75
 sustained by sexual harassment, 14–15, 72–73, 261
 and trade unions, 50–56, 65–68
 (*See also* Capitalism Labor market behavior)
Jockeys, 87–90
Johnson, George, 259
Johnson, Lyndon B., 258
Jokes about sexual harassment, 32
 last laugh with women, 265
Jungle, The (Sinclair), 58–59
Justice Department, 38, 112–14, 181, 183, 223, 251–52

Kasindorf, Martin, 239–41
Kasper, Harold, 166
Kellor, Frances A., 64
Kennedy, Richard, 207–08, 217
Kentucky State Human Rights Commission, 46–47
Knipe, Humphry, 34
Korbel, Bill, 222–23
Korbel, Connie, 13, 144–45, 222
Korda, Michael, 218–20
Kramarsky, Werner H., 168
Kreps, Juanita, 71, 99

Labor market behavior of women, 69–76
 begins early, 161

downward mobility, 72
financial dependence on marriage, 74
higher absentee rates, 70, 71
higher unemployment rate, 69
high job turnover, 69–72, 125–26
job segregation and earning power, 73–76
lower rates of continuous employment, 70
low female wages, 72–74
real economic need to work, 72–73
service sector, increased importance, 75–76
 and job segregation, 75–76
sexual harassment a negative influence, 69
teenage girls, 70
"Ladies," 36
Lawyers, 111, 117–18, 190, 234
 male, and sex harassment cases, 223–25
Lee, Jennifer, 236–39, 242–43
Legal redress for sexual harassment, 165–91, 262–63
 assessing cases individually, 174–175
 "characteristics not peculiar to one gender," 180–82
 court rationalizations, 187–88
 different strategies, 174–75
 forms of action, 165
 largest award to date, 167–68
 neutral rule, and increased action, 175–91
 punitive damages, 172–75
 reluctance of lawyers, 223–24
 right to unemployment insurance, 165–68
Legal redress, case histories:
 advertising secretary, 167–68
 bank employee, 183–85
 broadcast journalist, 112, 172
 clerical workers, 174–78
 factory worker, 172–74
 financial analyst, 112, 172
 office worker, 184–88
 police clerk, 168–72
 public-information aide, 112, 180–81
Lerner, Gerda, 63
Lewis, Alfred, 80, 81
Lewis, Augusta, 54
Lewis, Edwin C., 78

Libel and slander laws and suits, 47–48, 194–95
Librarians, 111, 129–30
Little Women (Alcott), 61–62
Look, Sally, 88–89
Los Angeles *Times,* 252
Lowell Female Labor Reform Association, 57
Lowell Manufacturing Company, 58

Machismo:
  and male insecurity, 229–30
  and racing, 88–89
McClure's Magazine, 62–63
McCombs, Phil, 82–83
Maclay, George, 34
McPheeters, Jean, 13
Madar, Susan, 13
Male attitudes, changing of, 220–232
  hypocrisy, 230
  lawyers and hostility, 223–25
  and personal involvement, 221–223
  stubborn belief in female submission, 225–27
  uncertainty and confusion, 220–221, 225–26
Male Chauvinism, How It Works (Korda), 218–19
Male Machine, The (Feigen-Fasteau), 218–19
Male mythology, blasts at, 32
Male prejudice against women workers, 78–79, 83, 119
Male rule (*see* Patriarchy)
Male status assertion, 36, 218–20
Managers, 111, 114–15
Manpower, 80
Manpower Administration, 166
Man-Trap, 247
Marriage, financial dependence on, 74
Marshall, Patricia, 80
Martin, Galen, 46
Maryland General Assembly, 159–161
Meat-packers, 58–59
Medical students, 101
Merrick, Lewis, 228–29
Meyer, Susan, 12
Michaels, Pat, 192–93
Michigan State University, custodial staff, 206–17

"Micropolitics" of power, 34–37
Migden, Chester, 240–41
Mill, John Stuart, 19
Miller, Margaret, 177, 183–84, 185, 187
Millon, John R., 127
Minnesota Department of Human Rights, 168–71
Models, 243–45, 246–47
Moffat, Bill, 226–27
Monge, Olga, 172–74
Monroe, Marilyn, 239
Monthly Labor Review, 205
Moon, Mary, 152–53
Morgheim, Virginia, 111–12, 172
Munger, Guy, 217
Murphy, Betty S., 128
Murphy, Jan, 199, 200

National Labor Convention of 1869, 54
National Labor Relations Board, 128
National Office Management Association, 37
National Organization of Women (NOW), 12
Nature of Deference and Demeanor, The (Goffman), 34
Nelson, Joan, 213
Nemy, Enid, 12
New Conscience and an Ancient Evil, A (Addams), 64
Newman, Pauline, 66–67
Newsweek, 259
New York American Civil Liberties Union, 189–90
New York City Human Rights Commission, 12
New York Daily News, 38, 256
New York magazine, 252
New York *Post,* 256–59
New York State Department of Labor, 166
New York State Division of Human Rights, 133, 136
New York State Human Rights Commission, 46–47, 168
New York State Unemployment Commission, 115
New York Telephone Company, 31–32
New York Times, The, 13, 253, 256, 258–59
Nolan, Kathleen, 242

Non-compliance, penalties for, 33, 40, 46–47

Norton, Eleanor Holmes, 12

NOW (see National Organization of Women)

Nurses, 111

O'Connell, Robert, 38

Officials, 111

Olivera, Michael, 195

On-the-job training (see Training)

On the Subjection of Women (Mill), 19

Organizations, working women's, 263–64

Ostreich, Janet, 146

Page, Norm, 198

Passivity, feminine, 35–36

Patriarchal relations, root of working women's problem, 14, 31, 49, 72–73

and capitalism, 49–53

Patriarchal relations (cont.):
and legal rationalizations, 188

Patriarchy, this society one, 14–17, 31, 49, 58, 261

Pay, less for women, 15–16, 49–53

Pemberton, John J., Jr., 189–90

Penalties, job, for non-compliance, 40–41

for job quitting, 44

Perlman, Laura, 166

Personal space, violation of, 34–35, 37, 92

Physicians, 111

Pidgeon, John, 169–70

Pimps, pimping, 64, 196, 242–43

Pincus, Ann, 256

Police patrol work, 80–87, 251

"Politics of Touch, The" (Henley), 35

Pope, Tom, 196

Poverty, and women's wages, 74

Powel, Harford, 218

Price, Leon, 177–78

Prisoners of Poverty (Campbell), 60

Professional women, 111–23

Prostitution, forced by labor conditions, 57–58, 64–65, 95–96, 195–96, 246, 248, 260

Prostitution in the United States (Woolston), 65

Pullano, Cindy, 140–41

Quinn, Sally, 258

Race, and sexual harassment, 121–123, 126–27, 131, 155–57, 227–29

Racing, women in (see Jockeys)

Radecki, Catherine, 36

Rape, 33–34, 46–47, 83, 85–86, 103, 148–50, 160, 188, 212–13, 219, 261

parallel to sexual harassment, 22, 29, 46–47, 103, 241, 264–265

Ray, Elizabeth, 252–57, 259

Reactions, women's, to sexual harassment, 40–48

Reader's Digest, 30

Receptionists, 21–22, 37, 130–31

Redbook, 40, 258

Redress, for sexual harassment, 45–48

(See also Legal redress)

Redwood City Tribune, 22

Reeves, Richard, 252

Reppin, Herbert D., 177, 185–87

Resistance and retaliation, specific instances, 151, 158, 199

Rich, Adrienne, 34

Richey, Charles R., 180–82, 189, 190

Ridgeway, James, 256–57

Ridicule, and oppressed people, 31

Rights of Women, The: An American Civil Liberties Handbook (Ross), 176

Rivers, Caryl, 258–59

Roby, Pamela Ann, 93

Romero, Mario Cesar, 229–30

Rosen, Sol, 224–25

Rosenberg, Rina, 167

Ross, Lena, 127

Ross, Susan C., 176

Rubaii, Sandy, 13

Rugoff, Marvin, 205

Salas De Vila, Madeline Leon, 38, 112, 172

Sales workers, 126

San Francisco Chronicle, 40, 82

Satire, and oppressed people, 31

Sauvigne, Krean, 12
Saxbe, William, 177, 181
Schneiderman, Rose, 66
School teachers, 52–53, 108–09, 111
Scientists, 111
Screen Actors Guild, 237–44
    action against sexual harassment, 241–44
    great power of, 241
Seaberry, Jane, 80–81
Seals, Connie, 47
Secretarial Ghetto, The (Benet), 131–32
Secretaries and stenographers, 30, 31–33, 36, 37, 92, 126, 131–32, 135–36, 220, 251
Senna, Cheryl, 97–98
Servants, 36
Service sector, 56, 72, 75
Service workers, 131, 143–44
Sex, as a commodity, 234
Sex-role conditioning, 34–36
Sexual attractiveness, and hiring policy, 34, 37, 74–75, 125, 126–31
    (*See also* Age; Employers; Employment Agencies)
Sexual denigration, verbal, 34
Sexual game stereotype, 31
Sexual harassment:
    in the academic world, 91–92, 98–111
    age and experience, penalization for, 74–75, 131–38
    analogous to rape, 22, 29, 46–47, 103, 241, 264–65
    in the art field, 90–92
    atmosphere created, 124–25
    blame in society's hands, 67–68, 260
    and "casting couch" cliché, 233–36, 249–51
    coercion, element of, 36
    compliance, and perpetuation of the pattern, 90
    considered ludicrous, 188, 216
    credentials no protection, 119
    description of, 32–34, 230–31
        further particulars, 188–89
        illustrations, 33
    devastating financial damage, 71–72, 73, 113, 114–15, 119–22

in the entertainment field, 233–51
and fast-food industry, 152–55
flirtation, ritual, 220–21
hiring policies, 33–34, 37, 74–75, 125, 126–28
in horseracing, 88–89
and husbands' attitudes, 223
ignored in socialist reform, 66–68
and job-hunting, 138–40
jokes and cartoons about, 30–32, 265
    put on the defensive, 32
    women's feelings ignored, 31
large incidence of, 37–41
    in agencies against sex discrimination, 37–41
    in UN, 39–41
loss of autonomy, 36–37
male dominance and "etiquette," 34–37, 43, 79
male retribution for rejection, 142–43
a new awareness, 32
nonreciprocal actions, 36, 261
of older women, 45, 134–38
and on-the-job training, 93–97
"part of the job," 79
part of patriarchal society, 13–14, 31, 49, 260–61
in police patrol work, 80–87
possible remedies, 261–65
    civil legal recourse, 261–63
    criminal prosecution, 262
    integrated work force, 261–62
    women becoming more active, 263–65
and premature death, 56, 61–62, 67–68
press indifferent to, 28
in the professions, 111–23
prosecution of difficult, 22, 28, 40–41, 48, 57–58
psychological damage, 122–23, 157, 261
racial factors, 122–23, 126, 131, 155–57, 227–29
retaliation for resistance, 33, 40–41, 47–48
sex as a commodity, 234
and sex-role conditioning, 34–36, 43–44, 46–47, 79, 226–228

Sexual harassment (cont.)
  since women became wage-
    earners, 30, 56
  society indifferent to, 46–47, 92,
    97
  stress and disruption, 36, 46–47,
    48, 62, 104–05, 115–17,
    146–47
  teenagers, 45–46, 147–61
  violation of personal space, 35,
    37, 92
  and waitress work, 143–48
  and Washington sex scandals,
    252–60
  women's reactions, 41–48, 124–
    125
    attempts at redress, 45–48
    competition, 124–25
    compliance, 42, 44, 90, 97,
      104–07
    enjoying it, 43
    fear, concern for future work,
      43–44
    holding on, 42, 44
    quitting the job, 41, 42, 43–46,
      97, 104–05, 151–52
  work the key element, 29, 43,
    260
  (See also Capitalism; Case his-
    tories; Employers; Job seg-
    regation; Labor market be-
    havior; Legal redress; Social
    coercion; Trade unions)
Shop girls, 62
Sigworth, Heather, 178–80
Silverman, Diedre, 13, 108
Sinclair, Upton, 58
Singer, Linda, 177
Skirts, length of, 30, 145
Slander and libel laws and suits,
  47–48, 194–95
Slavery, and exploitation of black
  women, 63
"Sleeping their way up," 251
Sloan, Harry, 240, 242
Smelser, Neil, 50
Social coercion, 238–39, 240–41,
  243–46, 249–50
Social workers, 111, 139
Sommers, Suzanne, 245–51
  and female stereotypes, 247–50
  quasi-modeling, 246–47
  and social coercion, 249–50
Staring, 34, 249–50
Status assertion, male, 36

Stein, Robert, 73
Stenographers (see Secretaries)
Step-'n'-Fetch-It, 31
Stereotypes, 31, 32, 35–36, 247–50
Stern, Herbert J., 185–87, 190
Stewardesses, airline, 30, 182
Story of O, The, 219
Strasser, Adolf, 53
Stress and disruption, 36, 46–47,
  48, 62, 104–05, 115–16, 146–
  147
Students, 36
Sulzer, William, and Mrs., 59
Sun-Sentinel (Pompano Beach,
  Florida), 88
"Swinging" female workers, 193
Switchboard operators, 37, 130

Taibi, Barbara, 168
Taxicab driving, 97–98
Teachers (see School teachers)
Teaching, college, 108–111
Teenagers, special problems, 148–
  161
Tenure, academic, 91, 103
Terwilliger, Sue, 146–48
Texas Federation of Business and
  Professional Women, 39
Textile workers, 52–53, 54, 56–57
Thomas, Heather, 13
Threat display, 34–35
Three's Company, 246
Time magazine, 252, 259
Title VII (Civil Rights Act of
  1964), 16, 37, 78, 87–88, 112,
  165, 175–91, 254, 263
  key concepts, 176–81
  landmark decision, 181–83
  and lawyers, 190, 224
  and unions, 204–05
  varying interpretations, 176–88
Tomkins, Adrienne E., 176, 185–
  186, 190
Touching, 34, 35, 36, 37
  study of female response, 36
Trade unions, and sexual harassment, 50–51, 203–17
  changing discriminatory pat-
    terns, 205–06
  case of Michigan State Uni-
    versity, 205–17
  International Ladies Garment
    Union (ILGU), 66–67
  and job segregation, 50–56, 65–
    68

287

Trade unions (cont.)
  maintaining male domination, 203–04
  most women not union members, 203, 204
  Screen Actors Guild, 238–43
Training, 93–97
Transcript, job interview, 23–27
Tully, Ed, 82
Typesetters, 54–55
Typists, 126–27, 130

Unemployment rate, women, 69–70, 132
  compensation rights, 45–46, 165–67
  minority races, 155–57
  young girls, 153
Unions (see Trade unions)
United Nations Secretariat, questionnaire, 39–41, 45
  confiscated by UN, 39
  reported sexual harassment in UN, 39
U.S. Civil Rights Commission, 37
U.S. Department of Health, Education and Welfare (HEW), 38
United States District Court of Appeals, 177
U.S. Environmental Protection Agency, 38
University of Delaware Commission on the Status of Women, 99–103, 109–10

Victorian era, 56–59
Village Voice, 256, 257
"Vindication of the Character and Condition of the Females Employed in the Lowell Mills, A" (Bartlett), 56–57
Vocational training (see Training)
Vogel, Irene S., 87
Voice of Industry, 57

Wages, women's, and economic survival, 72–74
Waitresses, waitress work, 36, 62–63, 97, 126, 128–30, 143–48, 251
  double jeopardy, 144
  (See also Case histories)
Walker, Mary, 209–12
Wall Street Journal, The, 38

Walter, Jessica, 241–43
Washington Newsworks, 126
Washington Post, 80–82, 256
Washington sex scandals, 224, 251, 252–60
  Elizabeth Ray scapegoat and red herring, 255
  public reaction, 259
Washington Star, 252
Weaver, Warren, 255–56
Webb, Sidney, 51
Webel, Glo, 13
Wechsler, James A., 256
Wilensky, Howard, 76
Willens, Harold, 259
Willers, D. K., 195
Williams, Diane, 38, 112–14, 177, 180–83, 185, 223, 254
Williams, Spencer, 183–84, 187
Willingham, Carol, 127
Wolfe, Leslie, 37
"Woman's place," 49–51
Women Office Workers (New York City), 32, 132–33, 264
Women's Bureau, 69, 93, 131, 144
"Women's jobs" (see Job segregation)
Women's reactions to sexual harassment, 42–48
Women's Rights Office (U.S. Civil Rights Commission), 37
Women's Trade Union League (WTUL), 66
Women View Their Working World (Hogg Foundation), 38–40
Wood, Carmita, 12, 115–17, 166
Woolston, Howard B., 65
Work pressures, against noncompliant women, 33–34, 40–41
Working women, male opposition to, 78–79, 82–83, 119
Working women's organizations, 264
World War I, 51
World War II, 52
Wright, F. L., 153–54

Yackin, Ellen, 12, 115
Young, John, 253–54, 259
Younger, Maud, 63

Zabel, Les, 240
Zoccola, Brian, 199–200